Gaddis jerked again so violently that for a moment Sir Howard thought the man was going into convulsions. "We need help."

"You're goddamned right, we need help," Horne said crudely.

"It won't help becoming hysterical," Sir Howard said. "Exactly what documents does Sir Robert have with him? I mean are they in themselves sufficient reason to suspect he may have been kidnapped?"

"Yes," Gaddis said. "Sir Robert has with him a numbered set of our latest war scenario manuals."

"Our contingency strike plans?" Sir Howard snapped. "I haven't seen them yet—but surely they're not so terribly different from the old set that has been published everywhere except in *Punch*."

"I'm afraid they're quite different, Sir Howard. Explosively different. . . ."

Charter Novels by Sean Flannery

THE KREMLIN CONSPIRACY
EAGLES FLY
THE TRINITY FACTOR
THE HOLLOW MEN
FALSE PROPHETS
BROKEN IDOLS

BROKEN IDOLS

SEAN FLANNERY

CHARTER BOOKS, NEW YORK

BROKEN IDOLS

A Charter Book / published by arrangement with
the author

PRINTING HISTORY
Charter Original / April 1985

ISBN: 0-441-08126-6

Charter Books are published by The Berkley Publishing Group,
200 Madison Avenue, New York, New York 10016.
PRINTED IN THE UNITED STATES OF AMERICA

This novel is for Laurie

There are four classes of idols which beset men's minds . . . of the tribe, of the cave, of the market-place and of the theater.

—*Francis Bacon*

A fifth to try men's souls may be the desires of shattered dreams . . . broken idols.

—*Anonymous*

☆ **PART ONE** ☆

✯ ONE ✯

As is so often the case, newspaper stories surrounding the disappearance of NATO General Sir Robert Isley Marshall contained only the barest of facts that even taken as a whole gave absolutely no indication of what really happened. Most accounts, for instance, got the time that Sir Robert disappeared from NATO headquarters outside Brussels, but only a few even hinted that he might have carried sensitive documents with him. The time, of course, meant little or nothing. The fact that he did carry documents, the Genesis Plan files, meant everything.

A few of the stories did mention the arrival of a dozen gentlemen, most of them Department of the Army civilians, air, naval, and trade mission attachés from as many NATO member countries, soon after Sir Robert's disappearance. They had been spotted coming individually through Brussels's Zaventem Airport without the usual customs checks. Whether on purpose, or merely by accidental oversight, no editor seemed to make the intuitive leap that in many instances air, naval, and trade mission attaché titles are merely covers for secret service positions. The Air Minister at the British embassy in Moscow, for instance, is an SIS man. The Italians have their SISMI chief of station at the embassy in Mexico City working as the naval attaché. Curiously, he's an old army man. And the new U.S. trade delegate to Peking is a CIA observer.

One story got all the facts correct about Sir Robert's driver, Stewart Merrick, who had been given the afternoon off. But it missed the important detail that Sir Robert often dismissed his driver and chauffeured himself.

Still another account got it straight that Sir Robert was chairman of the NATO Nuclear Defense Affairs Committee, but no one connected it with the fact that NATO had recently scrapped its defense plans and therefore had to have come up with something new. General Sir John Hackett and the others who had written the popular book *The Third World War: August 1985*, had not foreseen the new plan. Nor did the public sector have an inkling as to the nature of the NATO plan or its importance to Western security. . . .

It was just four in the afternoon. A Friday. October 14. The weather across Belgium and most of Europe was absolutely terrible. A low pressure system had passed and then had stalled southeast around Zürich. It would hang on for days, bringing with it gusty winds, dropping temperatures, and a chill rain that in the late evening and very early morning hours changed to fitful spits of snow.

General Sir Robert Marshall (ret.) emerged from his office and set his apparently heavy briefcase on the carpeted floor in front of his secretary's desk.

("He seemed bemused," she later testified. "Almost as if he was looking at the room, at me, for the last time. As if he knew, or at least suspected something was afoot.")

Marshall was a very tall man, well over six feet. And he was thin, almost to the point of asceticism. With a clerical collar, or better yet, a monk's habit, he could have passed as the curator of a dusty museum, or an exchequer of some sort, at a remote monastery. His face was angular, although surprisingly he did not have the sunken, hollow cheeks of so many seventy-year-olds. His nose was long, hawkish. On the battlefield during the Second World War, he had been nicknamed "The falcon commander" not so much for his decisiveness in combat—although he was decisive—but for his angular beak and his quick, birdlike motions whenever he was in a hurry or distracted. His complexion was a mottled red and white, a few blue veins crisscrossing his nose. Ravages of age, not drink, for Sir Robert had never been a heavy drinker.

"Clouds the mind and absolutely wrecks one's judgment," he said on more than one occasion.

But he never held it against a man for drinking. His favorite story was the one about the highly successful U.S. Civil War general, Ulysses S. Grant, who had been criticized by his fellow generals for drinking too heavily. Upon hearing the complaints, President Lincoln had ordered a case of Grant's brand of whiskey sent to each of his generals.

Nevertheless, no heavy drinker ever lasted long on Sir Robert's staff.

His hair was absolutely white and thinning, and somewhat on the longish side for a military man. It was his one obvious vanity. No hairpiece for him, no namby-pamby hair coloring either. "If I were a recruit, my sergeant would have me on report for my hair," Sir Robert was fond of saying. "I can still grow it long, and do a lot of other things as well." This last was always said with a twinkle in his eye.

As if to offset his rakish hair style, Sir Robert's dress was impeccable at all times and strictly correct. On that afternoon he wore his Army uniform, the Sam Browne belt highly polished, his shoes gleaming, his brass polished, and his rows of decorations in perfect order.

He had worked all day, yet his tie was still properly knotted and snugged up. But he seemed distracted, his abrupt motions noticeable as he seemed to flit about without apparently moving from where he stood.

"Are you going away, then, for the weekend, sir?" his secretary asked, coming around the desk and fetching his overcoat from the stand. She was an older woman, plumpish, and had been with him for years.

He turned his back to her and held out his arms so she could help him on with his coat. "I think not, Maggie," he said. His voice was on the hoarse side.

He turned back, and she helped him button his coat. "Get yourself right home and have Lady Sidney fix you a hot toddy. And stay there," she added, giving him a pat.

He stared at her for a moment, his pale eyes the most violent blue she had ever seen them. It gave her goose bumps.

"Good-bye," he said. He retrieved his briefcase and without another word left the office.

She stared after him for no definable reason, but then she looked away, suddenly feeling foolish. She went back to her desk.

" 'Good-bye'?" she muttered, picking up the phone and dialing for the garage. "Sounded like he was planning to go away and never come back." She shivered.

"Parking four. Merrick."

"Mr. Merrick, Sir Robert is on his way down."

"Yes, ma'am."

"And Merrick?"

"Yes'm?"

"He is in a strange mood. Don't upset him."

"Of course not," Merrick said, and Maggie Byrne hung up.

After a bit she covered her typewriter, then got her

hat and coat from the closet and put them on. Before she left, she checked Sir Robert's office. Nothing was out of place, his desk tidy except for the photograph of his wife, Lady Sidney. It had been turned around so that it was facing out; it was the last thing Sir Robert had seen as he left his office.

Maggie Byrne stared at the photo. She shivered again.

Lady Sidney was a lovely woman in every sense of the word. She was tall and somewhat on the thin side. As a younger woman her figure had been boyish; now it was the epitome of svelte.

She was trying very hard not to be rude to the man who had shown up a few minutes ago to see Sir Robert, apparently with an appointment, but it was difficult. He seemed boorish, and her thoughts were drifting to her husband's recent preoccupation.

"I'm dreadfully sorry, Mr. Langford—you were saying?"

"It's Langdon, Lady Sidney. Thomas Langdon, *London Daily Mail*. I spoke with Sir Robert on the telephone two weeks ago. He said it would be better if we met here than at his office. He said four-thirty. I'm sorry I'm a bit late."

"Yes," Lady Sidney said. Bobbs had shown the man into the drawing room. The drapes had not yet been drawn, and although it was gloomy and raining she could see out the French doors, across the veranda, and down to the gardens. The summer, she thought wistfully. If only it hadn't left.

Where Sir Robert's face was long and angular, hers was round and gentle. Her eyes were dark, wide, and guileless, a few laugh lines at the corners. Her nose was small, but her lips were well formed, sensuous, and her complexion was still nearly flawless. She almost always went with little or no makeup.

"May I ask you a few questions while we wait?" the

journalist said. He was a short man with jowls and
fleshy lips. His clothing was slightly wrinkled, as if he
had slept in his suit during the car ride over. Bobbs had
evidently taken Langdon's wet overcoat and hat.

"I assume Sir Robert's office sent your editor confirmation of the appointment?"

"Of course," Langdon said, flustered. It seemed
studied. He dug in his pocket for a crumpled telegram
that he handed to Lady Sidney.

She unfolded it gingerly, trying to hide her squeam-
ishness. There was a large grease stain on the telegram.
But the message was authentic, as far as she could tell.
The man seemed to have a legitimate appointment with
her husband.

She handed it back. "Won't you have a seat, Mr.
Langdon? Sir Robert should be here in a moment."

He took the couch, and she perched on a Queen Anne
chair across from him.

"I don't know if I can be of much help to you if you
have come to interview Sir Robert."

"I'm not a political writer, Lady Sidney. I'm a fea-
ture writer. Human interest pieces. I did the series on
Lady Di . . . the last big spreads?"

Suddenly she thought she remembered. "What sort
of an article do you wish to do about Sir Robert? Surely
not one with him in a bathing costume?"

Langdon laughed. "No, Lady Sidney, certainly not.
The story I have in mind to do is based on a remark
made recently by Margaret Thatcher."

"Really?"

"Yes, ma'am. She spoke in Parliament on the Soldiers Appropriations Bills. She said we owe our people
in uniform a debt of gratitude that must never be
forgotten. I think Sir Robert has become a forgotten
man." Langdon smiled.

Lady Sidney got the impression that the journalist
was lying to her. She could stand almost anything but

lies. "Forgotten by whom?" she asked. She didn't like the tone of this at all.

"Why . . . by the people of Britain, of course."

Lady Sidney wore several large tea rings on the fingers of both hands. She studied them for a long moment, a gesture at once odd for her, and rude. "Just what has my husband done for Britain, in your estimation, Mr. Langdon, that merits such attention from the press?"

The journalist seemed just as surprised by the question as she was that she had asked it.

"He was on the Versailles Team. I don't think there are many who know that."

Lady Sidney smiled inwardly, remembering those days. She and Sir Robert—he had been plain Bobby then—were married in 1942, but she had known him years before. She had had her eye on him ever since she was twelve years old.

"During the Second World War he was nothing short of brilliant. In North Africa they called him 'the falcon commander.' And he was one of the Nuremberg court's administrators."

"You have done your homework well, Mr. Langdon."

"Thank you. But there are a few years in the early fifties I'm not so certain of. I believe he may have worked with our secret service, although I don't really suspect anyone will tell me that. I do know he was in Berlin when President Kennedy visited to look at the wall. And then it wasn't long after that when he came to the NATO staff."

"Sir Robert did work as military liaison to our embassy in Bonn for three years," Lady Sidney volunteered.

Langdon smiled, and he licked his lips. "Oh yes, I almost forgot about that. It must have been a quiet time in your lives."

"Whatever do you mean by that?"

Langdon was immediately apologetic. "Heavens, Lady Sidney, I meant nothing personal, absolutely nothing untoward."

Lady Sidney was beginning to boil inwardly. She could feel her blood pressure rising. It had to be age, she told herself. That and concern about her husband that made her so thin-skinned just now. "It is I who should apologize for getting the wrong impression. It's just that . . ."

Langdon sat forward very fast. "Yes?" he asked eagerly.

"It's just that this has been a particularly trying day for me. The weather is miserable, and I am coming down with a nasty bug of some sort."

She could see that the journalist hadn't completely bought her story. But there was little she could do that wouldn't be grossly rude. She wanted desperately to be rid of him, and yet the damnable man had an appointment. Her husband had apparently wanted this interview, though for the life of her, she could not imagine why.

"I'm sorry. I've overstayed myself," Langdon said, starting to rise.

Lady Sidney got up. "No. Please," she said. "I'll just telephone Sir Robert's office. If he has been detained, I shall find out when we can expect him."

Langdon had gotten to his feet. "I would appreciate that, Lady Sidney. I did want to speak with Sir Robert."

"If you will just remain here, Mr. Langdon," she said. He inclined his head, and she turned and left the drawing room. She crossed the stairhall and used the front hall telephone. Her call was answered on the second ring.

"You have reached the evening recording for the administrative offices of the North Atlantic Treaty Organization. *Vous avez . . .*"

She hung up and went around to the foot of the stairs where she hesitated a moment. Then she went up to her study where she found her copy of the NATO staff directory. It was marked Confidential. She looked up the number for the parking garage and dialed it.

"Parking four, Chansois."

"Monsieur Chansois, is Mr. Merrick there by chance?"

"May I ask who is calling?"

"Mrs. Robert Marshall."

"Ah, Lady Sidney. *Non.* Monsieur Merrick is not here. The general dismissed him earlier."

"How long ago?" Lady Sidney asked, something clutching at her heart.

"I do not know for certain, *madame,* but I believe it was around the usual time . . . around four o'clock."

"I see."

"Is there something amiss?"

"Of course not," Lady Sidney said. "Thank you for your help." She hung up. Her heart was pounding, but she had no real idea why such a fright had come over her.

Langdon was still downstairs. She felt his presence as a pressure on her. An unpleasant, unwarranted pressure.

She rang for Bobbs on the house phone.

"Yes, madam?" he answered.

"Mr. Langdon is in the drawing room. Please offer him a drink. Tell him I'll be with him in just a moment or two."

"Very good, madam," the houseman said.

On the back pages of the staff directory were the mobile numbers for the various staff cars. She found her husband's, dialed for the mobile operator, and gave the number.

The connection was made, and she could hear the mobile phone ringing. Four times, five times. But there was no answer.

"I am sorry, *madame,* but there is no reply," the operator said with a very heavy French accent. "Would you care to try later?"

"Thank you," Lady Sidney said. She hung up.

She was being silly. More than that, she was acting as if she were a complete fool. Sir Robert often drove himself home. Often he stopped at his club. And more often than not, just lately, he had become forgetful of her. Stopping places, seeing people, inviting others to their home—such as the journalist downstairs—without telling her. Yet it was no reason for her to get herself into such a state.

But this time it seemed different to her. Put it down to women's intuition, she told herself, but this time she was worried.

She looked up a third number, and with shaking hands dialed it.

"NATO Security, Officer-of-the-Day, Captain Glynnis."

"Captain Glynnis, this is Mrs. Robert Marshall speaking. I'm General Sir Robert's wife."

"Lady Sidney, yes, of course. How may I help you?"

"Could you tell me the time Sir Robert signed out?"

"Of course," the O.D. said, and a moment later he was back. "Four-oh-seven, ma'am."

"What time did he clear the gate?"

The O.D. hesitated. "Is there something the matter, Lady Sidney?"

"What time did he leave the compound, Captain?" she asked firmly.

"Three minutes later. Four-ten."

"He didn't return?"

"No, ma'am. Could you please tell me if there is something the matter?"

"There is nothing the matter, Captain. He is merely late for an appointment, that's all."

"If there's anything at all I can do . . ."

"Yes," Lady Sidney said, forcing a lightness to her

voice. "Whatever you do, don't push the panic button. Sir Robert would never forgive either of us." She laughed.

The O.D. chuckled. "Of course, Lady Sidney. I understand. Have a good evening."

"Thank you," Lady Sidney said, and she hung up. She looked at the watch pinned to her blouse. He had signed out an hour ago. He was long overdue.

If there had been an accident, she would have heard by now. There were diplomatic plates on the staff car. High-priority plates that would alert any police officer.

It was not an accident, she told herself, rising. She went into her bathroom where she splashed some cool water on her face, then ran a brush through her short, boyishly cut light brown hair.

Her eyes were a little puffy, and her complexion was a little more sallow than usual. Other than that she would seem fine to anyone who did not know her well. She managed a slight smile, then went back downstairs to the drawing room.

Langdon was just sipping a small cognac. He put the snifter down and got to his feet as she entered. He smiled uncertainly. "You spoke with Sir Robert?"

"Unfortunately, no," she said. "And actually I'm quite cross with the old dear, but he's been detained. Some staff conference or another. He forgot to telephone me. Completely forgot." She hated lying, yet that's all she had been doing here.

"Will he be long?" the reporter asked.

"I couldn't say for sure, Mr. Langdon, but I suspect it will be several hours."

Langdon started to speak, but she adroitly held him off.

"There's certainly no need for you to apologize," she said. "I can understand your busy schedule. But I will have Sir Robert personally telephone you first thing in the morning." She stepped over to the drawing room doorway and pressed the staff buzzer.

Langdon looked at his watch. "There's no possibility he'll make it home within the next hour or so?"

"None, I'm afraid," Lady Sidney said. Their house-man, Bobbs, a former gunnery sergeant with the Royal Welsh Fusiliers, appeared from the stairhall.

"Madam?"

"Mr. Langdon is just leaving."

"Very good," Bobbs said. He went to get the journalist's hat and coat.

"I'm terribly sorry," Lady Sidney said. "But I'm certain that Sir Robert will be so apologetic tomorrow that you will be granted an outstanding interview."

Langdon finally managed a grin, although it was clear he was disturbed. "You're very kind, Lady Sidney. Thank you."

Bobbs returned with his things. Langdon said his good-byes and was gone.

From an upstairs window, Lady Sidney watched the dreadful man leave in his rented car, then she went back into her study where she poured herself a very large brandy, drank half of it, then sat down at her desk and picked up the telephone.

Something was wrong. Something had happened. She just knew it. She dialed a number she knew well, and it was answered almost immediately.

"Air Vice Marshal Sir Howard Scott's residence," the houseman answered.

"This is Lady Sidney. Let me speak with Sir Howard."

"Of course, madam."

Several moments later, Air Vice Marshal Sir Howard Scott, commander of the Allied Maritime Air Force, Channel, and best friend of Sir Robert and Lady Sidney, was on the line.

"Sidney, what a lovely surprise," he said lightly. "Tell me you want to leave that old poop you're married to and run away with me," he joked.

"Something is wrong, Howard. Something dreadful."

"What is it?" Sir Howard said in alarm.

"It's Robert."

"What about him, Sidney?"

"He's not here. He hasn't shown up from the office."

"Have you telephoned there?"

"He drove himself, and there is no answer at his mobile number, though it did ring."

"Anyone else?"

"The O.D., Captain Glynnis. Robert left the compound at ten minutes after four."

She could almost see Sir Howard looking at his watch.

"He's not terribly late, Sidney. This *has* happened before."

"I know, Howard, I know. But he had an appointment here at the house. A journalist all the way from London. It's not like him."

There was silence for a moment.

"Women's intuition, Sidney?"

"Would you check for me, Howard?"

"Of course, dear. And when I find him I intend giving him a good swift kick in the seat of his pants."

Sidney laughed despite herself. "That would be a sight to see, Howard. A rare sight."

✶ TWO ✶

Of course there wasn't one newspaper account of exactly how the Americans got themselves involved, although even the most naive of political observers could hardly have expected the Americans not to get involved. Despite the openness of the American press owing to the Freedom of Information Act, and despite the congressional attacks on the Central Intelligence Agency, which tended to lift the roof off operations for all to see, the inner sanctum, as it's called out at Langley, is very tight. Immune, if you will, to the day-to-day squabbles of power. Immune even to the vagaries of elections and political appointments.

Professionalism is a term of endearment among the drones: so-and-so is a Democrat in a Republican administration, but his coups of '78 and '82 saved him. Not even a Reagan would fire him. He's insulated, don't you know. A bloody professional. Untouchable.

And among professionals a secret is a secret that even wild horses couldn't drag out.

Yet all in all, it's curious that no bright *New York Times* journalist, or hotshot *Washington Post* editor caught even the slightest glimmer of the goings-on across the river. They already were focused very sharply

on the Agency because of the deaths of its director,
Franklin Lycoming, and its deputy director, Lieutenant
General Stearns McNutt, in an airplane crash. But if
they even guessed at what was going on, they printed
nary a word of it. Although had it been possible for
them to do their homework, the public would have
ended up with a far different and certainly more frightening perception of what actually happened.

At the very moment Lady Sidney was speaking on the
telephone with Sir Howard Scott, a very angry Sylvan
Bindrich was charging into an elevator five time zones
to the west. His bodyguard, Donald Page, punched the
button for the basement and they started down.

It was just one in the afternoon of a lovely Virginia
day. It was warm, and the sun shone in a nearly cloud-
less sky. Within the bowels of the Agency complex at
Langley, however, no one was smiling or whistling a
pleasant tune. They all were on emergency footing.

Bindrich, a short, somewhat stern-looking man not
given to rash statements or to hurrying, impatiently
watched the elevator indicator as he slapped a file folder
against his leg.

Until Lycoming and McNutt's stupid accident two
days ago, he had been deputy director of Operations
(clandestine services), one of the professionals who
along with the deputy directors of Administration,
Science and Technology, and Intelligence, and the chief
of the Office of Computer Services, ran the Agency.
That had ended Wednesday night in the Maryland countryside four miles short of the runway at Andrews Air
Force Base.

The accident had occurred a few minutes after 8:00
P.M. By midnight Bindrich was at the White House
listening to the President tell him what a terrible,
awesome responsibility the director of the Central Intelligence Agency carried on his shoulders. Even if it
was only a temporary appointment.

From his office in isolation on the fifth floor to the

director's suite on the seventh, with its magnificent view
of the Virginia countryside, was a lot farther to go than
merely twenty feet straight up.

He wasn't ready for the job, he had argued. Good
Lord, he had barely gotten his feet wet with his job as
deputy director of Operations, which had been handed
to him less than six months ago. There were others more
qualified. Paul Reid was a capable administrator, after
all. Or Tom Foster, the DDI, who handled the overall
analysis function extremely well would be a better
choice.

But no. Operations were, in the last analysis, the
backbone of the Agency. It wasn't a bone thrown to a
dog. All other departments were in support of that goal.
Who better to become acting DCI?

He had his plate full already. There were fully a dozen
sensitive operations underway. More to be mounted.
Delicate relationships to be nurtured. Complex scenarios to be worked forward and backward.

What better position to mount them from than the
DCI's chair?

Thursday morning had been a time of shock, of
course. In addition, the assignment of a bodyguard to
him was a terrible invasion of his privacy. And Bindrich
was a very private man.

By afternoon Protocol was working out the funeral
arrangements, and Bindrich was wading through briefs
and memos that seemed to go on without end, as did the
telephone calls. Lycoming had clearly not planned on
dying so abruptly.

One of Bindrich's first acts as DCI was to change the
private number of the telephone on his desk. It was
amazing the people who knew the DCI's classified
phone number.

By Thursday night, Bindrich, who most definitely
was not a man given to hasty conclusions, found what
he took to be a glitch in the fabric of Lycoming's administration. This morning, Friday, he had pursued it,

anomalies blossoming like flowers in a cherry orchard in April, only with a rotten odor. Very rotten indeed.

A half hour ago he had telephoned the whiz kid, Eric Kopinski, the majordomo of computers, and all things that stored information, down in Archives, for a line summary of Franklin Lycoming's five years in office. There were a half-dozen projects in particular that Bindrich wanted to see. Some of them were as recent as five months ago.

But Kopinski and his machines had drawn a blank on those items, to which Bindrich had fumed, Impossible. He had taken his *wallah* in tow and immediately charged downstairs.

The elevator door slid open to the main Archives entry corridor. Straight across was a metal door marked RESTRICTED AREA: AUTHORIZED PERSONNEL ONLY.

Bindrich and Page stepped off the elevator and went through the door into the security anteroom where a civilian guard, armed, was seated behind a small desk. He jumped up when they came in.

"Good afternoon, sir," he said. He held out a pen for Bindrich to sign the incoming roster.

"I want no one in here and I want no one out of here until I give the word," Bindrich said as he signed his name. He straightened up and turned to his bodyguard. "I want you to wait out here, Don."

"Yes, sir."

"Mr. Bindrich, I don't understand, sir," the guard said. He was very nervous.

"If anyone comes down on the elevator, they can remain here or they can return to their offices. But they will not be allowed inside. And I want a list of their names."

"Yes, sir," the guard said. "And no one is to leave?"

"That's right," Bindrich said. He turned and went through the narrow wooden opening, then through the bulkhead door into the air-conditioned coolness, the

odor of electronic equipment all pervasive. He headed
down the wide corridor toward the main computer terminal that housed the Agency's most sensitive records.

One of Kopinski's people stepped out of his office
and immediately spotted Bindrich. "Good afternoon,
Mr. Director," he said.

"Kopinski is back at the main terminal?"

"He's expecting you, sir."

"He'd better be," Bindrich growled, passing.

At the far end of the corridor were a pair of sliding
glass doors that were electrically operated. They would
open upon demand unless an unusually sensitive run
was being produced inside, and then they were switched
off.

The doors silently slid open for Bindrich who stepped
inside. He stood a moment looking at nothing other
than the backs of the equipment until the doors closed,
then he reached back and switched them off.

He made his way through the equipment consoles to
the main control terminal itself, where Kopinski sat
smoking a pipe and drinking coffee.

Kopinski was a younger man, in his mid-thirties. He
was tall and lanky with a thick, luxuriant beard and
mustache. His eyes were very dark, and at this moment
hollow. He wore no jacket, his tie was loose, and his
brown corduroy trousers were rumpled.

No one else was in the large, normally very busy terminal room. The computer was working, printouts were
being made on a dozen printers, data flashed across a
dozen terminal monitors, but there were no clerks, no
technicians, no girls to do the running. Just Kopinski
who looked up.

"You'd better have a good explanation for this,"
Bindrich said without preamble, dropping the file folder
he had brought with him on top of the terminal.

"The best," Kopinski said, putting his coffee cup
down and getting to his feet. His father, Stan, had
worked for the Agency in much the same capacity as his

son until a few months ago when he had suffered a near
fatal heart attack that forced his retirement.

Stan Kopinski had lately been fond of telling anyone
who would listen that the days of the big ledger book
and the rows of file cabinets were long gone. "Now-
adays it's bytes and chips, CRTs and color graphics. It's
a wonder any of us can keep up with it at all."

"I took a line sampling of the top ten upper-echelon
projects and broad-sweep policy decisions for the first
quarter of 1980. The quarter was arbitrary. I wanted a
control run."

"What did you come up with?"

"See for yourself," Kopinski said. He went across the
room to another terminal, which had printed out a short
run.

Bindrich brought the file folder with him. Kopinski
pulled out several sheets of printout paper. They were
loaded with summary lines; brief informational para-
graphs and addresses for the hard copy of the actual
documents in storage.

"There were two case reference numbers you gave me
for this quarter," Kopinski said, scanning the rows of
numbers. "I tried to bring them up at first but was told
in no uncertain terms that no such case numbers
existed."

"Impossible."

"Yes. Then I asked if there were perhaps some lock-
outs preventing mere mortals from having a peek.
Nothing."

"So you pulled up the entire quarter. Enterprising."

"Only the important projects."

Bindrich opened the file folder and referred to the top
document number. Lycoming had mentioned a meeting
in Geneva as part of some project he was personally
overseeing.

Kopinski glanced back. He looked at the file, then at
Bindrich. "If that's the reference you asked for, forget
it. It doesn't exist."

Bindrich extracted the memo. It had been stamped with the appropriate file references, it had been marked top and bottom TOP SECRET, and most importantly it had Franklin Lycoming's initials at the bottom. Bindrich knew those initials well. He handed the memo to Kopinski.

"What does it look like to you?"

Kopinski glanced again at the document. "It doesn't look forged. Has his secretary seen this, sir?"

Bindrich shook his head. "This was in his personal file."

"Maybe it was never entered."

"It has a number. There at the top. Plain as the nose on your face. If it were an animal it would bite. It has a number, it has an entry."

Kopinski handed the memo back. "I'm sorry, Mr. Director, but the document is not in my computer."

Bindrich, as an old communications hand, and for a number of years assistant to the deputy director of Operations, had known and worked with Kopinski's father. Although they had never been close friends—there was too much of an age difference—they had developed a good working relationship. But Eric would never do. He was a computer whiz kid, a genius, but like his machines he was too hard around the edges, too strident. His mind was in the eighties, but his style, in many respects, was still in the rebellious sixties. It was a wonder he worked for the Agency at all.

"Bring it up on the monitor."

"I've tried. With all the numbers you sent down." It was clear Kopinski was barely holding his temper in check.

Bindrich could feel his own anger rising. "You tried every single number?"

"Every one, sir. And there is nothing. There was nothing then, and there will be nothing now."

"For me, Eric. Won't you do just this one little thing?"

Kopinski sighed heavily, but he sat down at the monitor, cleared the screen—the hard copy printer jumping up several lines—and looked up. "The number, sir?"

Bindrich gave it to him slowly, enunciating each digit and letter with great care, and looking over the younger man's shoulder to make sure he got it right on the screen.

Kopinski punched the retrieve instruction key and sat back. The computer answered at once:

UNKNOWN REFERENCE ADDRESS

He looked up, a faint grin on his lips. But Bindrich wasn't having any of this. After all, it was nothing more than a machine. An incredibly stupid machine, if you were to believe the experts. An idiot, but with a penchant for information storage, quickness of operation, and infinite patience.

"Tell your machine that we would like it to look over every document Lycoming ever signed and see if such a number exists."

"It does that automatically."

Bindrich was incredulous.

"Actually, it looks at Lycoming's signature *and* the number to see if there is a match with anything in its memory. Same difference."

"Then let's forget the reference number for a moment. Let's describe the document. It has to do with Geneva, Switzerland. There was some sort of a meeting."

"What exactly do you want to ask?" Kopinski said. Bindrich was certain the man was being purposely obtuse.

"Let's have a list of any and all meetings Lycoming either attended in Geneva, Switzerland, or indirectly participated in during that quarter."

Kopinski nodded, and his fingers flew over the keyboard, the muted clacking soft and almost toylike here.

The building was constructed into the side of a hill overlooking the hilly compound. One side of the basement was actually open, while the opposite side was well back into the hill. Beyond this room, behind the computers, was Archives itself where the actual paper documents were kept in cardboard bins stacked shelf upon shelf in rows and tiers.

There'd been a move afoot in the Agency for several years to do away with the paper documents on the grounds of redundancy and of sheer lack of space. Already the older material was being stored in a warehouse in the southern part of Virginia, along with other classified government documents for which the GSA acted as caretakers.

To kids like Kopinski, information not in the computer was less than worthless; it was a cumbersome waste of time. Cross-referencing a million pounds or more of paper files was an impossibly slow task for an army of archivists. One person at a keyboard of a decent machine with a good program could outshine a dozen researchers and a hundred file runners.

But for Bindrich, numbers across a screen had no real substance. Even the hard printouts appeared to be nothing more than someone's fabrication. There were no signatures, no authorization stamps, nothing solid, nothing real. Hell, high school kids with home machines in their bedrooms were breaking into top-secret government computers.

"Nothing," Kopinski announced. Bindrich focused on the screen, which read

NO INFORMATION

"Which means what?" he asked.

"It simply means the DCI was never in Geneva during that period, nor was he involved in any project, meeting, or operation there. *Finis.*"

Bindrich angrily held the memo with Lycoming's signature in front of Kopinski's nose.

"I don't know what that means, Mr. Bindrich," Kopinski said without even looking at the memo. "I honestly can't tell you. Maybe it was something he intended to do but never got around to. We don't file intentions down here. Where'd you come up with the file anyway? Perhaps there's a clue there."

"In with his personal things."

"He hadn't planned on departing so suddenly."

Bindrich had had the very same thought earlier, but hearing it from Kopinski's lips he was offended. The young had little or no respect. Oh, Bindrich knew he was being crotchety, old and definitely unsympathetic beyond his actual years. But at times the smugness and self-assured attitudes of young people got his goat.

He looked through the other memos in the file, most of which, unlike the Geneva meeting, did not refer to any actual event by name, but only to reference numbers. References that should have been filed within the computer and matched with an address for an actual paper document somewhere back in Archives. But there was nothing in the computer. He hadn't wanted to believe Kopinski before. Now he had to. The younger man was staring at him. Bindrich focused.

"Do you want me to run the other references through again?"

Bindrich shook his head and leaned back against one of the consoles. "Let's make an assumption for just a moment, shall we? Not a big assumption really, more like a fair probability."

Kopinski said nothing.

"Is it possible that these documents were filed according to SOP but then later someone erased the references?"

Kopinski started to speak, but Bindrich held him off.

"Had that happened, would any trace of that action be found within the computer? Some instruction? Some holdover?"

Again Kopinski started to speak, but this time he held himself back, a thoughtful, faraway expression crossing his rebellious features. The static electricity level seemed to rise around him like a halo.

"Yes?" Bindrich prompted carefully. God, how he hated prima donnas.

"It's not possible. Not that."

"But?" Bindrich asked. Kopinski was on to something. It was clear.

"The reference memos you found. That was it? There was nothing else in each file?"

"He had a lot of paperwork up there. These I picked out because they hadn't shown up in the preliminary records scan. You called me on it yourself."

"I don't mean that. I mean for each individual reference . . ." He reached up and took the file folder from Bindrich and extracted one of the memos from it. "Here. For this one. For this number. Were there any other documents to go with it? Any files? Photos? Diagrams?"

"No."

"Not even a jacket? He hadn't left the jacket laying out?"

"What are you getting at?" Bindrich asked. He was sure Kopinski was on to something, and for the moment he forgot his mild dislike of the man.

Kopinski swiveled back to the keyboard. He propped up the open file folder and quickly entered two document numbers: the first, one number above the memo in Bindrich's file; and the second, one below it.

Moments later the machine began spitting out information. One of the documents was a field report on a banking investigation in Bern six months ago, and the second was a change in the Geneva Station staff directory. It too was dated six months earlier. There was an address for both files in Archives.

"Bingo," Kopinski said softly.

"What is it?" Bindrich asked.

Kopinski shook his head. "Something really weird here," he said. "There's a gap between these two addresses. It means something is back in Archives that isn't listed on my machine."

"Lycoming's memo?"

Kopinski shrugged. He asked the computer for the name of the document in the missing Archives address. The machine immediately answered

NO INFORMATION

"Bullshit," Kopinski swore, jumping up. He tore off the printout. "Let's go have a look-see, shall we?"

Bindrich snatched the file folder with Lycoming's memos and followed the younger man out a rear service door, down a short corridor, and then into a side entry to the vast storage area for the Agency's paper records. The place smelled of dust, age, and mustiness.

Kopinski consulted the printout, then hurried down one of the long aisles that receded into the dimly lit distance. Bindrich was close on his heels. Someone was whistling a tuneless melody, and to the left two people were talking in hushed tones.

There was something to it after all, Bindrich kept thinking. But why had the numbers been removed from the computer records? It gave him a very cold feeling at the pit of his stomach. He just hoped to God he hadn't stumbled upon some kind of a cover-up. He did not need that kind of a hassle.

Lycoming had always been an aloof DCI, ensconced in his ivory tower. During the past few years especially, fewer and fewer people in the Agency had had any real contact with the man. Even Bindrich, as DDO, rarely saw the man more than at the Monday morning briefings and pep talks. And yet within the Agency there had been a gradual resurgence in pride of workmanship that could only be attributable to the direction of its leadership; it came from the top down. Lycoming had been the man, in a manner of speaking, for the Agency. But now Bindrich was nervous and just a bit angry.

Kopinski turned down several aisles and went back up several rows, until he found the address. He had to pull over a tall ladder on wheels, then scramble up it. Matching the addresses on his printout with the numbers on the cardboard bins, he finally found the correct one, pulled it out, and hurriedly thumbed through the files it contained.

He stopped suddenly and let out a low whistle. Bindrich was looking up at him.

"What is it, Eric? What'd you find up there?"

Kopinski shoved the bin back in place and slowly climbed down the ladder. He held a buff-colored file folder.

"This is your missing number."

The file folder was too thin, too light. Bindrich opened it. The folder was empty.

Very carefully now, aware that he may have ruined a good piece of evidence, he held the folder by one corner between his thumb and forefinger. Kopinski was watching him, his eyes owlish, his lips pursed. It was very quiet back there. Or at least it suddenly seemed so to Bindrich. Sounds were muffled. The real world seemed very far away.

"I want you to run through the rest of the memo numbers the same way you did this one. But I don't want you to touch a thing back here. Put pink slips between the jackets."

"For what? Until when?" Kopinski asked. He was angry. "What is going on here?"

Bindrich stepped a little closer, careful of the folder he was holding. "None of your goddamned business, Kopinski. Not now, not ever. You're to do as you're told, and beyond that you're to keep your goddamned nose out of it."

Kopinski wanted to say something. He was gritting his teeth. In another circumstance he would have looked comic. But here and now it was very serious.

Bindrich softened somewhat. "I'm calling Technical Services Division out from the city. I want them to look this over."

Kopinski calmed down. He nodded. "I'll have the files marked."

"Very good."

"But . . ." Kopinski started.

"Yes?"

The younger man suddenly looked sad. "The bastard must have erased the computer's memory."

Bindrich nodded.

"That's impossible without me knowing about it. I mean . . . it's impossible."

Bindrich said nothing. The kid was bright, but he did have a lot to learn.

✦ THREE ✦

Detective Inspector Richard Matin of the Brussels Metropolitan Police Division got out of his car and stepped around to the black Citroën CX Chapron. The car was parked half up on the sidewalk along a very narrow side street just off the Place Poelaert, its parking lights on.

A half-dozen blue and white police cruisers, their lights flashing, blocked either end of the street. A small crowd had gathered even though it was late, nearly midnight, and the weather was cold with occasional snow flurries.

Matin was in a foul mood this evening. But then on most nights when he was called out he felt like that. He had risen to the height of his career several years ago, and every move for him since had been merely lateral.

"One day they will shove me aside to the dustbin, Emille," he was fond of telling his secretary of late. "Until then, one does his best, *n'est-ce-pas*?"

The oval plate on the back of the car was marked with a large letter A for Alliance, the North Atlantic Treaty Organization. Diplomatic plates. Apparently his department had received a telephone call some hours ago asking for assistance in locating the vehicle. The press was not to be called in.

He threw up his arms in defeat. A dozen newsmen, including the television people, were gathered just beyond the barricade on the far side of the Division of Criminal Evidence van. How could the fourth estate be kept away from anything? They monitored all the police channels.

Sergeant Jean Rubaix, the senior officer on the scene, came up to Matin and saluted lazily. He was a fifteen-year man.

"No need for you to have come out here tonight, Richard."

"They're getting nervous downtown. What have we come up with?" Matin said after a bit.

Behind him, across the broad Avenue Louise, the massive Palais de Justice rose up into the stormy low overcast, the spotlights gone soft with halos in the mist and snow. Within its massive dome were the relays for Eurovision, which brought television to much of Europe. Half of Brussels thought the building was a joke; the other half was divided in opinion. Had its designer, Poelaert, intended his creation to be Greco-Roman or Assyro-Babylonian? Or did it really matter?

"Absolutely nothing. The car was driven here, its parking lights left on because of the narrowness of the street, and it was abandoned. Simple."

"Fingerprints?"

"The automobile is clean. It has been polished."

"Inside?" Matin asked, moving around to the door on the driver's side. He peered in through the window, which had not misted over too badly because the car was protected in the lee of the building it was parked beside. The keys dangled from the ignition. Matin straightened up.

"The doors are locked. We were waiting for NATO Security," Rubaix said.

"They've been called?"

"Of course, Richard," Rubaix replied.

Matin took the man aside. The news people were beginning to clamor to be let past the barricade. Matin waved to the uniformed officers to hold them back. Not

to let them through. Several of the newsmen protested.
He'd hear about it from Girardin in the morning.

"Have we discovered just yet to whom the automobile is registered?"

Rubaix shook his head. "It's a diplomatic plate, that
is all. NATO. They'll come to claim it. They've been
looking all evening."

"I know," Matin said. He was a tall man, and very
thin. Rubaix was short and stocky. There had been a
cartoon pair in the American newspapers some years
ago. He couldn't quite remember the names, but he
remembered the characters. Rubaix just now reminded
him of the shorter one, and he supposed he might appear to be the lanky fellow always getting himself into
trouble. Matin's older brother, who had emigrated to
the States just after the war, had written a book about
the cartoons.

Matin shook his head. A hell of a time for memories.
He took out his notebook and silver pencil, and went
back to the window on the driver's side and looked in.
Sergeant Rubaix joined him, curious.

"Shine your flashlight in here," Matin ordered.

Rubaix unclipped his light from his belt, switched it
on, and directed the beam through the window onto the
steering wheel.

"On the radio console. The telephone," Matin said.

Rubaix complied.

"Bon," Matin said. He wrote something in his notebook, then straightened up and went back to his car,
leaving Rubaix for the moment staring through the window. The flashlight beam shone on a small placard
above the telephone handset. On it was the mobile
telephone number.

Inside his car, Matin radioed Central Dispatch with
the Citroën's mobile phone number and asked for a
trace. While he waited for the information, he stared at
the car. He was not a man of instincts or hunches, contrary to the popular misconception of an inspector. At
least he usually was not. But this business tonight was

definitely interesting. Earlier, the dispatcher had seemed excited when he had called in. And now Rubaix had mentioned that NATO Security had been looking for the car all evening.

One of their people had wandered off, apparently. Possibly with a prostitute. Possibly it was worse. It gave him a headache thinking about it. In the years he had worked in this city—or at least since 1966 when NATO headquarters had been moved to Brussels from Paris—there had been the odd bit every now and then. Someone's important secretary turned up missing. A decidedly Slavic-looking gentleman found dead in a grassy field. A bit too much of the party atmosphere from time to time when the North Atlantic Council would meet. Mostly the trouble involved junior staffers and the housekeeping personnel. But the end result was usually the same. Or at least it was for the department. Slap them on the wrist—gently now, lest we offend some delicate sensibility—and send them packing. Not for the border, mind you, but just back to their nannies at the monstrosity they had built for a headquarters complex.

Matin passed a hand over his face. He was getting bitter in his dotage. Time to get himself down to Paris, or even Amsterdam. Martine had been after him lately. The only trouble was, no place really held any appeal for him.

Central Dispatch was back. The voice on the radio sounded like Inger's, the young Danish girl they'd just put on nights.

"The car is registered to the Alliance, with A diplomatic plates."

"I understand that," Matin said dryly. "What about the mobile telephone number? It is for the personal use of whom?"

"From our directory, sir, the number is registered for the use of General Sir Robert Marshall. Do you wish his address?"

"Yes, please," Matin said. "But first, his position. Is it important?"

"I would say so, sir. Your general is chairman of the Nuclear Defense Affairs Committee."

Matin let his breath out slowly. He copied down the address, thanked the girl, and then just sat there staring out at the car.

Bloody hell, he thought. Inger had called the man who had got himself missing, *your general*. It couldn't be farther from the truth. Once the NATO Security people got here, General Sir Robert would be nobody's man but the Alliance's, and God only knew what was going on here.

Headlights flashed behind him, and Sergeant Rubaix came back around the Citroën. Matin drew up his overcoat and got out of his car as two men climbed out of a Mercedes that had been passed through the barricade. They had their identification out before he could even think to ask them, and they went immediately to the car.

And still the night seemed to go on without end as Air Vice Marshal Sir Howard Scott stepped out of the CINCHAN operations room with Thomas Gaddis, chairman of the Defense Planning Committee, and Colonel Oliver Horne, chief of NATO Security. The door hissed shut, and they walked down the long corridor, their heels echoing like pistol shots on the tiles.

Gaddis, who was actually Dr. Gaddis, a specialist in nuclear engineering, had requested they step around to his office the moment they found out about Sir Robert's automobile. He had seemed decidedly shaken by the news, and his reaction had deeply affected Sir Howard. From what anyone knew of Gaddis, the man was a pillar, the Rock of Gibraltar, unflappable. He didn't seem so steady at the moment.

Sir Howard was of moderate height, had a fair build despite his age, which was nearing seventy, dark but pleasant eyes, snow white hair, and a luxuriant country-gentleman mustache that he had grown forty years ago and had never shaved since.

He and Sir Robert had been stationed together in North Africa during the war, for a short time with a Home Office detachment in London, then again in Germany, and finally here.

Until the death of Sir Howard's wife Daphne four years ago, the two couples had been nearly inseparable. Harold Wilson, when he was P.M., had joked that it was simply impossible to invite either the Marshalls or the Scotts alone to dinner. One couple simply wouldn't come without the other.

After Daphne had died, however, it seemed as if some of the spark had gone out of the rest of them without any of them actually knowing what to do or say to change things.

"That's the bit about getting old that's not so cozy," Sir Howard had told Sidney Marshall. "All your friends who were to be at your side to the end, all the people you're closest too, start to die off."

They rounded the corner, crossed the intersection of four broad corridors, and entered Gaddis's large office through his secretary's. The outer office was in darkness, but inside, his fluorescents had been switched on over a large drafting table to one side of the room, and a brass table lamp glowed warmly on a huge walnut desk. The desk was veneer, Sir Howard suspected.

Gaddis closed the door and turned to them without so much as offering them a seat or a drink.

"We have trouble, gentlemen," he said. His voice was low, almost guttural, with a flat Midwestern United States accent, or something else. Perhaps Bostonian. Sir Howard thought the man had attended MIT. He was too small and too thin for such a voice, although his thick eyebrows somehow seemed menacing.

"Pardon me, sir, but is there something I should know?" Colonel Horne asked. He was a very large black man. He had been with the military police and military intelligence since he joined the U.S. Air Force at the age of eighteen. He had fought in Korea and in Vietnam.

"You know him best of all, Sir Howard. Any idea where he might have gotten himself?" Gaddis demanded, ignoring the security chief's question.

"What is it?"

"You tried his club. His favorite restaurants. And there was nothing. But there has to be something. Think, man!"

"Good Lord, Gaddis, what in heaven's name are you trying to say?" Sir Howard asked. There were no windows open, but nevertheless he felt a very cold wind blowing on him.

As chairman of the Nuclear Defense Affairs Committee, which was one of fifteen principal committees on the North Atlantic Council, Sir Robert had worked closely with Gaddis. He had never said much about the man except that he was "damned efficient" and that he was a "cold fish."

"I have to ask you a very personal question, Sir Howard. And I must have the truth."

Sir Howard nodded.

Gaddis hesitated a moment. He glanced at Horne, his expression almost a mute appeal for help. He was in trouble. Deep trouble. It was obvious from his manner.

"Do you know if Sir Robert has ever . . . has he ever been involved with another woman?"

Sir Howard could feel the blood rushing from his face. The question absolutely staggered him. "The man is seventy years old," he heard himself muttering as if from a long way off. Horne was turning to him. The man was saying something about cooperation.

"I'm sorry, but it is important, Sir Howard." Gaddis was suddenly speaking again. "Is it even remotely possible that Sir Robert has a mistress somewhere?"

Sir Howard could only think of Sidney. Thank God she wasn't here. Thank God!

"Sir Howard, Dr. Gaddis does have a valid point," Colonel Horne said. He was dressed in his uniform, whereas Gaddis was dressed in a rumpled jumpsuit. It made for quite a contrast with Sir Howard's dinner jacket and black tie. He had come directly from cocktails after Sidney had telephoned.

He shook his head. "No. Sir Robert does not have a mistress."

"But he has been preoccupied lately," Gaddis snapped.

Sir Howard blinked. "Yes, but he's been that way on and off for as long as I've known and worked with him. When he is in the middle of a project—when he has the bone in his teeth—he's on to it to the exclusion of nearly everything and everyone else."

"Single-minded," Horne interjected.

"He has a singleness of purpose, I should say. He's certainly aware of the periphery, though. That certainly does not mean he has a mistress."

Gaddis said nothing. He was clearly in turmoil.

"What is it?"

"You can think of absolutely nothing that could help?"

"I might if you would only tell me why you brought us here like this," Sir Howard said.

"You can remember nothing he might have mentioned to you in passing? A trip? A meeting? Anything?"

"What the hell are you holding back, Dr. Gaddis?" Colonel Horne asked.

Gaddis brought his hands together as if he were praying, and he shook his head slowly. "We're going to need help. And we're going to need it fast." His eyes began to fill. "It was the very first thing I went looking for when I found out he had turned up missing."

Sir Howard was truly alarmed now. But he had no idea what to say to the man. Gaddis looked as if he were shell-shocked. Sir Howard had seen cases during the war who had looked just like him.

"You think he's been kidnapped?" Colonel Horne asked.

Gaddis jerked as if he had been shot, but he nodded.

"And he had something with him? Sensitive documents?"

Gaddis nodded again, and Horne groaned.

"Christ," the security man said, bunching up his fists. "Why didn't you tell us that in the first place? By now they could have him halfway to Moscow!"

Gaddis jerked again so violently that for a moment Sir Howard thought the man was going into convulsions. "We need help."

"You're goddamned right, we need help," Horne said crudely.

"It won't help becoming hysterical," Sir Howard said. "Exactly what documents does Sir Robert have with him this evening? I mean are they in themselves sufficient reason to suspect he may have been kidnapped?"

"Yes," Gaddis said, recovering a bit of his composure. "Sir Robert has with him a numbered set of our latest war scenario manuals."

"Our contingency strike plans?" Sir Howard snapped. "I haven't seen them yet."

"There were only five sets. Sir Robert was selected to serve on the final review group before submission to the entire DPC."

"And he took them out with him?" Horne asked incredulously.

"Don't worry, it's not your fault," Gaddis said sharply. "It's done all the time."

Horne appealed to Sir Howard, who merely shook his head. "I haven't seen them yet," he repeated. "But surely they're not so terribly different from the old set that has been published everywhere except in *Punch*."

"I'm afraid they're quite different, Sir Howard. Explosively different. If they got out . . ."

"What is the classification?" Colonel Horne asked.

"Top secret, of course," Gaddis said.

Horne shook his head. "If he's here in the city, we will find him. Beyond that we'll need outside help."

"That will have to come from the Secretary General," Gaddis said glumly.

Horne looked from Gaddis to Sir Howard and back, then turned on his heel and left the office.

For what seemed like a very long time, Sir Howard and Gaddis stood facing each other, listening to the sounds of the building, listening, it seemed, to the pulse of the creature that had possibly been let loose. *Explosively different*, Gaddis had said of the new contingency strike plans. It made Sir Howard sick at heart to think about Sir Robert out there. Time was of the essence now, more so than finesse.

Sir Robert had checked out at the normal time, had dismissed his driver, and had left the compound. It was the last anyone had heard from him.

Sidney had tried to telephone him a short time later, but he had either already parked his car, or had been prevented from answering his mobile phone.

In any event, they knew nothing of substance. Sir Robert had presumably driven into town, parked his car on a narrow side street, and then vanished into the night.

"It's called the Genesis Plan," Gaddis was saying.

Sir Howard shook his head in frustration.

"He got his hands plenty dirty with this. He was the resident expert on—"

"The Secretary General will have to be called," Sir Howard interrupted.

Gaddis swallowed. "He was in Vienna. He's on his way back now."

"We will have to inform all the member nations, of course. We'll have to be . . . ready." Sir Howard turned away, not able to face Gaddis any longer, although he understood that none of this was the man's fault. Good Lord, was anyone at fault here? *Explosively different*. "We're going to have to have help," he said. Then he left.

•   •   •

Alone, Sir Howard made his way back to his own offices in Section Channel Command, having to sign through again with a very nervous young corporal with pimples. He felt old and very much alone now; it was as if the world had become entirely too big and too cold a place for the likes of him.

An uncle who had served in the King Edward's Own Cavalry had made the same allusions to his age at the start of the Second World War. He was in his eighties then, and the thought of the sophisticated weapons, the far-reaching ships and planes, the radios and a hundred technical wonders, had made him feel that the world had passed him by, that the world had forgotten him.

His secretary was gone, of course, but his office lights were still on. He sat behind his desk and dialed an outside number.

It rang only once before Sidney Marshall answered. She sounded out of breath, as if she had just run up a flight of stairs.

"It's me," Sir Howard said.

"Have you found him?"

"No, Sidney, we haven't."

She read fear in his voice. She stifled a sob. "Is he dead?"

"No. We found his automobile downtown. Parked near the Palais de Justice."

"But he wasn't there? Not a trace of him?"

"Listen to me, Sidney. You're going to have to be very brave now."

"What is it? Is it terrorists? Is that it?"

"We don't know. He is carrying some very sensitive material. There is a possibility he may have been kidnapped."

She moaned with fear.

It was four-thirty in the morning when the telephone beside Wallace Mahoney's bed rang, and he answered it immediately, almost as if he had been expecting a call.

The day before had been nothing special, nothing out of the ordinary. He had risen early, with the dawn, and had taken his first cup of coffee onto his rebuilt dock that jutted out into Shultz Lake just north of Duluth, Minnesota. The leaves had begun to turn because of the recent cold spell they had been having, and as the sun came up, illuminating the trees across the lake, it was as if the entire shoreline was on fire. He had worked on the nearly finished cabin until noon, when he fixed himself a light lunch, then had taken a short nap. In the late afternoon he had gone fishing, but his mind hadn't been on what he was doing. Instead, he was thinking about his wife Marge who had died what seemed like a century ago; about his son Michael, dead in Montana; about his only grandchildren and daughter-in-law, killed right here in an explosion; and finally he thought about his son John, his only surviving genetic link with the world, with life. He hadn't heard a thing from John in nearly six weeks. There was no answer at his house in Los Angeles, and his supervisor at the lab at Monsanto Chemical had said John had taken a leave of absence for an indefinite period. Mahoney had wondered, as he watched some inane television show the previous evening, how much more he could possibly take. The cabin was nearly finished, and when it was done he had no idea what he would do with his days. He had gone to bed early, had read for an hour or so, and then had drifted off, but only lightly, as if he knew something was coming. He wasn't surprised that it was Sylvan Bindrich on the telephone from Langley, and he would later admit to himself that in some sort of a perverse way, he was even relieved.

☆ FOUR ☆

The day was lovely. It was just a few minutes after noon when Wallace Mahoney stepped out of the busy terminal at Washington's National Airport. He was, except for his thick shock of silvery white hair, an undistinguished-looking man of moderate height, with sloping shoulders and a slight paunch even though he had lost a bit of weight recently. A retired businessman, or perhaps a professor of history at some small East Coast school, with that air of bemused detachment. His nondescript look was at once studied and hereditary, he joked. No one notices the spy who looks as if he's someone's kindly uncle.

He stopped a moment at the edge of the busy sidewalk filled with passersby and piles of luggage waiting to be picked up, and sniffed the mixed odors of spent jet fuel and car exhaust that was very unlike northern Minnesota's clean air. But it was exciting, all the same. He had forgotten that Washington, D.C., had a vibrant pulse that quickened his own, despite his protestations to the contrary. Yet all he really wanted now was to be left alone so that he could spend his remaining years with his memories. Although he was barely sixty-five, he felt as if he had lived a dozen lifetimes. All damned difficult, he might add. Although memories were all he had left, he consoled himself by thinking he should be grateful for at least that.

You're burying yourself too early, his wife Marge might have said. At times he could hear her, feel her substance very close to him. After all, thirty years of marriage during often difficult times counted as something toward one's own fabric.

It seemed odd, however, to be coming back to Washington like this even though it had only been a few months since he had been here last, talking with the DCI, Franklin Lycoming, trying to make some sense of the assignment in which his daughter-in-law and grandchildren had been brutally murdered. The events that followed had shaken the entire fabric of the Agency. Now it was as if he were a stranger, coming to the capital for the first time.

On the plane coming in, he had been like a tourist, picking out the Capitol, the Washington Monument, and the Reflecting Pool.

Don't let yourself grow stagnant, old man. It wasn't something Marge had ever said, but it was something she might have.

Mahoney supposed his odd, contradictory feelings arose out of his morbid preoccupation with his retirement. He *was* retired, goddammit. He had told that to Sylvan Bindrich this morning on the telephone.

"You're coming to the funeral, I presume."

"I hadn't planned on it, Sylvan," Mahoney had replied tiredly, looking at his bedside clock. It was still pitch-black outside. "You didn't telephone this early for that." Why hadn't he been surprised by Bindrich's call?

"He was the DCI, for Christ's sake!"

"I hardly knew him. And we didn't part on the best of terms."

There was silence on the long-distance line for a second or two.

"Are you on the seventh floor now?" Mahoney asked.

"For the moment. But something has come up, Wallace. Something I'm going to need your help with. I thought if you were coming to the funeral we could get together. Talk."

Something had always come up. "Leave me alone, Mr. Director. I don't want to hear whatever little dirty problems you have on your hands."

"It has to do with your last assignment," Bindrich said guardedly.

Mahoney could feel the old, familiar clutch at his chest. Christ, wasn't it over with yet? He had suspected there might be repercussions. Franklin Lycoming had expected them as well. Before Mahoney had left Langley for the last time, the director had told him everything would be taken care of. The loose ends would be picked up.

As far as your involvement is concerned, this investigation is completed. I will arrange to have the pieces picked up and swept under the carpet if need be. If you pursue this further, I will have you arrested and charged under the Secrets Act.

Those had been his exact words. In the past four months, hadn't he accomplished his goal? Was there more?

"There's nothing I can tell you that you wouldn't be able to find in the records or in the DCI's personal files," Mahoney had mumbled.

"Someone has tampered with those records. With a lot of them," Bindrich said. His voice had sounded far away and muffled. Mahoney remembered that now. There had been an ethereal quality to it.

"Not I, Mr. Director," he had shot back harshly.

"And not merely with the last assignment that you were involved with," Bindrich plowed on.

There had been a mole. Two of them in fact, within the Agency. Darrel Switt had been the most surprising of all. And Bob McBundy, who had been killed in Geneva, had been the most hurtful. McBundy the old friend. The confidant. The one man in the Agency who should have worn the white hat at the end. It still rankled . . . it still hurt.

"Wallace?"

Bindrich was laboring under intense difficulty, Mahoney could hear it in the man's voice. He was evidently stuck deeper in a quagmire than could be expected from his new appointment as acting DCI.

"I won't get you involved. I promise you that. The Company owes you a great debt of gratitude. But I need your help. Information, I'm asking for. Nothing else. It's all I'm asking."

Stanley Kopinski, looking wan and tired, stood next to an Agency limousine. He had lost a lot of weight since his heart attack. The skin hung slack on his thin neck and birdlike face. He smiled when he spotted Mahoney coming across the broad sidewalk.

"At least you're looking fit, Wallace," the former chief of Archives said. Even his voice had changed. It sounded reedy now, with a breathless quality to it. They shook hands.

"How are you feeling, Stan? Is your retirement treating you well?"

Kopinski just looked at him for a long moment. "Are you shitting me, or something?" he said. "I miss work like crazy. You?"

Mahoney shook his head. "Not a bit."

"Bullshit," Kopinski said mildly.

Mahoney tossed his suitcase and overnight bag in the front seat, and he and the older man climbed in the back, and they were off, their driver maneuvering expertly through the heavy weekend traffic. Fall, along with the spring, was an especially pretty time in Washington. A lot of tourists were here, along with Congress and its hundreds of staff.

The funeral was scheduled for two. There was time for lunch. Kopinski droned on about his own problems as they drove north, past the Pentagon, past the entrance to Arlington National Cemetery and finally into

Georgetown on the Key Bridge. But Mahoney wasn't listening to him. Instead he was seeing himself as an excited young man, just back from the war, Marge on his arm, as he prepared to take up his life.

Washington hadn't been so different then. Except perhaps there had been a certain innocence to them all in comparison to what they had become.

For a few halcyon years, it seemed as if most of the evil were being eradicated from the world. All that remained was to mop up. But then in 1947 came the establishment of the Central Intelligence Agency. Mahoney went to work for them, and his eyes were suddenly and very permanently opened.

He shook his head.

"Here we are," Kopinski said, and Mahoney looked up to find that they had pulled up in front of the Rive Gauche, on Wisconsin Avenue and M Street. It was a restaurant that Mahoney, Kopinski, McBundy, and a lot of the other old hands used to frequent. Seeing it suddenly brought another flood of memories to him, not all of them bad.

"I've been coming here a lot lately," Kopinski said. He seemed very tense all of a sudden.

"What is it?" Mahoney asked. But Kopinski got out of the car and started across the walk.

Mahoney followed him. Inside, the maitre d' immediately escorted them toward the back of the busy main dining room. He did not spot Bindrich sitting in the corner until they were almost on top of him. He recognized Don Page, one of the Company's strong arm types, seated at the next table.

"Sorry," Kopinski said sheepishly.

"He insisted?" Mahoney asked.

Kopinski nodded. "I'll drop your bags off at my place. You're bunking with me."

"Will I see you at the funeral?"

"Yes," Kopinski said. "You'll be riding out with me." He nodded to Bindrich, then turned and left.

Mahoney sat down. A moment later their waiter came and he ordered a Kentucky whiskey, straight, no ice or water. He lit a cigar, and sat back.

"I thought we'd have lunch before the funeral," Bindrich said. His voice was soft. It was obvious he hadn't gotten much sleep lately.

"I don't suppose you're going to want to conduct business in here."

"No," Bindrich said dryly. Clearly there was a lot on his mind. Mahoney had seen the same preoccupation in other men promoted above their level of competence. Some of them grew with the job; others failed. In over their heads, they all had the same anxious, tense look that Bindrich displayed now.

"I don't know how much help I'm going to be to you, Sylvan."

"You can give me your side of the story. I can put it together from there," Bindrich said. His face was round and soft, his eyes moist.

"I doubt it."

Bindrich cocked his head. It was an odd habit of his whenever he heard something that was just outside his ken. "What are you trying to tell me in your oblique manner? Was Lycoming into something nefarious? Did he have a mistress on the side? Perhaps a Russian?"

Mahoney smiled. "Nothing like that. You knew him better than I did, in any event. You should be better able to answer that kind of a question."

"Don't play cat and mouse with me."

"We weren't supposed to be conducting business here," Mahoney said. "Wasn't that the idea?"

Their waiter came with Mahoney's drink, and they ordered lunch, only soup and a small salad for Mahoney, a fillet of sole for Bindrich.

When the waiter was gone again, Bindrich leaned forward, lowering his voice. "I told you this morning that you would not have to get involved. But I do need your help."

"I'll do what I can for you, Mr. Director. But you must understand that I'm not going to have all the answers."

Bindrich sat back. "Oh, I think you'll be a help."

There were a lot of military men as well as the crowd from Harvard—Lycoming's alma mater—at Arlington for the DCI's simple but elegant funeral. Many were old men, their white hair ruffling in the light, warm breeze. The Vice President was there, comparing Lycoming to the old war-horse heroes of the past. And the Secretaries of State, Defense, and of the Interior had sent their representatives.

Lycoming *had* done a lot for the country in his Eastern-establishment sort of way. Buckley had once written that Lycoming was the last paragon of virtuosity in an increasingly unvirtuous town.

He had brought the CIA back from its position as the favorite sniping target of the liberals to a position of strength. Most recently, of course, this was because of President Reagan's posture of strength on the international scene, but it was due to an equally large extent to his own strength of purpose.

No one, but no one, had ever steam-rollered Franklin Lycoming. There wasn't the mechanism large enough for the job. The man simply had too much integrity.

There was a certain amount of press at the funeral, though not as much as Mahoney might have expected. Lycoming's wasn't a household name, although he had commanded a certain public respect, especially in recent years, and especially in the print media.

His widow, a son and two daughters-in-law were gathered with the minister and Bindrich and several other people Mahoney didn't recognize—family, he supposed.

They were not too far from the Oliver Wendell Holmes Memorial, which in turn was just up from the

JFK Eternal Flame. The limousines were parked along the drive, snaking back toward the Arlington Memorial Gate.

Mahoney stood well back with Kopinski during the brief service. Finally the coffin was lowered into the grave, and the final words were said.

"How did lunch go?" Kopinski asked as they started back to the car.

"It's not your fault, Stan, so don't worry about it. He telephoned early this morning to ask for my help."

"With what? I thought you were out."

"I am. Lycoming apparently did some kind of a cover-up on the network thing."

"The Geneva business?" Kopinski asked, his eyes widening.

"Right. Bindrich needs me to hold his hand."

"Can't say as I blame him. How about your son? I hear he's doing well these days."

Mahoney was just climbing into the limo. He backed out. "What?"

"John," the older man said. "He's finished with his training. Eric was telling me about . . ."

There was a terrible clutching at Mahoney's heart. He turned away from Kopinski and looked back toward the crowd around the open grave. The service was over. Nearly everyone was coming back to their cars. Bindrich was still at the graveside with Lycoming's family.

Was the destruction of Mahoney's family nearing completion now? The single question raced through his brain. His son Michael had been killed in 1979 by Russians trying to strike back at the Agency. Marge was dead. His daughter-in-law and grandchildren were dead in an explosion, and now was John involved in the business?

"Don't tell me you didn't know," Kopinski was saying.

Mahoney turned back to him. "Who recruited him?"

"I don't know, Wallace. Eric just mentioned his

name once or twice. Weeks ago. Thought he was your son. He was down at The Farm outside Williamsburg. Doing well from what Eric heard."

"Is he still there? Or is he here in town?"

"I don't know. He was still in training as of a couple of weeks ago."

John had been out of touch for at least nine weeks. It was about the length of the Company's primary training school. Hand-to-hand combat, psychological stress, equipment, weapons, techniques. A potpourri of tradecraft. The school served to pump the proper esprit de corps into the new recruits. Sometimes the spirit lasted a month or two, but it always faded in the end. Reading foreign newspapers and making friends with foreign government officials and their families was generally not the work the new people had envisioned. But now and then something would come up, something dangerous. Most of the new ones had no idea what was happening to them; The Farm hadn't really prepared them. If they were lucky, they survived. After a few field assignments on which they were lucky, they became pros. Most did not make it that far.

It was not the life Mahoney wanted for his son. Not after all he had lost.

"Are you going to stick with me this afternoon?" Mahoney asked sharply.

Kopinski, a definitely worried expression on his face, shook his head. "I'm to be dropped off in town, and then you're to be taken out to the Agency. Bindrich will be there by then." Kopinski shook his head. "I'm sorry, Wallace."

"Nothing to be sorry about, Stan. It's not your fault."

"I have the uncomfortable feeling that you're going to be hunting scalps."

Mahoney managed a slight smile. "Whatever gave you that idea?" he asked. He got in the car before Kopinski could reply.

• • •

Mahoney's name was on the clipboard with the guard at the main gate, and after he had signed in at the reception desk just inside the front door of the large building, he was escorted up to the director's suite on the seventh floor where he was handed over to Bindrich's secretary, a spinsterish old woman with her eyeglasses on a silver chain around her neck.

"Ah, Mr. Mahoney," she said. She picked up her telephone. "He is here, Mr. Director," she said softly. Then she hung up. "It will be just a moment, sir."

A half minute later, Don Page came out of the office, leaving the door ajar. "Good afternoon, sir. Are you carrying any weapons?"

"No," Mahoney said.

"Please go in," Page said, stepping aside.

Bindrich was staring out the large expanse of glass at the rolling countryside below. He turned. "It was a nice service."

Mahoney strode across the large office as the door closed behind him. "You son of a bitch," he swore. He could feel the blood singing in his ears.

Bindrich was genuinely startled. "What?" he sputtered.

"My son. You were DDO. You were responsible for recruitment."

"He was Lycoming's project. You didn't know?"

"Lycoming? DCIs do not involve themselves in such things. He would have handed it down to you."

"I'm sorry, Wallace, but John was recommended directly to Lycoming. I had nothing to do with it. Policy—"

"Recommended by whom?"

Bindrich, his round face puckered, looked at Mahoney. "Why, by Bob McBundy, of course, before he was killed in Geneva. You were there . . ."

"How?" Mahoney asked. He could hear his voice

from a long way off. He was beginning to feel detached.

"There apparently was a memo to that effect. I don't really know, though. I wasn't told."

"That was six months ago."

"These things take time. You know that," Bindrich said. He shook his head. "I swear to you, Wallace, I assumed you knew."

Mahoney nodded. "Where is he now?"

"Right this moment?"

Mahoney nodded again.

"Probably down at The Farm. He'll be finishing soon with his class. He's at the top, you know."

Was Bindrich lying? "And then what?"

"A subregional desk here. Then assignment."

"No," Mahoney said.

Bindrich opened his mouth.

"No," Mahoney repeated. "John is out. He will not be working for you. You're going to fire him. Send him back to his job in California."

"He's a responsible adult . . ."

"Don't give me that crap! You know what I can—and will—do."

"Don't threaten me, Wallace," a different Bindrich said. Before he had been on what he considered shaky grounds. Now, for just a moment, he was on his home turf; self-righteousness. "You had a long, distinguished career with the service. Don't ruin it now."

"You think you have troubles with missing documents? Wait until I'm finished. It'll be a nightmare."

Bindrich stared at him. "Because of your son?"

"Because of my son."

Bindrich turned away. "There's nothing I can do."

"Fire him. You don't need to give him any explanations."

"It's not that easy."

"Then I'll do it for you."

Bindrich said nothing. He was looking out the windows again. There was something about the set of his shoulders, one lower than the other, just then, that bothered Mahoney.

"You lied to me."

Bindrich maintained his silence a little longer.

"You've already sent him off. He's out there somewhere already. Isn't he? You've got him listed as an expendable."

"Now just a minute," Bindrich snapped, turning back. He was puffed up. "I don't have to stand here and take that! No one here is expendable."

"He's finished with his schooling, and he's already off, isn't that so, Sylvan?"

Bindrich sighed deeply. He nodded. "Yes. We couldn't keep him."

"Where is he?"

"In no danger. I swear to you."

"Where?"

"We couldn't keep him down. I had Dobyns, the acting DDO, send him out on a field assignment. Something came in just last night. He left early this morning."

"While we were talking on the telephone, you bastard?"

"I thought you knew that he was here."

"You never bothered to ask."

"Your parents, your wife were not asked by the Agency when you went to work for it," Bindrich shot back.

"This is different, goddammit, you heartless bastard! I lost Michael, and John lost his family."

"Which is one of the reasons he wanted in so badly."

Mahoney's eyes narrowed. What was Bindrich saying? His heart ached.

"I don't now all the details—no one can . . . but your son wants this more than anything else. He says it. His profiles say it. His physical testing is all positive. He's at the top of the scale in almost every category. The psychologists say he has one of the strongest instincts for survival that they've ever seen."

Just the smallest bit of pride crept into Mahoney's breast, and it frightened him. "No," he said, more as a cry of anguish than a command, more a sense of self-denial, than rejection of the idea.

There were bandages around John's neck. He seemed very pale. He had lost weight. "Christ . . . Christ . . . Dad, they killed Elizabeth . . . and the babies! The bastards! Oh God . . . the bastards!"

He had told his son it was over then, but apparently it was not.

Bindrich came around the desk. He poured Mahoney a drink, and directed him to a chair across the room.

"Cigar?" he asked. He held out a box of Cuban Gondoliers. Mahoney took one, and absently went through the routine of lighting it.

Bindrich sat down on the couch just across the long coffee table from Mahoney. "You always were a pragmatist, Wallace. I wouldn't want to change that in you."

Mahoney looked at him. He was still thinking about John, and about Geneva.

"I'll offer you a trade."

"My son for your information?" Mahoney asked bitterly.

"No, of course not. Your son is not mine to give or take . . . nor is he yours. What I had in mind is a simple trade of information. You tell me what I want to know, and I'll tell you where John is."

"And what he's working on?"

Bindrich hesitated a moment, but then he nodded.

"What was he offered?"

Again Bindrich hesitated. "I don't know, Wallace. I swear it. Monsanto wasn't enough for him, but it wasn't money."

No, it was never money, Mahoney thought. His son was out there somewhere. Alone. Oh, he had the organization behind him, but he was alone nevertheless.

☆ FIVE ☆

Going back over all that had happened months ago was much easier than Mahoney had thought it would be. There was little or no pain associated with the retelling, although the memories themselves—not so sharply defined in the actual recall as he thought they would be—were prickly. Lycoming, McBundy, Darrel Switt, McNiel Henrys. They were all figures from some past stage drama. In many respects, at least, it seemed that they had no basis in reality, past or present. Yet Mahoney found he was able to gently fool himself into such a belief, so that in that respect as well, the recall was less painful than he might have expected.

It had begun, he told Bindrich, with the existence of a mole in the Mossad, Israel's secret intelligence service.

Mahoney was already retired by then, living at the cabin in Minnesota, when his contact, a young woman from Tel Aviv, had shown up on his doorstep.

They wanted him to work free-lance. Clean house for them. His would be the unexpected face on the scene. Before anyone would know what to make of him, the Mossad hoped, he would have cleaned out their gremlins.

And he had. But it had led to a network of moles. An information exchange service from several secret services through a high-ranking British Secret Intelligence Service officer.

The network had been smashed, the final confrontation coming in Geneva, Switzerland, where McNiel Henrys, the head of the clandestine group, had been killed.

"But what did Lycoming have to do with it?" Bindrich asked. Like the others before him, he was having a lot of trouble accepting what Mahoney was telling him. Even within the Agency at the time it had happened, there were only a handful of men who knew the story. Most of them were dead now.

"Not a thing until later," Mahoney said. "He didn't want any of this to get out, though."

"God no!"

"He covered up. Senator Aronson was coming out later that month to poke around."

Bindrich sat back with his own inner thoughts. Mahoney watched him carefully. He had been told that every new DCI went through a period of incredulity and shock for the first few weeks. The secrets he was asked to accept, the status quo of the job, the constant sniping by the public, the immense pressures were so intense that nine out of ten men new to the job, given the chance, would gladly quit.

This now was just one part of Bindrich's incoming education as DCI. Even as deputy director of Operations, he had no real understanding of the vastness of the organization. He had been a virgin.

"Who was our contact with McNiel Henrys?" Bindrich asked.

"There were two of them, actually," Mahoney said softly.

"They're not in jail?"

"No."

"They couldn't simply have been allowed to go free. Or could they . . ."

"No," Mahoney said. Bindrich was coming to it himself. It was evident from the look in his eyes.

"They were killed."

Mahoney said nothing.

"McBundy. The DDO. My boss."

Mahoney got up, went to the sideboard, and poured himself another drink. He took it over to the window. The sun was going down, casting long shadows across the wooded, rolling hills. For a moment, as he looked out, he forgot what he had come here for. These were the Bureau of Public Roads grounds. There were a few buildings north of here. And there was an old cemetery out there. In the early days there wasn't even a sign on the highway announcing that the Agency was back here. From time to time they'd get an occasional car at the front gate, the driver lost, wondering what the hell he had gotten himself into when he was surrounded by armed guards.

The secret that wasn't finally sank to such a ludicrous state that a small sign was posted on the highway, announcing that the Central Intelligence Agency was at the turnoff.

Mahoney, his thoughts turning outward again, found that he didn't really give a damn about Bindrich's problem with the new job. He had his own problems dealing with the past, as well as with his son's future.

The telephone chimed softly. In irritation Bindrich got up and answered it. He spoke for a moment or two, then hung up.

Mahoney turned back to him.

"Who was the second man in with us?" Bindrich asked impatiently. Evidently the call had been more trouble on his already full plate.

"Darrel Switt."

Bindrich nodded. He wasn't surprised any longer. That was the second thing, after worry, that the job did for you. It knocked out your ability to ever be surprised. "Both of them your friends?"

"Yes."

The office was very quiet then. No sounds came from outside or from the other parts of the building. The director's suite was soundproofed as well as electronically clean. It was a cocoon. It did not seem such a safe place to be, though.

"And that's the end of the story?"

"When I returned here, Lycoming told me I was finished, that he'd take care of picking up the pieces and sweeping them under the rug."

Bindrich nodded. "There were references to some occurrence in Geneva about that time."

"Then you knew?"

"No," Bindrich said heavily. "It's why I called you here. There were references in Lycoming's personal papers. References he apparently had planned on destroying at some later date. The documents and case files his notes referred to were destroyed. We found only empty jackets in Archives. The computer had been wiped clean."

"Evidently he had planned on replacing the material with something else."

"We'll never know who did the actual legwork. I had the jackets themselves dusted. No prints. It was done well."

"Then that takes care of my part of the bargain."

"St. Albans. That mean anything to you?"

"Yes," Mahoney said. "It was part of the operation. Was it another blank spot for you?"

"Yes."

"I suggest you do as Lycoming had intended."

"What's that, Wallace?"

"Destroy the rest of the files or memos or whatever it was he left behind. Destroy it all, and then forget about it."

Bindrich seemed to give deep consideration to Mahoney's suggestion. He stared at the telephone on his desk.

"When you get right down to it, Sylvan, you only have two choices. You can complete Lycoming's cover-up. Or you can plan on briefing the next DCI, and laying it in his lap."

Bindrich blinked. "There's more to it than that." He ran his fingers through his hair. "Another drink?" he asked.

Mahoney shook his head.

"I have your story now . . ." Bindrich started. But then he looked at Mahoney with a different expression. "I *do* have your story, don't I?"

"The important bits."

Bindrich nodded. "Then there is more. A lot more, if the blank spots are any indication."

Mahoney didn't understand. Bindrich could see that.

"Your project in Geneva with the moles. It was the subject of only a few memos. There are a lot of others. Franklin Lycoming was a busy man."

Mahoney knew that what Bindrich was telling him should have a significance. But he found it difficult to concentrate on it. Lycoming was dead. For him it was over. Unless he had left some mechanism in place, his passing was all that was significant. And if he had left machinery behind, Bindrich would be the man to dismantle it. He was already on the right track.

"I envy you, just now," Bindrich said out of the blue.

"What, my retirement? Tired already?"

"No. My nose is a little closer to the grindstone than that. I envy you your ability to wrap things up in neat little bundles. I can't."

Mahoney started to laugh, but he stopped himself short when he realized the man was dead serious. "Don't let this Lycoming thing get out of proportion. The man is dead. It's over."

"I don't like it."

"It was his own way of doing business, Sylvan. His stamp. His mark." Bindrich wasn't buying it. "If he had left tons of notes, all in undecipherable code, would you feel better?"

Bindrich sighed but didn't answer the question. He didn't have to. "Now the quid pro quo, I suppose."

"Where is John?"

"In Brussels."

"Doing what?"

"Looking for a NATO general who has either been kidnapped or has defected."

It sounded fairly tame. "Who is our man over there?"

"Pierre Renelaux."

"He's with the embassy?" Mahoney had never heard of the man.

"No. Malcolm Conwell is chief of Brussels station. Renelaux is liaison at NATO itself. He has a seat on the ININ board."

"A Belgian?"

"He was born in Spa. But he was raised and educated here. Toledo, I think. He's been back in Belgium now for only a year. But he is a good man. He gets results."

"Why did we send someone over?"

"Renelaux asked for help."

"I should think his office would have been able to handle something like this with relative ease. If it was the Red Brigade or Baader Meinhof or some other group like that, Interpol could be tipped off. If it's a defection and the general is already in the Soviet bloc somewhere, there's damned little we could do about it."

"There's a bit more to it than that," Bindrich said.

Mahoney was getting a sense of déjà vu. He had heard words to that effect many times before.

"Half of Europe is looking for him. The other half is scared witless."

"The general took something with him?" Mahoney asked. He was definitely getting the sense that this was old home week.

"Contingency strike plans," Bindrich said. "We don't have our copy yet. Evidently it was something they had just developed. Our general was on the review committee."

"No clues to where he got himself off to? Who might have snatched him?"

"Not one, except they did find his car parked downtown."

"I still don't understand why you sent John."

Bindrich sipped his drink. "It's possible the general defected. Now, if that is indeed the case, there isn't a hell of a lot we can do about it except go through the motions."

"So you sent John," Mahoney said. He was having trouble getting a handle on Bindrich's motivation for sending a green agent into the field like this. "Aren't you a little concerned that in his present state of mind John might be dangerous? Anything could set him off."

"We don't see it that way, Wallace. We believe your son is stable."

Mahoney exploded. "His wife and children are dead a few months, and you believe he's stable? For Christ's sake, Sylvan, stable men do not simply walk away from their careers to become Central Intelligence Agency agents. Legmen. That's what he specifically requested, wasn't it? Field work?"

Bindrich nodded.

"But you people didn't give a good goddamn!"

"This is the real world we're dealing with now," Bindrich said. "I just want to head off your next charge that we're just sending cannon fodder out there."

"Aren't you?"

"Give your son, if not us, the credit for some intelligence. We think that in time he will make a damned fine field man. A rarity. Like it or not, Wallace, your son is very talented . . . very resourceful."

"If he survives."

"You did. He has so far."

Mahoney set his glass down, then turned to look out the window again. The sun was nearly below the horizon. The sky to the west was blood red. "I'm going to Brussels to see him."

"And?"

"Talk him into quitting."

"That's your prerogative, Wallace. I won't stop you. In fact I'll telephone ahead to clear you with Renelaux and Conwell."

"I'll leave first thing in the morning."

"I'll call this evening."

"You should get someone ready to take John's place."

"That won't be a problem . . . if it comes to that. But this could escalate."

"I don't care," Mahoney said.

"You don't care about the details?"

Mahoney turned back to once again face Bindrich. "I'm not some knight in shining armor, Sylvan. I'm not a seeker after the holy grail. I found out a long time ago that there isn't such a thing."

"Don't tell me fairy tales now—" Bindrich started, but Mahoney cut him off.

"I'm just going after my son. He's all I have left."

Bindrich studied him for a second or two. "Perhaps you're right. But ask yourself: What does *he* have?" He picked up his telephone. "Mr. Mahoney is leaving now. Have someone escort him down, sign him out, and have him driven to Stan Kopinski's home in Arlington."

"I'm going to get him back," Mahoney said as Bindrich hung up. "He doesn't belong in this business. I've got my stars up in my parlor window. I've given up all I'm going to give."

"I understand. I truly do."

Mahoney went to the door. Before he went out he looked back. "This general . . ."

"Sir Robert Marshall."

"Is he that important? Are the strike plans that vital?"

"Very. I'll send over a brief."

It was quite late in Brussels, after midnight. Wind-driven rain beat against the windows in the drawing room, and although the fire was well built-up on the grate, it somehow didn't seem able to provide any warmth. Lady Sidney shivered in her thick velour robe.

"Where is Renée?" Sir Howard Scott asked. He had

arrived just a minute ago. He stood with his back to the fire, warming his hands behind him. Bobbs, who never went to bed unless the household was completely settled, had gone to fetch him a drink.

"Upstairs. Asleep I should think. She was exhausted."

"And you look all in yourself, Sidney."

"The tablets don't help. And besides, I couldn't stand to be knocked out knowing that . . . that Robert is out there somewhere."

It had been thirty hours since Sir Robert had disappeared. So far not a trace had been found. Renée, his and Sidney's only child, had flown in from London this morning over her physician's protest. She was ill with a flu virus. Sidney had put her to bed early. She wished she could do the same.

"We've heard nothing."

"It's been so long. He could be anywhere."

"No news is good news in these sorts of circumstances, I'm told," Sir Howard said.

Even in her present state, however, Lady Sidney saw through the lie. She saw something else as well. Only she didn't know if she was going to be strong enough for whatever it was he was most certainly going to ask of her.

"Everything that can be done is being done. Besides the Brussels police and the Belgian National Service, Interpol has been called in."

Lady Sidney burrowed deeper into the couch, holding her robe close around her neck. "All any of them have done so far is to surround the place, and to put a tape machine on the telephones."

"They've given you a switch. You only have to record whatever you want to."

She said nothing.

"Very soon the French will be in the fray, and the CIA man—Renelaux—has been at it. I suspect he has or will be getting additional help from the States. So you see, we have a lot of help."

"Are our own people doing all they can?"

"Of course, Sidney. Belgium is being gone through with a fine-tooth comb. So is England, on the chance he went back there."

Sidney looked up, suddenly more alert. "On the chance he *went* back there?"

Sir Howard blinked.

"What are you telling me now, Howard? Was Robert kidnapped, or wasn't he?"

"We don't know for certain," Sir Howard said uncomfortably.

"For God's sake, what do you know? Tell me the truth! I demand it!"

Someone knocked discreetly at the door. They both turned toward it as Bobbs came in bearing Sir Howard's drink.

"Thank you," Sir Howard said gratefully.

"Will there be anything else, madam?" the burly man asked.

"No, thank you, Bobbs. You'd best retire now."

Bobbs left, and Lady Sidney turned again to Sir Howard. "What are you trying to tell me? Was Robert kidnapped?"

"We don't know."

"And now you don't think so. Is that it?"

"There are usually ransom notes by this time."

"Has he been assassinated, then?" She was trying very hard to hold herself together.

"Not that either, Sidney, and for the same reason. If someone had . . . done something to harm Robert, they would have let us know by now. They'd be bragging about it."

Lady Sidney felt light-headed. "Why do I get the impression that this is going to be a very long evening?" She looked up. "Howard?"

"There are some . . . delicate questions I'm going to have to ask you."

"You think he may have simply walked away?"

Sir Howard shrugged, an uncharacteristically non-committal gesture for him.

"What sort of delicate questions? Is he on medication? Is he a diabetic? Odd bits such as those? You can fetch that sort of trivia from his records." She shook her head. "But no, those are not so delicate after all. Robert has walked off, you think. Perhaps with another woman?"

"I can return later—" Sir Howard started, but she cut him of. She was incredulous.

"My God, you're serious! You think he *has* toddled off on his own."

Sir Howard downed his drink in one swallow and placed the tumbler on the mantel. He came across to where Lady Sidney was seated and perched on the edge of the couch beside her. He took her hands in his. He could feel that she was shivering.

"We've checked everywhere, Sidney. Train depots, the airports, buses, car hire firms. Just everywhere. No sign he'd ever passed that way. Which leads us to believe he is still in the city, or he was whisked away by a private car."

"Or drove away of his own volition."

"That too," Sir Howard said. "But we cannot do this alone. At least not as effectively as we could with your help."

"What help can I give you, Howard? You know Bobby. He's as kind as the day is long. And he's loyal to a fault."

"There've been no signs lately? A wife would be the first to . . . suspect."

"Oh, God," Sidney said, raising her knuckles to her mouth and turning away.

"I know this is damned difficult. But if there's to be any hope whatsoever that we'll find him, we'll need your help."

She turned back. "It's not another woman, Howard. I know that for a fact. In this you must trust my judgment. I will not have his name smeared like this."

"All right. I believe you, Sidney. I was just as shocked and hurt as you when it was suggested. But there is something, isn't there?"

She looked into his eyes for a long time before she finally nodded. "Yes," she said in a very small voice. "At least I think so."

Sir Howard waited.

"Lately, over the past month or so . . ." she began, but then she stopped.

"It's all right, go on," Sir Howard prompted.

She was thinking back to an incident nearly a year ago. A small thing, actually, something one wouldn't ordinarily remember beyond a day or so. But now it stuck out very vividly in her memory.

"Robert has been preoccupied lately. I was going to say it has been going on for the past month or so, but it has been longer than that. It's been a year."

"What is it, Sidney?"

"It was odd. He was on the telephone, upstairs in his room. It was very late. I couldn't sleep, so I went in to see him." She was looking within her memory of the incident. She could see him seated at his small writing desk. His back was to her, so he wasn't immediately aware that she had come in. Someone was speaking to him on the telephone. Loudly. She could hear the rasp of the voice even across the room.

"No," Sir Robert said sharply. *He was angry.*

Lady Sidney blinked. "Suddenly he became aware that he was no longer alone in the room. He turned to me. There was the strangest expression on his face. I'd never seen such a look before."

"Like how?" Sir Howard asked. "Angry? Sad?"

"Both," Lady Sidney said. "Perplexed. But as if he had been hurt somehow."

"What happened? What did he say?"

She shook her head. "That's what was so odd, Howard. He simply hung up the telephone without a good-bye or a single word to whoever was on the other end. Then he got up and came across the room to me."

"Did you ask who it was?"

"No," she said. "No, I guess I didn't. The next day it was like a dream, and then I forgot about it until now. Strange."

"It wasn't a woman?"

"No, it wasn't," Lady Sidney snapped impatiently. "I've already told you that such an idea is ridiculous. Simply out of the question."

Sir Howard nodded. "That was the first incident. You started to say that Robert had been acting strange."

"Yes. Forgetful. Not showing up for dinner. Being hours late—never this late—but hours late. Inviting guests to the house without informing me beforehand."

"You mentioned that earlier. Who was this newspaper chap yesterday afternoon?"

"Langley. Langford. Something like that." She groped for the name. "No. Thomas Langdon. The *London Daily Mail*. He did the last things on Lady Diana. I remember it now."

"He had an appointment with Robert?"

Lady Sidney nodded.

"To discuss what?"

"I don't know. Some sort of article about Bobby as the forgotten soldier. Something like that."

☆ SIX ☆

Coming from the lovely weather in Washington, D.C., to the cold, rainy weather over the European continent was like going from day to night, or summer to winter. For Wallace Mahoney, though, it suited his mood just fine.

He had taken the British Airways Concorde across to London, and from there a Sabena flight to Brussels's Zaventem Airport.

The CIA liaison to NATO, Pierre Renelaux, had been told to expect him, but no fanfare was to accompany Mahoney's arrival. Because of the NATO general's disappearance with highly sensitive documents, the city was in a minor uproar. It would do no good to add fuel to the fire by announcing the arrival of still another CIA operative . . . even a retired one.

He took a cab out to the Duc du Brabant et du Rhine, an inexpensive hotel near the Gare du Nord. Travel Section had suggested the hotel to him on Bindrich's signature. It was clean, he would be out of the way of the fray, and Renelaux would be able to make contact with no trouble.

He was in time for an early dinner in a small Italian restaurant across the street from the hotel, and then he went to a phone booth in the railway station and called the number Bindrich had provided him. No one was supposed to know he was in Brussels; nevertheless, he felt more secure taking the precaution of not phoning from his hotel.

A woman answered.

"Hello," Mahoney said. "I would like to speak with Pierre Renelaux."

"One moment, please."

It was Sunday. The train station was nearly deserted, as were the streets outside. Mahoney shivered, a sudden chill spreading up his back.

The woman was back. "Who is calling, please?"

"Wallace Mahoney."

"Welcome to Brussels, Mr. Mahoney," a man said. Pierre Renelaux, Mahoney presumed.

"I have come to speak with my son."

"Yes. I understand. I will have him meet us at your hotel," the man said. "He does not know you are here."

"I see."

"I would wish to speak with you for a few minutes first. Would that be possible?"

The pitch was coming. Bindrich must have spent a long time on the secure line with Renelaux last night or this morning.

"I'll be in my room," Mahoney said, and he hung up. For a minute or two he remained in the phone booth looking across the cavernous depot with its vaulted ceilings and cold marble floors. A million people had passed this way. Ten million people. He could almost hear their chatter, their heels slapping against the stone; it was as if a thousand million ghosts were rising from their graves and moving across a cemetery. His ghosts were among them. Again a deep chill rose up his back, raising the gooseflesh on his neck.

How many among the ghosts had he known? he wondered. And how soon would he be joining them? Suddenly he had a strong sense of his own mortality, something he hadn't felt since just after Marge died. It had been an empty feeling then. Now, however, it was almost comforting.

He shook off his morbid thoughts and went back to the hotel, and directly up to his room. He had not bothered to unpack his bags, and he didn't do so now. At worst, he figured, he'd merely be staying overnight. He'd catch the early morning flight to New York. Hopefully with John in tow.

There was no television in his room, but there was a very old-fashioned coin-operated radio. He dropped in a few ten-franc coins and switched it on. It didn't work. He contemplated calling down for a television set to be delivered but decided against it.

In the tiny bathroom he splashed some cold water on his face, then he sat down by the window that looked down on the Boulevard St. Lazare. The street glistened in the rain.

A large truck passed, turned the corner, and then was gone.

The worst part of it was that he had known John would do something like this, and yet he had been powerless to prevent it. John had always been the conservative one in the family. Where Michael had been impetuous, John had been the one to stand back and reason things out. But once he had his mind made up, nothing could sway him.

Mahoney worried about that now. John could very well have backed himself into a corner, and in that case, no amount of persuasion on his father's part would change his mind.

But what had Lycoming said to John? What bait had he dangled? What visions, what tales had he spun? What promises for surcease of sorrow had Lycoming made?

What were the motivations that drove a man? Scratch a hundred men and you'd find a thousand reasons.

His son was the special case. A certain faction within the Company had always preyed on his type. Had used them to great advantage. So-and-so pulled his coup: less than a kilo of horse; a lost weekend, a woman, a case of Johnnie Walker; a cute boy from one of the Greek isles for the forty-year-old engineer who had just lost his wife. Christ, the business was dirty. The list was endless.

Malleability was a complimentary term . . . for the agent runner, not the agent.

Part of it, of course, was the tremendous rush of power. At least for the young it was. (Don't kid yourself, old man . . . not just for the young.) The Central Intelligence Agency. Fighting the bad guys. Against the Russians. Adventure with a capital A and with no answer to normal lines of authority. A voice over a telephone. A signature on a written instruction. Ultimately a tie back to Langley. But Christ, what power. It was akin to an adult Disneyland for jaded spirits.

Mahoney knew it all. His son was just guessing. Making all the mistakes. Make a friend, use a friend, lose a friend. The litany of the Company. Damn, how Mahoney knew its verse and lines.

It was perplexing, he thought, what turns our lives took. In what direction they rebounded when dealt a heavy blow.

A dark Opel sedan with only a driver came down the street in the opposite direction the truck had gone, then turned the far corner.

Mahoney watched. A minute later the man came back around the corner on foot, crossed the street, and approached the hotel.

Bindrich's brief had described Renelaux as tall and dark, with a mustache and prominent nose. The man below was certainly tall.

Not really knowing why he continued to take these precautions—old habits, he supposed—he got up from the window seat and slipped out of his room. He went down the corridor where he stopped just around the corner away from the elevator and in plain view of the stairwell door.

About two minutes later the elevator came up from the lobby. Its doors opened, and a tall, dark man with a mustache approached Mahoney's room and knocked on the door. His right hand was in his jacket pocket.

Mahoney watched him for a moment or two. "Monsieur Renelaux," he said softly.

The CIA operative was startled. He spun around. Almost instantly, however, he visibly relaxed. "Mr. Mahoney," he said. "You surprised me."

Mahoney came down the corridor. "I saw you come across the street. I wasn't sure it was you."

"It may have been wise for you to take such precautions," Renelaux said. They shook hands and went into Mahoney's room. Renelaux peeled off his raincoat and hung it on the back of a chair. "Have you been briefed?"

"No. I don't know what you've been told. But I'm here merely to speak with my son."

Renelaux looked at Mahoney. "I appreciate that," he said. "I really mean it." His complexion was dark, as if he had lain in the sun for a long time. But that wasn't it. He was naturally dark. He had cruel eyes and thin lips. Bindrich, in his brief, had written highly of him. Instinctively Mahoney did not share the feeling. The man looked like a Paris used car salesman.

"You said you wished to speak with me, and then John would be arriving."

Renelaux nodded.

"How long before he will be here?"

"A half hour, perhaps a little sooner. Mr. Bindrich has asked me to inform you of the developing situation here, and from that you could make your own decision."

"My own decision about what?"

Renelaux shrugged, the gesture typically Gallic. "About your son. About yourself, presumably. He did not specify."

Mahoney decided he would make it no easier for the man. He went to the window, glanced down at the street, then sat down on the bed. "The meter is running."

"Sir?"

"Your half hour has begun."

Comprehension dawned on the man's face. "Ah," he said. "You are angry."

"Yes."

"With me?"

Mahoney stared at him. "Not yet."

The Belgian nodded. "General Sir Robert Marshall, chairman of NATO's Nuclear Defense Affairs Committee, disappeared from his office Friday afternoon. He carried with him certain . . . sensitive documents. We have been looking for him, without success, ever since."

"What has John been doing for you?"

"Shadowing the French and the Italians."

Mahoney sat forward. Slowly. "The SDEDC and SISMI are involved?"

"Naturally."

"Why do you have a tail on them?"

"I thought it best. This is important. There are many people who would like to find out where Sir Robert has gone."

"Who else?"

"The West Germans, the Swedes . . . every secret service within the Alliance."

"They're all here? In Brussels?"

Renelaux nodded. "All looking for Sir Robert. All wanting to snatch the documents before they get loose."

Lisbon had been like that during the war. It would have been ludicrous in those days, except for the fact that no one had been playing games. People got killed for their grubby little secrets. He feared now for his son more than he had before.

He wanted only to talk to John, to convince him to return to the States with him, and they could get out of there.

There was one detail that bothered him, however. It was something that Renelaux had apparently hinted at in a conversation with Bindrich.

"You don't believe Sir Robert was kidnapped?"

"No, I do not."

"You believe he defected? To whom? The Russians?"

"To them or the East Germans."

"What makes you think so?"

"No one knew he was going to be alone at that precise moment, so no kidnap plan could have been evolved. No one knew that he would be taking such documents with him. There was no sign of a struggle. His car was clean. Only his prints and those of the garage personnel were found."

"But word has gotten out that something big is afoot. Otherwise the other services wouldn't be here."

"We notified the committee, of course," Renelaux said, "which leaks like a water tap in an old apartment."

"And if indeed he has defected, there is little we would be able to do about it."

"Other than minimize the damage he has done to our position. If we knew for sure who has the papers . . ."

"My son is superfluous, then. There is no need for him to be here."

Again Renelaux shrugged. "I was told to arrange for your meeting, but first to brief you."

Mahoney glanced at his watch. There was still plenty of time before John was due to arrive. Something in the situation wasn't making a lot of sense to him.

"Sir Robert is an old man."

Renelaux nodded. "Seventy, but still sharp as a tack."

"He's a military man."

"General Sir Robert. Retired. Absolutely brilliant tactician. British Army.

"How long has he been on the NATO committee?"

"Off and on since the early seventies, I believe . . . with the Alliance, that is. Only the past four years on the Nuclear Defense Affairs Committee. Highly respected, but somewhat of a radical at times . . . if you know what I mean."

"No, I don't."

"Outspoken for a man of his rank and position. Some Brits, depending upon who you talk to, think of him either as an eccentric, dangerously meddlesome, or absolutely right on. There's no in-between."

"He heads an important NATO committee. Someone in power must think a great deal of him."

"Oh, don't get me wrong. Sir Robert is a member of the British establishment. He is *Sir* Robert, after all. He's given his entire life in service of England."

"Doesn't sound like a defector to me. Had you known him personally?"

"No," Renelaux said.

Was there something the man wasn't telling him? Mahoney wondered. But then again, operations almost always began like this . . . the odd bits that didn't seem to add up. It still offended Mahoney's sense of orderliness. But anomalies were the key; they had always been the key to understanding.

"Who is coordinating the investigation?" Mahoney asked after a moment.

"Oliver Horne, in name. He's chief of NATO Security. But in actuality no one has a firm hand."

"What's his nationality?"

"American. He was with the Air Force Intelligence Service before he retired. He's been with the Alliance now for a half-dozen years. A good man."

"How about you? What are you doing?"

Renelaux shook his head. "Nothing more than watching. There's little else we can do without stumbling over Horne's people, the Belgian police, Interpol—and of course the Brits have half a battalion of SIS people in the field."

Why did he care? Other than John's involvement with the affair, Mahoney had no connection with it.

"Has Sir Robert any family or friends here in Brussels?"

"His wife, Lady Sidney. They have a home near Anderlecht, just outside the city proper. His best friend would be Air Vice Marshal Sir Howard Scott. He's a commander of Allied Maritime Air Force, Channel. They go way back together, from what I understand.''

"Anyone else?"

"Their daughter, Renée Swearington. Thirty-six, divorcée. Lives outside London. She arrived yesterday.''

"You have files on them, as well as on Sir Robert?"

Renelaux nodded. "But not very complete, I'm afraid. They are the friendlies, after all.''

"The Russians?" Mahoney asked softly. "Are they looking for Sir Robert too?"

Renelaux drew himself up. "I know what you're going to say. If the Russians are looking for him—and they are—that he could not have defected to them.''

Mahoney held his silence.

"They're here, all right, along with the East Germans, the Poles, and a few other Warsaw Pact services. But it's all an elaborate smoke screen. They need time to get him out. Make sure he's not a herring." Renelaux almost seemed angry. Something was eating at him.

"Do you have the Russians identified?"

"They have a team here on a more or less permanent basis. It's run by a fellow named Konstantin Demin, who supposedly is in charge of the Aeroflot office downtown. Everyone knows who he is. Malcolm Conwell and his people out of the embassy take care of them.''

"Who else?"

"A couple of heavies came in. An Aeroflot transfer, and one of them with their embassy's travel section, we're led to believe.''

"What about Demin? Is he any good?"

"Yes, but we all have an understanding. If he doesn't push too hard, we don't push back. Keeps the natives happy.''

"Comfortable arrangement," Mahoney said.

Renelaux had perched on the edge of the chair. He jumped up. "You don't understand how it is here.''

"No, I don't," Mahoney said, but he was beginning

to get a measure of the Belgian.

"Since the war the Belgian people have been sensitive about . . . certain foreigners, and certain happenings within their frontiers."

"Like the Germans and their intrigues?" Mahoney asked.

The Belgian's face contorted. "The Russians, the Germans . . . they are of the same cloth." He was getting worked up, and he knew it. He forced himself to slow down. Mahoney could read the effort from his face, from the way he held himself.

"What is it, Renelaux?" Mahoney asked gently. "What's your rub with Sir Robert? Where have you known him?"

"I haven't known him."

"But you've known his type, is that it?"

"I don't know what you're talking about."

"Is it that Sir Robert is an aristocrat here in Belgium, telling the Belgians how to run their lives? Is that it, Pierre?"

Renelaux said nothing. Mahoney felt he had hit wide of the mark. It was something else.

"You are supposed to be briefing me. Isn't that your order?"

"What do you want, Mr. Mahoney? I understand that you were coming here merely to speak with your son. Talk him into returning home with you."

"You had seen Sir Robert's defection coming. I believe those were Bindrich's words. Curious."

"Not so curious."

Mahoney smiled. "Then you have an idea why he may have wandered off, and where he might have gotten himself to."

"The Soviet Union. East Germany. Poland. The Warsaw Pact. He'll probably work on *their* Nuclear Defense Affairs Committee. He's gone over. I know it."

"You've said that," Mahoney replied dryly. "The question I put to you is, *how* do you know that? What makes you so sure? How did you pick that idea? Certainly not out of thin air. Where's your rationale, Pierre?''

The elevator bell chimed. Mahoney was conscious of it even though he had been talking, just as he had been conscious of the passage of time.

He looked toward the door. The corridor was carpeted, so it was impossible to hear footfalls, yet he imagined he could hear a man coming their way. Then someone knocked at the door.

Renelaux glanced toward the door. "It is your son." There was no animosity left in his eyes, just a professional neutrality. "He is much like you, I think. You will have a hard time convincing him to stand down."

The knock came again. Mahoney remained where he was; Renelaux had more to say.

"If you are still here in the morning, and you wish more information, we will meet again. Meanwhile, I shall leave you." Renelaux went to the door and opened it. "Come in, monsieur," he said, moving aside.

John stepped into the room. When he saw his father he was momentarily surprised. But that faded. "Hello, Dad," he said.

"Hello, John."

"If you need my help, I will speak with you in the morning," Renelaux repeated, and he left.

For a long time, it seemed, John just stood by the door. He was a tall man, half a head taller than his father, and at nearly forty his hair had already begun to turn seriously gray. He had that huskiness that could either go toward chubbiness or toward athletic bulk. In John, at least so far, it had leaned toward the latter. In fact, Mahoney could not remember when he had seen his son looking so fit. At least outwardly.

There was that hint in John's eyes, though, that gave away something of the nature of his inner turmoil. He was a man obviously driven. In athletes such drive won competitions. In scientists it produced discoveries. But in operatives, in field men, it was a very dangerous mental state.

Like any parent, however, Mahoney could see his son through rose-colored glasses. It was John, no one else standing by the door. John as a college graduate. Marge had cried nearly the entire day and apologized for being so weepy that night. He could clearly see John as a high school student. As a swimmer. As a football player. It was easy even now.

"This reminds me of when you were a little boy, and I caught you with your hand in the cookie jar," Mahoney said, finally breaking the silence between them.

A flicker of a smile crossed John's lips. He came the rest of the way into the room, went to the window, and looked down at the street. He did not stand directly in front of the window, just as they had taught him at The Farm. Instead he stood well to the side, to present less of a target. Whatever it was he was looking for, he seemed satisfied after a moment that it wasn't there.

"What are you doing in Brussels, Dad?"

"Bindrich sent me."

John turned around. "I'm not going back yet. I have a job."

"Yes, at Monsanto Chemical in Los Angeles. You are a chemical engineer."

"Not now."

"You're not an operative."

"I did pretty well in Geneva," John said sardonically. After his wife and children had been killed in the explosion meant for him, he had gone after McNiel Henrys. Against all odds, he had very nearly succeeded. He displayed a natural talent for it. Or perhaps it was just luck.

"Hell of a motivation for a job."

"What do you mean?"

"You became a chemical engineer because it fit your sense of orderliness. You've become what you think is an operative for revenge."

The remark stung.

"It's time for you to begin forgetting, son."

"Never! The bastards . . ." He cut it off.

"If not forgetting, at least don't let it dominate your life this way."

"For Christ's sake, what the hell are you talking about, Dad? Why did *you* start with the Company in forty-seven?"

"It was all I knew."

"No. It was simple idealism. You wanted to fight the bad guys. You wanted to wear the white hat."

Mahoney shook his head. "It is infinitely more complicated, and certainly a lot less noble than that, John."

"Right," his son said. It was the answer he had evidently wanted to hear. "My motivation is not so noble either. But it's mine, and I'll live with it."

"Can you understand why I don't want you in this business?" Mahoney cried. He could feel his blood pressure rising.

"Yes I can, Dad. Michael is dead because of it. I can understand you wanting to protect me now."

"You know something of the ache."

"Mom is gone, which leaves you alone except for me. What would you do if anything happened to me . . .?"

The remark hurt. "Am I that selfish?"

John was suddenly contrite. "Christ, I'm sorry, Dad. But I'm not going back."

"I could have you fired," Mahoney said, but then he waved off John's objection. "I won't do that. But your job here, as you call it, is probably not what you think it is."

"You mean Renelaux? He's such a raging anti-German that he'd rather play footsie with the Russians than trust our own allies."

"You don't like him?"

John smiled. "He's all right once you come to understand him."

Mahoney got the uncomfortable feeling that John would be working here with his back door wide open. If and when he got in over his head, there'd be no help.

"You're out, John," he said, standing up.

"I've already told you . . ."

"I don't care what you told me," Mahoney said harshly. He came very close to John and looked directly into his son's eyes. "You'll return to Washington in the morning. Talk to Bindrich. All this is his doing."

"And if I don't go?"

"I will have you declared *persona non grata* in Belgium. And believe me, son, I can have it done."

"Why, goddammit?" John swore, raising his voice.

"Because I don't want you here. No one wants you here."

"I can't believe you're doing this to me," John said desperately. He turned away, unable for the moment to face his father. He was shaking with rage and frustration.

Mahoney wanted to reach out and touch his son. Make him understand what a field assignment was all about. Oh, John had had more than his share of grief and heartache. Good Lord, how much more could a man be asked to withstand? And he thought now that by working for the Company, through whatever logic, it would somehow help him salve his conscience, somehow let him strike back at the forces that could do such things as kill women and children.

Mahoney wanted to explain to his son how it really was, and yet standing here in this shabby hotel in Brussels, he wasn't at all sure he even knew the answer himself.

He had spent his lifetime chasing after . . . what? Adventure like some cowboy? How many times had he been called away in the middle of the night, no explanations, to be gone—totally out of touch—for months? How much worry had Marge endured in her life with him?

Mahoney wanted to somehow communicate with his son, to make him see clearly the perfidy, the lies and cheating, the deceit, the manipulations—all the terrible things one person could do to another—that would either be done to him or that he'd have to do to someone else.

"John," he said gently. "You don't belong here."

John whirled around. "And you do?" he cried. "The ultimate spy? The perfect operative? The Company's best?"

"You don't understand—"

"Understand?" John laughed harshly. "Understand? Jesus Christ, I've understood all along. We all did, every time you ran off. Every time we'd hear mother crying. Oh, yes . . ."

"I meant this is the big leagues now. This isn't The Farm, and this isn't Geneva where blind luck and instinct saved your life."

"Oh . . . you *are* the ultimate spy! You're an old man. Retired. You don't belong here!"

"I'm not going to play games with you any longer, John," Mahoney said tiredly. He turned to the phone. He no longer gave a damn if this line was tapped or not. He was going to end this here and now.

"It's time for you to quit, goddammit!" John shouted. "It's time for you to step down so you don't fuck this up like you fucked it up in Moscow!"

Mahoney's knees suddenly went weak. He could feel the blood draining from his face. He didn't dare turn around.

Moscow? The orders had gone out to a special KGB unit operating out of Denver. They had snatched Michael and had run. Three hours later his son was dead.

Mahoney's revelation, when it came, unfolded like the layers of an onion. John had been told nothing about the Moscow operation afterward. Not by him, not by his mother. John was here now with a value judgment certainly fired by the emotional heat of the moment, but it was a judgment based on some understanding of the situation nevertheless. Bindrich had called at a terribly off time. The funeral, the anomalies in Lycoming's personal files . . . ploys? The tools of the trade in order to move the proper man to the right spot?

He turned around to face his son. Lycoming may have recruited the son, but Bindrich had maneuvered him here to Brussels with just the right amount of information so that when the father took the bait, when Mahoney came here to talk John out of the assignment, the confrontation would come. The heat would rise. And things would be said that should not be said. The incredible bastard had done it.

It's an incredibly dirty business, but the outcome oh, the outcome is what we're after. If the bleeding heart liberals only knew.

His son looked frightened. Would he understand? Could he understand?

"You're going to have to leave," Mahoney said. His heart was aching, but he could no longer help his son, and he could see that John realized too much had been said.

The line has been crossed. Once over there's no use looking over your shoulder, because there's no way back.

"Are you taking this assignment?" John asked woodenly.

"I think so."

"Why? I thought . . ."

"It's what I do, John."

For a long time they stood looking at each other. John wanted to say something. Ask for forgiveness? Press the argument? Mahoney wanted to say something too, but there was nothing left to say.

✪ SEVEN ✪

The rain had stopped overnight, but the weather was still quite cool and blustery. Nevertheless, Oliver Horne was waiting at an outdoor café across from the Grand' Place at noon when Mahoney showed up after seeing John off at the airport.

Surrounding the square were ornately decorated seventeenth-century guild houses, dominated by the Hôtel de Ville, its belfry rising 320 feet into the gray sky.

Horne, a very large black man with a sour expression, was dressed in civilian clothes, a bulky blue overcoat wrapped tightly around him. He sat back, watching the heavy noon traffic. No one else was outside, and the waiter serving him was very curt.

Horne rose and extended his hand. "You don't mind sitting out here?"

"No," Mahoney said. "Thanks for seeing me like this."

"I checked you out. You're legitimate, otherwise I would not have given you the time of day." Horne's voice was deep and very rich. His accent was slightly Southern.

They sat down. The waiter came, and Mahoney ordered the same kind of beer Horne was drinking. The security officer ordered another.

"I should think we would attract attention out here," Mahoney said. The damp cold was penetrating.

"Probably," Horne said. "You're here representing the CIA. I thought that was Pierre Renelaux's department. Are you a supernumerary then?"

Mahoney smiled. "No. I was asked to come over and poke around a bit."

"This city is filled with people 'poking around a bit,' as you put it, Mr. Mahoney. Have you a special talent?"

"Anyone giving you a particularly hard time?" Mahoney asked, ignoring the question.

"No more than any other. Is there a significance?"

"I wondered, Colonel, why you had such a chip on your shoulder. Or is it simply because you are black?"

Horne's nostrils flared slightly. "You don't mess around. I like that."

Their beer came. "Will there be anything else, *messieurs*?" the waiter asked imperiously.

Horne looked up. "Perhaps," he said. "We'll let you know."

The waiter left, and Horne turned back to Mahoney. "I don't know what I can tell you. I didn't know the general personally. I can give you a list of his movements, the people who knew him, the Belgian police officers' report on his car, details like that."

"Later," Mahoney said. "I'm looking for first impressions. What do *you* think happened to him?"

Horne looked at Mahoney for several long seconds as if he were appraising an opponent. "Do I think he walked off, or was kidnapped. Is that what you want to know?"

Mahoney nodded.

"Beats the hell out of me. Really. Two days ago I would have bet almost anything that he was snatched. The Russians, probably. But now . . . ?" He let it trail off.

"But now?" Mahoney prompted.

"There is no hard evidence that he was kidnapped.

No struggle. No one tried to contact us afterward. Nothing.''

"Had the Soviets, let's say, taken him and the material he had with him, might they not keep very quiet about it?"

Horne's eyes went flinty. "You had better hope, Mr. Mahoney, that the Soviet government does not have the material Sir Robert walked off with. If they do, you had better put your head between your legs and kiss your ass good-bye. There'll surely be a war."

"I've not been briefed on the content of the documents. I was only told that they were NATO's new war scenarios."

"If any of the Warsaw Pact nations were to see the material, Chernenko would make immediate political hay with it. We'd be years recovering. The entire Western world would be years regaining any face. We'd all be labeled as warmongers." Horne looked up as a large bus rattled by. "They would not keep quiet. On the contrary. Besides, Demin and his people are in the fray as much as we are."

"You don't believe their activity is a smoke screen?"

"No."

Mahoney sipped his beer. It tasted as if it had been made with strawberries. It was very sweet, like a Swiss beer. "What's your best guess, then?"

"That's the point. I don't *have* a best guess. He was *probably* kidnapped, yet it *appears* as if he wandered off on his own. There's no way of knowing at the moment. But he sometimes seemed eccentric of late, so almost anything could have happened. I mean, for Christ's sake, he left HQ with the entire scenario. That's not sane."

"Eccentric? I thought he was establishment."

"He was. And a genius, too." Horne looked at his watch. "We're going to have to finish this some other time. Out at my office. I'll have your clearance ready for you. I can give you the poop sheet we have on him, as well as his entire jacket if you want it. You can speak with Maggie Byrne, his secretary. She knew him better than most. Who knows? You might just ask the one question the rest of us hadn't thought of."

"How about Sir Howard Scott?"

"If he'd talk with you, he'd be a valuable source. He and the general were very close. I mean *very* close. Their wives—Sir Howard's is dead now—went back as friends for years. I think even before the war. At the moment he is very busy with his own people, as well as with the general's wife, Lady Sidney."

"Tell me about her."

"Nice lady," Horne said. He finished his beer and got up. "You will have to excuse me, Mr. Mahoney, but I have to get back."

"You said Sir Robert was eccentric. What did you mean? Can you tell me that much?"

"Not really. Not without giving you a lot of background on him, some of which has surprised the hell out of me, I don't mind telling you."

"Just a word," Mahoney pressed. "Characterize him."

Horne smiled. "You are persistent." He looked away for a moment as he searched for the right word. "Charismatic," he said.

It struck Mahoney as odd. "Like the religion?"

"No, not that. Sir Robert has charisma. Like a movie star. Someone famous. A politician. A Kennedy."

"And his wife, Lady Sidney?"

"His Jacqueline."

Finding Sir Robert and Lady Sidney's large home near Anderlecht outside of Brussels presented no problem for Mahoney. He rented a car at the hotel and simply asked at an Esso station in the small town where Erasmus had lived in the 1500s. His troubles, however, began at the front gate.

The approach to the house was along a gravel road blocked a hundred yards off the highway by a tall iron gate. Several cars were parked on either side of the fence. Mahoney pulled up and wound down his window as an elderly man stepped out of the gatehouse and toddled over.

"I'm here to see Lady Sidney Marshall," Mahoney called out.

Almost instantly his car was surrounded by a half-dozen grim-faced men, handguns drawn. The old gate-keeper straightened up, a pistol in his hand, and slowly approached.

Mahoney was very careful to keep both of his hands in plain sight on the steering wheel.

The gatekeeper, who up close was not old but only made up to look that way, reached out and opened Mahoney's door. He stepped back. "Get out of the car, please," he said. He spoke with a British accent.

Mahoney eased out of the car, keeping his hands out in front of him, well away from his body. There was a great deal of electricity in the air. But he figured these men were SIS. Professionals.

"Who are you?" the gatekeeper asked.

"Wallace Mahoney. Central Intelligence Agency. You may check with Oliver Horne, chief of NATO Security. We were together in town two hours ago."

One of the men lowered his weapon, turned, and hurried back into the gatehouse.

"Are you armed?" the gatekeeper asked.

"No."

Another of the men holstered his pistol beneath his dark overcoat and approached Mahoney. "Please unbutton your overcoat, sir," he said. His accent was slightly cockney, with a nasal quality to it. This one had come up the hard way.

Mahoney did as he was asked, the wind very cold. The agent efficiently frisked him, then stepped back. "Clean, sir," he said to the gatekeeper.

"What are you doing here, Mr. Mahoney?"

"I've come to speak with Lady Sidney, if she will see me."

"She is not receiving visitors," the man snapped. "What are you doing in Belgium?"

Mahoney smiled. "I think that is obvious."

The gatekeeper started to say something, when the man who had gone into the gatehouse, presumably to telephone, stuck his head out. "He's legitimate, sir."

"Who've you got on the line?"

"Colonel Horne himself."

"He's positive?"

"Yes, sir."

The gatekeeper stood back as he lowered his weapon. He holstered it, and the others did the same. Mahoney lowered his hands. His arms were beginning to ache.

"As I said, Mr. Mahoney, Lady Sidney Marshall is receiving no visitors."

"I appreciate your position, Mr. . . . ." Mahoney said, but the man would not be drawn out.

"Please get into your automobile and return to Brussels. If you report to NATO, I'm quite certain that Colonel Horne will brief you."

"If you would be so good as to telephone Lady Sidney, and tell her that I am here and wish to speak with her, I would be grateful."

"Do you know her, then?"

"No," Mahoney said.

"Get out of here, Yank," one of the other men snapped.

Mahoney turned toward the man. "Are you here simply to guard Lady Sidney from harm, or are we all here to find Sir Robert?" he asked, his tone and manner pleasant. Before anyone could answer, he turned back to the gatekeeper, who evidently was the one in charge of this detail. "I don't have the time to waste arguing with you, young man. Telephone Lady Sidney, tell her who I am, what I am in Belgium for, and that I wish to speak with her."

The gatekeeper, who was a man of about Mahoney's

height but slight of build, remained stock-still for a long time. Finally he nodded. "I'll telephone her. But she will not see you." He turned and went back to the gate-house.

"Tell her one other thing," Mahoney called after him. The man turned back. "Tell her that I understand exactly what she is going through . . . the same thing happened to me not so long ago."

The house was a very large three-story stone and wood-beamed affair that looked very old, probably dating back at least two hundred and fifty years. One of the SIS men from the gate rode up with Mahoney. He got out of the car when Mahoney did, but he didn't come up the stairs to the front veranda. He remained leaning against the hood.

Before Mahoney could knock, the large, ornately carved front door opened and a huge, pugnacious-looking man in morning clothes stood there.

"Mr. Mahoney?"

"Yes," Mahoney said. "I'd like to see Lady Sidney."

"Please come in, sir," the large man said, moving aside.

Mahoney found himself in a very large stairhall. To the left was the living room. Beyond it, through open double doors, he could see what appeared to be a formal dining room. To the right of the stairs a wide corridor led toward the back of the house, and to the right of where he stood was a set of highly polished wooden doors. Objets d'art were tastefully placed throughout as much of the house as Mahoney could see.

The houseman took Mahoney's coat, then directed him toward the double doors. "You may wait in the drawing room, sir," he said, but at that moment Lady Sidney appeared at the head of the stairs.

"It's quite all right now, Bobbs," she said, starting down, her left hand trailing on the wide banister.

Bobbs looked up, nodded, then left.

The first things that struck Mahoney were what a beautiful, elegant woman she was, and as she came closer, how drawn, wan, and tired she seemed to be. She wore dark, flowing trousers, a white silk blouse with large sleeves, and a long, sleeveless sweater-vest. There were several tea rings on both hands, but she wore little or no makeup.

"Mr. Mahoney, I believe they told me. Are you Irish?"

"Fourth-generation American."

She smiled, offering her hand. "Then I shouldn't be at all concerned about your being a terrorist."

Her hand was warm and dry in his. There was a definite magnetism about her. Her voice was cultured, her bearing and carriage regal, and her manner gracious, yet there was an earthiness about her.

"No," Mahoney said. "I've come to offer my help."

She pursed her lips, the fine lines around her mouth tightening momentarily. "Am I to understand that you have been through a similar circumstance?"

"My wife was taken from me not so very long ago. The situation was very much different, but the loss you are feeling now, I'm certain, is no different than mine was."

Lady Sidney looked at him, searching his face. She managed a very slight smile. "What a kind, sensitive thing for you to have said."

"My questions may not be so outwardly kind."

She raised her right shoulder. "Anything to help, Mr. Mahoney," she said. Then she indicated the drawing room doors. "Shall we go in? You may pour us a drink."

They went into the drawing room, which was a big, high-ceilinged room with floor-to-ceiling bookcases, a leather-topped desk in front of French doors overlooking a lovely garden and lawn, a fireplace, and a grouping of softly upholstered furniture.

Mahoney poured Lady Sidney a glass of white wine and himself a small cognac. They sat across from each other.

A fire burned in the grate. They could hear the chill wind blowing outside. It was a very pleasant, substantial room. But lonely just now. That feeling pervaded the entire house.

"I'm falling apart, you know," she said out of the blue. She smiled sheepishly. "I'm sorry. You've only just come, and I don't know you . . ."

"It's all right," Mahoney said softly.

"But I feel as though I can trust you. I can, can't I?"

He nodded. "Has anyone else been out to see you, Lady Sidney? Other than the gentlemen from your Secret Intelligence Service?"

"The police of course, and then a man from Interpol this morning. They were nice. Howard was here, naturally."

"Sir Howard Scott?"

"Yes," she said. "He is a dear friend. I suppose I should telephone him now. Let him know that you are here."

"I will be seeing him later today, or perhaps in the morning."

Lady Sidney let her gaze drift to the fire. "You're going to ask me next, what I think happened. As if I knew, or could give you any kind of answer you want." She looked back. "If I knew, I would go fetch him personally."

"Did he wander off, or was he taken?"

"Taken," she said. The word seemed to leave her breathless. "I suspect he was taken, but odd things have been happening lately."

"What kind of odd things?" Mahoney asked as gently and noncommittally as he possibly could. These were the moments when the stray bits of information—the odd feelings and impressions—came out that often became the crux of an entire operation.

Lady Sidney explained to Mahoney about her husband's strange telephone call of a year ago, which led her in stages to tell of Sir Robert's recent odd, forgetful behavior.

"I'd find him at the club. Or Maggie—his secretary —would ring up and say that he had gotten off all right, and was now in Africa, or Berlin, or Washington, or someplace like that. But he had never mentioned it to me. He always apologized later, of course. Forgetful. So very much on his mind."

"More now than, let's say, ten years ago?"

"Oh, yes. Just in recent months he's been very preoccupied. I knew he was working on something terribly important to him. Howard suspects it may have been the documents everyone is so lollygag about."

"But you don't?"

"That I would not know, Mr. Mahoney. My husband shared his work with me, but only in the most general of terms. I have no interest in bearing terrible secrets. It would drive me mad. I leave that for others."

"But Sir Robert was bothered by something?" Mahoney prompted.

"Bothered, that is the term. Yes, he was more than preoccupied of late. He was bothered. I hadn't thought of it in quite that light. But it's apt."

"It had to do with NATO?"

"With the frightful nuclear mess we seem to have gotten ourselves into since the war. He knew it would happen, you know."

"When?" Mahoney asked.

"For a long time. Since before the wall."

Mahoney wasn't quite sure just what she was referring to. She picked it up.

"The Berlin Wall, you know. He was there when it was put up. We both were. We drove up from Bonn when we heard the news." She was back there. "Bobby wept. Tears filled his eyes, and he simply wept when he saw it. 'Such a terrible, terrible thing,' he said. 'This is the beginning of the end.'

"When your President Kennedy came to Berlin,

Bobby advised him. Told him about Germany, and
especially about Berlin. He told him that there would
always only be one Berlin. And that for a German, to be
a Berliner was supreme.''

"You were at Bonn then too?"

"Bobby was military attaché to our embassy. We
would have preferred Berlin, until the wall was put up,
of course, but then when the trouble started, we came
here.''

"What trouble was that?"

"The KgU. But that was blown all out of proportion.
Thank God it never reached the press."

"I'm sorry, I'm not following you."

"The *Kampf gegen Unmenschlichkeit* . . . Fight
against Inhumanity. They called themselves a political
action group. A Munich lawyer working in Berlin, Edward Juengst, was its leader. And Robert was quite
taken with them for a time.''

"What sort of group was this KgU?" Mahoney
asked. He had never heard of it, although Germany had
always had its political organizations and groups. It was
a national pastime.

"We were all taken in by it, you know. Juengst was a
very persuasive man when he had to be. He was a trial
lawyer, I believe. In any event, it was shortly after the
wall had been put up and the first shootings began that
the group was organized. It was Juengst's idea to accomplish two things: help Germans caught in the
eastern zone to escape, while at the same moment gener-
ate political awareness in Germany. Specifically in
Bonn, at the federal level.''

"Where did Sir Robert come into it? Was he a friend
of Juengst's?"

"Heavens no, although for a time the man was our
periodic house guest," Lady Sidney said, thinking back.
She held her wineglass in both hands. "From what I
gather, he had become quite successful in getting people
out of the eastern zone, but he wasn't having much ef-

fect on his own government.'' She looked up. ''At the time, you understand, the Federal Republic was very much frightened of what the Russians might do next. They were in no position, they felt, to upset the very delicate balance between them and the DDR.''

''Juengst had other ideas?''

''Indeed,'' Lady Sidney said. ''He felt that if he could not get through to his own government by the front door, he would have to try another way. With the British. Beginning with Robert, who had been so moved by the construction of the dreadful wall.''

''Then Juengst had had contact with Sir Robert at an earlier date?''

''No contact as far as I know. But Mr. Juengst had heard of Robert from others. He had had some American connections as well, including some who had been close to Kennedy. In any event, he showed up on our doorstep—almost literally—one afternoon.''

''And Sir Robert helped him, just like that?''

''Not at first, of course. Juengst was too much of a radical for Robert. But as I said, he was persuasive. He and Robert talked, off and on, for several months. Finally Robert went up to Berlin for a visit, which tipped him over the edge, I believe.''

''How?''

Lady Sidney smiled wistfully. ''My husband has always been''—she searched for the word—''something of an idealist. Juengst was trying to save lives. Kennedy was shot to death. The Cuban missile crisis still had us all in a tizzy.''

''And Sir Robert saw the wall again.''

She nodded. ''When he returned home he was so sad for a time, I became frightened for his health. 'They have no right,' he shouted. 'They're all monsters. We're poised on the edge of Armageddon.' And other things like that.''

''He began to help Juengst and the KgU after that?'' Mahoney asked.

"I presume so, although I never knew directly."

Mahoney sipped his drink.

Lady Sidney smiled. "I suppose I sound like some simpering idiot who remains home doing the mending while her husband goes out to do battle." She shook her head. "Throughout our marriage, there have been things from which Robert has insulated me. Some of his projects during the war, and then afterward, were best kept in isolation from everyone. But we used to argue at times. I would get my way occasionally, and then wish I hadn't." She looked deeply into Mahoney's eyes. "Robert has his politics and his intrigue. I have my art and my home. Now I want my husband returned to me."

"That's why I am here, Lady Sidney," Mahoney said. "You mentioned some trouble concerning the KgU."

"At first the wall wasn't really a wall in the sense of what it has become. It was merely barbed wire and guard posts. But the KgU had become too effective. As the escapes increased, so did the killings of poor people trying to cross to the West. The real wall was begun, and Juengst was found in his car beside the autobahn, shot to death. He was on his way to Bonn. To see Robert."

"There certainly must have been an investigation. Was Sir Robert named?"

"Yes, of course," she said. "Juengst was carrying documents with him that named Robert as a supporter. We were asked to leave Germany shortly after that."

"You came here to Brussels then?"

"No. To England for a couple of years, then to Paris, and finally here."

"What became of the KgU and its other supporters?"

"I don't know," Lady Sidney said. "We lost contact of course."

"Might there still be a connection?"

"What? Between the KgU and Robert's disappearance?"

Mahoney nodded. He knew he was fishing.

"No," she said simply. "It has been too long. No."
She set her wineglass down and got up. Mahoney got up
as well. He was being dismissed. She seemed tired, suddenly.

"Thank you so very much for seeing me like this,
Lady Sidney."

She offered her hand again. This time it was cool and
moist. "Find Robert, Mr. Mahoney. He is an old man.
He cannot take much . . . physically. I want him back in
one piece."

"I'll do my best. We all will."

They left the drawing room together. Bobbs appeared
from the back of the house and helped Mahoney with
his coat.

"I don't know if I have helped with my prattling, but
I hope so," Lady Sidney said.

"Had Sir Robert been late before?" Mahoney asked
on impulse. "Recently."

"Often," Lady Sidney said as they went to the door.
"He has been getting so forgetful. He had an appointment here at the house that very afternoon."

"Appointment?" Mahoney asked, keeping himself in
check.

"Yes. With a newspaper fellow from the *London
Daily Mail*. Thomas Langdon. He was here to do a story
on Robert."

"What sort of a story?"

"On Robert as the forgotten soldier, or some such
nonsense as that."

⭐ EIGHT ⭐

The SIS man who had ridden up from the front gate was gone. Mahoney got into his car and started the engine. He looked up at the house. There was a movement at one of the windows upstairs, but then it was gone. Someone had been watching.

Although it was still fairly early in the afternoon, a gloom had settled over the countryside. Wisps of fog curled around the treetops and at the dripping eaves of the large house.

There was a terrible sadness here, Mahoney thought. Sir Robert had wept when he first saw the Berlin Wall. He had been a sucker for a smooth-talking Munich trial lawyer who had played parlor games with terrorism against the Communists. He had advised President Kennedy, and no doubt he had been distraught when Kennedy had been assassinated. Over the past year Sir Robert had been preoccupied. Bothered. Distant and forgetful even with his wife.

All signs of age? Mahoney asked himself. He doubted it. The pattern was too consistent over too long a period of time. Sir Robert was probably an emotional man. But there was more.

Mahoney again looked up at the second-floor windows. There was more. Sir Robert was brilliant, but he also was a driven man. A man taken to causes. The Berlin Wall had clearly been an issue of deep emotional significance to him. So deep, in fact, that he had joined the KgU terrorist group of Edward Juengst.

Mahoney had to give the old boy marks for at least a modicum of caution, though. Lady Sidney had said it had taken him some months to soften to Juengst, to actually join the group. In the end it had taken a trip back to the hateful wall to turn the general's head.

It led to an intriguing thought. Juengst evidently was a smooth character who understood people. Certainly he must have spotted Sir Robert's emotional weakness right off the bat. Spotted it and exploited it.

The talks over a few months had softened the general. The final blow was the trip to the wall. Juengst's suggestion, no doubt.

That was then. Was there a new cause célèbre that had again turned the general's head? Something in the documents he had carried out with him? Something within the broader structure of NATO? Something he had read in the newspapers, seen on the telly? Something one of his cronies at his club had talked about? Was there another Edward Juengst out there who had come to see Sir Robert?

Two possibilities came immediately to mind. The first was the NATO documents themselves, which Sir Robert had apparently taken with him. The fact that the material was on the loose was creating as much or more consternation than the general's disappearance.

Obviously, whatever was in the documents had affected the man, otherwise he would not have walked off with them. But was something within the material the *cause* of his disappearance?

The second possibility was the *London Daily Mail* reporter Lady Sidney had said had come to interview Sir Robert the afternoon he disappeared. Thomas Langdon. He would be easy to find. Had he been with the general on other occasions? And had he been the bearer of some catastrophic news?

Mahoney put the car in gear and headed slowly around the long circular drive that went through a couple of hundred yards of woods before it came to the gate.

He glanced at the house in the rearview mirror. He'd have to be careful not to fall into the trap of singleness of thought.

Sir Robert had probably wandered off on his own. It was consistent with his past behavior, even if his wife was blind to it. But—and it was a large *but* in Mahoney's mind—past actions indicating probable present behavior were not iron-clads for fact. Despite what Sir Robert had been, he still could have been snatched because of his position, because someone knew he would be carrying the documents, because of any of a dozen reasons. Yet somehow none of that seemed to ring true.

He wound down his window as he slowed for the gate. But one of the SIS men swung the gate open and waved him through.

Mahoney nodded as he passed, and then he was out on the highway, accelerating back toward Brussels. His next step, of course, would be a complete briefing by Oliver Horne's office at the NATO complex outside the city.

He wanted to see Renelaux again. Inadvertently, John may have stumbled onto a key when he said the Belgian hated Germans so much that he was willing to play footsie with the Russians.

He did not know if the rift that had opened between him and his son could ever be healed. They had gone across the street to the small Italian restaurant, where they had shared a bottle of wine and made small talk about almost nothing.

They had, of course, avoided the issues at hand, although when they got to the airport, John insisted that he was not giving up the Agency.

"I've got a new career now, Dad. It's odd thinking I was ever a chemical engineer. It's so . . ."

"Mundane?" Mahoney suggested.

John grinned wryly. "Mundane," he said.

They shook hands.

"I'll see you when I get back," Mahoney said.

"Take care, Dad."

And there had been nothing more.

A cream-colored Rolls-Royce, going very fast, passed from the opposite direction and disappeared in the distance. Mahoney had seen a chauffeur behind the wheel and a passenger beside him in the front, but there was no one in the back. It struck him as mildly odd.

He was still thinking about it five minutes later when the car came up behind him, its horns blaring.

Mahoney glanced in the rearview mirror, then pulled over to the side of the road to let the car pass. But the Rolls slid in behind him and slowed as he did. This time there was someone in the back.

He brought his own car to a halt and wound down the window. One of the SIS men from the gate of the Marshall residence jumped out of the back seat of the Rolls and hurried up. The man pulled open the door. "Please get out of the car, Mr. Mahoney."

"Am I under arrest?" Mahoney asked, getting out of the car.

"No, sir. But Air Vice Marshal Sir Howard Scott would very much like to speak with you. He's sent his car. I shall return your automobile."

Mahoney glanced at the waiting Rolls, and then at the SIS man. He was the one with the cockney accent. "How will you know where to return the car?"

"The license tags are coded, sir. Sir Howard is waiting."

"I see," Mahoney said. He had come for information. Sir Howard was high on his list of persons with knowledge of Sir Robert.

He went back to the Rolls, the chauffeur held the door for him as he got in, and the other man—he looked like a bodyguard, probably military—nodded but said nothing. They pulled around the rented car and raced down the highway. Sir Howard not only wanted to speak with him, he apparently was in a great hurry to do so.

If anything, Air Vice Marshal Sir Howard Scott's home was even larger and more imposing than Sir Robert's. If the two men had been engaged in a contest of one-upmanship, Sir Howard would have won easily. Even inside, the house had just the correct touch of class, with none of the discordant notes that often were found in a bachelor's or widower's digs.

The chauffeur dropped him at the front door, and a pretty young woman in a black dress and starched white cap and apron showed him to the study at the rear of the house.

A dapper-looking man of medium height and build, with hair that matched Mahoney's in its whiteness and a luxuriant mustache, stood looking out the windows. He turned.

"Mr. Wallace Mahoney?" he asked stiffly. He was obviously angry.

Mahoney crossed the room, extending his hand. "Sir Howard," he said. "I am pleased to meet you, sir."

They shook hands. "Quite," Sir Howard said. He was dressed in a business suit. Apparently he had just come from work. His briefcase lay on his desk where he had tossed it, scattering papers.

There were a lot of books in the room, most of them bound in leather. Classics, most of them. There was the odd trophy here and there, and two walls held certificates and photographs from the man's long military career.

"Have you spoken with Colonel Horne about me?"

Mahoney asked. Sir Howard was evidently angry that Mahoney had approached Lady Sidney on his own, and Mahoney wanted to head off any serious trouble here and now. If he had to work against this man, and the SIS because of it, his own investigations would be in serious jeopardy.

"He mentioned your name in passing," Sir Howard said, barely able to conceal his anger. "But see here, you can't go running around the countryside terrorizing innocent people." Sir Howard was excitable.

"I hadn't thought speaking with the wife of the man we are all looking for could be construed as 'terrorizing innocent people,' as you put it."

"I want you to stay away from her."

"You are Sir Robert's friend. Had you noticed anything odd with him over the past few months?" Mahoney asked.

"Dammit to hell, man, I gave you an order!"

"Yes," Mahoney said dryly. "You must understand that the United States is vitally interested in finding Sir Robert and in recovering the documents he took with him. That in itself is irregular, from what I gather."

"I could have you sent out of Belgium."

"I don't think so. In any event, what are you trying to hide? Do you know where Sir Robert went?"

Sir Howard's face turned red. For a moment Mahoney thought the man was on the verge of a stroke.

"Lady Sidney evidently telephoned you. Did she say what we spoke about?"

"I want you to leave. Now!" Sir Howard said.

"No. Not until we get this straightened out. I've come to help find Sir Robert. Won't you allow me to help?"

"It's not an American problem."

"The Russians are here in Brussels, from what I understand. So are the Poles, and the Hungarians, in addition to all the NATO member countries. It's become very large."

"Then remain as you wish," Sir Howard said in frustration. "I cannot fight you on that. But you will stay away from Sidney."

Suddenly out of the clear blue it struck Mahoney what Sir Howard's difficulty was. The man was in love with Lady Sidney. He was in love with his best friend's wife. The insight was amazing and brought with it a number of thoughts, all of them intriguing.

How long had Sir Howard known he loved Lady Sidney? Was his love reciprocated? And finally, was this in all actuality nothing more than the eternal triangle? Would it turn out to be a messy murder case, with Sir Robert's body eventually found floating down some river, weights tied to his legs, or buried in some shallow grave far outside the city?

Mahoney doubted it. Lady Sidney seemed to have too much integrity for such a tawdry affair. In the brief time he had been with her, several things had been crystal clear: she was in love with her husband and desperate to have him back, and she was innocent of any knowledge of his whereabouts.

"I'm sorry if I have upset you, Sir Howard. I understand what strain you have been working under, and believe me, if I could conduct my investigation in any other way, I would. But if I am to continue effectively, I must have more information. Such as Edward Juengst and an organization called the *Kampf gegen Unmenschlichkeit.*"

Sir Howard visibly paled, then stepped back a pace as if he had suddenly lost his balance. When he recovered he shook his head. "Good Lord, she told you about that?"

"Yes. She said ultimately it was the reason they left Bonn and eventually came here to Brussels."

Sir Howard was nonplussed. He said nothing for the moment. It seemed as if he were trying to catch his breath. One hand had gone out and touched his desk top for support.

"I got the impression that Sir Robert is a somewhat emotional man."

"What do you mean?"

"He was deeply affected by the Berlin Wall, from what I understand. It was the reason this Juengst could get to him. He also had a great feeling for President Kennedy."

"He thought the man was a saint. A view we did not all share," Sir Howard said softly. His eyes were liquid. He motioned to a chair. "Perhaps we should sit. Would you care for tea?"

"Please," Mahoney said. He sat down while Sir Howard rang for tea. They waited until it came, then Sir Howard began.

"I've known Robert and Sidney since before the war. We practically grew up together. For years my wife Daphne and Sidney were a conspiracy. Of course Robert and I had our club, and our work. We were very . . . complete in those days."

"Until Germany?" Mahoney prompted.

"Even there at first, although I was never directly involved."

"Has Sir Robert always been that way?"

Sir Howard blinked. "What way is that?"

"Taken to causes."

Sir Howard thought back. "I suppose he was. The war affected him differently than it did the rest of us, you know. We all were glad when it was over. We wanted to sit back with our feet up and let the politicians handle picking up the pieces. But not Robert. He was very much interested in the reconstruction." Sir Howard shook his head with the memory. He looked directly into Mahoney's eyes. "You see, Robert always thought the Second World War was partly his fault."

"What?" Mahoney asked.

Sir Howard smiled. "It's not what you are thinking. He wasn't off his rocker. It's nothing like that. Before the war, before Poland and for a month or so afterward, Robert headed what was called the Versailles Team.''

"I hadn't heard of it.''

"Wasn't widely publicized. Not a popular view at the time, and especially not afterward,'' Sir Howard said. "Robert felt that the Germans had been given a terrible deal at Versailles after the First World War. From the time he became aware of the world outside of himself, he predicted that the Germans would go to war again. They would have to. It was inevitable, in Robert's opinion.''

"Sir Robert went to Germany? Spoke with the government?''

"Spoke with Hitler himself. On more than one occasion. Thought he was a madman but one who could be swayed. Felt Hitler could be made to understand that what had happened at Versailles could be reversed. Germany had a place in European politics, and it was one of leadership, not aggression.''

"Poland must have been a blow.''

"It was. Afterward, Robert kept saying how if he had only been a better speaker, a better negotiator, had more charisma, he might have done better.''

Mahoney sat forward. "What did you say?''

Sir Howard blinked. "I said Robert wished he had done a better job of convincing Hitler—''

"No. Charisma. Did Sir Robert use that term?''

"I don't know what you're getting at.''

Mahoney tried a different approach. "What else did Sir Robert say about Hitler? Besides the fact that he was a madman.''

"That he was smart. That he had a raging inferiority complex.''

"Charming?''

"At times. Robert said the man was filled with magnetism, that being around him was a heady experience.''

"Charisma? Did Sir Robert ever say Hitler had charisma?"

"Yes, he did. Often, as a matter of fact," Sir Howard said. "What are you getting at? Are you trying to say that Robert admired Hitler?"

"No, not that at all. How about after the war was over? The extermination camps must have affected him."

"Not as much as you might have expected," Sir Howard said. He was being completely open now with Mahoney, although if questioned why, he would not have been able to give a valid reason.

"What then?" Mahoney asked. It struck him as an odd, incongruous fact. Someone as emotional as Sir Robert would have to have been affected.

"He worked very diligently on the Nuremberg trials, of course, and then in Berlin on political reconstruction. That was very early in his marriage, and Sidney used to complain that she never saw him. That the Germans may have lost the war, but in the end they had captured her husband."

"How about after that? The fifties?"

"Back to England. He taught for a time at Oxford— three or four years it was—then he was posted to our embassy in Bonn as military attaché."

"What did he teach at Oxford?"

"Modern European history and military interventionism. He was most fond of his ongoing seminars with the young Rhodes scholars. A bright bunch always."

"Then Bonn and the KgU?"

"Yes," Sir Howard said. "That period is best left unmentioned. It was quite a mess when Juengst was found shot to death with Robert's name on all sorts of papers."

"British military documents?"

Sir Howard's eyes widened. "Good Lord, what a suggestion! Of course not! He may have made a judgment error with Juengst, but Juengst wasn't a spy. No, the papers Juengst carried with him were petitions and statements he meant to distribute in the eastern sector. They were meant to stir up dissent. Robert told me that Juengst had wanted to start a human tidal wave across the border, one so large that the Russians wouldn't have a hope in hell of stemming it.''

"But why Sir Robert's name on the petitions?"

"There were others. French. American. Juengst wanted to convince those in the eastern sector that they were not alone, that their plight was recognized by the powers in the West so that when the exodus began they wouldn't be fed to the wolves. What better name on a petition than that of a British general, the military attaché to the embassy in Bonn?''

Mahoney tried to digest what he had been told. It further supported his understanding that Sir Robert was a man who followed after causes.

"Was it ever established who murdered Juengst and why?"

"I think that's obvious. The KGB. They certainly couldn't allow Juengst to continue as he had."

"But there was no proof?"

Sir Howard shrugged. "From what I understand, the way in which the man was assassinated pointed to the Russians. Of course I never knew all the details. I had no interest other than extricating Robert and Sidney from the mess that was brewing.''

"You were instrumental in having Sir Robert pulled out of Bonn?"

Sir Howard nodded.

"Did he know?"

"He suspected, but he never actually knew. He used to chide me about it.''

"Lately?"

"No."

Mahoney's tea had grown cold. He set the cup aside. "How about just lately, Sir Howard?"

"What do you mean?"

"Sir Robert is a man of causes. Before the war, and after. Long after it. How about these days? Was anything his committee worked on a cause?"

"Do you mean is Robert an anti-nuker or some such rubbish?"

Mahoney nodded.

"Bloody hell, of course not."

"He *was* a man of causes."

"Yes, but not that one. Good heavens."

"Lady Sidney said he was worried about the frightful nuclear mess we had gotten ourselves into."

"Of course. We all are. We'd hoped your SALT talks with the Russians would have worked out."

"And cruise missiles?"

Sir Howard ducked the question. Mahoney suspected it was because the issue was just too sensitive and too fresh.

"Sir Robert was definitely not anti-deterrent force. On the contrary, he was strongly pro-military. Make no mistake about that."

"What was his latest cause, then, Sir Howard?" Mahoney asked quietly.

Sir Howard said nothing.

"He is a man of causes. There must be something. Lady Sidney says that for the past year he has been preoccupied. Forgetful. What has been stirring him these days?"

Sir Howard hung his head. "I don't know, Mr. Mahoney." He looked up. "I wish to God I did. Sincerely. I would tell you without hesitation, no matter what it was."

"Had you noticed his preoccupation lately?"

"Yes. All of us who knew him well did. We put it down to age. He was due for forced retirement in less than a year."

Another brick fell into place for Mahoney. "I see," he said. Whatever it was Sir Robert had been thinking

about, whatever had occupied him, his impending retirement had possibly forced his hand.

"I have a question for you," Sir Howard said. "In all
this, I'm getting the impression that you're convinced
Robert walked off. Perhaps even defected. There was
not a hint of kidnap in your questions."

"What do you think?"

"He could have been taken."

"For the documents he carried?"

Sir Howard nodded. He didn't look very certain,
though.

"But?"

Sir Howard sighed deeply. "I think it was unlikely he
was kidnapped. I think he walked off."

"To do what?"

"I don't know."

✯ NINE ✯

The divided highway was lit a ghostly yellow by large
sodium lamps on spindly-looking aluminum stanchions.
The weather was continuing its unpleasantness, the
rain changing to snow as the temperature dropped. It
would be a very long, hard winter for Europe, Mahoney
thought. There would be widespread heating fuel short-
ages. Cars and buses would slide off bridges. There
would be train wrecks, and heroic rescues.

It was Monday night. Sir Robert had been missing
since Friday afternoon, a full seventy-two hours. Almost anything could have happened to him in that time.
Almost anything could still happen. Mahoney had gotten Sir Howard's grudging cooperation, and he had
insisted they begin immediately. There were so many
possibilities to consider, so many avenues to explore,
that it would be a crime to relax while they were still
undone. They came in Sir Howard's Rolls-Royce, the
chauffeur driving very fast, the big car occasionally
slewing left or right as they careened over bridges that
were icing over, the windshield wipers flapping, soft
music playing over the barely audible but powerful beat
of the engine. Off across a long, treeless field the North
Atlantic Treaty Organization's sprawling complex stood

surrounded by lights. It looked more like a military
school or apartment development for senior citizens
than the seat of the allied military power in Europe.
There was nothing else around it. Yet for all its plain-
ness, it was obvious that something vastly important
went on here on a daily basis. There was a lot more traffic than Mahoney would have expected at that time of
the evening. It was past seven. But he supposed that
because of the missing general and documents, the entire organization was on emergency footing.

They came smoothly around the off-ramp, past the
broad outer parking lot, and pulled up at the sentry
gate. The uniformed guard stepped out, saluted, and as
Sir Howard powered down his window, he brought over
a clipboard.

"Good evening, Air Vice Marshal. Would you please
sign in your guest?"

Sir Howard took the clipboard, scrawled something,
and then handed it back. The sentry straightened up,
saluted again, and waved them through.

They drove up the main approach, sliding in beneath
the broad concrete canopy that covered the wide glass
entry doors. The chauffeur opened the car doors for
them, and Mahoney followed Sir Howard up the ramp
and through the electric doors.

A large circular counter where the information clerk
normally sat during the day was dark and empty now.
Several brochures were scattered on the countertop,
along with a half-full Styrofoam coffee cup.

Mahoney could feel the life of the building. It was a
low hum, somehow discordant now that the fabric of
the organization had been wounded. He cocked his head
as if he could hear the note and somehow translate it.
Hard decisions were being made. Frightened men and
women were scurrying back and forth like rats in their
warren, threatened by catastrophe so great it could only
be spoken of obliquely, and then only in hushed tones.

Sir Howard had started down the broad corridor. He

stopped and turned back when he realized Mahoney was not with him.

"Let's go, then," he called, his voice hollow. "They'll be waiting."

What was it he was hearing? Mahoney wondered. His own uncertainties? Was it the same as at the Gare du Nord where from the telephone booth he had heard the footsteps of a million ghosts? It was happening more and more often these days, and he had to wonder just who was pursuing whom.

He crossed the entry hall and fell in step beside Sir Howard. They went up on the elevator, getting off on the third floor, and halfway down that corridor they came to a door marked CINCHAN CONFERENCE. Sir Howard went in without knocking, Mahoney directly behind him.

It was a large room dominated by a long, highly polished conference table. Two men sat at the far end. One of them was Oliver Horne, the NATO Security man. The other, a tall, thin man with bushy eyebrows, Mahoney had never seen before.

"I hope you know what you are doing, Howard," the thin man said, rising.

Horne got to his feet as Sir Howard and Mahoney came around the table. "Mr. Mahoney," he said. He looked rumpled. Mahoney suspected he had not gotten much sleep since Friday night.

"Sorry for the hour," Mahoney said. "But I don't want to waste any more time." They shook hands.

"No," Horne said.

"Let me present Dr. Thomas Gaddis," Sir Howard said. "He is the chairman of our Defense Planning Committee."

Mahoney held out his hand, but Gaddis ignored it, turning instead to Horne.

"I don't want any part of this," he said peevishly. "Are you certain of his clearance?"

"I have spoken with the Secretary General about

this," Sir Howard said. "And he agrees. We must co-operate. Fully."

"Has Mr. Renelaux been informed?" Gaddis asked. Mahoney thought the man was frightened of something.

"This is simply a briefing to bring Mr. Mahoney up-to-date."

"If he is here representing the interests of the Central Intelligence Agency, why isn't he working with Pierre Renelaux? Just what is going on here?"

"I spoke with the Director of Central Intelligence himself," Horne said.

Gaddis was silent.

"He personally vouched for Mr. Mahoney."

"He must have stood in line. How many personal vouchers does that make now? How many dozen do we have running around with a free hand?"

"The dragon is loose, and it's got you scared silly, hasn't it," Mahoney said softly.

"You're damned right . . ." Gaddis began, then he shook his head. "Christ. The entire thing will have to be scrapped. There's nothing else for it, providing we're not at war within the week."

"Meanwhile, we're to find Sir Robert."

"I don't know what to tell you. This sort of thing is . . . alien to me. I'm a scientist."

"Can we sit down?" Sir Howard asked.

Gaddis looked at him, but then he nodded and they all took their places at the end of the table. He seemed trapped. "What is it you want?"

"I don't want the details. Not now," Mahoney said. "Tonight I merely want an overview. I believe Sir Robert took with him some . . . particularly sensitive documents."

"Explosive," Gaddis said, mopping his brow.

"I gathered as much," Mahoney said.

"He took a scenario book. The Genesis Plan is its code name."

"As 'in the beginning'?" Mahoney asked.

Gaddis looked at Horne in a mute appeal. When Horne did not respond, Gaddis turned back. His hands were folded in front of him on the table. "In simple terms, we have outlined plans for a reply to a breach of the East-West European border."

"It's more than that," Sir Howard said.

Gaddis flinched. "If East German tanks roll across the border, and we are forced to fight a conventional war, we will lose," he snapped.

"You are advocating a nuclear reply?" Mahoney asked. His sense of déjà vu was getting stronger.

There was a deathly silence in the already quiet room. Horne and Sir Howard looked uncomfortable. Gaddis was very much on the defensive now.

"Germany began the last two wars. Laid waste to Europe."

"What are the primary targets?" Mahoney heard himself asking.

"There are no . . . primary targets, as you call them," Gaddis said.

Sir Howard sat forward. "What Dr. Gaddis is trying to say, is that a conventional war—in Europe—has simply become impossible."

"We do not want an escalation," Gaddis said nervously. "At all costs."

It was not what Mahoney had expected. He was at a loss. "What, then?"

Once again Gaddis looked to Horne and to Sir Howard for support. They said nothing.

"What, then?" Mahoney repeated.

"We have laid out what we call . . . the last line of tactical nuclear confinement."

A cold wind suddenly blew. Mahoney shivered.

"The French had the Maginot Line," Sir Howard said.

Horne was looking away.

"We would recommend removing many of the tactical nuclear weapons from Germany," Gaddis said.

" 'Many'?'' Mahoney asked.

"All," Gaddis said. "We'd leave, of course, conventional weaponry systems."

"And if the Warsaw Pact tanks rolled . . . ?"

"The war would be fought exclusively on German soil," Gaddis said.

"Germany the . . . buffer zone?" Mahoney asked.

Sir Howard turned back. "We're talking about war here, Mr. Mahoney. It's not pretty. Contained, it would be considerably less ugly than its potential."

"Sir Robert was part of the planning committee? A member of the group that came up with this plan?"

"He was our resident German expert."

Mahoney said nothing.

"He knows everything there is to know about the East German military machine. He was one of our key members."

"How long had he been working on this?"

"A year. Fourteen months."

"Maybe that's why he left," Mahoney mused aloud. He turned to Sir Howard. "Do you suppose his work had an adverse effect on him? Could he have hated it so much he just left?"

"To where?" Horne broke in. "Are you saying he went over?"

"I don't know," Mahoney said. "Perhaps just into hiding. He took the document itself with him. Maybe he's holed up somewhere thinking it out. Rethinking it. Maybe he's come up with an alternative. He's a sensitive, intelligent man, after all, isn't he? Maybe the thought of an all-out nuclear war is repugnant to him. Maybe he had another idea."

"He could have been taken," Gaddis said.

"Was it known he was involved with the strike planning?"

"There were those who knew."

"Outside the committee?"

"Yes."

Mahoney turned to Horne. "Had you known about the others?"

The security chief nodded. "We've covered all those angles. We're watching anyone questionable."

Peace, Mahoney thought. Was that Sir Robert's new cause? And if so, what did he think he could do about it with the Genesis Plan? What was his intended line? Where would he take it?

Mahoney got to his feet, suddenly very weary. There was nothing else for him here. "Thank you," he said to Gaddis.

Sir Howard jumped up. "Don't you want to stay? There's more."

Mahoney shook his head. "I don't think so. I'd like to get back to my hotel. I'm tired, after all. Jet lag."

Gaddis was a frightened man. There was no doubt about it in Mahoney's mind. Another thought occurred to him.

"Have NATO bases across Europe been placed on alert?"

Gaddis and Sir Howard looked at each other. Sir Howard nodded. "DEFCON-four."

"The lowest."

"Yes," Sir Howard said. "But it's subject to hourly review, and it's in conjunction with a routine exercise. We do this sort of thing all the time. No cause for suspicion on the other side."

"Unless they had the Genesis Plan."

Sir Howard took a deep breath. "We've taken that into consideration."

"The Warsaw Pact is on alert as well?"

Sir Howard hung his head, but then he nodded. "Yes," he said. "Yes they are."

A NATO staff car brought Mahoney back into town. But he had the driver drop him off at the north side of the Botanical Gardens. He wanted to walk.

He stood for a while at the head of one of the broad paths through the park, the trees and bushes dark and somewhat foreboding in the damp evening's cold. The wind moaned through the branches, a familiar sound in northern Minnesota but oddly out of place and mournful here in the heart of a big city. After the very bright illumination around the NATO complex, the streetlights here were very dim, furthering the air of mystery.

Stuffing his hands into his pockets and gathering the bottom of his coat around his legs, he headed through the park to his hotel.

Sir Robert was a man of high emotion. A man given to causes. But he was a brilliant military man. Had been all of his adult life, though much of his military career had evidently been spent at the sidelines of government and politics. Oftentimes not so much on the sidelines as directly within, Mahoney was beginning to suspect.

Sir Robert may have been given to some inner urging, but as a military man he had to be pragmatic enough to understand the necessity of at least some sort of containment scenario.

Mahoney hadn't wanted the details about the Alliance's position because he knew them. There was no way in which NATO forces could win a conventional war in Europe. They were outgunned, 84 divisions to the Warsaw Pact's 170. Around 750 aircraft to their 4,500, 13,000 tanks to their 42,500.

Those numbers were not secret. They were very well publicized, in fact, as was the likelihood that NATO would have to resort to nuclear weapons when the big crunch came.

Regrettable. But everyone understood.

As a military tactician, however, even Sir Robert must have seen the fatal logic in the Genesis scenario: lose one country, lose them all. Yet he had come up with the plan. Or at least he was one of the men responsible for setting the notion down on paper.

Was it the scenario that had caused Sir Robert to

flee—if indeed he had fled? Was it the scenario that had caused the opposition to snatch him—if he had been kidnapped? Or was it something else?

Behind him, traffic moved along the Rue Royale, but here in the gardens there was nothing, only his own footsteps on the wet sidewalk. Even the city smells seemed to give way for just the minutes he was within the park.

He came around a sharp bend in the path that led out to the Boulevard St. Lazare, a lot more traffic here because of the railway station just down the street.

He crossed by the restaurant he and John had eaten in the night before, suddenly conscious that he was hungry, and entered his hotel.

The desk clerk handed him a message along with his room key. "The gentleman waits for you in the bar."

"Thank you," Mahoney said, opening the message where he stood. It was typewritten. *You and I have something in common—we'd both like to see Lady Sidney happy.*

There was no signature. Mahoney looked up. "Did he say who he was?"

"Non, monsieur."

"How long has he been waiting?"

"An hour. Perhaps more."

Mahoney glanced across the lobby toward the entrance to the hotel bar. The routines were about to begin, the opening notes in an extemporaneous ballet the prelude of which was Sir Robert's disappearance. It would have an international cast.

He turned again to the clerk, who had been watching him with keen interest. "If the gentleman should happen to come out and ask for me, tell him that you expect me within five minutes."

"Oui, monsieur," the clerk said. This was a hotel. He had seen many strange things happen. Besides, this was an American.

Mahoney turned and hurried out of the hotel. He

crossed the street and went down to the railway station. He entered a phone booth just within the main doors, and dialed the number for Pierre Renelaux.

The same woman as before answered.

"This is Wallace Mahoney. I would like to speak with Pierre Renelaux."

Renelaux was on the line a moment or two later. "Good evening, Mr. Mahoney. I understand you were successful in convincing your son to leave."

"I will need a weapon. A handgun. Have it delivered to my hotel this evening."

"What have you found?" Renelaux snapped.

"Nothing yet. Can you have the gun delivered?"

"Yes, certainly, but—"

Mahoney hung up and stepped out of the phone booth. Why didn't he trust Renelaux? he asked himself, hurrying back to the hotel.

He had been gone only a few minutes. The clerk assured him the gentleman had not stirred from the bar. He went in. There were only a half-dozen customers, including two couples seated together in one corner. A young man was playing the guitar at the far end of the room.

Two men were seated at opposite ends of the bar. One of them glanced toward Mahoney, then hopped off his barstool and came over.

He was very short, somewhat on the dumpy side, with a fat face and thick, wet lips. He held out his hand. "Mr. Mahoney, I'm so glad you've come. I'm Thomas Langdon. *London Daily Mail*."

Mahoney shook his hand. It was limp, cold, and damp. "You've come to do an interview with Sir Robert Marshall?"

"Yes, but I'd like to ask you a few questions if I may."

"When you tell me how you know my name, this hotel, and my connection with Lady Sidney, I'll talk to you."

"Fair enough," Langdon said. "May we use your room?"

"Here will be fine," Mahoney said.

"A tape recorder might be a bit conspicuous."

"There won't be a tape. I won't give you an interview, although I may answer a question or two."

"I see," Langdon said.

They went back to where the journalist had been seated. Mahoney ordered a bourbon, no water, no ice, and Langdon another Beefeaters martini on the rocks.

Langdon offered Mahoney a cigarette, which he refused, then lit himself one. "Your questions are fairly easy, Mr. Mahoney. I've been watching the Marshall house for the better part of two days. A few NATO types show up first, including Air Vice Marshal Sir Howard Scott, a close family friend, which tells me Sir Robert has gone bye-bye, probably been snatched. Saturday morning the place is surrounded with SIS boys." Langdon grinned. "But don't bother asking how I knew that one. Every British journalist worth his salt can spot an SIS man a mile off. They all have the look."

Their drinks came.

"How am I doing so far?"

Mahony said nothing. Instead, he busied himself with the routine of opening and lighting a cigar.

"I checked with some old friends among the local gendarmes who tell me they found Sir Robert Marshall's automobile—abandoned. No fingerprints other than his own and that of the NATO service garage personnel. No sign of a struggle, either."

"The name of your contact with the local police?"

Langdon smiled. Mahoney wanted to hit him. "Not a chance."

"Fine," Mahoney said. He started to get off his barstool. Langdon panicked.

"Hey, now! Just a minute!"

Mahoney looked at him.

"You can't make me reveal my sources."

Mahoney said nothing.

"Jean Rubaix. A sergeant with the Brussels police." Langdon blurted. "But if you tell him who told you, I shall deny it in print."

Mahoney sat down again. "Go on," he said.

It took Langdon a moment or two to settle down. "So I figure it's for real. Sir Robert has indeed been snatched. Back out at the homestead I see all sorts of comings and goings, most of them easily identifiable, but you I couldn't peg. You were driving a hired car. I had it checked."

"Rubaix?"

Langdon nodded. "Registered to Wallace Mahoney at this hotel." He looked at Mahoney. "You're a cop, aren't you? American. My guess would be CIA. My guess, with all the other activity, is that Sir Robert probably went missing with a briefcase full of nasty secrets."

Mahoney took a sip of his bourbon. "What about Lady Sidney? What is your connection with her?"

"None," Langdon said. "I had an appointment to do an interview with Sir Robert. I spoke with her for five minutes or so Friday afternoon. When the old boy didn't show up, I bugged out of there. She's a lovely bit for her age though, isn't she?"

"What sort of an interview?"

Langdon blinked. He stubbed out his cigarette and immediately lit another. "That's my business."

"Lady Sidney said it had something to do with her husband being, in your words, a forgotten soldier."

"Yes, well . . ." Langdon grinned. He sipped his drink.

"She didn't believe that any more than I do. What did you come to interview him for? What's your story line, Mr. Langdon? Your slant, I believe it's called."

"Why should I tell you?"

Mahoney shrugged. He was working very hard to keep his manner light and pleasant. "Let me give you a little something. Sir Robert is missing, of course. You're perfectly correct in that assumption. And none of us has a clue as to who took him. Frankly, we need all the help we can get. And I can tell you another thing: whoever provides the help will not be forgotten, if you know what I mean."

Langdon was skeptical. Yet it seemed clear that he wanted to believe he would be on the inside of a large story if he cooperated.

Mahoney smiled and nodded encouragingly.

Langdon made his decision. He put down his cigarette and leaned a little closer. "General Sir Robert Marshall may be the forgotten soldier all right, but it's not because he's an old war-horse out to pasture. No. It's because men of his stripe have to keep it low-key. You know what I'm talking about?"

Mahoney shook his head.

"He's a spook."

"With the SIS?"

"No, with the German BND."

"He's a West German spy?"

"You're bloody damned right. But the good part of it is, Sir Robert *always* was a German spy."

Mahoney looked at the contemptible little man for a long while. Langdon began to fidget.

"I'm sorry, Langdon, I'm dim or something, but I'm just not following you. Spell it out in plain English for me."

"Lookit. In the late thirties Sir Robert spent more time in Germany than he did at home. He was pals with Canaris and even with *der Führer* himself. Met with the paperhanger up in his Eagle's Nest. During the war he was in the middle of it, too. He was on the Enigma team . . . you know, breaking the German code. It took them a long time to get it done. It's my guess Sir Robert slowed that down a bit. After the war he hightailed it back to Germany and helped the Americans set up the BND with Reinhard Gehlen, who after all was said and done was just another Nazi. But Gehlen was okay because he hated the Russians, and they had become the bad guys. Then Sir Robert got mixed up with the group that was bringing wretches over the Berlin Wall. Did you know the story behind that escapade?''

"I heard about Edward Juengst. He was found dead in his car.''

"You bet. Rubbed out by some of the Germans he helped bring over.''

"Why?''

Langdon laughed. "What sort of a scam do you think they were running? Are you naïve or something? Juengst, with our general's help, was bringing East Germans over the wall, all right. For a few thousand marks a head.''

"And you're saying Sir Robert knew about this?''

"Knew about it? Hell, he set it up!'' Langdon said. He finished his drink. "That's why he got hustled out of Bonn so damned fast. He was getting to be an embarrassment.'' He looked at Mahoney with a new expression. "Don't tell me you were believing the noble crap stories about the old boy?'' He chuckled. "That's rich. That's bloody rich.''

"So you came to do an exposé.''

"You're damned right, Mahoney. And I still will. Only now I'm waiting for the final chapter. See which pond the old boy is found in.''

"What do you think happened to him?''

Langdon laughed out loud this time. "That's the easiest question of all to answer. It should be obvious what happened to him after everything he's done.''

"You've lost me again.''

"They were Jews he and Juengst were getting out of the DDR. So look to Tel Aviv, Mahoney. For God's sake, look to Tel Aviv. Some Jew has snuffed him. Mark my words.''

Mahoney nodded, laid a few bills on the bar, then slid off the stool.

"Hold up there a minute, Mahoney,'' Langdon said.

Mahoney stared at him.

"I kept my part of the bargain. I answered your questions. Now I have a few of my own."

"I didn't make any bargain," Mahoney said. And when Langdon started to protest, he stepped in a little closer. "If you get in my way, you miserable son of a bitch, I'm going to run right over you. And it won't be pleasant for you."

Alone in his room, Mahoney sat by the window looking down at the street. It was snowing in earnest now, and it was pretty. The snow made everything seem clean and new, as if the world were getting a fresh coat of paint but done by an artist.

Room service had finally brought him a roast beef sandwich and a couple of bottles of Grolsch, which was a very good Dutch beer popular in Belgium.

Someone knocked at his door and he turned around, surprised. He hadn't seen anyone come up the street.

"Yes?" he called.

"Room service, Monsieur Mahoney."

Mahoney went to the door and opened it on its chain. One of the bellmen stood there. He held a small package wrapped in brown paper.

"A delivery for you, sir."

Mahoney opened the door the rest of the way, took the heavy package from the bellman, and gave him a hundred-franc note.

"*Merci, monsieur,*" the man said, then turned and was gone.

Inside, the door once again locked, Mahoney opened the package. Inside was a small carton containing a Smith & Wesson snub-nosed .38 revolver and twelve dumdum bullets, crosses cut in the soft lead for maximum dispersion and, therefore, maximum killing power.

The extemporaneous ballet was beginning.

✭ TEN ✭

John Mahoney figured that at forty he had lived an entire lifetime, and he was beginning all over again. It was like being born, only without the bliss of ignorance.

The first time around, it had taken nearly forty years to complete his education, first prep school and then college and then marriage. This time around it had only taken him nine weeks at the Agency's school.

There were a lot of other differences between this life and the old one. The first time around he had fallen in love. There'd be none of that for him this go around. When you were in love, he told his fellow trainees, you were vulnerable. It was as simple as that. Vulnerable with a capital Victor to any son of a bitch who wanted to set you up for a potshot; to any third-rate director of people's lives who wanted yours in a basket; to anyone, in fact, who wanted to get at you for any reason. All they had to do was grab your love and you were theirs in a neatly wrapped package. But you were mostly vulnerable to yourself, he would say at the drop of a hat— especially if he had been drinking. Vulnerable to your own stinking, miserable heart.

There hadn't been too many people in his life for whom John had had any affection, with whom he had opened himself completely. The first, of course, had

126

been his mother. She had been called "Margery with the laughing eyes" when she was young. He had found the inscription under her photograph in her 1937 college yearbook. He was ten years old when he had read it, and for several days he had gone around looking at his mother's eyes. Smiling at her. Making silly faces until she discovered the cause of his behavior. Now he had difficulty bringing up a clear image of his mother's face because of how she had looked in the hospital just before she died of cancer.

There had been his brother Michael. In John's very earliest memories, there had always been Michael who was only a few years younger than John. Michael had been right there at the door when John went off to kindergarten, had worshipped his brother the high school athlete, had been proud of his brother the chemical engineer, and had been John's best man. His death had been nearly impossible to take. At the time, John could not conceive of anything more difficult. Anything more painful would not be possible to bear.

But the explosion that had killed Elizabeth and his children had very nearly shattered his life forever. Hardly an hour went by when he did not think about them, when he was not hearing the terrible explosion, seeing the fire, the flames leaping high into the night sky, smelling the burnt plaster dust.

On that day, six months ago, his life had stopped. It was only a defense mechanism, some sort of mental legerdemain, that allowed him to function at all. Sometimes, it seemed, he worked on instinct alone. Shaving, eating, sleeping were all automatic gestures.

And yet he had gone after McNiel Henrys and the network that was responsible for Elizabeth's and the children's murders. Against all odds he had caught up with the man, and he would have killed him except that McBundy had beat him to it.

He returned to Washington, D.C., and then went out to Minnesota. His father had cooked for him. Had gotten him up in the morning to go fishing, or walking.

Had fed him. Had taken him into town to bookstores, to movies, to restaurants. Had treated him like a man recovering from a very long, very serious illness.

But the day came when it was time for John to return to Los Angeles. Once there, though, he had closed down the house. He was not able to face the children's rooms any longer, much less the room he and Elizabeth had shared.

He had had trouble facing his job as well. None of the people at Monsanto Chemical knew what had happened to him, of course, other than the fact that his wife and children had been killed in an accident. They had assumed he had gone off his rocker for a time as any of them might have, given the same set of circumstances.

The worst part of it was their solicitousness. Everyone walked on eggshells around him. It had been terrible. Lycoming's telephone call from Langley had been a life-saver that John had lunged at like a drowning man will lunge at anything thrown to him.

"Life has to have meaning in order for it to be worth continuing," the DCI had told him.

John knew the meeting was highly unusual. It did not matter. Here was a man throwing him a lifeline. He was not pussyfooting around.

"I don't even know why I came here," John had said. "What do you want of me?"

"I want you to go to work for the Agency. Your father was the best this Company has ever known, bar none. There are those of us who think you could be even better."

"There's nothing else, is there," he had said bitterly. California was out, as was Monsanto.

That was the old life, John thought as his Sabena flight from Paris touched down at Brussels's Zaventem Airport. This was the reincarnation.

But had he now lost his father?

He got through customs with no fuss, took the moving sidewalk out to the main hall, then hurried across to the front doors where the cab stands were located. It was Tuesday morning. For most of the night it had snowed here, but it hadn't in Paris. It was quite a contrast.

Renelaux had told him to go along with whatever his father demanded. "If he wants you to leave, then leave. Go to Paris, John. Have a night on the town. Get some rest. Then come back in the morning, and we can get to work."

He had taken the shuttle to the airport Holiday Inn outside Paris where he had remained in his room, reading newspapers, reading *Time* and *Newsweek*, and watching television.

At six he got up, took a shower and got dressed, then went back to the Sabena departure gate where he presented himself for the early flight back to Brussels.

He felt guilty, somewhat like a traitor. But his father simply did not understand what this assignment meant. He could not.

Pierre Renelaux was waiting in his dark blue Opel just behind the taxi ranks. He waved. John spotted him immediately and angled across the broad sidewalk.

"How was Paris?" the Belgian asked, grinning.

"The Holiday Inn was fine. I didn't get any farther," John said, tossing his bags in the back seat.

They got into the car, and Renelaux pulled out away from the cabs. They headed from the airport at a fast clip.

"How's my father doing? Is he still here?"

"Oh, yes," Renelaux said. "He went out to see Sir Robert's wife after you left. Later in the evening he showed up at Alliance headquarters with Sir Howard Scott."

"Was he briefed?"

"Tom Gaddis said he was told everything."

For a moment John drew a blank with the name, but then he remembered. Gaddis was the chairman of the Defense Planning Committee, and Renelaux's major source within NATO. "What else?"

Renelaux shrugged. "Your father is a very sharp man. I'm not going to risk my job by having him followed. He'd spot my people immediately."

"My father is an old man," John protested.

"Yes. But he's a professional. He needs no protection. Especially not now."

"What do you mean?"

"Last night he telephoned me for a weapon. I sent him a pistol."

"Oh, Christ! What's going on? What is he up to that he thinks he needs a weapon?"

"I do not know. Honestly. Perhaps he feels better to be armed."

"He doesn't like guns. He never has."

"I do not know, John. He would not tell me. He simply asked for a weapon, so I supplied him with one. It's not my place to question."

"You're the goddamned operations man here."

"I spoke with Conwell. You haven't met him. He's chief of station here."

"And?"

"I told him what happened, that's all."

John sat back. "Then what am I doing here? I thought you would be able to convince him to leave. I thought that once I was gone, he'd return to the States. It doesn't sound like he's giving up."

"He may go ahead and conduct his own investigation. We will conduct our own. We have more help. He is only one man."

"I don't like this."

"I didn't imagine you would," Renelaux conceded. "If you truly want to return to the States, I am sure it will not go against your record. Your father did interfere."

John said nothing. He was seething with a dozen conflicting emotions. Stay or go. He wished with everything within him that there was some way he could take back the things he had said to his father. He wished that he could go back; he wished fervently that he could be satisfied with his old job at Monsanto Chemical in Los Angeles. He wished for peace. Oh, God, how he wished for peace, and for his wife and their kids, and his life that had a future.

"Whatever you decide, there is one thing I will need your help with. It will take only a day or perhaps two."

John looked at him. "You need a new face?"

"Exactly," the Belgian said. "It is why I have kept you isolated here. You are to be our secret weapon."

John didn't know if he liked the sound of that, yet returning to Washington, D.C., and facing the people back there was too much like admitting defeat. It came uncomfortably close to a return to Monsanto and his old life. It was what his father wanted.

Renelaux's office was at NATO headquarters, and his apartment downtown was not too far from the Gare du Midi, Brussels's other railway station. He was married and had two small children whom he sent away to boarding school in Switzerland. He had never tried to make any secret of the fact that he was an American citizen and that he worked for the Central Intelligence Agency as a liaison officer with NATO. Outwardly he was proud of his position.

Actually, his openness was a cover for an extensive network of informers within NATO itself.

This was not spying. Not in the real sense of prying into the affairs of an enemy state. This was more like keeping an ear over the fence for any backyard gossip that might come his way. At least Renelaux felt that way about his real work.

Thomas Gaddis was a perfect example. He was a brilliant scientist but a man with hardly any common sense. Renelaux had befriended him some time ago. They would often meet for coffee during the day, and at least once a month Gaddis and his wife would come to the Renelaux apartment for dinner.

They would talk, of course. As couples. Sometimes the men would adjourn to the other room while the women tidied up, for Madame Renelaux was just as adept as her husband at drawing out her friends, making them talk about themselves, about their husbands, about life in general. In fact, because of this, the couple were considered some of the best conversationalists in Brussels.

For the two days John Mahoney had been in Brussels before his father had shown up, he had stayed in the Renelauxs' guest room.

Madame Renelaux—never Marie—had taken a liking to the young Mahoney. Although she was barely six years older than he, she had adopted an almost motherly attitude toward him.

When her husband returned from the airport with John, she was visibly pleased and kissed him on both cheeks, welcoming him back.

"All this intrigue," she said. "It makes the blood run, *n'est-ce-pas*?"

"Good morning, Madame Renelaux," John said politely. He did not know yet whether or not he liked the woman. She was a bit too flamboyant for him.

"Are you to stay with us a little longer?"

John nodded. "I believe so . . ."

"Non," Renelaux said. "Later, perhaps. For now there is work for both of you. This very afternoon." He pulled off his coat and hung it on the hook.

Madame Renelaux brightened. "You want my help?"

"Oui. This afternoon you will pay a courtesy call on Lady Sidney in Anderlecht."

"Of course. But what information do you wish?"

"From you, nothing. You will simply pay your respects. I am involved in this business, you see. It is common knowledge. You could not help but visit the distraught woman for the afternoon."

"Yes?" Madame Renelaux said. She knew something else was coming. Anticipation was written all over her face.

"Exactly one half hour after you arrive you will suddenly remember that you must make a very important telephone call to the city. It is something you must do."

"And where will I telephone?"

"I will supply you with the number, my dear. The number will ring eight times, there will be no answer, and you shall hang up. You will immediately try again, this time letting it ring only three times. As soon afterward as you feel comfortable, you will take your leave. Your work shall have been completed."

"Work? What work?"

Renelaux turned to John. "You are a chemical engineer, so you understand technical matters. You will have one dangerous time, but afterward all will be easy."

"We're doing something to Lady Sidney's telephone?"

"*Oui*. I believe that we may go very far in this investigation if we can only know what telephone calls the lady receives."

"I would have thought the SIS or at least Interpol would be monitoring her telephone calls. In case it is a kidnapping."

"The SIS have placed monitoring equipment on her line, but they are gentlemen. They have given her the means of connecting the recorders only when she wishes to."

"What if I am caught?" John asked.

Renelaux shrugged. "You are merely doing your job. You would be ejected from Belgium, of course, but there are other assignments."

The new ones were always set up to be the fall guys. Long after this assignment was completed, one way or the other, Pierre and Madame Renelaux would be here. One way or the other, John would be gone.

He decided he didn't give a damn. Whatever Renelaux was or wasn't, he certainly was correct about Lady Sidney's telephone. If they could listen in, it would be a virtual gold mine.

•   •   •

Madame Renelaux's automobile was a well-kept Mercedes 240D, with a lovely metallic maroon paint job and an expensive and quite complicated stereo system. She had bought the car with her own money, she explained to John on the way out to Anderlecht, and it was absolutely the only thing she had that was her very own.

She was a twitterer, with a high-pitched voice that dripped with sympathy for everything except how John was driving on the snowy roads, and how he would treat her car later this afternoon.

"I shan't forgive you if you put her into a ditch somewhere," she said.

The car felt very solid on the road. Most of all, John was glad to be doing something other than reading endless briefs on NATO, on the Genesis Plan, and on General Sir Robert Marshall.

Renelaux suspected that the old boy had walked off. Had probably defected either to the Russians or at the very least to the East Germans. Gone off his rocker, the Belgian maintained.

John had formed no solid opinion yet. He had told Renelaux that, and the man had agreed wholeheartedly that John's was the more enviable position.

"Keep your mind open, that's what I always say. That way, whatever happens, you will be ready and able to receive it. No preconceived notions."

His tool kit and the small but powerful transmitter were locked in the trunk of the Mercedes along with several packages. He had understood what he was supposed to do as fast as Renelaux had explained it to him. The operation was actually quite simple. The only problem would come if someone chanced along and saw him up on the pole.

Just before they left, Renelaux had taken John aside and had given him a Beretta .380 automatic with an extra clip of ammunition.

"I'm not going to shoot at some Belgian cop," John protested.

"It's not for them, John. Listen to me. There are others wanting Sir Robert. Dangerous men."

"I thought you said the Russians were merely throwing up a smoke screen."

"Yes. That is what I believe. But I am not willing to bet your life on my belief. Are you?"

In the end, John took the gun. It lay bulky now beneath his coat on his left side. Heavy with implications for what would happen if he actually had to use the thing.

"It is here," Madame Renelaux said softly.

John slowed down as they came to the turnoff for the Marshall residence, and eased slowly up the narrow driveway. They were stopped at the gate. John powered the window down as the gatekeeper Renelaux had told him about came from the gatekeeper's shack.

"Good afternoon," John said. "I have brought Madame Renelaux. She has an appointment with Lady Sidney Marshall."

The gatekeeper glanced in the back seat at Madame Renelaux, but then he turned his attention to John. "Who are you?"

"I am Madame Renelaux's driver. I will not be staying."

Madame Renelaux leaned forward. "He is John. I am sending him into Anderlecht to pick up a few things for me. When he is finished he can return."

The gatekeeper looked deeply into John's eyes, then nodded. "Just a moment—someone will ride up to the house with you."

A younger man in a dark suit and mountain parka came from behind the gatehouse, climbed in beside John, and the gate was opened.

John drove the rest of the way up to the house, where he helped Madame Renelaux out of the car.

"Bonne chance," she said to him under her breath.

And then louder, "One hour, no more, John. I will see you here then."

"*Oui, madame,*" John said.

She turned and went up to the house. John and the SIS agent drove in silence back to the gate, where the agent got out of the car, and John continued back to the highway and headed into Anderlecht.

As far as John was able to tell, no one followed him from the Marshall residence into the small town of Anderlecht. Nevertheless, he stopped at a government liquor store and purchased a bottle of brandy so that he could slow things down. Pausing outside, he glanced across the town square and back toward the highway he had just come in from. No one seemed to be paying him any attention. There were no foreign types hanging around, no big, mysterious automobiles, no windowless vans with too many antennae as they had warned him about in school.

Already the paranoia was beginning. He almost always had the urge to stop and look over his shoulder. Christ, and he had just begun.

He drove out of town on the same road he had come in on, but about a mile west of the driveway to the Marshall residence, he turned onto a narrow country lane barely wide enough for one car.

The road had been recently plowed, the snow piled up in dirty heaps at either side.

John stopped a half mile in, the forest pressing darkly on both sides, and took the map Renelaux had sketched for him from the glove compartment.

He got out of the car and looked both ways up the road. A curve was shown on the map. He could see it a hundred yards or so ahead. Just after the curve, the telephone lines that served the Marshall residence along with several other large houses in the area crossed the road.

John got back into the car and drove the rest of the

way, coming to the telephone lines and stopping again. Quickly he went to the trunk and took out his tool kit and climbing irons. He glanced at his watch before he strapped on the spikes, then plunged into the snow off the side of the road.

Madame Renelaux had been with Lady Sidney for slightly less than twenty minutes. Soon she would be making her telephone calls. He was going to have to hurry if he was going to be ready for them.

About eighty yards into the woods, the road no longer visible, he came to the telephone pole Renelaux had specified. A metal tab about seven feet off the ground listed a seven-digit number Renelaux had given him. This particular pole was at an optimum distance from the road and from the logging paths that criss-crossed these woods. It was not likely anyone would happen by while John was doing his work.

He scrambled up the pole as best he could, the sharp spikes biting securely into the creosoted wood. Near the top, where the wires were attached, he tied himself off with his safety belt and took a screwdriver from his tool kit.

Within two minutes he had the junction box cover off. It took another two minutes to identify the eight pairs of wires that represented eight individual phone lines.

He took out his tester, clipped the black lead to the frame of the junction box, then glanced at his watch. It was time in one minute.

He swiveled around and looked back toward the road for the car, but the trees were too tall and too dense in that area for him to catch a glimpse of it.

Directly toward the west, however, toward Brussels, the land sloped downward, giving a clear line of sight into the city.

He glanced at his watch again. It was exactly two. He shoved the sharply pointed end of the red probe into the first pair of wires, making contact with the bare copper beneath the insulation. The tester's light bulb lit a steady glow, indicating he had made connection. He waited several seconds, but the light did not flicker.

Madame Renelaux would be telephoning now.

He withdrew the probe and inserted it in the second set of wires. Again the tester's bulb lit but remained steady.

On the fifth set the light began flashing immediately. Someone was using the telephone. He watched the light flicker a second time, and then it remained steady. A few seconds later it flickered again, a second time, then a third time, then went steady again.

He had identified the telephone line from the Marshall residence.

It took him less than five minutes to set up the coupling device that would pick up the phone signals from the wires and the tiny transmitter that would send the messages to a receiver in Brussels.

He replaced the junction box cover, then climbed back down the pole. From the ground only the small wire antenna was visible only if you knew it was there. Everything else was contained within the junction box.

Back at the car, he replaced the tool kit and his climbing irons in the trunk, took the packages out and laid them in the back seat, and then headed back to the Marshall residence to collect Madame Renelaux.

Once he dropped her off at her home, he would take a cab to the address Renelaux had given him. It was an apartment on the top floor of a large high-rise building on the east side of the city. The receiver was located there, as was a tape recorder. The apartment was well stocked with food, a television, and everything else John would need for a few days.

If anything came up, anything important, he had a number to reach Renelaux. But it was to be used only if John learned something vital to their investigation.

☆ ELEVEN ☆

From the start, Mahoney's purpose here in Brussels was simply to fetch his son from the mouth of the lion. At some point, however, understanding Sylvan Bindrich's manipulations, he had crossed over into the other world of commitment. Riding in a cab across the city to the Quartier Léopold, he thought idly about other assignments, other cities, other uncertainties. Shot through each memory was the general feeling that although what he did might be necessary, it certainly had never been pleasurable, neither had it usually been satisfying in the end. And yet he kept on. Curious, he thought, to what lengths we put ourselves for duty and honor. Of course it wasn't all that noble. John understood that. But for want of a better peg on which to hang his emotion for the chase, duty and honor did quite nicely. This time it was for Sir Robert, whom Mahoney had begun to think of as "the old man." Which was another curiosity. Sir Robert was just a few years older. For all practical purposes, he and Mahoney were contemporaries. Sir Robert had a bit more background before the war. The man had been a bit older and wiser, had had more depth when the big crunch came. But all in all, Sir Robert had fought the same battles as Mahoney, had listened to the same music, had despaired of the same events.

The snow had stopped, but it was very cold this morning. The sky above the city was a dull gray blanket. There would be more snow. He had not slept much last night. He had risen early, had had a croissant and butter with his coffee, and then had ordered the cab.

The cabby dropped him off at the corner of a narrow side street leading off the Rue Belliard. He paid the driver, then waited until the taxi had disappeared down the street.

There were people out and about, all of them bundled up, walking fast, their heads bent low against the chill wind.

The Royal Museum and the Museum of Natural History were a couple of blocks away. The neighborhood here was quiet, sedate, well kept. Somewhat better than he had expected it would be.

He saw that the numbers ran odd on the southern side of the avenue, so he crossed over. The plaque for 13B was for the second floor of a three-story, nondescript stone building in a row of similar structures. There was a buzzer at the door. A speaker grille was set beside it. Mahoney pressed the button.

A bottle of milk was set on the narrow step. He bent down and picked it up. The glass was ice cold.

"Yes, who is it?" a man's voice rasped from the speaker in English.

Mahoney leaned forward. "My name is Wallace Mahoney. I've come to speak with Margaret Byrne."

There was no immediate answer.

"Is she here?" Mahoney asked.

"Who is this?" a woman's voice came from the speaker.

"I spoke with Colonel Horne last evening," Mahoney said. "He mentioned that I should talk with you."

The lock buzzed. Mahoney pushed the door open and stepped inside to a narrow, dark staircase. He'd started up when the door at the top opened, spilling light down.

A short, plumpish woman appeared at the head of the stairs. Mahoney hesitated.

"Well, come on, then. Don't want to make me late for work," she said.

Mahoney came the rest of the way up the stairs and then walked into the small, neatly furnished apartment. The man who had answered the buzzer was nowhere to be seen. He handed the woman the bottle of milk.

"Thank you," she said. "Have a seat, Mr. . . ."

"Wallace Mahoney."

"Right. Care for a cuppa?"

Mahoney unbuttoned his coat and took it off. "Yes, please. If it isn't too much of a bother," he said.

"None at all," the woman said. She disappeared into the kitchen.

Across the room on a small lamp table was a framed photograph. Mahoney went over and picked it up. It was a picture of Maggie Byrne and Sir Robert. It had evidently been taken some years ago. It was summer. They were in the mountains.

"That was in Germany," the woman said from the kitchen doorway.

Mahoney put the photograph down and turned around. "How long ago?"

"In the sixties."

"You were his secretary even then?"

"Oh, yes," Maggie Byrne said. "I've been with Sir Robert for a very long time."

Mahoney sat down on the couch as she poured them both a cup of tea from a small, cracked, porcelain pot. "Where did he go, Mrs. Byrne?"

"It's Miss Byrne, and I wish to God I knew where my general was. I would go fetch him." Her eyes suddenly glistened.

There was a noise in the kitchen. Mahoney glanced up. Maggie Byrne's eyes darted from the kitchen doorway back to Mahoney. "It's my brother Carl. He's come from London to help."

"With what?"

"With all the people after me. I'm frightened."

"But you know about me?"

She nodded. "I was told you might be showing up on my doorstep."

Mahoney sipped his tea. It was very good.

"Milk or sugar?" Maggie Byrne asked.

Mahoney shook his head. "What did Sir Robert say to you when he left Friday?" he asked. "How did he look to you?"

She gazed off. "He looked terrible. Like he was sick. I told him to go right home and have Lady Sidney fix him a hot toddy."

"Did he say anything to you?"

"About what?"

"Where he was going."

"No. He just said . . . good-bye. That's all."

"Good-bye?" Mahoney prompted.

"Right. It was odd. I told Sir Howard that. It was just odd. I mean he might've said 'Have a good weekend, Maggie.' Or perhaps, 'Don't be an old nag.' Something like that. Not 'Good-bye.' "

"Then what?"

"Then nothing," Maggie Byrne said. "I helped him on with his coat, and he left. I called the parking garage and told Merrick—he's Sir Robert's usual driver—not to upset Sir Robert, just to get him right home."

"But Sir Robert dismissed his driver."

"I didn't know that was going to happen. Sir Robert walked out the door, and I immediately called down to the garage."

"Why?"

Maggie Byrne cocked her head. "He seemed . . . upset. Something was bothering him."

"Just that afternoon?"

Maggie Byrne looked at Mahoney. "I don't know what you mean."

"You said Sir Robert seemed upset. Had he been

upset all week? All month?''

"He's been working awfully hard these past months.
I could see it was getting to him. He was all the time
rushing off, or spending hours, it seemed like, on the
telephone.''

"There at his office?''

"Of course. Where else, man?'' Maggie Byrne said
impatiently.

"Were Sir Robert's calls ever recorded?''

"Of course not!'' the woman exploded.

Her brother appeared at the kitchen doorway. He did
not look happy. He was a very large man. He was
dressed only in dark trousers and a sleeveless undershirt.
His shoulders were broad and hairy.

Maggie Byrne looked up at him. "It's all right,
Carl,'' she said. "Honestly,'' she added when it seemed
as if he was going to remain there. He went back into
the kitchen.

"I didn't mean to upset you,'' Mahoney said.

"Carl is a cabby, but you'd never know it to look at
him. He used to lift weights. Great bloody things clank-
ing about the house. We lost our parents in the Blitz,
and he's never been the same through all these years.''

Mahoney was impatient with her rambling, but he felt
that he was very near learning something of importance,
so he did not want to disturb her.

"He absolutely hates the Jerries. Still to this day.
Always wanted me to quit Sir Robert.''

Mahoney started to say something, but then he held
off. There it was again. The Germans. Always it came
back to Germany when Sir Robert's name came up. But
it had been so many years ago. Even his involvement
with the KgU had been in the sixties, twenty years ago.

"It must have been hard, leaving Bonn and returning
to England after the Juengst thing,'' Mahoney said.

Maggie Byrne shook her head. "Not really. Sir
Robert was always too sad about what was happening
over there for him to really enjoy himself. He told me

once that being in Bonn was like trying to live next door to the grave of a very old friend. Gave me the chills, it did.''

"So he didn't really mind leaving?"

"No, not really. He was genuinely glad to get away for a while, I think. Lady Sidney was, too, though she never said too much about it. Never said much about anything, for that matter."

"You went back with them, to London?"

"Oh, yes. He wouldn't leave me behind. He couldn't operate without me. And he knows it, too."

"Then to Paris?"

"Right. And finally here to this godforsaken city," Maggie Byrne said with some vehemence.

"You don't like Brussels?"

"No, and neither does Sir Robert. Doesn't trust the Belgians. Says they're sneaky people. Too stuck on themselves." She sipped her tea and grinned. "The Belgians—especially the ones here in Brussels—are modeling themselves after the Swiss. They're trying to be big-money men. Big wheeler-dealers."

"I understand that Sir Robert was going to have to retire next year."

Maggie Byrne put her cup down forcefully. "Don't you believe it!" she snapped. "Just don't you count Sir Robert out until the very last bell." Again her eyes glistened. "Although the poor dear certainly deserves a rest. Seems like he's been going night and day."

"For the past year?"

She nodded absently.

"How about Sir Howard Scott? What does he have to say about Sir Robert's work?"

"They're friends. But Sir Howard doesn't know my general like I do. No one does, you see, not even that wife of his. Isn't she the high and mighty . . ." Maggie Byrne cut herself off, realizing what she was saying and who she was saying it to. She straightened up. "What else was it you were wanting to know? I have to get off to work now."

"Sir Robert said good-bye and left. He didn't give you any indication where he was going?"

Maggie Byrne shook her head. She was remembering Friday afternoon. "No," she said. "I helped him with his coat, told him to go home, and he said good-bye and left. Funny thing, though. Before I left for the night, I checked his office. To make sure it was tidied up. I always do that if he leaves before I do."

Mahoney said nothing.

"His office was fine, except for Lady Sidney's photograph on his desk."

"What about it?" Mahoney prompted.

"It usually sits so that he can see it when he's working. But this time it was turned around."

"Facing out?"

Maggie Byrne nodded. "So he could see it when he went out the door."

Sir Robert *had* walked off. Mahoney was nearly certain of it now. And he could see that Maggie Byrne knew it as well. She had known it that Friday afternoon. But why had he flown, and where had he gone?

Mahoney put down his cup and got to his feet. "Thanks for your help, Miss Byrne," he said.

She looked up at him, then got up herself. "He'll come back, won't he?"

"I suspect so. But first we'll have to find him."

"To do what? Drag him back?"

"Just talk."

Maggie Byrne stared at him. "You mean it, don't you. You're not like the others."

"What others?"

"All the others. Horne. Mr. Renelaux. All the others out there. There's not one of them gives a damn about Sir Robert. All they care about is their precious documents."

Mahoney got his coat and pulled it on. "Thanks for your help."

"You'll find him, won't you?"

"I think so," Mahoney said. He went to the door, but

before he left he turned back. "Merrick, Sir Robert's driver. Where might I find him this morning?"

"At work, I should suspect," Maggie Byrne said.

"Thanks," Mahoney said again, and then he let himself out, went downstairs and out into the street.

Mahoney walked down to the Rue du Trone, where he caught a cab over to the Avis office on the Rue Américaine and got himself a new Chevrolet Celebrity. He drove out to the NATO complex thinking about Sir Robert and the pressures he must have been under. Self-imposed pressures, Mahoney supposed. The same as in Germany with the Berlin Wall, and with Edward Juengst, but difficult to bear nonetheless.

The roads were well cleared, but there were occasional patches of ice on the bridges. He had been issued a number and a pass, so that when he got to the NATO complex he was let through the gate with no bother, although he did have to sign in.

He drove around the back of the main building to the parking garage, where he got out and went through a service door. It was a very large garage. Many expensive cars were parked in one vast area. A big Mercedes sedan was up on a grease rack, a mechanic beneath it. Mahoney went to the office behind a glassed-in cubicle.

A small man with steel-rimmed glasses sat at a radio console. He was drinking coffee and eating a large sweet roll.

"What can I do for you this morning, sir?" he asked, looking up. His accent was German.

"I'm looking for Stewart Merrick," Mahoney said.

The little man put down his coffee and got up. "Who are you?"

"A friend of Sir Robert's," Mahoney said, holding out his NATO badge. "Is Merrick here?"

The little man stared at him for a long time, but then he nodded toward the back. "In the lounge."

Mahoney went back around the office and into the drivers' lounge, a small room overfilled with plastic furniture and vending machines. A tall, well-built man with thick eyebrows sat at one of the tables. He was reading a newspaper. He looked up.

"Are you Stewart Merrick?"

The man nodded. "You from upstairs?" he asked, his cockney accent thick.

"Colonel Horne suggested I speak with you."

"If it's about the general, I can't tell you anything more than I've already told the others. He showed up down here, told me to take the rest of the weekend off, and took the car himself."

Mahoney came across the lounge and sat down across the table from Merrick. The man seemed jumpy.

"Who else have you talked to?"

"Everyone—until they told me different," Merrick said defensively. "The newspaper blokes were the worst. Bleedin' sods!"

"And there's nothing to add?"

Merrick shook his head. "What're you around here botherin' me for?"

"You were the last person to see Sir Robert. That counts for something, don't you suppose?"

"I got nothing to tell you."

"Wasn't it a little unusual for a man of Sir Robert's position to be driving himself around?"

"He did it all the time."

Mahoney smiled. "How long have you been his driver?"

"Since he came here."

"It's been a while, then."

Merrick nodded.

"He always drives himself around like that. What'd he need you for?"

"I didn't say that."

"He's been taking off on his own now for the past couple of years."

"Something like that."

"For the past year?"

Merrick shrugged. "I don't know. I've not kept track. But something like that. Yeah."

"But not at the beginning?"

"No, not when he first came here. Only in the last year or so."

Mahoney decided that Merrick wasn't hiding anything after all. The man's defensive attitude was nothing more than his fear that he would be blamed for Sir Robert's disappearance. Mahoney also decided that he did not like the man.

"One last thing, Merrick."

"Sir?"

"The Citroën Sir Robert drove. Was that his car? Was it assigned exclusively to him?"

"Yes. It's a Chapron. A good automobile."

"Is a mileage log kept so you can keep track of your maintenance schedules?"

Merrick nodded.

"I want a copy of it."

"I'd have to dig through the records. Get it out front to a copy machine."

Mahoney took out a cigar. "I'll wait," he said.

It took Merrick nearly an hour to produce the mileage and maintenance logs for Sir Robert's automobile. Mahoney waited in the lounge. He supposed that the man had telephoned Horne, or someone else, for authorization. It didn't matter. If someone hadn't already gotten on to the idea by now, they would sooner or later.

The automobile was less than one year old, so the records Merrick brought only went back to when it was put into service. That was all right as well. Mahoney was primarily interested in the last year.

He left the parking garage, climbed into his car, and quickly thumbed through the documents. As far as he could see, most of Sir Robert's trips were of two mileages. A long mileage, and a short one. One out to Anderlecht, he suspected, and the other merely into the city.

Mahoney drove out of the complex, turning in his badge, and headed back into Brussels.

Sir Robert was almost certainly seeking after another cause. Everything seemed to point toward that direction, although whether or not the Genesis Plan scenario was his cause, or if it was merely coincidental that he left on the day he had the material with him, was not quite as clear.

His secretary Maggie Byrne knew—or certainly felt strongly—that her boss had walked off and had not been kidnapped.

Sir Howard was convinced his friend had gone off under his own steam, although he was afraid to take the thought much further.

Pierre Renelaux was convinced that Sir Robert had not only walked off, but that he had defected. Although he was not clear on the reasons.

Lady Sidney was frightened, and although anything she had to say would necessarily be colored by her love for her husband, she too had seemed to be holding something back.

All that was balanced against the opinion of one man —Thomas Langdon, the reporter from London. He was convinced that Sir Robert had been snatched by the Israelis and killed. Langdon's line of reasoning was the least plausible of anyone's in the entire mess, and yet it offered up the most intriguing possibilities. It opened an entirely different view of Sir Robert: the saint who had helped Edward Juengst's KgU to save East Germans, or the sinner who, along with Juengst, capitalized on the plight of innocent people. Mahoney didn't buy the latter.

By the time Mahoney reached downtown Brussels, he knew that he was being followed. The same older gray Mercedes sedan that had been behind him shortly after he had left NATO headquarters had made all the same turns, and now was behind him as he pulled into the Avis parking area.

He turned the car over to the attendant and went inside to sign his credit card slip. The Mercedes was parked across the street when Mahoney stepped outside.

There were four men in the car, and although at this distance he could not recognize them, he sensed that there was something odd about them.

He had expected routine surveillance sooner or later. Possibly even by Renelaux's people. Certainly by the Russians once they found out who he was. But there was something about the four across the street now that was disturbing. As if they were not professionals, only mindless thugs.

He hesitated a moment, noting the license plate, then headed up the street to the cab stand at the corner. He got a taxi and directed the driver to take him to his hotel, then sat back and relaxed. He resisted the urge to turn around and look out the rear window. The gray Mercedes would either be there or it wouldn't. At this juncture there would be no point in him trying to lose them, or to do anything to interfere with their routine. First he needed some information. And second, when the meeting came, as it would, he wanted it at the time and place and circumstances of his choosing.

No doubt whoever was following him was a part of the operation to find out what had happened to Sir Robert. Renelaux had said that John's duties had been to follow the French and Italian investigators. Was everyone watching everyone else?

He paid the driver when they got to the hotel, and as he went inside, the Mercedes drove slowly by. This time he caught a better view of the four men. They all seemed small, slight of build, somewhat swarthy of complexion. They all wore large hats, but Mahoney had got the distinct impression that the four were Indian, or perhaps Arab.

☆ TWELVE ☆

All afternoon John Mahoney had been able to relax in the apartment Renelaux had provided. For a time he had watched television, but with the sound down very low so that he would be able to hear when the telephone surveillance receiver kicked over. For a while he had simply stared across the countryside to the east of the city, imagining that he could see the telephone pole he had climbed earlier, that he could see the thin wire antenna sticking out from beneath the junction box cover, that the direct line of sight meant he could discern the actual thing as well.

But as night fell, as the dusk came over the city hastened by the overcast, as the lights came on in the apartments of other buildings, as cars and trucks and buses switched on their headlights, John began to think back, and he began to get jumpy because of it.

He was usually all right during the day. It took quite a bit then to set him off. But at night, unless he was very busy, working flat out on something that demanded his undivided attention, he would get into trouble.

It was at those times that he would be standing on a dock, looking across the mirror-smooth water of Shultz Lake in northern Minnesota. He was able to smell the odor of the pine trees that lined the shore. He could clearly smell the damp earthy odors and the heady bouquet of growing things that had died and were being pressed down into the marshy area on the north side of the lake. It was during those times that he was even able to feel the cool wind on his arms and his neck and his face, and resurrect the same feelings he had had about his father's apparent death. They were feelings that had caused his sleeplessness that night, had caused him to get up and go outside.

Like a man experiencing an all-too-familiar nightmare, John Mahoney knew what he was doing to himself, and yet he had little or no control over the process. He also knew what was coming, and yet when the explosion did come in his mind, when the night sky behind him lit up in an incredible white-yellow ball of expanding gases, and when he was shoved off the dock into the water by the pressure wave, it still came as a terrible, terrible shock to him. His wife, his children were in the cabin! They were dead! God Almighty, they were dead!

John shook himself, glanced at the receiver and automatic recording machine, then went into the kitchen and opened a beer. Back in the living room he sat down at the equipment table that had been set up in front of the large plate glass window, put his feet up, and lit a cigarette.

He had been sweating, and now it gave him a slight chill.

For a long time he had thought about revenge. But the closer he had come to it, the nearer he had actually come to pulling the trigger on the man he felt was responsible for the deaths of his wife and children, the less satisfying the prospect seemed, until near the end he did not know if he would have pulled the trigger or not.

There were times when he thought about Caroline Henrys, the daughter of the man he had sworn to kill. She had moved to France, finally. St. Tropez or perhaps Cannes, he thought. But meeting her, like almost everything else that had transpired, seemed now like a dream.

That had all happened in a previous life. It had nothing to do with his new life.

The surveillance receiver burred softly, a green light winking on the console, indicating that the telephone call was incoming to the Marshall residence. The tape recorder automatically started.

John sat forward and turned up the set's volume. The receiver burred a second time, and then the telephone was answered.

"The Marshall residence," a man said. It was Bobbs, the houseman.

"Put Lady Sidney on. This is Howard Scott."

"One moment, Sir Howard."

John thought Sir Howard had sounded shaky. He looked at his watch. It was barely seven. Scott was probably calling from his home.

"Howard?" Lady Sidney came on.

"Thank God you're there," Sir Howard said. "Are you all right, Sidney?"

"Oh my God; what is it? What's happened? Have you found him?"

John's stomach tightened.

"You're certain you're all right, Sidney? No one has come to the house?"

"What is it?" she nearly shrieked. The indicators on the audio level dials jumped into the red.

"Has no one been out there to see you?"

"Just the Renelaux woman this afternoon for early tea," Lady Sidney said, calmer.

"We may have a lead," Sir Howard said. His voice sounded distant. "Just a moment—they've arrived."

"Howard?" Sidney called, but for several long seconds there was no reply.

John stubbed out his cigarette and lit another. They had some sort of a lead. But what?

Sir Howard was back. "Doyle-Handyside is here."

"What's happening, Howard? You must tell me. I demand it, or else I shall come over there immediately."

"No. Stay there, Sidney. I don't want you moving out of the house."

"Then tell me!"

"This evening, just a few minutes ago, we discovered a message at the front gate."

"A message?" Lady Sidney asked incredulously. "What sort of message?"

"It was in the form of a cassette tape."

John turned the volume up. Lady Sidney stifled a sob.

"Sidney?" Sir Howard said.

"Is it . . . a ransom note? Have they taken him after all? Is it terrorists?"

"We don't know yet for sure."

"What do you mean, you don't know for sure? What did the tape contain?"

"Merely the message that Robert is in safekeeping."

"Oh . . . God . . . Howard."

"I don't know about it, though, Sidney. It may be a hoax. There was no mention of the documents."

"Who was it from?"

"We don't know that either. But we'll find out," Sir Howard said. John could hear someone speaking in the background. He assumed it came from Sir Howard's home.

"What shall we do? Did they ask for money?" Lady Sidney asked.

"No . . . no money. Not yet. But for now you're just going to have to sit tight. There is nothing you could do, in any event."

"I can't just sit here."

"You must! Take a tablet and go to bed. In the meanwhile, put Bobbs on."

"Oh, no! You will not give him instructions on my behalf. I will not be a prisoner in my own home."

"Then promise me you will stay there tonight, Sidney. Promise me!"

Lady Sidney hesitated, but finally she acquiesced. "I will remain here, Howard. Dutifully."

"I'll ring you up first thing in the morning. Get some sleep."

"Don't be an ass," Lady Sidney said, and the connection was broken.

John waited a moment, then he hit the rewind button on the recorder. While the tape was backing up, he telephoned Renelaux.

"I have something you'd better listen to," he said when he had the Belgian on the line.

The mileage records for Sir Robert's Citroën supplied almost nothing new even on closer reexamination. Armed with a map of the city and surrounding countryside, Mahoney spent the better part of an hour going over the daily logs and comparing the mileages with the distance from NATO out to Anderlecht.

On several occasions the mileage did vary. But it was not often, the variation was consistent with a trip into the city first, and there was no one occasion where the mileage varied greatly, indicating Sir Robert had taken a much longer trip.

He had not known exactly what he had expected to find; nevertheless, the records were disappointing.

It was nearly eight o'clock by the time he was finished and had changed his clothes. He stuffed the .38 into his coat pocket and left his hotel room. If the Mercedes was still out front, he would deal with what it implied here and now.

There were quite a few people in the lobby when he came down, many of them on their way out for the evening, some of them coming down from their rooms for cocktails before dinner, and others just arriving on the early evening flights.

Of course he should have telephoned Renelaux for help. Brussels was the man's city. He had the manpower and the vehicles to set up a lateral system of tails. Mahoney the rabbit, the four in the Mercedes the hounds, and Renelaux's people the watchers moving

laterally, ready to pounce at the instant the situation
heated up.

Standard tradecraft. It was in the book that Mahoney
had helped write after the war.

Another equally important chapter in the very same
book, however, strongly recommended that your rear
not be tended by someone who might stab you in the
back, given the provocation.

Use a rat as an informer, use a drug addict as a go-fer,
or use a foreign diplomat you've been able to blackmail
as a conduit for disinformation (that was an old trick
the Soviets had taught them in the fifties). But no matter
how desperate the situation became, never but never use
one of the untouchables to actually guard your back
door.

Mahoney had come to think of Renelaux as an untouchable, but in a more benign sense than someone
who might actually pull the trigger. The Belgian had
struck Mahoney—and apparently John, as well—as a
man of too many unusual self-interests.

Renelaux, by his own admission, was cozy with Konstantin Demin, the local KGB majordomo.

John had supplied the information that the Belgian
had a very large blind spot when it came to the Germans. He was back in the thirties and forties. He might
be working for the CIA, but the man was still a Belgian
nationalist at heart. He could never forgive the Germans
for what they had done to his country. He was the same
as a lot of Manchurians who could never forgive the
Japanese.

One of the dark-skinned little men from the Mercedes
was sitting across the lobby reading *Stern*, the German
picture-news magazine.

There had been three others, making the odds four to
one. It wasn't the numbers that bothered Mahoney.
Rather it was what such numbers meant.

One or two men were sufficient for tailing a single
subject. If four men were involved in the surveillance
operation, they'd be split up. But when four men

bunched together the way they were with the Mercedes, it meant serious trouble. They were out to hurt someone.

Mahoney crossed the lobby, stepped outside past the doorman, and without hesitation crossed the street, dodging the heavy traffic. From the corner of his eye he could see that the Mercedes was parked near the end of the block. He turned the opposite way and hurried toward the railway station.

Behind him, the man from the lobby raced outside, crossed the street amidst much blaring of horns and screeching of tires, and jumped into the waiting Mercedes.

There were a lot of pedestrians and cabs, and a few buses milling around in front of the station. Mahoney slowed down. He did not want to lose his tails. Not yet.

At the main doors he stopped a moment and patted his pockets, first his side pockets, then his breast pockets, and finally his trouser pockets as if he were a man who had suddenly realized he had forgotten something.

He half turned to go back to the hotel, catching a glimpse of the Mercedes pulling up behind the cab ranks, and then he found what he had apparently been looking for and wheeled around once again.

Only two men got out of the Mercedes, he noted with satisfaction as he entered the crowded, noisy station. He could see the reflection of the car very clearly in the glass doors.

He went directly to the ticket windows and purchased a round-trip ticket to Anderlecht. One left every hour at fifteen minutes past the hour until 11:15, which was the last train.

The most danger here in the station would come in the press of the crowd. Mahoney stepped quickly away from the ticket window and angled out into the middle of the huge main hall before he headed toward the stairs that led down to the trains.

He avoided the urge to turn around and scan the

crowds for his followers. One of them was surely behind him, while the other would be checking at the ticket window to find out his destination.

The timing now would be tight. He had managed to cut out two from the Mercedes. Now came the chance to separate the two on his tail, depending on how fast the ticket agent was.

Just before the stairs, Mahoney, again apparently thinking of something else, turned abruptly and walked off to the left, past the news kiosks, a bank where a long line of customers was waiting to exchange money, and a barber shop, to the broad corridor that led back to the public rest rooms.

He entered the men's room and quickly stepped into one of the vacant stalls, closing and locking the door. He stood looking through the gap in the door. The rest room was quite busy.

At the far end a black man with a huge Afro hairdo was shining shoes. At least a half-dozen sinks were in use. And all but three of the urinals were occupied.

One of the short, dark-skinned men from the Mercedes came around the corner, hesitated a moment as he scanned the faces, then went to a sink where he began washing his hands. Mahoney could see that he was watching the stalls in the large mirrors.

The other man would be finished at the ticket counter by now. He would know that Mahoney was headed to Anderlecht on the next train. He had probably purchased a pair of tickets there for safety's sake. If he had not seen Mahoney's detour, then he'd be on his way down to the trains now, expecting to meet up with this one on Mahoney's tail. If he had seen him duck into the men's room, he'd be coming around the corner at any moment.

The little dark man continued washing his hands as several men came and went. Still the other one did not show up.

Mahoney took out the .38, checked to make sure there was a shell in the next chamber the hammer would fall on, then stuffed it back into his coat pocket, keeping his finger loosely on the trigger.

He flushed the toilet, and a moment or two later unlatched the door of the stall and stepped out.

The small dark man looked up at Mahoney's reflection in the mirror, then shut off the water and reached for a towel from a stack on the counter. At that moment his eyes were diverted from the mirror. Mahoney quickly stepped across to him and touched his arm. The little man flinched, then started to turn. Mahoney restrained him.

"I hope you understand English, because if you do not, you will die right here," Mahoney whispered urgently.

The man looked into Mahoney's eyes. "Sir?" he said.

"Finish drying your hands, and then we will leave together. If you do anything to make me nervous, I will instantly kill you. Do you understand?"

The little man was Arab. There was no doubt of it in Mahoney's mind. But it was puzzling that they should be involved.

The Arab nodded ever so slightly. "Yes, I understand," he said. His breath smelled of cloves. He dropped the towel on the counter, then turned and with Mahoney directly behind him, left the rest room, not one person suspecting anything untoward had happened so nearby.

Outside, past the bank, the Arab started toward the stairs, but Mahoney touched his arm.

"Not to the trains. We're going outside."

"Yes, sir," the man said. They headed across the main hall, past the stairs.

The Arab angled toward the front door where, presumably, the Mercedes was still waiting. Mahoney prodded him straight across to the broad corridor that led out to the Rue du Progrès exit. Before terribly long the man who had gone down to the trains would realize that something was wrong and would come back up in a big hurry.

"*Lā*," the Arab said, stopping in his tracks.

People were coming and going. The station was very busy. There was a constant din. Announcements blared in English, French, German, and Flemish from the overhead public address speakers. Trains rumbled from below. And there was a cacophony of voices.

Mahoney glanced toward the stairs, and then at the main doors. There wasn't much time!

He reached inside his breast pocket awkwardly with his left hand, removed his wallet, and flipped it open to his identification.

"*Polizei*!" he said loudly in German as he pulled the .38 from his coat pocket and jammed it into the Arab's back.

The small dark man nearly fell over. He let out a string of Arabic. Only a few people nearest them realized that something was going on, and several stopped to watch until they realized Mahoney was holding a handgun, and then they began to scatter. Very soon, like the ripples of a pebble dropped into a still pond, panic would spread. They had to get out of there.

"Move," he said to the Arab, raising the pistol a little higher into the small of his back. "Move!"

The Arab took a couple of hesitant steps, but then Mahoney prodded him hard with the snub-nosed barrel of the pistol, and the man fairly jumped down the broad corridor and out the doors to the avenue.

They turned right, away from the front of the station on the Place Rogier where the Mercedes would still be waiting, and hurried down the street, the rumble of an incoming train rising from below.

Mahoney looked back. No one had followed them from the station. Someone in the crowd who had seen them would be calling the police, however.

Nearly to the end of the long railway station, Mahoney shoved the Arab into the doorway of a service entrance. They were in relative darkness in the deeper shadows.

He raised the pistol to the Arab's head. The little man

backed up until he was against the corner and could go no farther back.

"Why were you following me?" Mahoney asked softly.

The Arab just looked at him, a mixture of fear and deep hate in his eyes.

"I will not keep my patience very long," Mahoney said. "Why were you following me?"

Still the Arab said nothing.

Mahoney carefully cocked the hammer of the .38. He did not like guns. He was nervous now that the damned thing might actually go off. The Arab evidently read something of that in Mahoney's eyes.

"*Min fādlak* . . . please, eminent sir, I am merely dog excrement."

Mahoney pressed closer, jamming the barrel of the pistol against the man's cheek. The Arab began to shiver.

"Why were you following me?"

"To see where you were going," the Arab squeaked. His head was inches from the stone wall of the alcove.

Mahoney jabbed the gun barrel hard against his cheek. The Arab's head banged against the wall.

"You were sent to kill me. Why?"

The Arab's eyes widened. "No," he pleaded, his nostrils flared. "No, honorable sir, no, you must believe me. *Min fādlak* . . . *min fādlak*."

Mahoney jabbed again at the Arab, this time hitting hard enough to open a small cut on the little man's cheek. Some blood trickled down from the slight wound. It turned his stomach. There wasn't much time.

"Who sent you to follow me?"

"I may not . . . tell," the Arab said softly. His English was beginning to desert him.

"I will not allow you to leave this place alive unless you tell me what I want to know," Mahoney said as softly.

Cars and trucks were passing on the broad street, but no one had walked by yet. He had been lucky so far, but he did not think his luck would hold out much longer.

Holding the gun barrel firmly against the Arab's cheek with his right hand, Mahoney flipped open the little man's jacket with his left, intending to reach for a wallet.

The Arab flinched, moving sideways, away from Mahoney's hand.

A police car, its siren suddenly very loud and very close, careened around the corner and raced past them.

Mahoney half turned to look, but the Arab shoved out at him, intending to dislodge the pistol from his cheek. But he pushed too hard and the gun went off, bucking in Mahoney's hand, the single shot sharp and unbelievably loud in the narrow doorway.

The Arab's head smashed backward against the rough stone. Some blood came out of his mouth, along with a few bits of shattered teeth. His left eye filled with blood, and then he folded up, his knees buckling beneath him so that he ended up wedged in the corner, sitting on his ankles. His legs and arms quivered, and his head lolled forward, bumping against his chest as if he were having a minor epileptic fit.

Mahoney stepped away from the still slightly quivering corpse and looked both ways up the street. The sound of the shot had been muffled by the doorway and by the sounds of traffic, but someone must have heard it.

Other sirens were converging on the station, no doubt in response to the report of a man with a pistol.

Mahoney jammed the pistol in his coat pocket, then turned back to the dead man. Steam rose from the wound in his face. The bullet had not exited through the back of the head because it had been cut as a dumdum; when it encountered the bone of the skull, it had mushroomed into a broad, jagged-edged missile that cut and tore and mangled its way through tissue. In this case, brain tissue. There wasn't much else more effective at close range.

Mahoney hurriedly went through the man's pockets,

finding a long, sheathed knife on the right hip and a huge Graz Buyra automatic in a shoulder holster.

Mahoney, conscious of the beating of his own heart marking the scant time before someone would come, stared at the big weapon in the dim light. He recognized it without removing it from its holster. It was the KGB Department Victor's assassination weapon of choice. A very large caliber. Very much more reliable than the American military .45 automatic, certainly much more effective than the British Walther PPK, and even better than the Italian Beretta 9mm automatic.

There was no wallet, no passport, or any other identification. Only a comb, a packet of clove-flavored sucking candies, and a small amount of money—Belgian francs and a few other coins.

He had to go now. He had pressed his luck as far as he could.

He was about to stuff the money back into the man's pocket, when he realized that one of the coins was larger and much thicker than any of the others. It was silver. He held it up to the dim light.

It was a Libyan five-dinar coin. Worth about ten dollars.

Mahoney pocketed the coin, stuffed the rest of the things back into the dead man's pockets, then straightened up and checked the street. No one was coming. Yet. He stepped out away from the doorway and walked off into the night, just another passerby in the great city.

☆ THIRTEEN ☆

It was getting late and Detective Inspector Richard Matin was tired. There was quite a crowd of people and cars backed up beside the Gare du Nord on the Rue du Progrès. Uniformed traffic control officers had blocked off the street from both ends. The Criminal Investigation van and coroner's ambulance were angled side by side directly in front of the doorway, their headlights illuminating the murder scene.

Matin's back hurt like hell, his mouth was foul, and he could feel that his feet and ankles were swollen. He held his hands up to the light. His fingers were swollen as well. Martine, when he told her, would be on his back again about his high blood pressure. He had forgotten to take his pills that morning.

His car was parked just behind the coroner's ambulance. He leaned against the hood as he waited for the laboratory people to finish their work. Sergeant Jean Rubaix was with them along with the photographer and the coroner, all crowded into the death scene in the narrow alcove.

He had learned from the first officer on the scene that a large man anywhere from thirty to seventy years old,

with light-colored hair, brandishing a gun and claiming
in very good or very bad German (depending upon who
was giving the report) that he was a police officer, had
kidnapped the smaller, dark-skinned gentleman from
the depot.

Four cars had initially been dispatched to the station.
Minutes later someone had heard what he took to be a
single shot. Nevertheless, it had taken more than ten
minutes before officers on the scene found the body,
secured the crime scene, and summoned help. An immediate search of the area had been instituted, with no
results. They had simply been too slow.

The newspaper and television people were there, of
course. Matin glanced in their direction down closer to
the Place Rogier. Since that NATO general had disappeared, all of Brussels had seemed to go crazy.

"It is worse than Paris," he had lamented to his wife
just that morning. "And you want to go there? I tell
you, this city is filled with gangsters. Just go walking
alone at night, and it will be like Paris for you."

A train rumbled into the station, and then the street
was quiet. It was not raining or snowing, which was a
blessing, but it was very cold.

Jan Breezard, the homicide division's photographer,
broke away from the others and emerged from the
alcove. He headed across to his car, but Matin pushed
away from where he was leaning and intercepted him.

"What do you think, Jan?" Matin asked.

"Oh, good evening, Richard. I see they got you out of
bed."

Matin forced a smile. He did not like the nasty little
Fleming who, whenever he was given the chance, would
embarrass French- or German-speaking officers by
speaking rapid-fire Dutch. Matin *always* spoke to
Breezard first, in French, giving the photographer no
choice but to reply in French.

"How does it look?"

Breezard shrugged. "He was shot in the head. Close range. And he's obviously an Arab. What else can I tell you? I am a cameraman."

"How soon will you have the photographs on my desk?"

"First thing in the morning, Richard."

Matin glanced over toward the alcove. Rubaix had stepped aside and was beckoning. They had finished and were ready for him. He turned back to Breezard. He had a funny feeling about this. But maybe it was just the crazy week.

"You may collect some overtime this evening. I wish to have the photographs on my desk within one hour."

Breezard started to groan but then thought better of it. Matin was his superior. And Matin did have the reputation for being a tough old bastard. Breezard nodded. "They may still be wet, but they will be on your desk within the hour."

Matin went across to the alcove. Rubaix and the coroner, Dr. Alois Flaubert, a tall, distinguished-looking man who taught at the university, were waiting for him. It was surprising to see Flaubert there. Normally one of his assistants handled such routine matters.

"Good evening, Doctor," Matin said. They shook hands. "To what do we owe the pleasure of your presence?"

Flaubert looked at him, cocking his head. "Is that supposed to be some sort of a joke, Inspector? If it is, I do not see the humor."

It wouldn't be long now, Matin thought, before he was indeed moved aside and tossed into the dustbin. "I meant nothing by it, Doctor, believe me."

"Yes, well . . ."

Matin stepped into the alcove, then hunched down over the body crumpled on its ankles in the corner. A small amount of blood had trickled down from the wound in the cheek; more blood had oozed from the victim's mouth, and from his eye and left ear.

Dr. Flaubert stepped into the alcove. "A young male, probably an Arab, in his middle to late twenties. A single bullet to the head. I think when we get inside we'll find it was a mushrooming soft lead projectile. I suspect there is a lot of damage in there."

Matin reached out and gently held up the corpse's head. There was a grimace on the young man's face. The Arab had been in fear of his life at the moment it had ended. There was a small, half moon-shaped cut on the left cheek.

"How about a time of death?"

"I can't give that to you precisely, not yet. But I would say his time of death matches very closely with the reports of his abduction from the station."

Matin gently let the young man's head down.

"May we take the body now?" the coroner asked.

Matin got up. "Are the laboratory people finished here?" he asked Rubaix.

"Yes."

"How about his pockets? Any identification?"

"No. But he was heavily armed," Rubaix said. "And I think you should have a look at his arsenal."

Matin nodded. He turned back to the coroner. "Yes, Dr. Flaubert, you may remove the body. I would appreciate an autopsy report as soon as practicable." He turned again to Rubaix. "No identification, you say?"

"None," the sergeant said. "But someone went through his pockets. Two of them were turned half out."

"A robber?"

"His money was intact."

Matin turned again to Dr. Flaubert. "I would like to know when this man last ate . . ."

"Of course."

"And *exactly* what he ate."

Flaubert nodded. Matin glanced again at the body, then went with Rubaix out of the alcove and across to the back door of the Criminal Investigation van. Rubaix opened the rear door and stepped up into the van's warmth. Two lab technicians had just finished sorting their crime-site collection. Matin climbed up and closed the door. The lights inside were concentrated over a countertop that ran from front to back. Several clear plastic bags were laid out in a row on the counter. Matin saw immediately what had excited Rubaix. It was the big automatic.

"It's the Russian gun?" he asked, although he knew it was. He had worked in this city with all its comings and goings for too many years not to recognize it.

"Yes, sir," one of the technicians replied. "No serial number, of course, and no clear prints from the cross-hatched surfaces."

The Russian designers were clever. The weapon was extensively crosshatched so that no fingerprints would be found. The weapon itself, however, had become a clear enough fingerprint. Only Soviet intelligence officers used the big gun. KGB operatives. Someone on the payroll.

"What else?" Matin asked.

"About the gun, sir?"

"No, I mean what else did you find? There was no identification?"

"No, sir, none. And very little else."

It was a night for gut feelings, Matin decided. And his at that moment said that the sad little Arab lying dead in the doorway was in some way connected with the disappearance of the NATO general.

Brussels had its murders, as did other cities of its size. But just lately there had been too much activity here. Just now, this particular murder struck a responsive note in Matin's inner self that resonated to such clues.

He looked at Rubaix, who seemed to show up at almost everything of importance. "You're detached from this moment, Jean, to work for me on this."

Rubaix nodded solemnly. "Yes, sir."

Coming up the driveway to Sir Howard Scott's somewhat ostentatious house for the second time in a little
more than twenty-four hours brought a singular though
disconnected thought to mind: he had never chased
after money. Although the opportunities could have
been developed at any point along the line, it had simply
never occurred to Mahoney to seek a fortune. When the
kids were little, his career had carried him between New
York and Washington, D.C. Later, postings overseas
precluded them ever purchasing a home, a place of their
own in which they could have collected the bric-a-brac
of his career, of their lives. The nearest they had ever
come to such a thing was their little cabin on the lake in
northern Minnesota. But it wasn't much. A retirement
shack, he had called it. Now, dealing with a missing Sir
Robert, and a present Sir Howard, both men of long-
standing wealth and power, both men of long-standing
breeding and fine educations, Mahoney wondered if he
weren't just a bit resentful.

From the Gare du Nord he had walked a half-dozen
blocks over to the Boulevard Anspach beyond the post
office and had gotten a crosstown bus to the Porte de
Hal. He had taken a cab—for nearly all the Belgian cash
he had on him—out to the town of Wemmel, to the
northeast. There he had telephoned Sir Howard and
asked that he be picked up. The man had sounded agitated, but he had sent his car.

The large house was mostly dark, but there were three
cars parked in the front, one of them Renelaux's dark
Opel. Mahoney supposed something had happened.

It was colder out here in the country than it had been
in the city. He was met at the front door by one of the
house staff, an older man, and was shown immediately
back to the study.

Sir Howard was seated at his desk, a portable cassette

tape player in front of him. A recording of someone talking was playing. Sir Howard shut it off and rose as Mahoney came into the room.

A fire was burning in the grate. Pierre Renelaux sat to the left of it. Colonel Oliver Horne was seated to the right. A third man was present. He stood beside the desk. He was about forty, very tall and gangly. His hair was mussed, a five-o'clock shadow darkened his chin, and his dark gray suit looked as if it had been slept in.

"We tried to reach you earlier," Sir Howard said. He was definitely shaken.

"A ransom message?" Mahoney asked, indicating the tape recorder. He took off his coat and laid it over a chair.

"I take it you are Wallace Mahoney?" the third man said. He was very English.

"That's right."

"I've heard of you, sir. And I don't mind telling you it's a rare pleasure to meet you at last."

"Forgive me, please," Sir Howard said, coming around the desk. "This is Quentin Doyle-Handyside. He's acting as chief of SIS operations here in Brussels."

"Just for this business," Doyle-Handyside said. He and Mahoney shook hands.

Horne was staring at Mahoney. He seemed puzzled. Renelaux, on the other hand, seemed somewhat smug. The diversity of attitudes struck Mahoney as odd.

"We're keeping this quiet for the moment," Doyle-Handyside was saying. "We have an electronic analysis team coming over from London. Should be here within an hour. Sir Howard did the right thing, telephoning me. Kept the lid on it, if you know what I mean."

"Naturally I had to phone Sidney, and of course Oliver," Sir Howard said. "As chief of NATO Security . . ."

"It's all right," Doyle-Handyside said placatingly.

Evidently Sir Howard was feeling guilty. But what

about Renelaux? Mahoney wondered. No one seemed
to be ready to offer an explanation, and he wasn't going
to press it.

"Let's rewind the tape, then, and we'll start at the
beginning," Doyle-Handyside said.

Mahoney decided he didn't like the man. He was a
pompous ass. Where in God's name were all the good
ones? Where the hell had they all gotten themselves to?

Sir Howard rewound the tape, and Doyle-Handyside perched on the edge of the desk, motioning for
Mahoney to take the straight-backed chair off to the
side.

"One of Sir Howard's house staff, Norbert Winslow,
returning from town at about six-thirty, found a manila
envelope wrapped up with an elastic band attached to
the front gate," Doyle-Handyside began. "It was addressed to Air Vice Marshal Sir Howard Scott. Typewritten. Probably a manual portable."

The tape had finished rewinding. Doyle-Handyside
continued.

"Winslow plucked the packet from the gate and
brought it up to the house, where he naturally turned
it over to Sir Howard. Sir Howard opened it, found
the cassette tape—BASF, thirty-minute duration—and
played it."

"I telephoned Doyle-Handyside immediately, and
then Sidney . . . to make sure she was unharmed," Sir
Howard interjected.

"What did you tell her?" Mahoney asked softly.

Doyle-Handyside seemed startled by the question.

"Just that I had received a tape, and that she was to
remain at home."

"She agreed?"

"Reluctantly."

"You did not tell her what the tape contained?"

"Only that Sir Robert was being held, and that apparently he was unharmed."

Mahoney let his breath out slowly. He glanced at
Renelaux. The man was hiding something. "What are
you doing here?"

Renelaux started. "I happened to be in Horne's office
when Quentin telephoned," he said indignantly.

Mahoney turned back to the others. Bullshit, he
thought. Sir Howard seemed worn out; Doyle-Handyside seemed perpetually surprised.

"The tape," the SIS man said.

Sir Howard punched the button.

At first there was no sound, but then a man began to
speak, in English, but with a very definite Arab accent:

> Greetings, Honorable Air Vice Marshal Sir Howard
> Scott, from the Socialist Peoples Libyan Arab
> Jamahiriya. We have news of your Honorable
> General Sir Robert Isley Marshall. He is in good
> health and will be in no danger providing you do
> not attempt to contact him.

There seemed to be a scuffling noise in the background of the tape. The speaker had stopped. Mahoney
thought he could hear a whistle that hooted once, twice,
and a third time. But from very far away. Doyle-Handyside and Horne were listening very closely to the sounds.
They both sat forward, rapt expressions on their faces.

> We are not terrorists. We wish nothing at this mo-
> ment. Nor will we harm Sir Robert, providing you
> do as you are instructed.

Again the speaker hesitated. This time they could
hear him breathing.

> Please convey our assurances to Lady Sidney that
> her husband is in good health and will not be
> harmed. You will be contacted in fourteen days'
> time, Sir Howard, with further instructions."

• • •

Sir Howard reached out and stopped the tape. The others looked up. "That's all there was on the tape," he said.

"No further background noises?" Mahoney asked.

"None," Doyle-Handyside said. "Immediately after the speaker finishes, the machine is turned off. The remainder of the tape is pristine."

"What do you think?" Sir Howard asked.

"They're not terrorists," Mahoney said. "Or at least whoever made the tape has not been trained in any Eastern terrorism camp."

"I agree with Mr. Mahoney," Doyle-Handyside said to the others. "They do not act that way . . . the ones who had any kind of training."

"Are we dealing with amateurs, then?" Horne asked.

"Presumably," the SIS man said. "European Arabs, the displaced variety. I don't think, despite what the speaker tells us, that he is Libyan. I don't think Qaddafi would get involved in something like this. At least his activities to date have been directed against either Israel or the U.S., and not NATO *per se*."

"There have been no indications, so far as we have been able to determine, that Libya is involved," Renelaux said.

Mahoney's hand went to the Libyan coin in his pocket. Somehow this didn't add up in his mind. Somehow it was all too pat, almost as if it had been purposely laid out for him—or for whomever—to discover, to make the connection. Yet it certainly was possible that they were dealing with amateurs who had snatched Sir Robert.

They'd be harder to figure. Their motivations would be less clear. Their methods unorthodox.

"What about the fourteen days the speaker mentioned?" Mahoney asked. "Does that date have any significance for you, Sir Howard?"

"None," Sir Howard said, shaking his head. "I've

gone over it a hundred times. It's November first. It means nothing."

"No birthdays, anniversaries, nothing significant in Sir Robert's history?"

"Nothing."

Mahoney turned to Doyle-Handyside.

"We're searching his files at the moment."

"I'll personally look through the NATO archives," Horne volunteered.

"How about the Genesis Plan? Is the date significant?"

"No," Sir Howard said.

"I think the date will turn out to have no significance in and of itself," Doyle-Handyside said. "It is the time span. The fortnight that is needed for something or other."

Mahoney tended to agree. He was trying to put it together, from Langdon's idea about the Israelis to the dead man—possibly Libyan—in the doorway at the Gare du Nord. But the other three men in the gray Mercedes would be a lot more cautious. Would they turn around and go home? Or would they remain and continue what they had begun . . . only with more care now that one of their own was dead?

He decided that he could do almost anything alone, but this now needed backup. Any kind of business with Libya at this moment in history would demand a certain sophistication because of the Libyan government's unpredictability.

Sir Howard was not qualified to help, of course. Horne was merely a security officer but would be of some use here in Brussels. Renelaux certainly was capable, but the man was hiding something, and Mahoney did not want him at his back door. Which left Doyle-Handyside, an unknown. Rather keep them all distracted here, holding down one of the variables while another was explored.

He laid his bombshell.

"The speaker on the tape may be an amateur, which is puzzling to me, but he is probably Libyan."

"You can't know that with any degree of certainty," Doyle-Handyside said with a certain pompousness. "Not until our dialect man gets here."

"The horn in the background about two thirds of the way through the message was probably a ship's whistle. I'd guess the port of Tripoli."

"What have you got?" Renelaux asked.

Mahoney turned to him.

Doyle-Handyside realized that something was going on between the two men. But he misinterpreted it.

"If we let individual service differences into this equation, we'll never solve it," the SIS man said peevishly.

"It's not that at all," Renelaux said, "I assure you. But Mr. Mahoney has some information for us, I think. It is why he showed up here tonight."

It suddenly struck Doyle-Handyside. "But I thought . . ."

Mahoney shook his head. "No one called me."

"Then how did you know about the tape?"

"I didn't, although it did not surprise me. Not after what happened tonight." He turned to Horne. "Do you have any contacts on the Brussels metro police force?"

Horne nodded. "We work very closely with them as well as with Interpol."

Mahoney turned back to the others. "I was followed to my hotel this evening by four men in a gray Mercedes sedan," he said. He gave the license number to Horne.

"Did they follow you out here as well?" Sir Howard asked.

"No," Mahoney said. In concise terms he told them how he had left his hotel and made the first cut out at the train station, separating two of his followers from the other two. The second cut out was a bit more difficult, and he admitted to a tricky moment when he had held up his wallet and cried "*Polizei!*"

"They were Arabs," Mahoney said.

"Were you able to question the one?" Doyle-Handyside asked.

Renelaux's eyes were bright.

"Yes," Mahoney said. "He admitted that he had been following me, and he admitted he was under orders, but he refused to tell me who he was being directed by."

"There are ways—" Doyle-Handyside started, but Renelaux interrupted.

"No . . . no. What happened, Mr. Mahoney? He was a Libyan? Did you get a positive ID?"

"No positive identification, I'm afraid. But the man was possibly Libyan." Mahoney pulled the five-dinar coin from his pocket and handed it over to Doyle-Handyside, who studied it for a moment.

"It was in his pocket," Mahoney said.

"Along with Belgian currency, perhaps?" Doyle-Handyside asked.

"Yes."

"Then why didn't you assume he was Belgian?"

Mahoney shook his head. "He was an Arab."

"Was he armed?" Renelaux asked.

"Yes," Mahoney said. "He had a knife. But he also carried an automatic."

"What?" the SIS man demanded impatiently. "A Colt? A Beretta? What?"

"A Graz Buyra."

Doyle-Handyside stared at him for a long moment. "Bloody hell," he finally said. "Oh, bleedin' hell!"

"What about the other three in the Mercedes—" Sir Howard started to ask, but Doyle-Handyside cut him off.

"No. What I want to know is what happened to the little bastard with the Russian hardware?"

Mahoney sighed. "He's dead. The police have surely found him by now."

✭ FOURTEEN ✭

Perhaps only a few seconds passed, but it seemed like a mini-eternity to Mahoney. Renelaux had instantly put it together; it was written all over his face. Of course he had supplied the weapon, so he had been suspecting something like this all along. Sir Howard was horrified. He was a soldier. Murder was totally out of the question to him. Hydrogen bombs, fighter-interceptor strikes, missile launches were impersonal. Murder was . . . messy.

Doyle-Handyside was livid. He hopped off the desk. "That tears it," he said. He went across to the sideboard and helped himself to a sherry.

"Exactly how did it happen, Mr. Mahoney?" Horne asked. He seemed to be the only one not overly affected.

Mahoney explained it to him. In detail.

Sir Howard had turned away, but Doyle-Handyside listened from across the room as he sipped his wine. When Mahoney was finished, the SIS operative shook his head in disgust.

"Bloody hell, I say," he muttered.

"It'll appear to be some sort of an assassination, not a simple murder, I suspect," Horne said. "The news media will be in on it, of course. Sometimes in this city they get to the crime scene before the police do."

"We'll have to head them off at least for a few days," Mahoney said.

"I didn't think it was real," Sir Howard interjected, turning back despite himself. "I thought it was some sort of a hoax. Not once was the Genesis Plan mentioned. But now . . ." He gestured vaguely toward Mahoney.

"This could be nothing more than coincidence," Doyle-Handyside said hopefully.

"I can't believe that," Renelaux spoke up. "Libyans just don't start popping up all over the place out of pure coincidence."

"Which still leaves us the Genesis Plan," Sir Howard said.

"Maybe he threw it away. Maybe he stashed it before he was snatched. Who knows?" the SIS man offered. He sipped his sherry.

"I'll make a few quiet inquiries," Horne said. "See what they've come up with, where they're heading. If it looks bad . . . I'll play it by ear. I don't know."

"He's gone four bleedin' days, and there's nothing but a tape telling us to hold off for a fortnight," Doyle-Handyside said. "And on top of that we have a murder on our hands and some kind of a Qaddafi plot." He was speaking to Sir Howard.

"This won't do us any good," Sir Howard said. He looked frightened.

"Find out about the Mercedes," Mahoney said to Horne. "Perhaps you can get some help, but if the other three haven't already bolted, you might get on them. We might get a break."

Horne nodded. "You're not going to stay at the same hotel, are you?"

"No."

"Where are you going?" Renelaux asked, but Mahoney stood up. Horne got up too, and Sir Howard came around his desk.

"Has there been any significant movement from the

opposition?'' Mahoney asked.

"Do you mean the Russians?'' Sir Howard asked.

"Right.''

"None, other than the standard response to our DEFCON-four.''

"If they had the scenario, would they react differently?''

"Almost certainly,'' Sir Howard said immediately. "We met in DPC session this afternoon with the Secretary General.'' He glanced at Renelaux and Horne. "I had planned on speaking with you in the morning once the details were cleared. The DPC came up with a recommended course of preliminary action . . . namely, we are to do nothing but watch. If Warsaw Pact forces increase their alert status, so shall we. But in no event will we posture ourselves in any manner other than routine. The Secretary General also suggested, and all of us on the Defense Planning Committee agreed, that the representatives of each of the member nation secret services here in Brussels for this operation meet at once so that their efforts could be coordinated.''

Doyle-Handyside started to protest. Mahoney held him off.

"I think that's a wonderful idea.''

"They feel we're all stepping over each other. We need a concerted effort. And someone should be designated to direct the operation.''

"Sir Robert is British,'' Doyle-Handyside said. "I don't want the bloody frogs—or anyone else, for that matter—stepping all over me.''

Mahoney studied Doyle-Handyside's peevish countenance for a moment. "What about the Russians? Has anyone thought to keep track of them?''

No one said a thing.

"My man tonight was carrying a KGB assassination weapon. That is significant.''

"We've been watching Konstantin Demin, of course,'' Renelaux said.

"And?"

"His people have checked the airports, train stations, car rental agencies, all the usual."

"Have they made any effort to contact Lady Sidney?" Mahoney asked.

Sir Howard gasped.

"Not that we are aware of," Renelaux replied.

"If Qaddafi has taken him, we'll never see him alive," Sir Howard said. "And God only knows what that madman will do with the Genesis Plan."

"Hold it like a gun to our heads, I suppose," Doyle-Handyside said glumly.

"I'll go, then," Horne said. "There is a lot to do yet tonight if we're going to sidetrack the Brussels police." He started for the door.

"Who is your contact? Is it Jean Rubaix?" Mahoney asked.

Horne turned back, startled. "Yes. How did you know?"

"Just a lucky guess."

Horne looked pointedly at him for a moment, but then he turned and left. They could hear him in the stairhall asking for his coat, and then he was gone.

"I'm going back to town. I'll give you a lift," Renelaux said to Mahoney.

"No, go ahead."

Renelaux's gaze went from Mahoney to Sir Howard and then to Doyle-Handyside. "If there's something else . . . ?" he asked. "Something the rest of us should know?"

"It's nothing significant," Mahoney promised. "I want a few more details about the scenario itself, and about the administration of the DPC."

The Belgian did not believe him, but there wasn't much he could do about it. He nodded.

"I'll go with you," Doyle-Handyside said. He slipped the tape out of the machine and pocketed it, then left with Renelaux.

Mahoney could hear both of them out in the stairhall, then outside where two cars started and moments later drove off.

Sir Howard looked all done in. There were bags under his eyes, his skin hung slack and gray under his chin, and when he lifted a cigarette to his mouth to light it, his hands shook.

"We could have done this in the morning, Mahoney," he said. "In fact I'd prefer it, if you wouldn't mind awfully."

"I'd like to speak with Lady Sidney."

"Out of the question."

"Tonight. Right now. You can come along with me."

Sir Howard gazed at Mahoney as if he were looking at some new species of fool.

"I wouldn't ask this if it were not of the utmost importance."

"What more can Sidney possibly tell you that would have any significance?"

Mahoney held his ground, although he said nothing.

"It's late. She almost certainly will be asleep."

Mahoney got his coat and pulled it on.

"Perhaps we could telephone her?"

"Telephone if you will, and tell her that we're on our way. But I must speak with her in person."

Sir Howard looked toward the door. "It's about that Arab you . . . who was killed tonight. That and the tape. You think Sir Robert has been taken to Libya."

"It's possible."

"What in God's name can Sidney tell you? Haven't you got your sort of people over there? We can speak with Doyle-Handyside. Certainly he should be in on this."

"So we can step over each other? I believe those were your words."

"Bloody hell," Sir Howard said. He stubbed out his cigarette in the desk ashtray. "I'll tell you one thing straight off, Mahoney. Sidney is a delicate woman. I will not allow any browbeating of her. I absolutely forbid it, do you understand?''

Mahoney nodded, and they went out into the stairhall where Sir Howard rang for his car and driver, but got his own coat from the hall closet.

It was nearing midnight. Lady Sidney met them in the drawing room. Sir Howard had telephoned her from his car phone to expect them. She wore a dressing gown. Her eyes were red and somewhat puffy. Mahoney did not think she had been sleeping very much.

''This looks terribly ominous,'' she said to Sir Howard, kissing him on the cheek. ''Is it more about the tape?''

They all were standing. She looked to Mahoney when Sir Howard did not answer. ''What is it?''

''I'm terribly sorry to bother you so late, Lady Sidney, but I need some information that only you can supply.''

She was suddenly very frightened. Her lower lip quivered. ''Please sit down,'' she said.

''We're not staying long,'' Mahoney said. ''I merely want to know if your husband has, or has ever had, a friend in Libya. Perhaps from Tripoli or Benghazi.''

''He certainly does not,'' Sir Howard said crossly. ''Good Lord, man, I could have told you that.''

''No, wait,'' Lady Sidney said, touching his arm. ''That's not quite true, Howard. There is someone. With the Libyan National Banking Institute. He was a student, years ago, for a brief time, at Oxford.''

''When was this?''

''In the fifties, I suspect, although I can't possibly give you any exact date. I do remember that he stayed only a short while.''

''Yet you remember now?''

Lady Sidney smiled, but only as a reaction to an obvious question. ''I couldn't help but remember. Robert mentioned his name just six months ago, and again three weeks ago. He was here in Brussels. They met for lunch.''

"Where?"

Lady Sidney shook her head. "I don't know. It could have been anywhere. Is that significant?"

"Do you remember his name?"

"Yes. It was an odd one. Ali al-'Usta."

"Had you ever met him?"

"Yes. He came to the house to fetch Robert."

"What did he look like?"

"He had terribly large eyes. They were sad. I remember that now vividly."

"Anything else?"

"He was very tall, fat, and he moved ever so slowly. Will he have information about Robert? Is he somehow involved?"

"I don't know, Lady Sidney, but I'm going to need your cooperation now. Yours and Sir Howard's."

She nodded, but Sir Howard just looked at him.

"No one must know of this conversation. At least not for a few days."

Lady Sidney was not bothered, but the request startled Sir Howard.

"We can't keep this from the others. Surely you can see that I at least have a duty to Doyle-Handyside."

"And Colonel Horne?"

"Yes, to him as well. And your investigation surely must be cleared with your own people."

"I must ask you to do this for me. In return I will give you a favor."

Sir Howard was frustrated. "Whatever are you talking about, man?"

"There is a tap on the telephone in this house."

"The tape recorder," Sir Howard said nervously. "Sidney knows how to use it."

Mahoney shook his head.

"What are you talking about, then?"

"Pierre Renelaux has almost certainly put a tap on the telephone in this house, perhaps on your telephone as well."

"Renelaux . . . ? How could you know such a thing?"

"He knew about the tape."

"He was in Horne's office when I telephoned."

"But he was not curious. He had all the knowledge he needed. He must have gotten it from somewhere. When you mentioned you had telephoned Lady Sidney and had told her the contents of the message, I supposed that he had to have listened to your conversation."

Lady Sidney was alarmed. Her complexion had turned even more pale. "This man has listened to *all* my conversations?"

Mahoney turned to her so fast that he nearly tripped over himself. "Who else has telephoned here in the last few days . . . since Friday?" he asked, working very hard to keep his voice calm.

"My daughter's friends from London. Langdon, that dreadful newspaperman. Ever so many other journalists wanting to know about Robert."

She was lying. Someone else had telephoned her. "Did you record any of those calls?"

"No need to," she said. "I told that to the secret service men. The only telephone call I received of any significance to . . . Robert's disappearance, was from Howard."

Mahoney looked into her eyes. It made her uncomfortable. "Lady Sidney, I want you to listen very carefully to me now, because Sir Robert's safety may depend upon your answer, and my life may be placed in the balance."

"Here, I told you none of this . . ." Sir Howard sputtered.

"No," Lady Sidney said, her eyes wide. "It's all right."

"I must know if you received any other telephone calls. Any messages, any information in any form about Sir Robert."

"You are doubting my veracity?"

"I won't have this," Sir Howard said, raising his voice.

"I have nothing to tell you, Mr. Mahoney," she said, a hard edge to her voice. She turned to Sir Howard. "I'm terribly tired, Howard, you do understand."

"Of course," Sir Howard said.

She kissed him on the cheek, nodded to Mahoney, then turned and left the drawing room. Bobbs appeared a moment later.

Sir Howard was angry. "I came here this evening against my better judgment. I'm sorry I did." He started for the door. Mahoney stopped him.

"If you want to see Sir Robert again . . . if you want this business resolved, I need your help."

Sir Howard turned back. "I won't mention this to anyone, if that's what you want. But only so long as I judge that the investigation is not being affected adversely by my silence."

"And secondly, Lady Sidney is lying."

Bobbs shivered. Mahoney could see that the big gunnery sergeant wanted nothing more than to come into the drawing room and take him apart.

Sir Howard wanted to protest, but he could not. He nodded. "I believe you may be correct." He looked up. "If you are, however, and Pierre Renelaux does have a tap on these telephones, then he will know everything. I believe in that case you would do better to get the information from him rather than trying to browbeat Sidney."

Mahoney turned to the houseman. "The telephones in this house are being monitored. I suggest you conduct yourself accordingly."

Bobbs nodded uncertainly.

"It is also possible that Lady Sidney may be in some danger," Mahoney said.

"From whom?" the houseman asked.

"I would suggest that if any Arab gentleman, no matter his apparent credentials, shows up here, you not admit him no matter what your SIS contingent outside might have to say about it.''

Bobbs nodded. ''Is there anything else you can tell me, sir?''

''Not at this point.''

''Thank you, then, sir. I'll keep an eye out.''

''Do that.''

Sir Howard's driver dropped Mahoney off downtown, near the Gare du Midi, where he would be able to get a cab. Once the Rolls had disappeared around the corner, Mahoney walked across the nearly deserted street to the train station and entered one of a very long row of phone booths in the main hall.

All the newsstands, banks, and restaurants were closed. As Mahoney gave the overseas operator the number he wished to call, along with his international credit card number, he watched the service people do their cleaning. They operated two big machines that rode back and forth across the huge hall, sweeping the floor, washing and drying it, and then laying down a coat of wax, all in one continuous operation. Working together, two machines were faster on the job than one machine would be working twice as long.

It took nearly five minutes for the call to go through, and then the telephone was ringing. It was eight in the evening in Washington. Bindrich was home by now.

The acting DCI answered his own telephone. ''Yes?''

''I'm going to need some help,'' Mahoney said without preamble.

Bindrich picked up on it without hesitation. ''Conwell has complained. He says you are working autonomously.''

''I am.''

One of the big floor cleaning machines swept by. It was very loud. Mahoney knew it should mean something to him. It was a reminder, of sorts. He knew he ought to make the connection.

"Why have you gotten yourself involved?"

"I don't know, Sylvan. A lot of reasons."

Bindrich was silent for a very long time. When he came back he sounded cautious but resigned. "What sort of help will you need?"

"A cover. A very convincing cover that will have to hold up for twenty-four hours at least. Better yet, forty-eight."

"What are you up to . . . ?" Bindrich almost said Mahoney's name, but he caught himself in time. It almost certainly wouldn't make any difference on this line, but old field habits die hard.

"This might be difficult. I'll need it very fast—by tomorrow—and it'll have to be absolutely secure."

"Can't do much for you if I don't know what you want."

"I need to meet and speak with a man by the name of Ali al-'Usta."

"An Arab?"

"A member of the Libyan National Banking Institute. In Tripoli."

"In Tripoli," Bindrich repeated. "You want to meet him in Tripoli?"

"Yes. And he may turn out to be a hostile, at least as far as the investigation is concerned, so I'll need a plausible reason for being there."

The line was silent for a long while. Mahoney did not want to push it, so he held his peace. He watched the machines going back and forth in precise paths. Well planned. They had done this so often it had become routine. They belonged together. It was like a ballet.

It was strange, the errant thought crossed Mahoney's mind, but he had come here only to pull his son out of the business. He still did not know why he had gone ahead with this thing. Even now, he told himself, he could get out. First thing in the morning.

"You will have to meet with Conwell. There is no

other way around it," Bindrich said. "He will be able to provide you with the transportation in and out, and the documents."

"What have you got in mind?"

"Al-'Usta is a banker. You're going to him to talk about banking."

The Agency had its people there. Mahoney was certain of it. But they'd be deep-cover people. Most likely Arab-Americans. If they had anything whatsoever to do with an American, no matter how well kept a secret the contact was, their positions would immediately be suspect.

"I'll work with Conwell. But this must be kept from Renelaux."

"I can't find anything wrong with that. He has his hands full with his own operations. And I can understand your resentment, because of John."

Mahoney almost missed the significance of Bindrich's last remark. He had come here to pull John out, and he had done just that. Was Bindrich referring to the fact that John had worked for Renelaux?

"What?"

"I said I understand your feelings."

"I haven't the foggiest idea what you're talking about."

"I mean about your son."

"What about him? He's home, isn't he? Or have you sent him out on another assignment?"

"Christ," Bindrich swore, half under his breath.

"What's going on here? Goddammit, level with me!"

"John is there. In Brussels. He never came back. I thought you knew that."

Mahoney was short of breath. He passed a hand over his forehead. John was here. He must have flown to Paris, and then turned right around and took the next flight back. All this time he had been working with Renelaux. The son of a bitch. The miserable son of a bitch had kept it from him.

"I'm sorry," Bindrich was saying. "I hope you are not going to do anything foolish."

"No," Mahoney said. "Nothing foolish." He was having a hard time talking. "I'll speak with Conwell in the morning. Please get on this right away. I'd like to get this over with and get the hell out of here."

"I can put someone else on it—"

Mahoney hung up, left the phone booth, and went outside. He was conscious now that it was very cold. The streetlights and the lights illuminating the big railway station were very harsh. He got a cab and asked the driver the name of a nearby hotel.

"The Cecil is a nice hotel, *monsieur*," the cabby said. "It is by the Gare du Nord, on the Boulevard Jardin Botanique. There will almost certainly be a room for you at this time of year."

"That will be fine," Mahoney said, settling back in the seat. He'd have his bags transferred over in the morning. He could send a cab for them. No one would know where he had gone.

✯ FIFTEEN ✯

It was very late when Renelaux showed up at the apartment. John Mahoney had tried to get some sleep earlier, but he had not been able to. Now Renelaux paced back and forth across the small living room, and it made John irritable.

"Your father knows that I have a monitor on Lady Sidney's telephone."

"How can he know that? Did he follow me? Does he know that I'm here in Brussels?"

"I don't know how he knows anything. The man is a mystery." Renelaux stopped his pacing to face John, who was perched, in stocking feet, on the edge of the couch. "He went out to see Lady Sidney directly after the meeting broke up. Sir Howard took him."

John felt a sense of pride. He could have said "I told you so" to the Belgian. He had told the man about his father's abilities, his father's stubborn nature. He had to wonder, though, just how much his father actually knew and how much was speculation.

"He told her about the tap, then?" John asked.

"Almost certainly." Renelaux gestured at the equipment by the window. "It is all useless now. Nothing more will be said on the telephone from that house."

"There may be other incoming calls."

Renelaux went across to the equipment and rewound the tape. He had listened to the second, very brief conversation three times, and had replayed it in his head a dozen times since John had intercepted it earlier this evening.

"It will be too dangerous to remain here, John. We must dismantle the equipment and leave this morning."

"They cannot trace us here."

"Oh, but they can. They can make a telephone call, seizing the line and opening the transmission link here to us. From that point they will trace the telephone lines from the house. They will find the transmitter, and they will follow its beam here. It may take them some time, but do not underestimate the technology."

Renelaux pushed the play button. The telephone rang twice, and Lady Sidney answered it herself.

"Yes?"

There was silence for a second or two. Renelaux looked up at John, who was staring at the tape.

"Yes, who is this?" Lady Sidney asked.

"Robert sends his love. He is safe and well," a man's voice came from the speaker. He spoke English with a German accent. Renelaux could tell that the man had been educated in England. His English had that special softness and cadence peculiar to the upper class.

Lady Sidney gasped. "Oh . . . my God," she said, stifling a sob. "Oh . . . where is he?"

"He tells you not to worry. Everything will turn out for the best."

"I want to speak with him," Lady Sidney cried.

There was a very soft click on the line. She heard it.

"Hello?" she called. "Hello, are you there?"

Renelaux shut off the tape machine. He shook his head, then looked at John. "I do not know what is happening, my friend. But with your father's help, I believe we will find out."

"He's agreed to work with us? He knows I'm here?"

"No, nothing like that. He prefers to work on his own. For that I do not blame him. It will be up to us to find out what he is doing. He will be moving from his hotel by the Gare du Nord. Very likely he has already taken up new quarters. But his bags will not be moved until morning. He will send a cab, perhaps a messenger for them."

John knew what was coming next. He did not know if he was up to it . . . not in his skills, or in his heart.

"You will be at the hotel to follow your father's bags to his new quarters. And then you will follow your father."

"Why me?"

"You know him. You understand something of his habits. For you it will be difficult. I fear for anyone else it would be impossible."

The overcast had deepened in the night, as had Mahoney's impatience. Malcolm Conwell, whose official title was Special Assistant to the Ambassador but whose real job was chief of Brussels station for Central Intelligence Agency activities, was not due in until 9:00 A.M. That information had been gained only after a string of telephone calls and four times as many transfers from a young staffer in the political section.

From a phone booth outside a restaurant near the Académie des Beaux-Arts, Mahoney telephoned the Hotel Duc du Brabant et du Rhine and told them he would be checking out. His bill would be taken care of by the Agency's housekeeping section.

Across town, off the Rue du Congrès, he hired a cabby to go over to the hotel, fetch his bags, and deliver them to the American embassy on the Boulevard du Régent. The embassy would take care of transferring his things to his new hotel. It wasn't much of a cut out, but it was better than nothing.

All that had been completed by nine, and he showed up in front of the baroque, four-story embassy building situated near the Parc de Bruxelles, and directly across from the equally ornate British embassy on the Rue Joseph II, a half hour later.

Just inside the glass doors two clerks were busy processing visa applications behind a long counter. A third got up from her desk and came to the counter when Mahoney walked in.

"Good morning, sir," she said.

"I'm here to see Malcolm Conwell. Tell him it is Wallace Mahoney."

The woman looked at him. Nearly everyone within the embassy knew in truth what Conwell was. Among the junior staffers, such as this young woman, there was an aura of mystery about the man, and anyone connected with him, because of his position.

"Yes, sir," she said momentarily. She telephoned from her desk, spoke for just a moment or two, and when she hung up she was even more impressed than she had been at first. "If you will just come with me, sir."

Mahoney followed her around the counter, through a sagging swinging door, and down a short, busy corridor to an aging, creaking elevator.

It had just come down, and it opened immediately, two men deep in discussion stepping off and passing. Mahoney and the young woman got on. She seemed ill at ease. Mahoney was in no mood to help her, so they rode up to the fourth floor in silence.

Malcolm Conwell, a tall, heavyset, almost rotund man with only a fringe of gray hair below the top of his shiny bald head, was waiting in the broad corridor. There were the sounds of typewriters clattering, telephones ringing, and the hum of people talking. This was a very busy floor. Mahoney suspected this was the heart of embassy activities.

"Thank you, Karen. I'll take over from here," Conwell said.

The young woman nodded, looked at Mahoney, then went back down in the elevator.

"Mr. Bindrich called very early this morning," Conwell said.

Mahoney went with him down the corridor to an unmarked door. Conwell had to unlock it. They stepped inside, and the CIA chief of station flipped on a light switch. Fluorescent lights came on, and a small jewel light over the wall switch went from red to green as the door closed and latched.

"This is our screened room," Conwell said. "I thought we'd conduct our business in here this morning. Mr. Bindrich seemed . . . upset." Conwell's voice was rough, as if something were wrong with his throat. Behind it, though, it was evident the man was from the East Coast. Connecticut, Mahoney guessed.

A thick manila envelope, gray with a wide diagonal orange stripe across it and marked Top Secret, lay on the conference table.

"Did Sylvan tell you what I needed?" Mahoney asked.

Conwell motioned for him to sit down. "Yes, he did. You want to get across to Tripoli, to speak with a banker—Ali al-'Usta. It has something to do with the disappearance of General Sir Robert Marshall." Conwell fingered the envelope. "But Mr. Bindrich could not be more specific. Can you?"

Mahoney sat forward. "I do not want Pierre Renelaux brought into this."

Conwell's right eyebrow went up. "This business is in his bailiwick."

"I will withdraw if he becomes involved."

"I think that might be for the best, in any event," Conwell said. "Although the director seems to think differently."

"I'll need a bolt-hole. Preferably someone not already too deeply in place. I don't want to disturb whatever else we have going there."

"I've been on the telephone half the night with the Libyan desk at Langley, and with our new DDO. We think we have it worked out for you."

"One other thing," Mahoney said.

Conwell looked up.

"My son is here. Working for Renelaux."

"Yes?"

"What, specifically, is he doing?"

A faint smile played across Conwell's lips. "I really wouldn't know, Mahoney. I don't get myself involved with every individual legman. I leave those sorts of details to my officers, or agent runners."

"My son isn't an agent."

"No. He's a special operative. Still in training, actually." Conwell tapped the envelope. "Mr. Bindrich mentioned you were upset. Do you want me to pull him out of Brussels? I can have him on a plane for the States this morning."

The offer was tempting. But Mahoney shook his head. "No."

"Do you want me to put someone on him? Keep him here in the embassy, perhaps? What, Mahoney?"

"Nothing. Nothing at all. Now, what do you have for me? Are we dealing with Libya at all?"

Conwell stared pointedly at him for a second or two, then he opened the bulky envelope and spread its contents on the table.

"We certainly don't publicize it, but we do deal with the Libyan government," the CIA station chief said. "Your name is Wallace Morgan. We kept it close to accommodate monogrammed luggage or shirts or handkerchiefs, some such. You're an attorney for Manhattan International Bank. You've recently been in Paris and here in Brussels making inquiries about renegotiating some of the outstanding loans the Libyan government has with your bank. You're only on a preliminary mission to probe the intent of the Libyan National Banking Institute."

"How about Manhattan International themselves? Al-'Usta may check."

"Your background will hold up for a few days. From what I understand it's all you asked for."

Mahoney nodded.

"You're specifically asking to meet with al-'Usta because his name was mentioned by a mutual friend. General Sir Robert Marshall."

That part was neatly thought out, Mahoney felt. Not only had they built him a cover to enter Libya and to meet with the proper person, but they had constructed the legend in such a way that the prime motive for Mahoney's visit was immediately brought into the legitimate forefront.

"How soon will they receive me?" Mahoney asked.

"You're scheduled to leave this afternoon. Paris, then direct to Tripoli on Libya-Arab Airways."

"You haven't already contacted al-'Usta?"

"No. One of our Paris people coincidentally happened to be staying with a Libyan deputy consul from the embassy at the man's villa outside Paris. We got word to him, and he mentioned it. The deputy consul seemed very interested in having someone from Manhattan International speak with his country's banking interests, Qaddafi notwithstanding."

That part of it was a bit loose. If al-'Usta was hostile, he might ask about Mahoney's connection with the deputy consul, or at least with the man who approached him. In that event Mahoney figured he would have to pull the plug.

"What have you constructed in case of trouble?"

"Are you expecting any?"

Mahoney had decided not to say anything to Conwell about his confrontation with the four Arabs at the Gare du Nord. Renelaux had evidently not said anything about it. Nor had Conwell apparently made any connection between the death of the man and Mahoney's investigation.

"It's possible."

"Likely?"

Mahoney shrugged.

"There's a puppet show every night just now at the Suq at-Turk in Old Town. It is a covered marketplace. Very easy to find. If you are there during the show, it will mean you need help. Someone will contact you. He will ask about your mother's health."

"And then?"

"You will go with that person. A light plane will be standing by on an airstrip about twenty-five miles east of the city. Near the town of Homs. From there you will be flown out, beneath Libyan radar, to Malta."

They had worked it all out on very short notice. Mahoney suspected that Conwell and few of his staff had gotten any sleep last night.

"That will be a very dangerous alternative, however," Conwell warned. "For you as well as for our people. There are too many holes in the plan. But it was the best that could be done for you on such short notice."

"I appreciate your help."

"I must ask you two things. First, is it absolutely necessary that you get into Tripoli on such short notice?"

Mahoney thought about the young Arab lying dead in the doorway. He thought about the tape that had been delivered to Sir Howard's. And he thought about Lady Sidney, who almost certainly was hiding something. He nodded.

"Secondly, I would ask that you operate with the greatest of care and discretion while in Libya. You understand the political situation at this moment. We would much prefer that you speak with al-'Usta, then have a good night's sleep at your hotel, and the next morning fly back to Paris."

"I will try."

Conwell shook his head. "Why aren't I so optimistic?'' he asked rhetorically.

Mahoney didn't bother answering.

"Will you need a weapon?"

Mahoney again thought about the dead Arab in the Gare du Nord doorway. He could fight one of them, but not an entire country. He shook his head.

"Good," Conwell said, obviously relieved. "If you are in danger, go to the puppet show. We don't want a shoot-out."

The terribly hot October sun beat unmercifully down on Idris Airport to the southeast of Tripoli. Mahoney paused just a moment at the foot of the 727's boarding stairs, a chill playing up his back. This was Qaddafi's stronghold. Even the atmosphere seemed inimical. Something very bad hung in the air like a thin but palpable dust cloud: all-pervasive, foreboding, unreasoning.

He had a very good look at the city as they came in: white, cubist, giving the impression of being neat and very clean. There was nothing at this level, here at the airport, to dispel that impression. The terminal building fifty yards away was low, its broad glass windows reflecting the late afternoon sun. A half-dozen people stood on the rooftop observation platform watching Mahoney and the others from the plane walk across the tarmac. Two of them were dressed in military uniforms. The others were in traditional robes and headdresses.

Mahoney had spent the morning before his flight to Paris in the embassy's reading room, bringing himself up-to-date with background information. He had delved into the current state of the international banking business so that he could at least get the initial openings with al-'Usta correct, and then he had gone on to the Libyan situation reports and assessments themselves.

With the advent of Qaddafi, the name of the country had been changed from its simple form—Libya—to the

Socialist Peoples Libyan Arab Jamahiriya, the last word
loosely translating as "State of the masses." It was a
newly coined Arabic word, one analyst had written.

The same analyst had written another report sum-
ming up what he called the Libyan hate list. Qaddafi
had declared nine enemies of the State in their order
of danger to Islam: Capitalists; the Idle Rich; Ex-
ploiters; Those Who Cooperate with Foreigners; Cor-
rupt People; and, in Qaddafi's own words, "Shepherds
who consider people as herds of animals"; Selfish
People; Rumormongers; and Lazy People.

In broad strokes Mahoney had also delved lightly into
Libya's tumultuous history, beginning with the Phoeni-
cians who founded Tripoli, through the revolution in
modern times. In all of that there was nothing that set
Libya apart from any other Arab country except, of
course, Qaddafi himself.

He had set out, without much real hope, to find
another cause that Sir Robert might be hankering after,
another hook for the man's apparently unlimited capacity for empathy with someone else's inspirations. He
did not think it would be Qaddafi. He was too small. He
had no style.

There was a danger in thinking with blinders like that.
He had learned all about that in Moscow. If you believed all Russians were godless monsters, it would forever color any relationship you might be able to
develop. All Arabs were not terrorists. Had Sir Robert
found someone or something within this country to take
to his bosom?

Mahoney was in the middle of the line of people coming into customs from the airplane. They had been held
on the plane for fifteen minutes after they landed so that
their luggage could be off-loaded first and brought
around to customs. When it was his turn, the two officers were pleasant but thorough.

They put stamps on his single bag and his briefcase.

"The purpose of your visit, sir?" one asked.

"To discuss banking business with the National Banking Institute."

"You have, then, an appointment?" the other customs agent asked. He laid Mahoney's passport down.

Mahoney got the definite impression he was being watched, this conversation overheard. There was nothing he could do about it. He would have to cooperate. "Yes, with Mr. Ali al-'Usta."

"Ah, yes," the officer said. Neither of them had bothered writing down any of Mahoney's answers. They just stood there now. Faint smiles on their brown faces. Waiting expectantly.

"May I go?"

"Yes, of course you may go."

Mahoney gathered his passport, his bag, and his briefcase, then walked out of the customs hall to the money counter where he changed a few hundred Belgian francs into Libyan dinars. He had brought no American currency with him. Conwell had cautioned that he would be less conspicuous that way. But he felt very conspicuous at the moment. Not only was he a Westerner, he was obviously an American.

Outside, he took a cab into the city, directing the driver to take him to the Hotel Uaddan, which at one time housed a casino as well as a hotel. Those days were long gone, of course, but the hotel still had the reputation of being the best in Tripoli.

On the way into the city they passed the sprawling government hospital and then the old King's Palace and marvelously green grounds before they cut over toward the harbor where the hotel was located right on the Shar'a Adrian Pelt overlooking the Mediterranean.

He was given a lovely room on the fifth floor, its balcony facing the sea.

Once he was settled, he telephoned the National Banking Institute and asked for al-'Usta.

"I am so very sorry, but Mr. al-'Usta is not in presently," a woman, presumably his secretary, speaking very good English told Mahoney.

"He was expecting me. I am Wallace Morgan. Manhattan International Bank."

"Yes, of course, Mr. Morgan. He asks if you may join him for dinner this evening."

"Yes, of course," Mahoney said. "I have a room at the—"

"Of course, at the Uaddan. An automobile will pick you up at nineteen hundred hours."

"Thank you. I will be ready," Mahoney said. The secretary hung up. But he held the telephone to his ear a moment longer until he heard a very slight change in the tone of the line. His phone was being monitored. He would have almost been disappointed had it not been.

It had taken John Mahoney most of the afternoon to contact Renelaux, and when he finally did, the man came immediately over to the Hotel Cecil.

They met downstairs in the bar. It was around six o'clock.

"He is here?" Renelaux asked. He seemed agitated.

"No, he's not. I told you that on the telephone. His bags were brought over to the embassy, and then they were sent up here."

"You have not seen your father, then?"

John shook his head. He was getting alarmed. Something he did not understand was going on. "What is it?" he asked.

Renelaux looked toward the lobby. He seemed to make some sort of a decision. "Just a moment," he said at length. He got up and went out.

John waited a half minute, then he got up and followed the Belgian. Renelaux was at the front desk. He said something to the clerk, showed him something, and then the clerk handed him a room key.

John hurried across the lobby as Renelaux turned. Together, without a word, they took the elevator up, getting off on the fourth floor. Renelaux led the way to 407, where he let them in with the key.

A single battered suitcase had been set up on a stand and had been unpacked. Some of the clothes were hanging in the closet. John recognized them as his father's.

Renelaux had found a folder with papers in it. He was going through them when John joined him.

"These are the mileage records for Sir Robert's staff car."

"Where is my father?"

Renelaux looked up. "I do not know, John. I swear it."

"But he is gone. You do know that."

"Yes. He has disappeared. I have no idea where he has gone. No one does. Not even Conwell."

John glanced at the closet, a hollow feeling suddenly in his gut.

☆ SIXTEEN ☆

What had once been the hotel bar and lounge was now a restaurant on one side and a coffee shop on the other. The hotel was very well kept up, although just at the moment there did not seem to be too many guests. The few here, Mahoney was reasonably certain, were Russians. From the way one group of them talked through the lobby, they were engineers. Mahoney decided he'd bring that back as a little present for Conwell to pass on to Langley. It'd be worth points.

Mahoney wandered into the coffee shop as if he had the evening free and was trying to decide what to do with himself. But by seven exactly, the night cooling but still quite warm, he was out front.

A very large Mercedes 600SE luxury limousine slid up the palm-lined driveway and came smoothly to a halt at the front entrance. Mahoney supposed the car was for him, but he did not move from his spot, waiting to see what would happen.

The car's windows were smoked gray, so he could not see inside. The front door opened and the chauffeur, wearing a khaki uniform with military patches and insignia, jumped out and came around. He looked very stern.

"Mr. Wallace Morgan?" he asked.

Mahoney nodded.

"Please, sir," the chauffeur said, opening the rear door of the very large car.

Mahoney could see that a man dressed in Western business clothes was seated in the backseat. He stepped forward and got into the car.

"Mr. Morgan, I am so pleased to meet you," the small, dark, very intense man said. His eyes were round and very dark. His hair was jet black and oiled, and a pencil-thin mustache adorned his upper lip. His cuff links were diamond, his shirt, silk, his suit obviously hand-tailored.

"Mr. al-'Usta?" Mahoney asked, shaking the man's hand. This was not right.

"Yes, of course," the Libyan replied as if to ask Mahoney whom he had expected.

"I appreciate your being able to see me on such short notice," Mahoney said cautiously. Alarm bells jangled along his nerves. Either Lady Sidney had been mistaken with her description of al-'Usta, or one of the men—either this one or the one Lady Sidney had seen—was an impostor.

The chauffeur got back behind the wheel, and they moved slowly away from the hotel, turning down the next street away from the harbor.

"There is a very nice place to eat very near the Palace. It is the Lanterne. Perhaps you have heard of it?"

Mahoney hadn't.

"No? Well, it is a place of international cuisine. The last decent place in this city that does not serve cous cous. We can have a steak there, if you would like."

"That is very kind," Mahoney said.

They drove through the quiet streets for a minute in silence.

"You know, Mr. Morgan, although there is some danger in meeting like this, I mean considering the present . . . delicate situation, there can be precedent here for international banking."

Mahoney didn't quite know if he followed the man.

"Yes, that's it. We will set a precedent. A socialist working in harmony with a bastion of capitalism," the Libyan said with some enthusiasm. He touched Mahoney's knee. "You know, of course, that it is unfortunate, the relationship between our two nations. But it comes of your president's cowboy politics. His loaded-gun diplomacy. We can hardly relax our vigil when the Seventh Fleet continuously invades our territorial waters."

Mahoney said nothing in reply. There was nothing to say. But he was disappointed. He had come here expecting al-'Usta to bring up Sir Robert's name. But now he wasn't certain he was speaking with the banker. Who, then? he wondered. An operative from Qaddafi's secret service? If that were the case, there was going to be very big trouble here. Very big indeed.

They had driven past the old Libya Palace and National hotels, and they cut directly across town in front of the vast King's Palace grounds, finally coming around the corner to the Shar'a as-saidi. It was the same street that Mahoney had come in on from the airport, and for a moment or two he thought he was being driven back out there to be put on a plane and taken immediately out of the country. But they pulled up in the next block in front of a gaily lit restaurant, the only building in the block showing any life. The British embassy was just around the corner.

The chauffeur jumped out and opened the door on his boss's side. The Libyan got out, and Mahoney slid out after him.

Inside the nearly filled restaurant, they were given a choice table, and their drink orders were taken. Mahoney was surprised that alcohol was served here. He ordered a bourbon straight up, no ice, no water. The Libyan ordered a very dry martini.

Their waiter came with menus. "Good evening, Mr. al-'Usta. Welcome back."

"This is our little fiction," al-'Usta said when the waiter was gone. "There is no drinking of alcoholic beverages in this country. But our government recognizes the situations in which we must deal with the infidel from foreign nations. We must bring them here. Treat them well."

Their drinks came and the Libyan offered a toast. Mahoney raised his glass.

"To a successful negotiation between us, Mr. Morgan."

"And to a mutual friend."

The waiter had identified him as al-'Usta. Lady Sidney must have been mistaken.

"Oh?" the Libyan banker said pleasantly. "Who might that be?"

Mahoney watched the man's fingers curl around the stem of the glass. "Robert Marshall," he said. There was no reaction.

"Sir Robert? Has there been any further word?"

Mahoney shook his head, disappointed. "None. I saw a copy of the *Times* just before I left. There was nothing new."

"It is a shame, but I suspect that some overzealous commander—perhaps in Poland, or Albania, or even the German Democratic Republic—decided to take him. And now it is too late."

"Did he give you any indication that he was worried about being kidnapped when you saw him last?"

Al-'Usta looked sharply at him. "What are you talking about? It has been years since I saw the old man."

"I'm terribly sorry," Mahoney said.

"He is a high-ranking NATO general. Things like this . . . happen. One would assume he was taken."

"I was under the impression that you were recently in Brussels."

"How did you receive such an impression, Mr. Morgan?" There was suddenly a dangerous edge to the Libyan's voice.

"Someone—I don't recall just now who it was—was convinced they saw you and the general dining in Brussels some weeks ago."

"No," al-'Usta snapped. "I have not been in Brussels —or anywhere in Europe, for that matter—for eighteen months. And it has been years since I last saw Sir Robert."

Their waiter returned. He smiled. "Gentlemen, may I recommend—"

Al-'Usta cut him off. "No, you may not."

The waiter was taken aback. "If you need more time . . ."

Al-'Usta shoved his glass aside and rose. "I suggest our evening is over, Mr. Morgan . . . or whoever you are. But you certainly are not from Manhattan International. You are here looking for kidnappers."

Everyone in the restaurant was looking at them. Either this man was a very good actor, or he was for real. Whatever the case, it was definitely time to leave.

Mahoney got to his feet. "I am sorry if I upset you by coming here like this, Mr. al-'Usta. But Sir Robert is a mutual friend."

The Libyan glared at him. "Sir Robert is a colonialist. He is no friend of mine."

The waiter was beside himself with embarrassment. A short, very thin little man dressed in a tuxedo was hurrying from the back. He was probably the manager.

Al-'Usta said something to the waiter in Arabic, then turned to the manager. Mahoney caught the word "Uaddan." It was his hotel.

"A taxi will come for you. You will be returned to your hotel. I suggest you remain there. Leave first thing in the morning. Beyond that I would not trust for your safety." He said something else in Arabic to the manager, then turned and stalked out of the restaurant, leaving Mahoney where he stood.

"Please, sir," the manager said coolly. "If you will just have a seat, your taxi will be here momentarily."

"Yes, please, sir, this is no place in which to make a disturbance," the waiter added.

"I'm sorry . . ." Mahoney began to say, when he distinctly heard the screeching of tires outside. He moved as if in slow motion (although later he realized that his reactions must have been very quick), shoving the manager aside and heading as fast as his legs would carry him to the front door. Someone shouted something, but whether it came from inside the restaurant or outside on the street, he could not tell.

The next all happened at once, though Mahoney could pick out the individual elements.

There was a dry rattle of automatic weapons fire, the noise echoing off the buildings. There was the high-pitched whine of an occasional bullet ricocheting off the pavement. There were the sounds of glass breaking, and as Mahoney reached the door and cautiously opened it, he distinctly heard an urgent grunting as if a pig were rutting in a farmyard.

Al-'Usta seemed to be doing a macabre dance beside his car, his left leg held up over the head of his chauffeur lying in the street, while four men in some sort of dark-colored uniforms fired automatic weapons, the slugs ripping into his body. The grunting noises were coming from him.

The firing stopped as al-'Usta bounced against the open car door and crumpled in a bloody heap atop the chauffeur.

His assassins swung around, but Mahoney ducked back into the restaurant, where there was pandemonium. Half the patrons were on the floor, while the other half were shouting and demanding help.

Mahoney shoved his way back through the dining area and into the kitchen, where the cooks and helpers were crouched beneath the stainless steel preparation tables.

He was across the kitchen when several people screamed in the dining room and shots were fired. But then he was outside in the back alley, running off into the night, his leather soles slapping against the pavement.

He raced down the alley until he came to the broad avenue across which were the grounds of the King's Palace. He stopped just a moment to get his bearings. The Suq at-Turk, where the puppet show was held, was in Old Town. It was on the far northwest side of the city. It would take an hour, perhaps longer to find his way there on foot. All the while he would be very conspicuous.

He looked back. But why had they killed al-'Usta? And who had ordered it?

Mahoney hurried across the street, then behind the Palace grounds in the opposite direction from the restaurant.

Sirens began to sound in the distance. No doubt it was the military police. This was nothing for an American to be caught up in. Conwell would be disappointed in his performance here, and he himself felt like a used fool. But he still could not decide if this had all been a setup. If the man who had just been gunned down was al-'Usta, then who was the tall fat man of Lady Sidney's description?

On the east side of the Palace grounds, Mahoney came to a broad street along which some traffic flowed. A few cars and one battered blue and white taxi, no one in the back seat, were stopped at a traffic light.

Mahoney hurried across, his right hand raised. The cabby spotted him and pulled over. The young man hung out the window and said something in Arabic.

"*La vieux ville*," Mahoney said in a his limited French. He kept his mouth pursed, an attitude of bored impatience with the night on his face. He was not an American in trouble; he was a Frenchman bored with the city.

The cabby shook his head.

"*La vieux ville*," Mahoney shouted. He took out

some money and held it up. "Old Town," he cried in
English. "Do you understand? Chop-chop. Old
Town?"

"Ah, yes," the cabby replied in heavily accented
English, his face lighting up. "Old Town. By Suq al-
Mushir."

"*Oui. Oui,*" Mahoney said. The Suq al-Mushir was
at the main gate into the old section of the city. From
there the Suq at-Turk was very close.

There was only marginally more traffic downtown
than there had been around the King's Palace. When
they were several blocks away from the restaurant,
Mahoney craned his neck in an effort to see, but there
was nothing, and then they were speeding past the post
office, and he sat back.

That there was a Libyan connection to Sir Robert's
disappearance was almost a foregone conclusion. After
all, four probable Libyans chasing one American
through Brussels—at least one of them armed with a
KGB weapon of assassination—meant something. In
addition, Lady Sidney had indicated that Sir Robert not
only had a friend in Tripoli, but he had lunch with him
on two occasions over the past six months. And finally,
the man claiming to be al-'Usta the banker had been
assassinated on the very night he was having dinner with
an American investigating the disappearance of Sir
Robert. But the implications were ominously filled with
anomalies. Wherever he looked, contradictions seemed
to blossom like spring flowers.

The man Mahoney met this evening was most likely
al-'Usta. His secretary had answered for him at the National Banking Institute. He drove a very large, very
conspicuous automobile. And they had known him by
name at the restaurant. That meant the man Lady Sidney remembered as al-'Usta had to be an impostor.
Whoever Sir Robert had lunch with on those days could
have been anyone. Anyone at all.

As far as Mahoney understood it, no one else on the

investigation in Brussels had been bothered by the Libyans. Why just one lone American?

And finally, in the end, Lady Sidney was holding something back from him.

A single thread wove through all those odd bits. Mahoney was certain of it.

They passed the Grand Hotel and followed the harbor around to the northwest, the traffic increasing. The smell of the sea was strong through the open windows of the cab. But it did not smell fresh and clean tonight. It was the odor of death and darkness. It made Mahoney uncomfortable.

They pulled up across from the castle gate that led into Old Town. To the left, rising above the roofs of the bazaar, was a minaret. Mahoney got out, and he glanced up at the spire as he dug in his pocket for money.

"The Caramanli Mosque, boss," the cabby said through broken, yellowed teeth. "It is beautiful. But you must first get permission. Beautiful."

"*Merci*," Mahoney said, paying the driver.

"Very nice. Very nice view," the driver babbled.

Mahoney nodded and smiled. "*Merci, merci, mon ami*," he said, and he turned and hurried across the street, ducking through the gate in the thick castle wall. He pulled up short and stepped back.

The cabby was still there. The street was well lit, and Mahoney was able to see that the driver held a microphone to his lips. A moment or two later he laid it down and drove off.

Mahoney stepped back through the gate and blended with the crowd, going deeper into Old Town. He was bothered that he had so obviously been set up here in Tripoli. He only hoped now that his contact to get him out of there had not been compromised as well.

He stopped at a coppersmith's booth. The old, toothless man grinned and held up a broad-bottomed pot.

"Suq at-Turk," Mahoney asked. "The puppets?" He made gestures with his hands as if he were controlling a puppet. "Suq at-Turk?"

The old coppersmith pointed deeper into Old Town, then turned away, holding his wares up for other passersby.

Mahoney stumbled into the covered market and found the puppet show a few minutes later. The streets here were very narrow, twisting in every direction into a rat's maze of back alleys and surprising little squares filled with artisans. Tiny little shops with weavers, goldsmiths, and leather workers busy working on their wares competed for space with dozens of clothing shops, tiny little alcoves selling watches, radios, and even television sets.

It cost him less than a dinar to get into the puppet show, which was mostly attended by younger children and their parents, although there were quite a few other adults there too.

He stood at the fringe of the crowd, trying to see the tiny figures and hear their shouts and cries. The language did not sound like Arabic to Mahoney. It sounded almost like Turkish. The crowd laughed and clapped from time to time, and despite himself Mahoney found that he too was getting caught up in the show.

"It is more funny if you know the language," someone at his elbow said with a very heavy Russian accent.

Mahoney turned. A short, very husky man with heavy, dark features, thick eyebrows, and a lined forehead was watching the puppets. He was obviously Slavic. Mahoney's heart began to race. Had it been a Soviet plot all along? Had they lured him here to Tripoli to sidetrack him?

The Russian looked at him. "Tripoli is a lovely city, you know. I live here with my mother."

Mahoney nodded.

"Is your mother alive and well?"

"No," Mahoney said. A Russian? It made some sense, actually. The Russians were the only non-Arabs who could move around Tripoli these days with total freedom. He thought about his tip to Conwell about the Russian engineers in the lobby of the Uaddan, and he had to grin.

"That's it, my friend," the Russian said, turning back.

"I met with a man named al-'Usta this evening," Mahoney said. He looked at the puppets.

"I understand that. He is a deputy secretary with the National Banking Institute."

"They came to us at the restaurant."

The Russian looked around. "They? Who? What do you mean?"

"I don't know who they were. But they assassinated al-'Usta. And they came after me."

"This night? Just now?" the Russian asked in alarm.

"Yes. Twenty minutes ago."

"This is terrible. Most unfortunate. What did you do or say? Did you speak with anyone at the hotel?"

"No one."

The Russian was obviously trying to figure it out. He was frightened.

"There is a way out of here for me?"

"Yes. Right now. I will take you to the airplane. It is near Homs. You will be all right. But I will have to notify my friends."

"We will have to leave immediately," Mahoney pressed. He told the Russian about the cabby speaking on the radio.

"They have a loose tail on you. Have had since you entered the country."

"Here?" Mahoney asked.

"Shopkeepers. Cabbies. Hotel clerks. They all report foreigners," the Russian said absently. "But that is of little importance now. I am going to walk out of here. You must follow me. But do not get lost. If you lose me,

you will be on your own." The Russian looked into
Mahoney's eyes. "Do you understand?"

"Yes."

"Fine," the Russian said, and he turned abruptly and
headed away from the puppet show as the children
laughed.

Mahoney slipped away from the crowd and almost
missed the Russian turning a corner in the opposite
direction from the Suq al-Mushir, and he had to hurry
to catch up.

The Russian was turning another corner, and Mahoney quickly closed the gap between them, threading
his way through the crowd.

Once, the Russian doubled back suddenly and
Mahoney let him get behind, supposing the man wanted
to find out if anyone was following them. But there was
no one back there, and the Russian appeared, by the
book, out front again.

It took them nearly forty-five minutes like that to
traverse Old Town, and the Russian finally disappeared through a gate in a tall stone wall.

Mahoney ducked through the gate a moment or two
behind the Russian, finding himself in a wide, low
garage. A light came on in a battered Volkswagen.

"Get the doors," the Russian said, climbing in
behind the wheel.

He had the car started by the time Mahoney figured
out the latch and swung the doors open onto a narrow,
unpaved alley. The Russian backed the car out, and
Mahoney swung the doors closed, then got in on the
passenger side.

The Russian flipped on the headlights, and they drove
to the end of the alley where it made a sharp turn to the
left, and suddenly they were out on a broad, busy
avenue.

"If we are stopped, you will let me do the talking,"
the Russian cautioned. "*All* of the talking."

"Of course," Mahoney said.

They made a big circle through town, coming twenty

minutes later back to the Shar'a Adrian Pelt along the
harbor, where the Russian stopped at a phone booth.
He made two brief telephone calls, and then seeming
not quite so worried as before, got back into the car,
and they continued to the east.

"Will everything be all right for your people here?"
Mahoney asked as they left the city behind them.

The Russian kept checking the rearview mirror. He
glanced at Mahoney. "This business you had here . . . I
hope it was worth the trouble it caused."

"I think so," Mahoney said. He did not want to tell
the man that this had probably been a red herring.

"You think so," the Russian said. He was suddenly
angry. "I hope so. It will be difficult for us now."

"The Libyans suspect you?"

"No, don't be foolish. It is my own people. I think
this will be very hard to explain to them."

Mahoney understood now. The Russian was stationed here in the Soviet embassy. But in actuality he
was a double. Which meant he was not only spying on
his own embassy for the States, he was also watching the
Libyans. He was in a very delicate position.

"Why don't you come with me tonight?"

"On the airplane? To Malta?" the Russian asked incredulously.

Mahoney nodded.

"And leave my wife and children behind?" The Russian shook his head. "Perhaps you are not married, and
you do not understand. But I cannot get my family involved in this business."

Mahoney looked away, not bothering to try to explain the irony of that remark to the Russian double, the
intense blackness of the night serving his mood well. He
thought instead about Lady Sidney and about Sir
Howard's love for her. He had, at times, despaired that
his life was too complex to be enjoyed in any normal
way. And yet Lady Sidney's and Sir Howard's lives
were certainly no easier for all their apparent stability.
He also thought that he had come a long way with this

business. Even farther than he had ever expected to
come. His original intent, after all, had simply been to
bring John home. But now he was caught up with the
business of Sir Robert, a man whose background
Mahoney still had to learn before he could mount a
realistic search. The luxury of irony could come later.
For now there was work to be done.

And yet he still could wonder at himself. For weeks he
had known—or perhaps even hoped?—that the call
would come for him from Langley. There had been so
many assignments, so many foreign capitals, so many
personalities, so many mysteries needing unraveling that
it all had ruined him, he supposed, for any sort of normal life. Marge had understood it perfectly, in her own
way. And just now his ache for her swelled. They'd talk
sometimes through the night when he'd come back from
some particularly difficult business; never about what
he had just done, but about seemingly inconsequential
things that nevertheless always seemed to cut to the very
heart of what troubled him. If he began to lose faith in
people, she could somehow sense his trouble, and they
would speak of friends who had been loyal over the
years. If he was confused, she would speak to him of
what she called the mystery of life. *You have to feel it,
old man, to understand,* she would say. And just now he
thought he might understand his son's frustration,
though he knew he could not help him.

It's what I do, he had told John, as if his life had been
reduced to instinct. As if he had no choice. And perhaps
he didn't.

☆ **PART TWO** ☆

✫ SEVENTEEN ✫

Sylvan Bindrich waited for the dawn. One part of him was impatient to get on with it, while another part of him never wanted the day to come. With it would come a shattering not only of the darkness, but of the comfortable fiction that Franklin Lycoming was a hero of the free world, a dedicated servant whose place at Arlington was well deserved, as was his place in the history books.

Bindrich had always been something of a modern man, outward appearances to the contrary. Pressed hard he would admit a certain reluctance to accept the notion that history repeats itself, that as a race we were doomed to repeat our mistakes over and over again, variations in the pattern due only to the current technology. He was more of a pragmatist, operating on the assumption that today's problems could only be taken care of if addressed today. Tomorrow's problems would present themselves in due time, and would be taken care of in turn (he did understand prevention, of course) as they arose. And yesterday's troubles . . . well, they belonged to another age. Nothing could be done but adjust our thinking to the effects, and only the effects.

Franklin Lycoming was an historical problem that did

not fit the mold. Like the atomic bombing of Hiroshima and Nagasaki, which was still having vast repercussions, Lycoming's apparent perfidy could very well tear the fabric of the Central Intelligence Agency to such an extent that it could never be repaired.

In his mind, Bindrich likened what he had found to Richard Nixon's betrayal of the public trust, only with many more sinister implications. Lycoming had apparently freely shared U.S. intelligence data with the secret services of a dozen or more countries, including America's enemies, via some sort of an old boy network.

At first, of course, Bindrich had simply refused to believe what he had found. Such things were not within the realm of American possibility. There had been the Israel Beers of Israel, and the Kim Philbys of England. In the old days there had even been the Rosenbergs and Klaus Fuchs in the States. But America had become too sophisticated for such things to happen these days. There were too many cross-checks on a man's integrity for such things to happen.

Mahoney's testimony, the physical fact of the missing files in Archives, and Lycoming's own memos were damning evidence to the contrary.

Mahoney would keep his mouth shut. The jackets of the missing files had been physically removed from the shelves, and the computer records had been skillfully altered by Kopinski, once the young man understood the problem and its implications. The empty folders, along with computer readouts and the memos, lay heavy in Bindrich's briefcase at his feet.

He glanced down at it, then reached down and touched the clasp. All the evidence was there, and in Mahoney's head.

The eastern horizon was becoming perceptibly lighter. Bindrich tiredly got to his feet, went across to the sideboard, where he poured himself a cup of stale coffee from the coffeemaker, and went to the window.

It would be a beautiful day. The sky was clear. Overhead, the stars shone brightly from a black sky, but to the east the stars were already beginning to fade with the dawn.

By now Washington would be waking up. Senators would be rolling over. Congressmen would be taking showers. Aides and bureaucrats would be having their breakfasts, some of them already on their way into the city.

Bindrich looked at his watch. The man he wanted to speak with this morning was an early riser. He was famous for his dawn meetings. Still, Bindrich felt uncomfortable calling so early.

Mahoney would have to be summoned home, of course. His testimony would have to be entered in some sort of a record. . . .

Bindrich stopped himself at that thought, the coffee cup halfway to his lips.

What use were records? So that other people could read them? So that Lycoming's administration could be indicted?

Bindrich turned, put his cup down as he passed the sideboard, and went to his desk. He picked up his phone and dialed the private number he knew by heart but hoped he'd never have to call like this.

The number was answered on the first ring by a young man. "Yes."

"This is the DCI. I must speak with the President this morning."

Bindrich was a lot calmer now that the actual thing he dreaded most was coming about. He rode in the back seat of his limousine, his briefcase clutched to his side. They were let in through the west gate, and the driver took him smoothly up to the portico.

Bindrich opened his own door and was met just inside the White House by the President's assistant appointments secretary, a young man Bindrich had never seen before.

"Good morning, sir," the young man said. "If you will just come with me."

Without a word, Bindrich followed him down the west corridor, past the kitchen, and into the elevator hall. They took the car up to the second floor, then across the corridor to the President's study where the aide motioned Bindrich to wait, and then he left.

A moment or two later, the President, dressed in a suit and tie, appearing fresh and well rested despite his age, entered from the right.

"Good morning, Sylvan," he said, smiling as he came across the room.

"Good morning, Mr. President," Bindrich said. They shook hands.

"Have you had your breakfast yet? Would you care for some coffee?"

"No, thank you, sir," Bindrich said. "I don't think I could stomach it."

The President had been bustling. He stopped now, his head cocked, and looked at Bindrich. "That bad? The Middle East, Nicaragua? The Soviets?"

"None of them, sir. This is somewhat . . . delicate." Lycoming and the President had been personal friends for years. Bindrich had even considered hushing the entire thing up, on the chance that the President was somehow involved. But in the end he decided that he would not want to know about it if that were the case.

The President went to his desk and sat down. Bindrich approached, opened his briefcase, and began taking out the empty files, the memos, and the computer printouts of the search he and Kopinski had made originally for the missing documents.

"It's about Franklin Lycoming, Mr. President. I'm afraid I have discovered something quite disturbing."

•   •   •

The telephone on Bindrich's desk chimed. He picked it up.

"Your satellite call to Brussels is ready, Mr. Director," the communications man said.

"Malcolm, is that you?"

"Yes, Mr. Director, this is Malcolm Conwell."

"The moment Mahoney is finished in Tripoli, I want him back in Washington."

"I thought you might be calling about Mahoney. There was some trouble."

Something clutched at Bindrich's heart. But he was an old operations man, whereas Conwell always had been an administration type. Trouble meant something different to him.

"Is he out?"

"Yes, sir, he is. But he had to use our bolt-hole. It may have compromised everything there."

"Anything out of Quaddafi, or out of Moscow yet?" Bindrich asked. The circuit was encrypted. Their conversation was secure.

"Everything is quiet. I naturally assumed you had been informed."

"Any indication what happened?"

"We don't have the full picture yet, but preliminary reports indicate that al-'Usta may have been assassinated by an ultraloyalist splinter group. It was known, of course, that he would be speaking with American banking interests."

Bindrich tried to think this out. If they knew Mahoney was coming, there had to be a leak. Either in al-'Usta's office in Tripoli, which was the most likely, or somewhere there in Brussels, which was the most disturbing.

He was thinking like an operations man now. Automatically. Mahoney would need coverage if they were to flush the pipes to see if the informant was there at the Western end.

But then he shook his head in exasperation.

"I want him back here in Washington."

"Yes, sir," Conwell said hesitantly.

Bindrich picked up on it. "But what, Malcolm?"

"Frankly, Mahoney is living up to his reputation as a maverick. I don't think he'll listen to anything I have to say."

Bindrich smiled, again a purely reflexive action. Operations men were bred for individuality.

"Are you in contact with his son?"

"No. At least not directly."

"But you can get word to him without going through Pierre Renelaux?"

Again Conwell hesitated. "Are you trying to tell me something, Mr. Director?"

"Yes. I want Mahoney here. If he won't listen to you, send his son after him. It's important. Vitally important."

"What about Renelaux?"

"I want him insulated from Mahoney. At least for the moment."

"Can you tell me why?"

"No," Bindrich said tersely. "Can you get a word to John?"

"Yes, sir."

"Convey to him the urgency of the situation."

"If I better understood—"

"The President wants to speak with Mahoney. Is that urgent enough?"

"Uh, sorry, Mr. Director," Conwell said. "I'll get word to John immediately."

"Thank you, Malcolm," Bindrich said. "How's the weather over there?"

"Terrible," Conwell said, and the connection was broken.

Bindrich hung up the telephone and sat back in his chair. Someone knocked at his door and he looked up as his secretary came in. He could see his bodyguard, Don Page, seated in the outer office.

"Mr. Kopinski is here to see you as requested, sir."

Bindrich was having trouble focusing on the present. He kept seeing a montage of Archives, the President at his desk, Lycoming's casket being lowered into its grave at Arlington. He wanted to telephone Conwell again and set up a circuit of some sort, directly with Mahoney. But his better judgment ruled against it. Lycoming was dead. What they were doing was nothing more than cover-up. He didn't think Mahoney would mind leaving Brussels. A NATO general gone missing was nothing to crow about.

How many shabby hotels had he stayed at in his life? Wallace Mahoney wondered. How many late meetings had he attended? How many sleepless nights had he spent contemplating mysteries just beyond his ken? In the end the hotels and the meetings and the discomforts were always forgotten. The preference went to the mysteries themselves. How the puzzle was unraveled seemed somehow less important in the end than the fact it actually had been solved. At times they all were like little boys holding up their tin cups that were inscribed with their childish victories. His had been a lifetime of it, and he was finally sick to death of the job. But it was a job. It had to be done. And he was as good a candidate as anyone to complete this one. But Lord, he hadn't even caught his breath from Tripoli yet.

"I don't think I should be surprised that you came right back," he said. "I should have known better."

John had brought a bottle of Kentucky sour mash whiskey. He opened it and poured them both a drink, but he didn't say a thing.

"I was surprised that you showed up here tonight like this. I thought Pierre Renelaux was keeping you under wraps."

"Where did you go?" John asked. His voice was soft. He leaned back against the writing table.

"What do you mean?"

"I watched the hotel. I even came up here. I was here when your bags were brought over from the embassy. You never showed up."

There was so much for John to learn. You learned it all very slowly at first, until the very end when it seemed as if you were learning so fast it was impossible to keep track. But you learned that as well.

"If you can't keep track of me, how can you expect to find a missing general?"

John's expression softened. "I'd wager the man is not half as devious as you."

"Or as Pierre Renelaux?"

John's expression stiffened.

"Was it he who sent you after me? Sent you to watch me?"

"Yes. You wouldn't tell him anything. This is his investigation. He wanted to know what you had come up with."

Mahoney had arrived only minutes before John. It had been a harrowing trip to the tiny airstrip near Homs, but the drive wasn't half as harrowing as the flight aboard the tiny Cessna. His pilot was Libyan, half blind and mostly drunk, Mahoney figured. They just skimmed the waves to keep well under Libyan radar, and it seemed to take forever to make Malta, and then, via commercial airliners, to Sicily, Rome, and finally to Brussels. He was worn out. And at the moment somewhat disappointed in his son, although he felt he was beginning to understand what motivated him.

"Go home, John."

"Is that all you can say to me, goddammit?"

Mahoney took off his jacket and tossed it aside. He poured himself another drink and lit a cigar. He sat down and put his feet up. The whiskey was passable.

"Who sent you? Renelaux? Conwell?"

"How do you know anyone sent me?"

"Bindrich didn't telephone you. You have that look

in your eye. It's determined, not overawed."

The change that came over his son wasn't a pleasant thing to watch. For the moment John's loyalties were divided. He had what he felt was a job to do, and he wanted to get on with it. His own father was an apparent impediment. Mahoney didn't know if he wanted to press his son far enough, though, to see which way he'd actually jump. It was like the old maxim; never look back; you might see what's gaining on you.

"Mr. Conwell asked me to speak with you. Something is going on in Washington. Mr. Bindrich wants you back immediately. The President wants to speak with you."

Bindrich had evidently gone to the President about the Lycoming thing. He could not leave it alone. All hell would be breaking loose . . . but very quietly. No one wanted to make any waves unless it was absolutely necessary. The Company would suffer.

"There's more."

John shook his head. He wanted to say something, that was clear. And it was clear that he was having trouble framing his comments. He seemed confused.

"You helped Renelaux put a tap on Lady Sidney's telephone. And under his direction you began watching for me when I dropped out of sight."

"What's going on here, Dad?"

"It's called a field assignment. You went to school on it."

"I'm being used. Renelaux has me under wraps as his . . . secret weapon."

"It's part of the business."

"I can't believe this. Not you, too. With strangers, for Christ's sake, I can accept it, but not with you!" John cried out. He pushed himself upright and began pacing the room as if he were a caged lion who would go crazy at any moment if he weren't let free.

"There's a lot more to this business than you know," Mahoney said, knowing full well what that sort of a statement would do to John. He truly felt sorry for his son. Now even more so than just after Elizabeth and the kids had been killed. John had had his grief to mark reality for him. As terrible as it had been, the tragedy had been *real*. Now it must have seemed to him as if everything were an illusion. He was viewing the world through an ever-changing mist.

"Yes, but I'm trying to learn. I'm trying to help."

"Then keep Renelaux off my tail."

John stopped his pacing. "There's more to this than you are aware of as well, you know."

"I know that a tap was put on Lady Sidney's telephone. And I know that she received a call she is lying about. She is desperate to keep it a secret. When I told her that her telephone conversations were being monitored, she practically jumped out of her skin."

John looked at his father in amazement. "It's part of the job."

"How does it make you feel?"

"Rotten, goddammit!"

"Like a sneak thief in the middle of the night? A peeping Tom?"

"Yes, that too."

Mahoney shook his head, a heavy feeling coming into his chest. "Who telephoned her?"

Someone came into the room next door and slammed the door. They could hear the muted sound of the television coming on much too loudly at first, and then softer as it was turned down.

"I came here simply to pass along a message from the DCI. You're being recalled."

"Why wasn't Renelaux sent?"

Again the very odd expression crossed John's features. It was the same sort of look that a man who has found out his wife was going to bed with his brother might have. It was a look of betrayal.

"Renelaux is to be cut out of this?"

"No," John said quickly. "Mr. Conwell said he was

to be insulated. That's the exact word. I don't quite know what it means, though.''

"It means Pierre Renelaux will continue, in his own way, to search for the general. It also means that he will be able to continue doing what he's really stationed here in Brussels to do, secure that no one else will know about it.''

"Which is?''

"Do you want to hear this?''

John nodded.

"Spying on NATO.''

"Oh, Christ! Who else knows?''

"Malcolm Conwell, and of course the DCI, along with whoever Renelaux's control officer might be back at Langley.''

"Who is your control?'' John asked on impulse.

"I'm not on an assignment.''

"But the DCI has you on recall. The President wants to speak with you, goddammit. What's going on?''

Mahoney got up, poured himself another drink, and went to the window. There was still quite a bit of traffic. A car pulled up across the street, and a large man got out, looked across to the hotel, then crossed the street.

Mahoney turned back. "The President wants to talk to me about the Geneva thing. Sylvan Bindrich found some information that Lycoming had on the business. It has him worried.''

"Bindrich was McBundy's assistant . . .''

"It's nothing like that. And in any event, it's history. It can wait.''

"But the President . . .''

Mahoney knew he was taking a terrible chance. When the President of the United States called, you jumped. If not, heads rolled. But Bindrich would just have to cover for him. He was not going to leave. He could not.

"The President won't send the Marines after me.''

"You're staying then?'' John asked incredulously.

"For the moment.''

"What do you want me to tell Renelaux?"

"Good-bye."

"I'm not leaving!"

Mahoney glanced out the window again. The large man who had gotten out of the car was back across the street once more, apparently waiting for someone.

"What message did Lady Sidney receive? Who called her?" he asked, turning back.

"Did you hear me, Dad?"

"I heard you. Just keep Renelaux away from me."

"What am I supposed to tell him?"

"That you're following me. Nothing more."

"I'm to lie to him? Christ, we're on the same side!"

"Everyone lies to everyone else."

The simple statement seemed to have a tremendous effect on John. It almost seemed as if he had been physically rocked back on his heels. "I . . ."

"Apply it across the board, and then look for anomalies."

"I don't understand."

"Consider that everyone is lying to you. Trust nothing, but fit everyone's story together. The truths that three different sources give you will match. The lies, and there'll be plenty of them—some significant, some not quite so important—will clash. The glaring differences —the anomalies—are what you look for."

John tossed his drink back, then seemed to come to a decision. He put down his glass. "Someone telephoned her. It was a man. He said Robert sends his love, and that he was safe and well. He told her not to worry."

The entire business in Tripoli was a setup. Mahoney was almost a hundred percent convinced of it now. But who had set him up? And why?

"What else?"

"He told her that everything would turn out for the best."

" 'Everything would turn out for the best'? His exact words?"

"As close as I can recall."

"One other thing, John."

"Yes?"

"Did the man have an accent?"

John nodded. "German, it sounded like, but—"

"But?"

"If he was German, I suspect he learned his English in a British school. An upper-crust school."

"Oxford?"

"Perhaps . . ." John said, but then he clamped it off, suddenly realizing in what direction his father had just gone. "Christ."

Mahoney was a hundred percent sure about Tripoli now. But it was the only thing he was sure of.

John was still in awe of his father's refusing a Presidential summons. He shook his head. "I don't understand," he said.

"You will," Mahoney said softly.

John sighed deeply. "About the other night . . ." he started.

Mahoney said nothing.

"I'm sorry for . . . the things I said."

"I know," Mahoney said.

☆ EIGHTEEN ☆

Mahoney sat in Detective Inspector Richard Matin's office in the Brussels Metropolitan Police Headquarters on Hoogstraat. Matin had left for the moment, presumably to make sure Mahoney was who he said he was. While he was gone, Mahoney had picked up a photograph standing in a frame on his desk. It showed a lovely woman in a stunning, low-cut evening gown. She stood by a rose bush. It was the sort of picture that was taken in the backyard just before you were off to a ball or formal dance.

Matin's office was shabby. Piles of papers, books, and files lay everywhere. The walls were adorned with city maps, colored pins stuck here and there.

"She is my wife," Matin said from behind.

Mahoney turned as the inspector came in. "She is lovely."

"It was taken some years ago. It has always been my favorite of her." Matin took the photograph, gazed fondly at it, and set it back in the precise spot Mahoney had picked it from.

"I assume Colonel Horne verified my identity?"

Matin nodded. "Yes, of course. And you are here to discuss the disappearance of General Sir Robert Marshall. It has now been one week. Very strange."

"In what way, strange?" Mahoney asked. He had an odd feeling about Matin.

The Belgian detective held up a hand, then cocked his head. "Mr. Mahoney, you must understand the delicate position I now find myself in. The Central Intelligence Agency does not have a charter to operate in my country. We are not the enemy. We are not at war with the United States."

"Would you rather I be from the FBI?"

"I would much prefer it."

"Would you like me to produce such credentials, Inspector?" Mahoney asked, a hard edge to his voice. "It might take me an hour, perhaps two. But if you wish the fiction, I can certainly supply it."

Matin looked at him through shrewd eyes. At length he sighed. "I will retire soon, I suspect. Madame Matin wishes it. I suspect the department wishes it. And I feel that soon I too will wish it."

"Then it will be unanimous."

"Indeed. But I would ask you a question."

Mahoney inclined his head.

"The general has disappeared. There is no question about that, is there?"

"No," Mahoney said, sitting back.

Matin held his fingers together, making a steeple. "*Bon*," he said. "But has a crime against the Belgian people been committed in the act of the general's disappearance?"

"Such as kidnapping?"

"Or murder?"

"I do not think so," Mahoney said carefully.

"Then he has defected?"

"I don't know. It may be that he is simply in hiding."

Matin regarded Mahoney for a second or two. "Yet in the end it may be found that he was kidnapped?"

"Yes."

"I see," the Belgian policeman said. "What is it you

wish to know, Monsieur Mahoney?''

"Only routine details . . ." Mahoney began, but Matin laughed.

"Please."

"Have you a police record on Sir Robert?"

"No."

"Have you a record on Thomas Langdon?"

Matin's eyes narrowed. "It is a new name to me. Who is he?"

"A journalist for the *London Daily Mail*. He is . . . or was here in Brussels as of two days ago."

"What is his connection?"

"He came for an interview the same day Sir Robert disappeared. He thinks the Israelis may have kidnapped or assassinated the general."

"Whatever for?" Matin asked, startled.

"It has something to do with some business Sir Robert may have been involved with during the sixties in Berlin. I'm not entirely sure of the details myself."

"But you tend not to hold with Langdon's theory?"

"No."

Matin picked up his telephone. "Emille," he said. "I wish to find out what we might have on a British journalist. Thomas Langdon. He is apparently with the *London Daily Mail*."

Mahoney took a slip of paper from his pocket and handed it across. He knew he was taking a chance on precipitating his own arrest, but he needed the information.

"One moment, Emille," Matin said. He picked up the paper.

"It is the license number of a gray Mercedes sedan. It followed me from NATO. I would like to know who it belongs to."

Matin nodded. "I have an automobile registration number I wish you to check for me." He gave the number, then hung up. "Is the car perhaps registered to this Langdon?"

"No," Mahoney said.

"But you were followed?"

"Yes."

"And it was not a coincidence?"

"No."

"But there is something else, *monsieur*. Something you are hesitant to discuss with me. Something. Why do you hesitate? Perhaps we can begin with that . . ."

The man was bright, but he was in for two surprises. One about Langdon and his connection with this department. And the second about the Mercedes.

The telephone rang. Matin picked it up. "*Oui*, Emille," he said. He wrote something on a pad of paper, then looked sharply up at Mahoney. "Yes, I understand. What else?" He nodded. "Yes, I see. *Merci*." He hung up.

Matin had come up with something. It was obvious.

"*Monsieur*, it is my duty to tell you that I have sufficient information at this point to hold you in custody."

"On what charge?" Mahoney asked, outwardly calm. If it came to a confrontation, Bindrich would have to call in the State Department. He was not going to be delayed here.

"Murder."

Mahoney's eyebrows rose. "Whose murder?"

Matin was puzzled. But it was clear he was angry as well. "The automobile you tell me followed you is a staff car of the Libyan embassy."

It was not surprising. Mahoney just could not figure how the Libyans had been dragged into it. Or why.

"A young Arab was murdered near the Gare du Nord two days ago. Witnesses place a white-haired man in the vicinity. You were staying at an hotel down the street. Then you moved. Coincidence?"

"I can't answer that at the moment, Inspector. But what about Thomas Langdon?"

Matin thumped his fist on the desk top. "You probably killed that young Arab, and I wish to know what he was doing in Brussels carrying a Soviet assassination weapon. Just who are you, *monsieur*?"

"An investigator trying to find a NATO general."

"He carried something with him?"

Mahoney said nothing.

Matin nodded. "I see. He carried a bag filled with secrets. Nuclear secrets. Secrets about missiles and submarines and airplanes."

"I'm sorry."

"I tell you, Brussels is becoming like any other city. It is disgusting. Madame Matin wishes to make a vacation in Paris. I tell her we can stay here; the crime rate is the same." Matin shook his head.

Someone knocked on the door, but before Matin could respond, a tall, husky man barged in.

"I came as soon as I heard . . ." he started, but he cut it off when he realized Matin was not alone. "Oh, excuse me, sir."

"No, that is all right, Jean," Matin said. "What is it? You came as soon as you heard what?"

The man glanced nervously at Mahoney.

"It is all right. Monsieur Mahoney is here working on the NATO business. Now, what do you have?"

"Nothing, Richard. It is only about Langdon. I understand inquiries have been made."

Jean Rubaix, no doubt, Mahoney figured.

A flinty look came into Matin's eyes. "What about Langdon? Do you have information about him?"

Rubaix nodded. "Of course, but I . . ."

"Yes?"

"Well, I thought perhaps something had happened to him."

"You know Monsieur Langdon?"

"Yes, of course. He is an informant. Has been for several years. It was from him we got the information on the Giselle case."

"Ah, I remember now," Matin said expansively. "But no, Jean, Monsieur Langdon is fine as far as I know. Monsieur Mahoney was asking about him. It seems they know of each other.''

"I see," Rubaix said. He seemed very uncertain now. "Should I remain?"

"That is not necessary, Jean. I will speak with you later."

"Of course. A pleasure to meet you, *monsieur*," he said to Mahoney, and then he left.

Matin got up from behind his desk and went to the window. The weather finally seemed as if it would break. The sky was definitely lighter than it had been all week, although it was too cold to melt the snow that had fallen. It lay in wet, dirty little piles everywhere in the city.

"The Arab gentleman we found dead is certainly connected with this business," he said as if from a distance within himself. "But then too, I suspect, are the Russians. He was carrying a Soviet weapon."

Mahoney held his silence. If Matin was going to tell him anything, prodding would certainly not help.

"That is one bit of the puzzle. Another, apparently, is this Thomas Langdon, whom you say came to Brussels for an interview on the same day the general disappeared. Now it turns out that he is an informant to this department. Another piece of the puzzle, perhaps?"

Matin turned around.

"It does put Langdon in a rather good position," Mahoney suggested.

"I am sorry, I do not understand."

"I would like to be delicate, but—"

"Please, *monsieur*, do not spare my feelings. I am interested in the truth." He shook his head. "Perhaps that is why I should retire. Who wants the truth?"

"Langdon apparently has a connection with NATO as well as with your department."

"He sells information."

"It is a two-way street, Inspector. Give a little, get a little. I'm sure you understand."

"*Oui*," Matin said tiredly. To look at him now you would suspect it was midnight, not midmorning. "We should look, then, for a connection between Langdon and the Libyans?"

"Possibly."

"Did Langdon kill the young Arab?"

"I would doubt it."

"But then, what do the Libyans have to do with this business? Has Colonel Qaddafi taken your general?"

"I honestly do not know," Mahoney said. "But I would certainly hope not."

"I see. Then I shall continue with my investigations. I too wish to find General Marshall. To end the madness that has come over my city. I wish also to find the murderer of the young Arab, though I suspect I may not be as successful in that endeavor." He hesitated. "Is there more for me?"

"Brussels is a big city," Mahoney said, rising.

Matin looked at him. "And for you, where do your investigations take you now?"

"Here and there."

"Should I follow you?"

"There are others in Brussels."

"Yes, my city is filled with them. It does not make us happy. But we turn our heads. For now."

"Thank you for your help, Inspector Matin," Mahoney said. He held out his hand, but Matin ignored it, and after a moment Mahoney let it drop.

"Langdon is involved."

"Yes. Probably."

Matin shook his head. "And he has sucked poor Jean into it as well."

Mahoney wanted to tell him that Renelaux and Horne had a pipeline here to the department as well, but he figured he owed some of his loyalties to the Company. Matin's next comment could have been the result of mind reading.

"It is a desperate occupation you are engaged in."

Mahoney smiled wanly. "I have been retired now for several years."

"You should try fishing. I hear it is very relaxing."

"I'm told that," Mahoney said. He nodded, then turned and left the inspector's office. He took the elevator down, and outside took a cab over to where he had left his rented car in a parking garage a few blocks from his hotel.

He circled the area on foot three times, and finally deciding he was clean, ducked inside and got the car. A Cortina.

Mahoney drove out of the city on the Boulevard Léopold II, the radio tuned to a French classical music station and the heater on, although he had his window half open. The sun was actually trying to come out. For most of the way out to Anderlecht, Mahoney thought about Thomas Langdon. In one way or another, the man was probably a key to Sir Robert's disappearance. For a while Mahoney had figured Langdon to be nothing more than a crass but very good journalist who had poked his nose into almost everyone's business on his way to a scoop.

But the cultivation of a Brussels police officer was not an overnight thing that one did simply to get a story. It was a long-term, very deliberate business that needed a great deal of delicacy and patience to succeed. If Langdon had been a specialist on NATO or on Belgian affairs, he might better understand such devotion to a source. But Langdon was not, as far as Mahoney knew.

So where did Langdon get his drive? Where had he learned his moves? Why Brussels? Or was he simply a marionette being directed by someone else?

As he drove, Mahoney thought about other things as well. His plate was full at the moment.

John refused to cooperate, and that was worrisome. But he had done all there was to be done about that situation. His son was a grown man. He had to make his own life. He'd gotten over his initial grief about Elizabeth and the children. The rest of it he would have to deal with as best he could. On his own.

Bindrich would press him to return and answer to the President's noises. If so, he'd have to be made to understand the situation here. It would have to be explained to the President just what was at stake.

Here in Brussels, Malcolm Conwell was another matter. From what he knew of the station chief, Conwell was more of an administrator than a field man. Which meant he couldn't shoot worth a damn—neither could Mahoney—but he certainly knew how to pull strings. He would have to be dealt with, too.

And finally there was Renelaux, the one man in this entire business who could offer the most help and yet presented the least trustworthy picture . . . at least in Mahoney's eyes.

Conwell might hold him at bay for a time. And John might keep him sidetracked for a day or two. But in the end Renelaux would become suspicious and would come looking himself. When that happened, Mahoney wanted to be ready.

He stopped at an inn just outside Anderlecht, where he ordered a beer and then used the telephone, calling the Marshall residence. Bobbs answered.

"This is Wallace Mahoney. May I speak with Lady Sidney?"

"Yes, sir."

Mahoney went to the bar, got his beer, and came back to the telephone just as Lady Sidney was coming on.

"I do not wish to be disturbed by you any further, Mr. Mahoney," she said. "I wish to make that perfectly clear at the outset."

"Don't you believe I'm here to help?" Mahoney asked, giving her one last chance.

"Leave me alone, sir," she said.

"Robert sends his love and says he is safe and well," Mahoney said.

There was a deathly silence on the line.

"He tells you not to worry, that everything will turn out for the best."

"My God," she said softly.

"Your line was monitored, Lady Sidney. I'm not the only one who heard the tape. But I think I can help if you will let me."

"Oh, you bastards!" she cried. "Oh, you bastards! You're the same type who put up the walls, or take advantage of vulnerable people. You're—"

"No, Lady Sidney, I've come to help."

She said nothing.

"The first time we met I told you that I understood. And I do, even more than you could ever guess. Your husband is gone, but he sends you his love and tells you he is safe. Do you believe it? Do you think he is safe?"

Still Lady Sidney was silent.

"I know what you are going through. I understand your pain. But can you understand to what lengths . . . desperate people might be driven to?"

She stifled a sob. "Oh, God, I'm so frightened. So terribly frightened, Mr. Mahoney. No one seems able to give me an answer."

"I can't either; I've only questions. But I won't give up. I truly want to find Sir Robert."

"Come here, then," she said. "I will talk with you. I will try to answer your questions."

"You will have to inform the men at the gate that I am coming. I'm in Anderlecht now. I shall be there within a few minutes."

"I will," she said, and she hung up.

Mahoney took his beer back to the bar, finished it, and then left the inn. He hesitated at his car for a moment. This was not his fight. It was not his problem. He'd been having a lot of thoughts like those lately. Too

many. Make a decision, old man, and stick with it.
Don't vacillate. And don't bitch about it. Just do the
job.

He got behind the wheel, started the car, and drove
out to the Marshall residence, pulling up at the gate less
than five minutes later.

The SIS man posing as the gatekeeper came out and
without a word opened the gate once he made sure who
it was.

Mahoney drove slowly up the driveway, pulling up in
front of the house and shutting off the engine. He sat
there for a second or two. There were going to be a lot
of people hurt once this business was over with. Langdon, Renelaux, Rubaix, Matin, not to mention Lady
Sidney and Sir Howard Scott. Why had he done it?
Where had he gone? What was he hoping to accomplish?

He got out and went up to the house. Bobbs was at
the door before he could knock. Just inside, the houseman took Mahoney's hat and coat, and directed him
back to the drawing room where he had met both times
before with Lady Sidney.

She was seated in a chair by the French doors looking
out across the vast back lawn. When he knocked and
came in, she turned around but didn't bother to get up.

"Forgive me if I don't rise," she said tiredly. "I hate
to admit it, but I have just a touch of arthritis. It's so
pedestrian."

Mahoney crossed the room and perched on the edge
of the couch. "My wife was bothered with it. She used
to take warm baths."

Lady Sidney smiled. She looked all in. "This has
worn me out, Mr. Mahoney."

"Please call me Wallace."

She inclined her head, as if she were listening to some
inner voice. "I think Mr. Mahoney would be better. I
don't wish to be rude, but—"

"Sir Robert taught at Oxford?"

"Yes. For a time in the fifties."

"Do you still maintain ties there?"

Lady Sidney looked blankly at him for a long time.

"Do you and Sir Robert still have friends there? Perhaps among the staff? Perhaps former students?"

"What do you want, Mr. Mahoney? What is it you are looking for? Robert didn't go back to England. You won't find him in some cloistered halls. He did not go back for his youth."

"May I be frank with you?"

"Haven't you been all along?"

"Your husband is a seeker after causes."

Lady Sidney swallowed a laugh. "What are you telling me now? Don't you think I know that? Good God, I've lived with the man practically my entire life." She was exasperated.

"He's gone off before on his causes, hasn't he?"

"Yes, of course . . ." She let it trail off, but Mahoney suspected the finish of the sentence may have contained the word "idiot," as in ". . . you idiot."

"He went to Germany. Before the war, and again afterward. He went to Berlin to see the wall before he helped Juengst and his KgU."

"Do you think he's gone back to Germany to moon over the wall?" she asked.

"Did you know the caller?"

She shook her head. He believed her.

"Wherever Sir Robert is, he is doing something now that he has thought about for a very long time."

"What makes you think that?"

"He has been tense for the past year or more. His behavior has apparently been erratic. His secretary has said so. His driver has said it. You told me about his telephone calls . . . so he's not alone in this. He's been thinking about something—working up to something—for at least a year."

"What does it have to do with Oxford?"

"In less than a year, from what I understand, Sir

Robert will be forced into retirement.''

She lowered her head, and then nodded. "It bothered him a lot. He said there was so much he could do, now.''

"Now?''

She looked up. "Meaning with his experience. He said he was finally beginning to understand so much.''

"Sir Robert was not taken. Or at least I don't believe he was. And I don't think you believe he was.''

"He defected?'' she asked in a small voice.

"No. I don't believe he went to the Russians,'' Mahoney said. He shook his head. "No, your husband is off on another quest. The biggest of his life.''

"And if you are wrong?'' Lady Sidney asked. "What then?''

"Then I'm wrong. I can't offer more than that.''

She stifled a sob.

"Do you still have friends at Oxford?''

"What has it to do with Oxford?''

"I think he looked back. I think there may be some answers there. Al-'Usta, the Libyan banker you say was here twice recently to talk with Sir Robert, was an Oxford student. He is a link with the past. There may be others.''

"And that is the only link?''

"There is another, and you know it.''

She looked at him.

"The man who telephoned you. Sent the message that your husband was safe. He spoke with a German accent.''

She barely nodded.

"But he spoke English.''

Again she barely nodded.

"Oxford English?''

She lowered her eyes. "Yes.''

"Who is there at Oxford? Who can I speak with?''

"Stanford Hall. He's a professor of European history. He and Robert were close, although Stanford is much younger. Robert thought he was brilliant."

"They still have contact?"

"Yes. He was a junior lecturer when Robert taught there. He is a full professor now. If there is anyone at Oxford who knows anything, it will be Stanford."

☆ NINETEEN ☆

The timing worked well, and Mahoney managed to make a British Airways flight to London, arriving at Heathrow around early suppertime. He changed some money, took an A2 bus into London's Paddington Station, and made a connection by fast train up to Oxford, arriving in the university city shortly after 8:00 P.M.

It was dark and raining when he stepped off the train. Although it was much warmer here than in Brussels, there was a winter's chill in the air.

Outside the station he looked in vain for a taxi, or at least a vendor selling umbrellas, but this end of town seemed all but closed. He hunched up his collar, pulled his hat down, and started out on foot, coming within not too many minutes to High Street, the various colleges on either side, the Quadrangle off to his left, and an occasional student in his garb hurrying off to a pub or perhaps to a tutor. The business of the university was a comfortable constant here.

The rain intensified, and Mahoney ducked into the doorway of a photo shop, water dripping from the brim of his hat. He was very cold. He could see his breath in the harsh light from the streetlamps.

From what he had read, there were actually twenty-one colleges within the organization of the university. Among them were University, Balliol, and Merton— which were the oldest—and All Souls, which dealt with the law and with history.

Sir Robert had taught at All Souls, and Stanford Hall was now one of its most distinguished and apparently outspoken professors of history, European history from the Renaissance on. Mahoney had found his name in the English-language *Who's Who* in the Brussels National Library.

It had been a short entry. But it had been intriguing that Hall's fame had to do with his unique insights into militarism over the past six hundred years.

Sir Robert had taught European history and military interventionism here. Presumably he had had some influence on Hall.

After less than ten minutes the rain moderated, and Mahoney dashed across the street and around the corner to an extremely narrow, cobblestoned street that led behind All Souls College Law Library, and then off at an odd angle to a residential street.

He slowed down as he passed under the streetlight on the corner, a don or professor merely out for an evening stroll. As he walked, however, he studied the street. There were a couple of small automobiles, neither of a recognizable make, parked half up on the curb, their parking lights on. A group of three men turned the corner at the far end of the block, and then were gone.

A bell somewhere in a nearby tower chimed a deep-throated single note, marking the half hour, and then the city was once again silent except for the gentle drip of water from some eaves down into a puddle.

Stanford Hall lived at Number 227, up a short walk behind a dozen hooded bushes, their cloth coverings glistening in the rain.

Mahoney mounted the porch steps, hesitated a moment, then rang the bell. Moments later he heard someone coming from inside, and then the porch light came on. A second later the door swung inward.

A short, slight man of indeterminate middle age, with a white face and thick glasses in very dark frames, stood blinking. He wore a quilted smoking jacket over a white shirt and bow tie. His trousers were baggy and somewhat too large for him, and his slippers were definitely down at the heel. A bachelor, Mahoney suspected.

"Good evening, Professor Hall," Mahoney said.

"Good evening to you, sir. Do I . . . know you?"

"You do not," Mahoney said. "Lady Sidney Marshall sends her greetings."

Hall's eyebrows rose. He stood aside so that Mahoney could come in out of the damp chill. He closed the door.

"I was wondering when someone would be showing up at my doorstep," he said. His voice was very soft and contained a slight lisp. Mahoney couldn't help but wonder what fun the students made of his affliction.

"You were expecting me?"

"Not you specifically, but certainly someone," Hall said. He squinted at Mahoney. "But you're not English. American, perhaps?"

The house smelled musty, of books and closed-in living. Not dirty, simply messy.

"Yes, American."

"Here about Sir Robert's disappearance?"

"Yes. I suspect he's off after another cause."

Hall laughed. "You suspect I'll point you in the correct direction? My tail out, my forepaw bent, my nose on point? My dear man, you came all that way for a hope and a prayer?" He shook his head. "Good Lord, such gall at least deserves a drop."

He turned and shuffled across the stairhall, going into the small living room. A fire was on the grate, and Beethoven's Fifth Symphony in its second movement was playing on the BBC-1, the black and white picture snowy. Books lay everywhere: on shelves that lined most of three walls, on the floor, on end tables and a coffee table, beside the long couch, on two of three easy chairs, and on the broad windowseat, heavy curtains were held inward by untidy piles of books. A single floor lamp was lit over a wing chair in front of the fire. On a table beside the chair was a bottle of Asbach Urhalt, a good German brandy, and a single snifter, empty.

Hall pulled another snifter from a cabinet in the corner and motioned toward the couch. "Take off your hat and coat, and sit down, Mr. . . . ?"

"Wallace Mahoney."

Hall poured a stiff measure of brandy into the snifter. Mahoney took off his coat and looked for a place to lay it.

"Just anywhere," Hall said, handing him the drink.

Mahoney took it with one hand, then carefully laid his sodden overcoat on a clear spot on the floor next to the couch, his hat on top of it. He sat down.

Hall poured himself another brandy. He sat in the wing chair, a bemused expression on his face. He held up his snifter in a toast. "If you'd care to smoke, please do, Mr. Mahoney. Meanwhile, to Lady Sidney, one of the loveliest women England ever produced. Don't you agree?"

"Wholeheartedly," Mahoney said, raising his glass and sipping the fine brandy. He put the snifter down on a stack of books at his feet and went through the business of lighting a cigar.

Hall watched him. "Amazing," he said when Mahoney had it lit. "Opium I can understand. Even hashish. But tobacco? A poison."

"Like war?"

"Such as war," Hall agreed pointedly. "But all the more fascinating for its idiocy, don't you agree?"

"There has never been a good war."

Hall grinned owlishly. "But some have been more interesting than others," he said. "There should be an ashtray behind you."

Mahoney reached back and found the bottom section of a 55mm shell casing, a piece of cork glued in the center of it to use as a pipe knocker.

"How is Sidney holding up?" Hall asked seriously.

"Not well. It's all very confusing for her with the SIS and Interpol and a dozen other NATO-related agencies all running around asking questions, bugging her telephone, watching her twenty-four hours a day."

"But you're different," Hall said, a finger to the side of his nose. "Oh, yes, I can practically smell it. You are a soldier, of course, but the maverick, the night rider."

Mahoney had to smile. "No. Just an old man trying to unravel a puzzle."

Hall shook his head. "You're being modest now, I suspect. Ingratiatingly so. And irritatingly so. But you did not come all this way to kowtow, to lick my boots. Nor have you come to lay your cap at the altar of advanced learning, as it were. No, on the contrary."

Mahoney couldn't decide if he liked the man or not. Nor could he decide completely if he was being toyed with.

"Come, Mr. Mahoney, I will give you your first answer in all honesty."

Mahoney inclined his head. "You were expecting me, or someone like me to show up on your doorstep. Why?"

"Me or someone *such as* me," Hall said. But then he waved it off. "No matter. Of course I expected someone as soon as I heard Robert had gone walkabout."

"You don't believe he was taken?"

"Snatched?" He shook his head thoughtfully. "I dunno. You tell me. Is there any evidence of it?"

"No."

"No," Hall repeated. "I suspected someone would show up here sooner or later because of Sir Robert's association not only with this college, but specifically with me. I suspect his military records have been gone through. I suspect someone might even have dug up poor Edward Juengst's maggot-infested corpse from its grave. Good God Almighty, I suspect that every aspect of Robert's past would have been gone through."

"No one else has been here?"

"Not yet."

"Sir Robert hasn't called you?"

Hall puffed up. "Don't be a shit-heel, Mahoney. I agreed to answer your little questions. Don't insult me. Do you actually think I give a holy damn which side comes out on top? I'm an historian, and a goddamned good one, and I'll make my mark—not the one the stupid Hebdomadal Council already believes I've made —but a serious mark." He blinked. "Are you following me at all, Mahoney? Or are you a simpleton?" He poured himself another brandy. "More?" he asked, holding out the bottle.

Mahoney got up and held out his snifter. Hall splashed a good measure of brandy into it, and Mahoney sat back.

"You worked with him for three years?"

"Four and a term," Hall corrected. "And the man was marvelous. A bloody genius."

"What were you then? A student?"

"What was I then? Nothing. I mean absolutely *nada*. *Nada!* He had insights, don't you know. Not only did he have the scholastic learning, he had the practical experience. I mean, for heaven's sake, the man absolutely made history. He spoke with Hitler. Possibly influenced the decisions *der Führer* made. He was a living laboratory right here under our microscopes. And he could tell us what it felt like when we prodded him with our inanities. Christ!" Hall ran his fingers through his hair. "Christ, it was unique," he said.

"Why'd he leave?"

"All Souls?"

Mahoney nodded.

"This is the netherworld. The real world beckoned. Things were happening. He had a higher duty. An obligation. God . . . an obligation.''

There was a small metal box with a hinged top on the table beside him. He set his snifter down, opened the box, and withdrew a very small, poorly rolled cigarette. Mahoney suspected it was marijuana. As soon as Hall lit it, his suspicions were confirmed. The odor of burning fall grass filled the room.

"He wanted to be the great fixer. He wanted to ride off on his trusty nag and chase after windmills. He had his Dulcinea in Sidney, and he had his pick of lapdogs willing to play his Sancho Panza.''

"Who came closest?''

Hall focused on Mahoney. "Me? Howard Scott? I don't know. Robert was too aloof at the time.'' He looked away. "I was on my own quest for what I considered academic excellence. Howard Scott was—and as far as I know still is—an order taker. The penultimate soldier behind Robert.''

"What did he teach here?'' Mahoney asked quietly.

"Everything.''

"What drove him, Hall? What was his motivation? His raison d'être?''

Hall laughed. "My dear fellow, it sounds terribly much as if you have spoken at length with Howie Scott, the wild lover at Mods.''

"Moderations? The examinations?''

"That's right. Scott was in love with Sidney from the day he was a silly undergrad, taking his Mods.''

"He went to school here? I didn't know that.''

"Of course, of course. It's legend. I wasn't even a twinkle in my father's eye, but as concerns Oxford, the early nineteenth century or early twentieth are all of a mind. A flash. But his love was common knowledge to everyone except poor Robert.''

Mahoney sipped his drink as Hall paused long enough to take a deep hit from the hashish cigarette. His eyes seemed to glaze as if he were the kewpie doll at the top

of the hammer and mouse game at the fair, and someone had just rung the bell with a potent blow.

"He used to drive up here from London. That was
later, when Robert was teaching us our twos-and-fours.
Used to moon all over the place. They had a house on
Ronlee Commons, or some such as that, if I remember."

It was raining very hard again. Mahoney could hear
the downpour hammering the roof, and he shivered un-
consciously, although the room was quite warm from
the fire.

Hall's story began, Mahoney suspected, like his lec-
tures. He had to puff himself up first. Make certain his
audience fully appreciated his importance, his credentials, so that his pronouncements would carry the weight
he felt they should. And he began nearly at the point
Mahoney suspected he might, with Sir Robert's guilt
about the war.

It hadn't been too many years since Robert had been
a guest at the Eagle's Nest, and in Munich and even
Berlin. And it had certainly been even fewer years since
the war when he showed up at Oxford. In those days a
lot of them counted the time passed in months: it was
less than a hundred months since VE. Somehow the
event they all were frantically studying seemed more immediate to them that way, more accessible.

Of course no one could argue with him, as if anyone
had a mind to be so foolish. Robert Marshall was a man
with a singleness of purpose and a huge awareness of
who he was.

The invasion of Poland had been a blow, of course.
But there were certain of those within the college who
suspected that the blow as recounted in '53 was something larger than it actually had been in '39.

It wasn't that Sir Robert was a liar, or even an actor
who pumped up his own lines, his own emotions to suit
the mood of the moment. It was that he was a man

uniquely in tune—in absolute tune, mind you—with his time.

"Yet a lot of us thought he might have been a bit out of sync at times, you know?"

Mahoney didn't, but he let it pass.

Sir Robert was unique in a number of other ways as well, among them his fantastic memory for detail. He could describe at length each room of the Eagle's Nest. He could tell about the road approaching, about the elevator through living rock, about the colors, the textures, the feelings, with a scientific accuracy that boggled the imagination.

In the beginning they checked up on him. They simply had to. The first, or was it the second summer, a sabbatical was taken from tutorials, and a half-dozen scholars went over to Berchtesgaden and Munich and West Berlin to investigate whatever they could lay their hands on.

Within reason, everything the man had told them checked out one hundred percent. Not only was he a genius, he was a man gifted with the sight for "infinite detail," as it was popularly called at the time by students studying for Final Schools, preparatory to graduation.

"Then did the kudos and plaudits fly! You should have seen it! It was a bloody circus."

Everyone paid attention then. And it did not become so unfashionable to believe the war had been preventable. Think of it. Goddammit, Chamberlain had actually screwed up. There was no such thing any longer as foregone conclusions—destiny. The single-digit theory came into fashion then and actually held sway for as long as Robert taught at All Souls. For want of the nail, the shoe, the horse, the rider, the message, and the battle were lost. The little Dutch boy with his single digit had plugged the leak in the dike and saved the land. The individual could, and often did, have a much vaster ef-

fect on the course of events than historians had thought
possible.

Hitler was just a man, Mahoney offered.

So was Genghis Khan, which meant nothing. But
could the ordinary soldier, the ordinary diplomat, the
ordinary person affect history? Given the laws of
chance, of time and place, certainly. But could the ordinary man, thinking it out beforehand, go in and find
the fulcrum and the lever of sufficient length to affect
the course of history?

"The war was a mistake," Mahoney suggested.

Hall's already animated face lit up. "But such a
grand, colossal faux pas. Such a legacy of debates and
historical perspectives it has left us mere mortals."

"At the cost of how many millions of lives?"

Hall dismissed that with a wave of his hand. "Sir
Robert took time to develop his arrogance, his colossal
conceit, you know."

"No, I don't," Mahoney said dryly. He decided he
did not like Hall.

Hall laughed foppishly and waved his hands around
as if he were chasing away flies. "He didn't always
believe the war was his fault, you know. He had to talk
himself into it. And it took an awful lot of superficial
introspection . . . let me tell you." He laughed at his
own joke.

It was a very deliberate process. From the beer hall
putsch, Hitler's imprisonment, and *Mein Kampf* to the
establishment of the *Schutzstaffel* and the goings-on at
Prinz-Albrecht Strasse—to Dachau and Auschwitz and
even to Flossenbürg where Canaris was murdered—all
of that had been preventable. Not only on a one-to-one
basis, but in broad strokes.

"Robert believed that any major event—a flood, a
war, famine, any event—no matter how large or small,
could ultimately be reduced to an individual act or series
of acts," Hall said.

"The automobile accident is a driver's fault."

"Perhaps the engineer's fault who developed the faulty curve."

"The battle, the commander's fault."

"A war is reducible to an essence," Hall said. He took another hit from his marijuana cigarette. He nodded as if he were hearing music, then he looked up. "A charismatic Robert could have convinced Hitler in 1938 in Bavaria that Germany would be the next *political* power in Europe, and not the military nightmare that it became. And so the face of history would have been changed."

Mahoney held himself very still. There it was again. He had been looking for common denominators. Here was one in front of him. Charisma! But Hall was continuing.

"The man positively worked himself into a lather convincing himself that he was at fault for the war. We were watching the development of a Caesar, of an Alexander the Great, a Napoleon. We expected tremendous things from the man."

But nothing seemed to materialize. For a time, especially through the turbulent era of the French withdrawal and the American involvement in Vietnam, they were all certain that something very large was going to happen.

But it did not. Sir Robert went along his way as an apparently minor adjutant on the international scene.

"I don't mind telling you the entire sordid business with the KgU and silly Edward Juengst was a disappointment," Hall said. He took another hit. The cigarette was getting short.

"I was told an interesting speculation," Mahoney said. "That the people the KgU brought out were Jews who could afford a ten-thousand-mark ransom."

Hall laughed. "Money would never have changed hands. I knew Juengst. If he had wanted payment—if

Robert had wanted payment—it would not have been in money. It would have been in political activism." Hall shook his head. "No, Mahoney, whoever fed you that cock-and-bull story was doing a number on you."

"You knew Juengst?"

"Of course. He came here. Looking for his mecca, I suppose. Looking—like you—for a handle on Robert-the-Great."

"And you gave it to him?"

Hall's left eyebrow rose imperiously. "Of course I did. I'm an historian."

"You bastard," Mahoney said under his breath. Hall didn't hear him, or chose to ignore it.

Suddenly he went off on a tangent. If Robert was in love with the entire idea of historical influence, he could hate some things in just as sincere and boyishly enthusiastic a manner as well.

The Russians were the scourge of the earth. They were the blight upon the land, the tumor within the works of peace and common decency.

"But not the ordinary Russian, of course," Hall hastened to add. "The KGB. The Komitet. The State Security people with their disinformation and Department Victory assassinations, all the little nasties that spy novels are made of."

This was brand new. Mahoney had not been aware of any Russian connection, no matter the thrust, no matter the relative lack of importance or consequence.

"When did this all come out?" Mahoney prompted.

Hall blinked and just looked at him as if he were an idiot. He took another hit from the marijuana cigarette, then rolled the hot end between his thumb and forefinger. When the spark was out, he put the tiny stub into his mouth and ate it, licking his fingers afterward.

"That's the lovely thing about Mary Jane. You can smoke it, bake it into a muffin, boil it in a soup, eat it, stick it up your ass—almost anything—and it gives you a nice high." He grinned stupidly. "Too bad people weren't more like that."

"Was Sir Robert involved in the cold war before the Berlin Wall was put up?" Mahoney asked, trying to change the subject.

Hall looked at him. Then he got shakily to his feet and picked up the brandy bottle. "A little more?" he asked. His voice was surprisingly steady.

"The Russians," Mahoney prompted.

Hall stood there with the brandy bottle in hand. "Oh, hell," he said. "He had no love lost for the Russkies long before their stupid little wall. I mean, for God's sake, man, look at the Chinese. They put up a wall ten thousand miles long half a million years ago, and everyone from Nixon to Reagan goes over for a look-see. What's a puny little wall around Berlin? You know the great Chinese wall never worked worth a shit anyway."

Mahoney watched a play of emotions on Hall's face. Tiredness. Bewilderment. Disgust. But mostly envy and jealousy. Sir Robert had jumped into the real world with both feet. While Stanford Hall, who talked a good line, had stayed behind wasting away in safe, secure, cloistered academia.

"It's been a lot easier to criticize the world from your tower, hasn't it?"

"Don't be perverse, little man," Hall snapped. He forgot why he had gotten up with the brandy bottle. He put it back on the table and sat down.

"Sorry," Mahoney said, but he didn't mean it.

"You think it's been duck soup here? Peachy keen? Take the kiddies by the hand and lead them through the obvious? You think it's been a picnic trying to do any serious research?"

Hall jumped up again and went to the fireplace where he poked the logs to little effect. When he came back he again picked up the brandy bottle and poured Mahoney a good measure. He poured himself more as well.

This time when he sat down, it seemed as if he were a man who had suddenly realized he was doomed to repeat all of his stupid mistakes over and over again.

Mahoney suspected it was a malady common to historians.

☆ TWENTY ☆

It was still raining very hard. Mahoney could see that Hall was listening to it drumming on the roof. He seemed to find some comfort in the sound, because he began to relax; his body sagged, his expression softened, and it seemed as if he were sinking down into the chair.

"I tend to get a bit maudlin at times," he explained. "Especially at night. In the rain." He looked up at the beamed ceiling, and then at the books.

"It affects me that way sometimes."

Hall focused on him. "You *are* human after all."

"I've been accused of it."

Hall smiled. "He never had much love lost for Americans either. 'Dollar diplomacy,' he told the kidlets. Chop-chop. Ford-IBM-and-Ma Bell will get you."

"Bogeymen from the East as well as the West," Mahoney suggested.

"In the classic pincer action. Europe will be the ultimate battleground."

"Save me the anti-MX missile tirade," Mahoney said. He raised the snifter to his lips and inhaled the fumes. He felt as if he were playing Hall like a gigantic fish on a five-pound test line.

"Don't be an ass, Mahoney. I'm an observer."

"And you regret not being a participant?"

"Crap. Pure, unadulterated crap. Look what it has gotten our vaunted Sir Robert-the-Great."

"Did the Russians snatch him?"

"Look to Langley. It's just as likely the CIA took him. Though you've had your little bit of trouble just recently. Something about a nearsighted pilot, I believe."

Hall was wired into some source, but who? Or was it merely guesswork? Could he have put it together? Sir Robert gone, the investigators coming out of the woodwork? An American shows up. CIA? Logical? One thing for certain, Hall was one bitter man.

"So he was anti-American."

"And anti-Russian."

"Did he pass that along to his students when he was here?"

"Do you mean did he nurture budding terrorists out of these hallowed halls?"

Mahoney said nothing.

"You do know that we played a bit of an experiment in the fifties. A few Libyans, a few Iraquis, the Shah even sent a chosen few over from Teheran. Not exactly the Rhodes snot-nosed kids, but some of them weren't bad, if'n you could get past the anti-Anglo chip on their shoulders."

Still Mahoney held his silence. He reached for another cigar, but Hall held him off.

"For God's sake, mercy."

Mahoney shrugged. "He wasn't born hating the right and the left."

"Delicious," Hall said. He reached into the metal box and pulled out two marijuana cigarettes. He held one out to Mahoney.

"No, thanks."

"Really, you ought to try it. Somehow I don't think you ever have."

"No point."

Hall laughed. But he put one of the cigarettes back and lit the other. He sat back in his chair, holding the smoke in his lungs.

"No, Robert came here with at least that part of him fully developed," Hall said dreamily. "I always thought of it as a matched set."

"I'm sorry, I don't follow you."

"You know, bookends. The KGB and the CIA. Communists and capitalists. Oligarchists and democrats. I mean, who could match a Trotsky and a Lenin with a smokin' Joe McCarthy and a Tricky Dicky?"

"He hated us all."

"Europe was the battleground. He wanted you to go home across the Atlantic and them back across the Polish steppes."

"We didn't start the last two wars here."

"They were internal matters."

"Christ, Hall, what the hell are you trying to say to me now?"

"This is our battleground. Leave it to us."

"Are you such a complete fool?"

Hall laughed. "Bobby-the-Good is on NATO's Nuclear Defense Affairs Committee. He holds that belief."

"What belief?"

"Europe for the EEC."

"America hands off?"

"That's right."

"The hell with the Battle of Britain?"

"That's right."

"The hell with the Warsaw Pact?" Mahoney said. He didn't wait for an answer. "The hell with nuclear testing—the hell with missile deployments, tank forces, troop strength? Bury your head in the sand? Is that it?"

"It'll work out one way or the other."

"Come now, Hall, you can't be advocating that, can you? You're the historian; Sir Robert is the idealist."

"Not only are you human, my dear man, I detect a modicum of intelligence."

"Yeah," Mahoney said, slowing it down. "But where did he come up with it? His source?"

"Who knows? Pick a place. Gehlen, perhaps."

"Reinhard Gehlen? The BND? The German secret service?"

"*Jawohl. Der Bundesnachrichtendienst.* He was *your* baby. He hated the Russians. Pullach was where it happened. It was the beginning of the rape of Europe."

"Bullshit," Mahoney said. Hall sputtered, but Mahoney held him off. "Come on, Hall, I didn't bang on your door for this. I don't want the anarchist lecture. I need to know about Robert Marshall."

"A knight of the realm. Sir Robert-the-Jerk."

"Where did he get himself off to?"

"Beats the hell out of me."

Hall took another hit from the marijuana cigarette. Although he was slowing way down, it wouldn't be long, Mahoney figured, before the man was lying flat on his back on the floor.

"He knew Gehlen?" Mahoney asked after a minute or so.

Hall nodded. "Knew him and hated him. Called him the rotten quisling."

"Doesn't sound like a man who hates Russians."

"It had nothing to do with Russians; it had to do with loyalty to a cause."

"Gehlen hated Russians from the beginning."

"Gehlen was a man of the hour. Whichever way the wind seemed to blow best for him at the moment, is the way he drifted. And don't try to tell me anything different with your schoolboy politics."

After Eton and a short stint at Oxford, Sir Robert had been sent to Germany for his real education. His was to be a military life, and in those days—the Versailles Treaty and all it implied to the contrary—it was still thought that the Germans produced the absolutely best soldiers. It was in their genes, infused into the being and fiber of the people and their institutions, into their borrowed religion of Valhalla and Odin, and into the very air that blew mysteriously on both sides of the Rhine.

Expose a lad to the German university life, and some of that ambition, or rather that orderliness, would rub off.

"And it did, of course," Hall slurred. The marijuana was finally beginning to make him sloppy. "Couldn't ever really get close to him. He always had that barrier up. An aloofness."

"But he spoke of Germany with you?"

"He taught military interventionism. The war had just gotten over with. Of course he spoke about Germany."

"No. I meant about the past. His past as a young man in college there."

"About Heidelberg? No more than any of us talk about our youth. Sometimes we wish it could happen over again. Sometimes we wish we had paid a bit more attention."

Hall was wandering. Mahoney pulled out a cigar and went through the process of lighting it.

"Don't do that, for God's sake! It stinks up the house," Hall said.

Mahoney ignored him. He had gotten more information out of an irritated Hall than he had from a complacent, maudlin Hall.

"Christ," Hall said. Then he took another hit of his marijuana cigarette, his eyes glazed, and his head drooped.

"Did he go back to Germany this time?" Mahoney asked. "Is he hiding out there?"

"He hated *der Führer*. Called him the Austrian paperhanger." Hall chuckled. "We all called him that, but when Robert said it, it was worse than being called a Polack."

"I was under the impression that he thought Hitler was a genius."

"Oh, yes, he was that. And Bobby gave that to him. But Hitler had no class. No real concept of historical perspective. No understanding of his true mission, of where he could have fit into the realm of European politics."

Hall sat forward, his expression clearing. "Imagine a Europe without the war," he started, and he began to spin out his fancies.

Let's say Hitler stopped at Czechoslovakia, Austria, and of course East Prussia. Let's say he consolidated his position there. Perhaps he even sent arms across to the South Pacific to help Roosevelt in the war against Japan. He could have gotten his subs out there.

Then there was a Fascist Italy. Might he have taken it over eventually? In the name of peace? By that time Roosevelt would have been occupied with his war in the South Pacific. If *der Führer* had wanted war, he could have gone after the Soviet Union with total impunity.

"Who would have cried out when his troops rolled across the Polish border then? Hell, he needed a corridor to Russia. For years the Communists had tried to make inroads into German politics." Hall shook his head. "Do you think His Majesty's government would have given a good goddamn about the fall of Moscow?"

No one would have intervened. The atrocities Stalin had been perpetrating on his people were a scandal. No one would have given a damn if the blitzkrieg had wiped out Moscow.

Backing up, of course, they could have picked off Yugoslavia and Rumania and Bulgaria. And then they could have sat back and rested. They could have licked their wounds, because there would have been plenty of them. They could have consolidated and stabilized their new governments of occupation.

"You know that Hitler actually had a great respect for us English, though I can't honestly tell you how he came to such a foolish, ill-founded opinion. But somewhere along the line he could have become our ally."

Hall took another hit.

"And you English would have sat still over the 'final solution'?"

Hall waved it off. "No one likes Jews, Mahoney," he said. "You Americans knew all about the extermination camps and yet you didn't do a damned thing about it. Curious."

Freedom of thought and expression. Wasn't that what a university was all about? Yet it rankled. Hall was more than a bastard . . . much more.

"All that aside, think of it, Mahoney. Instead of the Soviet Union and the United States at each other's throat, we could have had a triumvirate: a powerful United States with her atomic bomb and her victory over Japan; us, with our impeccable manners and sense of administration; and *der Führer* ruling all of Central and Eastern Europe. All allies. All pals. There wouldn't have been a slant-eye or a darky ruling in the bunch. Think of it! Unless one of us wanted to start something, there would have been guaranteed peace for his thousand-year Reich, and for the rest of us as well."

Mahoney prodded him back to the subject at hand. "Is that what Sir Robert was advocating in those days?"

"No," Hall said, shaking his head. "No, he was more of a realist than I was . . . or still am, for that matter. No matter our desires, we can't go back. Makes for interesting speculation, though."

"He understood it was impossible to go back?"

"Very firmly. We used to lament together . . . I did the lamenting, he did the consoling, although it was obvious to everyone around him what a tremendous burden he was carrying around.''

"What sort of a burden?''

"Oh, you know. We already talked about it. He knew he couldn't go back, and he knew it was no use crying over spilt milk, and yet he took on this tremendously heavy weight around his neck: that had he only been a bit more persuasive, my grand scenario would have been possible. Had he learned his lessons better in Heidelberg and then later in Munich and Berchtesgaden, the war and its even more horrible aftermath would never have happened.''

"The aftermath?'' Mahoney asked. "What specifically bothered him most after the war?''

The doorbell rang. Hall looked toward the corridor. "It's starting hot 'n heavy now,'' he said. He glanced back. "The Russians on one side of the wall and you Americans on the other. Gehlen wanted to punch holes between the two, but just for the game of it. Robert hated him. Juengst, no matter how misguided he was, wanted to punch holes between the two to help the people. Robert loved him.''

The doorbell rang again, and Hall got up. "Excuse me for a moment. It's probably just one of my idiots.'' He walked unsteadily out of the room.

Mahoney sat back, puffed his cigar, and sipped his drink. It all pointed back to Germany again. Heidelberg. Munich. Hitler's Eagle's Nest. Then came the war. Afterward Berlin and then Bonn, then back to Berlin and the wall, and Juengst. And now NATO's Genesis Plan in which nuclear weapons would fly if and when Warsaw Pact tanks rolled across the border . . . in Germany.

The doorbell rang a third time.

He brought his brandy snifter to his lips when he heard Hall say "Heavens,'' and then there was a soft but distinctive plopping sound: once, twice, three times. It was unmistakable.

Mahoney set his brandy snifter down and jumped up as someone in the corridor grunted. There was a crash.

He was in the stairhall a second or two later, and unmindful of the danger to himself, he tore around the corner where he came to a stop.

Stanford Hall lay on his side, a small hall table crushed beneath him, blood streaming from wounds in his head and in his throat, his left leg twitching. The odor of gunpowder and of defecation was very strong. The front door was open. It was raining very hard.

Mahoney leaped to the door as a car door slammed and a powerful engine raced away in the night.

He turned back. Hall's eyes were open, his glasses askew. Surprise was registered on his face. He had not recognized his murderer. He had simply been surprised that someone would have the effrontery to pull a gun on him. His leg stopped bumping.

"I'm sorry. I should have known," Mahoney mumbled.

He turned and looked out into the street. There was no one there. "I'm sorry," he said again, turning back.

He hurried back into the living room, put on his coat and hat, then drained his snifter, wiped it inside and out with his handkerchief, and put it back in the cabinet. He took his cigar, then emptied the ashtray in the fireplace. He replaced it behind the couch.

Back in the corridor he looked down at Hall, and shook his head. The man had been shot with a high-caliber handgun. A Russian Graz Buyra? he wondered.

He felt very bad about leaving Hall like that. He bent down and carefully felt for a pulse at Hall's neck, but there was nothing. He straightened up, then left the house, closing and locking the door behind him. He hunched up his coat collar, pulled his hat down, and stepped off the porch into the cold rain.

He was in time to catch the last train back to London, where he took the bus out to the Penta Hotel right on the airport grounds after first picking up his bag where he had left it in a terminal locker.

He managed to call Lufthansa and make reservations for his flight in the morning.

He lay in bed, fully dressed, waiting for his heart to slow down, listening to the noises of the hotel, and seeing in the darkness Hall's surprised countenance in death.

There were so many questions. For each answer, a dozen new avenues opened up. But it came back to the single word he had heard over and over now: charisma. Sir Robert had needed it in 1938. From what Mahoney was learning, he had finally developed it.

It was midnight. Detective Inspector Richard Matin sat at his desk in his office at police headquarters. He looked out the window across the city. The sky had cleared, and now the stars shone as bright, hard points, clearly visible even above the glow of the city's lights.

Matin had been sitting there for several hours. He had telephoned his wife to tell her that he would be late. She had called back around ten to ask if he had had his dinner, and he assured her he had, and that he would be along soon.

His empty stomach rumbled now. Of course he hadn't had his dinner, nor had he eaten any lunch. It had been a terribly long day.

Matin figured he had known Jean Rubaix as long or longer than he had known anyone else other than his wife.

He and the sergeant had never been close, but they had worked with each other for most of the fifteen years Rubaix had been on the force.

In all those years Matin felt he had come to know the man. But sitting there now, thinking over the events of the past week, he realized just how little any of them knew about each other.

It was very sad. Or at least it struck Matin as very sad

and lonely that they could not be closer to one another than that. And yet there seemed to be no help for it.

He turned back again to the files on his desk. The buff-colored one on his left contained thin dossiers on three men: Thomas Langdon, a journalist with the *London Daily Mail*; Colonel Oliver Horne, the American chief of NATO Security; and Pierre Renelaux, Central Intelligence Agency liaison to the Alliance.

There was something else about Renelaux; there were a few facts that did not seem to add up, that would suggest he was something more than he presented himself to be. But Matin felt that such speculations would have to wait until another time.

The middle of three file folders contained telephone logs for Jean Rubaix's department over the past six months. This folder was thick. It had taken Matin the better part of twelve hours, spread over all of that day and evening, to go through each sheet, gleaning from the calls a pattern that Rubaix had not bothered to conceal.

The final folder contained Rubaix's service record. It was spotless. Almost too spotless for a fifteen-year man who had never risen above sergeant.

Matin had asked him about it some years ago, and Rubaix had merely replied that he was terrible at two things in life: taking tests and giving orders—both requirements for the job of lieutenant.

It was clear to Matin, however, that Rubaix had a third deficiency as well. And that was loyalty, or the lack of it.

Someone knocked at his door. Matin looked up. *"Entrez,"* he called.

The door opened and Rubaix came in. His coat was open, and he wore a sweater beneath it. He seemed curious but not suspicious. "I came as soon as I got your message, Richard. Something has broken on the Robert Marshall case?"

"Yes, Jean," Matin said. "Sit down. Some wine?"

"No. I had a late dinner. It did not agree with me," Rubaix said. He sat down across from Matin. "What do we have?" he asked, eyeing the folders.

Matin had a lot of prejudices. His wife said too many. Among them he hated liars, and he hated people who circled around an issue. The Americans called it beating around the bush, which he found apt. It was difficult now, however, to come directly to the point.

"I have three files here, Jean," he said. "The first is yours."

Rubaix smiled uncertainly but said nothing.

"It is a wonderful record you have compiled. You have done investigative work that should have been rewarded long ago."

"I do not want a promotion, Richard. We have already discussed that."

Matin held up his hand. "I know, I know, Jean." He tapped the thick, center file. "This folder contains telephone records for your department over the past six months. It has taken me many hours to sift through each number, matching them with times and dates. You have been a very busy man."

The first signs of alarm began to show on Rubaix's face. But he did not say a word.

"This final folder contains the dossiers of three men. You know them well. Intimately, we might say. Thomas Langdon, Oliver Horne, and Pierre Renelaux."

Rubaix's eyes narrowed. "I know many people. Langdon has been an informer to this department for some time now."

"I see. And Colonel Horne? He tells you about NATO?"

"He is a fellow police officer. I work with him just as I work with Henri at Interpol."

"You share information with Colonel Horne?"

"Yes, of course."

"And Monsieur Renelaux, a former Belgian who decided to become an American and yet lives here. A curious man. Do you share information with him? Is he another policeman such as Henri and Colonel Horne?''

Rubaix was beginning to sweat. "What is it, Richard? What are you getting at?"

Matin could taste the bile rising in his throat. He thumped his fist on the desk.

"With Colonel Horne I can understand, Jean. But with this Thomas Langdon, a journalist, I cannot."

Rubaix started to protest, but Matin held him off.

"There will be time at your review board hearing for you to speak. It is my turn now. When I am finished you will be relieved of duty, pending the hearing."

"Richard," Rubaix said in alarm. He got to his feet.

Matin looked up. "Horne, I understand, but you gave information about this department—privileged information—to a British journalist and to Renelaux, who spies on NATO for the Americans. You abused your position. You violated my trust."

Rubaix backed away. He had nothing to say.

Matin rose. "I will caution you, Jean, not to discuss this or anything else with these three men, especially not with Langdon who is almost certainly involved in General Marshall's disappearance. Go home. Get some sleep."

Rubaix made a strangled little noise, then he turned and fled from the office.

Matin remained standing for a long time, staring at the door. Way at the back of his mind, he had held the hope—silly actually, he thought now—that somehow when confronted, Jean would have had some logical explanation. Some perfectly sensible reason for what he had done.

But there had been nothing. It was both disappointing and frightening.

✫ TWENTY-ONE ✫

Mahoney arrived in Frankfurt before noon and rented a car for the short drive down to Heidelberg. It was a lovely if somewhat chilly day. The weather across the European continent had finally broken. Only a few puffy white clouds lingered. But he was not in the mood to enjoy it. He was on the move now. As soon as he stopped, the lines from Langley would reach out to ensnare him. Or whoever had killed Stanford Hall, and he had a fair idea who it was, would come after him. So far he had been very open about his movements, but as he drove very fast along the Ell autobahn, he kept checking his rearview mirror to see if he was being followed. There was a lot of traffic, but no one seemed especially interested in him, not even when he varied his speed from less than a hundred kilometers per hour to more than one hundred and fifty. He had not brought the pistol along with him, of course. It would have been far too complicated and time-consuming to take through airport security. It was rare for him to feel a need for such a thing, and yet at that moment he felt open and vulnerable without it. He did have to admit, however, that even if he had had the gun, he would not have been able to save Hall. That had simply been a terrible mistake on his part. He wasn't going to make any

more like that, although here in Germany he already felt
as if he were under a very powerful light on a micro-
scope stage, ripe for examination and perhaps even
dissection.

It took him less than forty minutes to reach the an-
cient university city. He checked into the Europaischer
Hof, a fairly expensive hotel but centrally located. He
had been here once before, years ago when the mark
was much cheaper against the dollar, and he remembered that the restaurant was very good. It was in the
days when McBundy was riding herd.

He had the bellhop bring his bag upstairs to his room,
then he went back out to his car and drove around to a
parking garage marked on his street map. He turned the
car over to the attendant, and for a very large tip in advance, he was assured that there would never be a delay,
day or night, should he suddenly want the car.

Afterward he found a small, charming restaurant
on the Necar River, near the old bridge, where he had
a stein of beer and a small plate of sauerbraten with
heavy, rich pumpernickel bread. He did not hurry
through his meal. The waitress, dressed in a pretty
dirndl and white apron, had seated him by the window
so that he could watch the traffic outside as well as the
goings-on in the restaurant. It was a very popular place.
He thought that Sir Robert had probably come here as a
young man. Maybe recently as well?

After his lunch he walked slowly up the hill, the castle
hanging over the city, almost mysterious, the tiered
gardens built for a queen's fancy impressive even at a
distance, and the narrow, twisted, sharply inclined cobblestoned streets reminiscent of a much earlier age.

Sir Robert had come here as a young man to absorb
from the German psyche something of a military spirit.
Sir Robert the student. Judging from the man's subsequent career, Mahoney suspected his sojourn here had
been quite successful.

He stopped at one of the many student pubs for a

small after-dinner wine, but more for the flavor of the quarter. It was noisy, almost boisterous in the *Gasthaus*. The students wore the flat-topped caps with variously colored horizontal stripes indicating rank and line of study.

A few of the students in the pub did take some notice of Mahoney, perhaps thinking him a visiting professor or maybe a tourist displaced from the beaten path. But no one approached him.

Later he walked over to the student jail, where in not so distant times past—in fact as recently as just before the war—students were punished by imprisonment for various infractions of university rules. While incarcerated in the tiny rooms, the students would draw silhouettes of each other on the walls with charcoal, then sign their names, the date, and perhaps some pithy or even sarcastic message for posterity. There were only a few tourists wandering through the rooms, so Mahoney was able to take his time, moving from cell to cell, from silhouette to silhouette.

After an hour he gave it up, thanked the caretaker, and left, starting back down the hill toward the university administration buildings.

Mahoney had not really expected to find anything in the student prison, and yet he had, at least for a little while, made a serious effort to find . . . what? The silhouette of Sir Robert as a young student? Almost certainly, as a foreigner, he would have gotten into some trouble. Perhaps next to the silhouette would have been the startling, all-telling inscription. Mahoney had to smile at his daydream.

Farther down the hill he began passing the various university buildings, some marked with brass plaques announcing the department: Anthropology, History, Mathematics.

He had steeped himself in the feeling of the city, of the student quarter. It was time now to go back to work.

At a small student bookshop, Mahoney bought a

guide map to the university and its environs. It was divided into the old university and the new sections built after the war. In both sections of the school, however, there was listed a Student Records Center. Mahoney chose the old center, oriented himself, and walked back up into the student quarter.

The building, its brass plaque announcing simply Records, was down a very narrow back alley, other buildings closing in around it, nearly blocking out the sun. It was a four-story gray stucco structure with a red tile roof. There were quaint little windows tucked up under the eaves.

He stepped inside and found himself in a neat little anteroom, the wooden floor highly varnished, the woodwork gleaming, and a pervading odor that was a cross between disinfectant, wood, and musty books or records. A young woman wearing a wild print dress and very big, very thick-rimmed glasses looked up from her work and smiled. She had very nice teeth.

"I would like to speak with someone about the records of a certain student," Mahoney said in his rusty German.

"These are only to 1940, sir," the girl said in English.

Mahoney switched. "I am looking for the records of a man who studied here in the twenties."

"The nineteen-twenties?"

"Yes."

"Would this person still be alive?"

"Yes," Mahoney said.

The young girl reached into the desk drawer and brought out a preprinted form. "The person whose records you are requesting must first fill out this Authorization to Release Data form. Or else there must first be a court order. You are perhaps from the court, perhaps a policeman?"

"No," Mahoney said, taking the form, folding it, and putting it in a breast pocket. "Could I speak with the . . . director of records?"

"Herr Klauser, the curator. He may be very busy, sir. But if you would wait for just a moment, I will see."

Mahoney nodded as the young girl rose from behind her small desk and disappeared through the door at the back. The curator apparently was there, because Mahoney could hear the girl talking, although he could not make out the words. A man murmured something, she replied, and then she was back. She left the door partially open.

"This would be in reference to whom, sir?" she asked.

"His name is Robert Marshall. He is an Englishman. As I said, he would have attended school here in the twenties . . ."

The door opened the rest of the way, and an extremely old, wizened little man, half bent over, hobbled into view. He wore a dark suit the coat of which was cut in a very old, almost theatrical style, hanging halfway down to his knees.

The girl stepped aside. She was obviously very respectful and perhaps somewhat frightened of the man. "Herr Klauser . . ." she stammered.

"Who are you?" he snapped in German.

"Wallace Mahoney. I am a friend of Sidney Marshall. Sir Robert's wife."

Klauser eyed Mahoney for several moments. His gray hair was very thick, as were his eyebrows and mustache. Mahoney guessed him to be at least in his early to middle seventies. And perhaps even older.

He turned and went back into his office. "Come in, then," he growled.

Mahoney stepped around the desk. The girl was wide-eyed. She was frightened. And she was not very good at hiding it. He knew that he could get from her whatever it was, but the curator was waiting.

Klauser's office was large, and although it was filled with books, folios, maps, and what appeared to be trophies or mementos of some sort, it was exceedingly neat. Mahoney got the impression that every single item had its place and always remained exactly there.

"I am Franz Klauser. I am chief curator of records," the old man said from where he stood in front of his desk. "What do you want with Robert Marshall's records?"

"Sir Robert has been missing from his office in Brussels since a week ago Friday. I have been employed, on his wife's behalf, to find him."

"You are a private detective, then?"

"In a manner of speaking," Mahoney replied.

Klauser had not offered Mahoney a chair, but he went around behind his desk and motioned toward one now. When they were settled, he began filling a very old pipe.

"Evidently you are aware that Sir Robert is missing. You are familiar with his name," Mahoney said.

"I read the newspapers," Klauser snapped. Mahoney could not tell if the man was angry or if his brusque attitude was the norm. It was disconcerting.

"I thought I might find some information here about Sir Robert's past that might help my investigation."

"What sort of information?"

"Perhaps old friends. Perhaps there would be someone still around, someone who might have knowledge of his whereabouts."

"The newspapers mentioned kidnapping."

Mahoney shrugged. "It is possible he was kidnapped."

"But you do not believe it likely?"

Mahoney took his time answering. Something was going on here. He could see it in Klauser's eyes, in the way the curator held himself. He shook his head at length. "No, I do not believe it likely."

The door had been left open. Klauser looked up beyond Mahoney. "Motti," he called softly. A second later the young girl appeared at the doorway. Her eyes were wide behind her glasses. "No disturbances," he said. "Close the door."

Her hand shook as she closed the door. Mahoney turned back to the curator who had finished packing his pipe and had lit it. The smoke was very aromatic, but not sweet, such as some pipe tobaccos.

"How did you become aware that Robert Marshall attended this institution?" Klauser asked.

"The information was in his service record, of course."

"You are not from All Souls?"

Was there something in the morning's newspapers about Hall already? Mahoney hadn't seen anything at the airport that morning."

"No," he said. "But I understand Sir Robert taught there in the fifties."

"That is my understanding as well, Herr Mahoney. But it is still not quite clear in my mind exactly who you are."

"I am conducting my investigation on behalf of Lady Sidney Marshall. We are interested in returning her husband home."

"You are an American. A policeman? Are you perhaps with the Central Intelligence Agency?"

Mahoney sat back and stared at the old man. "Will you cooperate with me in my search, Herr Klauser? Or will I be forced into securing a court order to see Sir Robert's records?"

"I doubt that you would be successful," Klauser snapped, the nearest thing to a smile Mahoney had seen so far creasing the old man's face.

"Then you do not wish to cooperate with me," Mahoney said harshly.

Klauser spread out his hands. "Alas, my wishes mean nothing in the face of facts, although for certain I would not cooperate with someone such as yourself in any event."

"What do you mean?"

"Very simply, Herr Mahoney, Robert Marshall's records are no longer here."

The building had been very quiet all along, but Mahoney suddenly became aware of just how quiet it was. No noises penetrated from outside or from the outer office, and there wasn't even the ticking of a clock.

"His records have been moved? Perhaps to the new student record section?" Mahoney asked.

"I mean that his records are not here."

"Has someone stolen them? Is that what you are trying to tell me, Herr Klauser?"

The old man rose. He hobbled from behind his desk and went to the door as Mahoney got to his feet.

"Now, I have much work to do," Klauser said. He opened the door, then turned and went back to his desk. He did not bother looking up as Mahoney went out, closing the door behind him.

The secretary, whom Klauser had called Motti, was not at her desk. Mahoney went around the corner and looked down a flight of stairs.

"Motti," he called softly. But there was no answer. After a moment or two he went back into the anteroom, looked at the door into Klauser's office, then left the building.

There would be nothing to be gained here, he thought as he headed back into town. Klauser was not going to cooperate. The girl would remain out of sight, and breaking into the building at night and searching for Sir Robert's records—even if such a thing were feasible—would be inviting disaster. If he were arrested, he would be easy prey for whoever had killed Stanford Hall. His safety, at least for the time being, was in his constant movement.

He returned to his hotel where he took a quick shower, changed his clothes, then checked out. The clerk was apologetic, but he had to charge Mahoney a full night's lodging. Somehow he seemed to have the same attitude that Klauser and the girl had had. A slight fear. Something in the eyes.

His bag in hand, Mahoney left the hotel and walked to the parking garage, taking a roundabout route, doubling back on himself, suddenly stopping to look in shop windows, suddenly crossing the street, then stopping and looking to see if anyone followed. But by the time he got to his car he was reasonably certain that he wasn't being tailed, although he was beginning to wonder if he weren't getting somewhat paranoid, seeing dark, hidden, forbidding secrets behind every German's brow.

He cleared Heidelberg by 5:30, and by dark, driving very fast, almost recklessly, he had already passed Augsburg and was barely twenty miles outside of Munich, still certain that no one was behind him and yet almost as certain that no matter what happened he would not get any cooperation here.

At least not directly.

He spent the night in his room at the Pension Beck, a small, very inexpensive hotel in central Munich, after first finding a parking lot near the airport. In the morning he booked a Bad Reichenhall-Berchtesgaden tour that included entry to all attractions, lunch in the Bavarian Alps on the Austrian border, and return by four in the afternoon.

He boarded the sleek Mercedes bus in front of the American Express office on the Promenadeplatz, along with twenty other people, most of them older couples, many of them American or Japanese.

The bus driver, wearing a microphone on his chest, repeated everything three times—in German, English, and then French—as they slowly wound their way southeast from Munich.

They stopped often on the autobahn to see and

photograph the sites. Each time they did, Mahoney watched behind them to see who else pulled in. He was not being followed. And it bothered him to an extent. He understood that his tradecraft was rusty, but he also understood that even the best of legmen would sooner or later make a mistake, especially if the subject knew what to look for.

He kept to himself for the most part, and as much as possible—given his state of intense preoccupation—he tried to enjoy the magnificent scenery. This was the fairy-tale land of the Bavarian Alps. Of kings and trolls and maidens and castles. But nearly forty years ago he had come to this place at the close of the war, with a Russian intelligence officer. It seemed so very long ago, and yet the intervening time seemed like nothing, almost as if it had never happened, or had happened to someone else.

It was a measure of his career, he supposed. The time had passed and he had barely noted its passing. It was frightening, in a way, that he had never really stopped to enjoy his life. He had been too restless for it. He wondered if he weren't being sentimental, being an old fool for his regrets.

The best times, he decided, had been when John and Michael were little. Six or seven years old. When for them the world was a very fresh, brand-new place of discovery. Where around every bend in the road lay a brand-new adventure—the zoo, a movie, a trip to the ocean. Everything was discovery.

For Mahoney, almost everything was old. He'd been nearly everywhere. He'd personally experienced nearly every sort of perfidy; he'd been shot at, shot, and once even left for dead.

It was a pity, the thought came to him, to be so morose in the midst of such magnificent scenery. But forty years ago all the civilians—mostly peasant farmers —had been driven out of the immediate area of Berchtesgaden so that Hitler's people could maintain some sense of security. This was to have been the area of the famed National Redoubt where Hitler and his elite troops and scientists were to wage the final act of war: drawing the fighting out for years, until, it was hoped, the Americans finally gave up and went home. Then *der Führer* and his loyalists were to emerge from the mountains and exact their retribution with marvelous new weapons and an old resolve of the German peoples.

There was a bloodlust inherent in these mountains, it seemed. Plans for the conquest of the world were drawn up here. Lies were told not only to the outside, but to the German people themselves.

They passed through Bad Reichenhall, the driver promising his passengers that they would stop for lunch on the return from Berchtesgaden, which was barely ten miles farther to the south.

The Austrian border was very close here, the mountains very tall but heavily wooded at the lower elevations, a lot of snow higher up, starkly white against the dark evergreen forests.

It had clouded over, and there was a sharp chill in the air. It was snowing in the upper reaches to the south. In another month, perhaps less, these roads would become treacherous, their driver told them in three languages.

For now, however, he promised they were safe.

They turned off the highway they had been following onto a much narrower road that kept switching back on itself as it climbed. The driver had mentioned earlier that there would be a treat in store. It was what Mahoney had come for.

He had been here—exactly here—days after the war was over. He remembered now coming up in a convoy of jeeps. There were a lot of reporters and photographers from all the major newspapers and magazines, *Look* and *Life* included.

The mountain road eventually wound its way to the top of a flat ridge where the Berghof was located. It was Adolf Hitler's Bavarian retreat. Beyond it, farther up the twisting road, was the tunnel and the elevator, blocked then as now by massive bronze doors that rose 350 feet up to the Eagle's Nest itself. In the old days it contained nothing more than a reception room, a kitchen, and a glassed-in balcony. Mahoney had no idea what it contained now. And he didn't care.

A young woman guide was waiting for them in the parking lot of the Berghof when they descended from the bus, and in three languages she began chattering as she led the group off.

Mahoney angled off toward the back where he had spotted what appeared to be a caretaker's house through the woods on the way up.

He followed a flower-lined path around the side, then across a concrete patio. An old woman came out.

"*Entschuldigen*," she said. "Excuse me, *mein Herr,* but you are not supposed to be back here."

"Pardon me," Mahoney said in German. "But I was at this very spot once before, a very long time ago. I was just remembering."

The woman looked at him. She was short and rotund. Her white hair was done up in a bun, and she wore billowing skirts and a stiffly starched white apron. She looked as if she had just stepped out of a chamber of commerce advertisement.

"*Ja*, but now is different. You are here on the bus?"

Mahoney smiled. "I just wanted to see, that's all. I was here with friends."

"Everyone is gone. All gone," she said. She spoke loudly. Mahoney suspected she might be hard of hearing.

"It has been many years, *gnädige Frau*," Mahoney agreed. "It is just my memory. It brought me back. But then you were not here in those days. It means nothing to you."

The old woman puffed up. "I was here!" she snapped.

"During the war?" Mahoney asked eagerly. "I do

not remember you. In 'forty-five . . .''

Her lips pursed. "Not during the last year."

"But you came back. Ah, so, I understand. I suppose many come back."

"Oh, yes," she said. "There are a lot of them who come back to see. A lot of them, some from the old party . . ." She stopped.

Mahoney smiled and held up his hand. "It is all right. I understand. It is the very reason I have returned."

She looked suspiciously at him. "You are an American."

"Yes, now. But before the war . . . well, I was here with friends. British friends."

The woman's eyes widened.

"We weren't the enemy. Not really. We were friends, and still are. *Verstehen Sie, Freunden?*"

"What do you do here, like this? Go back to your group. I have work to do."

"I have something for him. For my friend," Mahoney said, staring directly into her eyes. She was very frightened. Just like Klauser had been. Someone had gotten to her.

"Go away!" she shouted, and she started to turn away.

"*Gnädige Frau*, I am trying merely to find my friend. I wish him no harm. I wish to help him. He is . . ."

She turned back to look at him.

Mahoney made a circular motion at his temple. "He is . . . sick. I would like to help him. His wife would certainly like to help him."

"I do not know what you are talking about!" the old woman shouted. "Now, go away! I will call the *Polizei!*"

"Sir Robert was here. You saw him!"

"Go away!" the old woman cried.

The bus driver came around the corner, below the patio, and called up. "There you are. It is time to go back."

✯ TWENTY-TWO ✯

Mahoney would forever remember this period as a time of discovery, although he was moving so fast that he hardly had time to catch his breath. One event seemed to pile on top of the next. One seemed to lead to the next. It seemed, he recalled, that he was being pursued along a dangerous, twisting path toward some end he knew was there but couldn't see, by some compelling force just beyond his ken. Of course he was light-years ahead of everyone else still running around back in Brussels. The media, in its typical fashion, had since relegated the disappearance of Sir Robert to the back pages or to the occasional update on the evening news. Nothing seemed to be happening, in their minds, to hasten his recovery. That was in the positive sense. Nothing seemed to be happening in the negative sense either. An important NATO general had disappeared. The world held its collective breath for a few short days, expecting . . . what? The worst? The end of the world? The nuclear holocaust? Some Red Brigade or Baader Meinhof demand? A snigger, perhaps, from a Qaddafi? Or a news conference by the general himself in Moscow? When nothing happened, everyone sighed in relief and turned his attention to more pressing, more urgent problems. *Nearly* everyone sighed in relief. *Nearly* everyone turned his attention elsewhere.

It was just four o'clock when the tour bus disgorged its passengers in front of the American Express office in Munich. Many of them stayed back to thank the driver, but Mahoney hurried off to find a cab, which he took to the offices of the *München Arbeiter Zeitung* on Prinzregentenstrasse. The newspaper, one of Munich's largest, was housed in a modern office building obviously built after the war.

A bronze casting of the globe flanked by brawny German workers, massive hammers held in their muscular paws, rose from the center of an otherwise pretty courtyard. The fountains at either side of a garden had been turned off for the season, but a lot of people strolled about or sat on stone benches.

Mahoney entered the main reception area through large double doors and approached the pretty young woman at the reception desk. He took off his hat. There was an air of hustle-bustle in the building even though it was a Sunday. A broad staircase curved from the center of the hall up to offices on the second floor. Two elevators were up there as well.

"May I be of assistance, sir?" the receptionist asked, looking up and smiling.

"I wish to do some research . . . of a private nature," Mahoney began diffidently.

The receptionist nodded her understanding. "Then you wish perhaps to see our clippings files?"

"I could begin with that, yes," Mahoney said uncertainly. "But I might also wish to see some actual back issues. Perhaps for the past year. No more."

The woman pointed across the main hall. "Issues going back three years would be in our reading room." She wrote out a pass. "You may remain in the library, where our clippings files are located, for as long as you wish," she said. "It is open twenty-four hours a day."

"Thank you," he said.

"Just up the stairs to the elevators, and then to the editorial department, which is on the fourth floor. You will be directed from there."

"Thank you," he said again, taking the pass. He turned, crossed the hall, climbed the stairs, and then took the elevator up to the fourth floor. Just through a set of glass doors, a young man with a pencil behind his ear sat behind a counter. Beyond him were the busy news offices.

The young man looked up from a piece of copy he had been editing. Mahoney handed him the pass.

"Just around the corner to your left," the young man said, glancing at the pass and then handing it back. He went back to his work.

Mahoney followed his directions and found himself in a long, narrow room that probably ran across the entire west side of the building, front to back. Except for an open area just within the doorway, it was seemingly filled with file cabinets, racks, and shelves, floor to ceiling, arranged in tight little rows like a library.

Two work tables had been set up in the open area, separated from the stacks by a short counter behind which sat a very old woman. Two much younger women, pushing roll-about carts loaded with files, worked in the back.

Mahoney approached the counter and handed across his pass. The old woman examined it a moment, then looked over the top of her glasses at him.

"I wish to conduct some research," he started.

She reached into a deep tray and pulled out several small pink slips of paper. "For each subject for which you wish to gain information, make out a request. Be very specific, *mein Herr*. Think of our filing procedures."

Mahoney took the slips back to one of the tables. He laid his coat and hat over one of the chairs, then sat down.

"Be very complete, also," the old woman said. The

two younger ones had stopped their work and were staring out at Mahoney.

It was very quiet here, except for a deep-throated,
almost subaudible rumbling that seemed to come from
within the bowels of the building. He suspected it was
press time, and he was hearing, or feeling, the gigantic
printing machines somewhere below.

On the first slip of paper he wrote Edward Juengst's
name. Munich lawyer. On the second, Thomas Langdon, British journalist, *London Daily Mail*. On the
third, Stanford Hall, professor of history, All Souls
College, Oxford University.

The old woman behind the counter was watching
him. A husky man, his sleeves rolled up, his tie loose,
no jacket, came in, dropped a couple of files on the
counter, glanced at Mahoney, then left. The old woman
rang a bell, and one of the young women from the back
came up, took the files, and went back to the stacks.

Mahoney wrote on another slip of paper: NATO,
military interventionism in Germany. Plans.

Finally, he wrote General Sir Robert Marshall's name
on a slip of paper. He started to print the word NATO
beneath it, but then he scratched that out and wrote
Friend of Germany instead. It was the only one he
wanted.

He got up and went back to the counter, and handed
the slips across. The old woman fanned them out and
picked them up one at a time with her left hand while
holding her glasses with her right. As she read each one,
she looked up at Mahoney as if to inquire about his lack
of intelligence, or his audacity to seek such information
here.

Mahoney watched her face very carefully as she read
each slip. When she came to the one with Sir Robert's
name, her eyebrows rose a fraction of an inch, and her
fingers tightened on her eyeglass frames.

She looked up, her eyes locked into Mahoney's, and
she rang the bell. A second later one of the young

women came to the counter.

"See to these, Katrina," the old woman said, handing the clerk all but the slip with Sir Robert's name.

The younger woman scurried back to the stacks.

"This file is presently in use, *mein Herr*."

"I see," Mahoney said. The air in the room seemed suddenly thin. "May I inquire as to who has the files?"

"Certainly," the woman said. She sat down and typed something on a keyboard.

Mahoney looked over the edge. It was a computer terminal.

The woman looked up a moment later. "Walther Mueller."

"Is he here today?" Mahoney asked respectfully. His heart was beginning to race.

The woman picked up a telephone and dialed three numbers. *"Ist Mueller hier?"* she asked. She looked up at Mahoney. "There is an American here who wishes to see the files on Robert Marshall. Mueller has them." Her hair was done up in a bun, and wisps of it had worked loose. "I will tell him. *Danke*," she said, and she hung up.

"Yes?" Mahoney asked.

"Unfortunately, Herr Mueller is not here. He has the files with him."

"Will he be back tomorrow?"

"They do not expect him for at least a week. Perhaps longer."

The young girl came back with one of the files he had requested. She laid it on the counter. The old woman glanced at it, then handed it to Mahoney. "You may not remove the file or any of its contents from the library, however . . ."

"That is not necessary," Mahoney said. "I was primarily interested in seeing the Robert Marshall clippings."

The woman's eyes seemed to bore into his. "You do not wish to see the other files, then?" she snapped.

"No. Thank you. Perhaps I will return to see Herr Mueller. But I thank you for your assistance."

He went back to the table where he got his coat and hat. Both young women and the older one were staring at him. When he reached the door he turned back.

"Pardon me," he said. "But about Herr Mueller . . ."

"Yes?" the old woman asked.

"What is his position here? What assignments does he cover?"

"He is our chief correspondent covering affairs of the German Democratic Republic."

Once again outside, Mahoney quickly left the entry courtyard and strode down the busy avenue, almost totally unmindful of his surroundings. Just at the back of his mind, just barely out of reach, was a tantalizing understanding of how all the pieces fit. His surprise was complete. He had thought, naturally, that by now in his life he was beyond such shocks. East Germany. Mueller was the newspaper's chief correspondent for East German affairs. He had Sir Robert's file. What did it mean? What in God's name did it mean?

Renelaux was convinced Sir Robert had defected. He had suggested East Germany among the possibilities.

Lady Sidney had worried about her husband's strange preoccupation over the past year. She called her husband an idealist. He was a seeker after causes.

But good Lord, he had the Genesis Plan. Had he brought it to East Germany with him? Was that where he was at this moment? In conference with military planners? Giving them the details of NATO's strategies?

Superficially it seemed a plausible explanation for the facts at hand. For *many* of the facts at hand.

The Libyans had been put onto Mahoney to throw him off, to lure him, if possible, to Tripoli where he would be assassinated along with al-'Usta. His contact in Libya, after all, had been a Russian. The weapon the young Arab in Brussels had carried was a KGB weapon of assassination.

Stanford Hall had been assassinated to keep Mahoney from learning about Sir Robert's German connections. The murder had come too late, but that simply had been a mistake on their part. Konstantin Demin, in Brussels? Had he masterminded this entire affair?

Sir Robert had apparently had a love affair with Germany since long before the war, a war that he ultimately came to feel was his fault.

Disturbed with the way Europe was headed toward almost certain nuclear disaster, especially in light of the new NATO contingency plans—the Genesis scenario—he had defected. To East Germany. The Russians, of course, would have become involved and perhaps unbeknownst to Sir Robert had begun covering his tracks.

It fit most of the facts. But not all of them.

What about the business on the tape about the fourteen-day deadline? What about Sir Robert's message to his wife? What about the British journalist's involvement in this business? But even more importantly, what about the attitude he had felt from Klauser in Heidelberg and from the old woman up at the Berghof? This was *West* Germany. If Sir Robert had defected to the East, why was his presence being felt here, on this side of the wall?

The anomaly was disturbing. And just now Mahoney began to feel, rather than know, that he was soon going to require help. This was going to get too big for him to handle alone.

Mahoney felt a certain sense of urgency as he crossed the busy broad street to a taxi rank, and he looked over his shoulder to see who was back there. There were many people, of course, but no one after him. The newspaper building was several blocks back, already out of sight. In his haste to get away he had not even bothered to watch in which direction he had walked. He had just left.

"The Hofbräuhaus," he told the cabby, and he sat back for the short ride over to the famed beer palace that could trace its history back to before 1600, although this building was less than a hundred years old.

More important, however, to Mahoney's inquiries at the moment was the fact that the Hofbräuhaus had been the seat of the German political psyche since after the First World War.

This was Hitler's old stomping grounds. All the party hacks had come here to quaff beer and scheme in the *Schwemme* (which literally meant trough), in the garden, or upstairs in the great *Festsaal*, or in the smaller rooms.

Military officers from the occupation forces met here after the war, and their presence gradually gave way to the Social Democrats, and the Greens and the other parties and factions that ruled, or wanted to rule, now.

The cab turned onto the Platzl, then pulled up in front of the great building, the huge curving sign on the front very famous.

Mahoney paid the cabby and entered the building, passing directly through to the garden. There were a lot of people seated at the outside tables despite the chill.

He picked the end chair at a long table at which several men and women were already seated. They looked up, smiled, and nodded toward the empty chair. A few moments later a heavy-chested waitress, carrying several one-liter steins of beer in each hand, came by.

"*Dunkles oder helles?*" she asked lustily.

"The light, *bitte schön*," Mahoney said, and she plunked down a big stein of the beer and was off.

Mahoney raised his stein in toast to the others at the table. "*Prosit,*" he said. The others returned his toast and then went back to their discussion.

For a time, he remained in the garden, drinking the

excellent beer and feeling the weight of the building around him. He could imagine that he heard the babble of a thousand voices plotting in the dark corners.

He remembered how it had been in Germany after the war. The country was shattered. There was little left of the people; even their will seemed to have been as completely wrecked as their buildings. But now, forty years later, Germany had once again become one of the most prosperous countries on earth.

He tried to listen to some of the conversations around him, but he couldn't get much. An occasional word, a scrap of a phrase, no more. Here were no dark secrets. Here were no plotters.

In the center of the garden was a fountain out of which rose the statue of the lion for which Löwenbräu got its name. Trees, starting to lose their leaves now, rose out of the garden toward the pretty blue sky. In the summer, he thought, this would be pleasant. At any time it was so . . . peaceful.

He finished his beer, paid, and left through one of the low arches. Instead of going out the front doors to the street, he turned left and meandered up the wide stairs to the second floor.

There were a few workmen doing something to the stage in the great hall. Row after row of long wooden tables had been set up, around each of which were sixteen chairs. Of course—this was the end of Oktoberfest time. Every night this place had been a madhouse.

He turned away from the Festsaal just as a buxom waitress, carrying at least a half-dozen steins of beer in each hand, entered one of the private rooms down the corridor.

There was no one else there at just that moment. He started down the corridor, the wooden floor creaking, the odor of tobacco and stale beer very strong.

He reached the doorway when it opened and the waitress stepped out. Mahoney caught a glimpse of a smoke-filled room, a large table around which at least a dozen men were seated, and a large stag head on the wall. Several of the men happened to look up and they caught Mahoney's eye. But the waitress closed the door.

"*Moment, bitte, Fräulein*," Mahoney said.

The waitress turned back. "*Frau*," she corrected. "May I help you with something, *mein Herr*?"

"I am looking for my friend."

"He was supposed to meet with you here today?"

"Not exactly today," Mahoney said.

"I don't understand, *mein Herr*," the waitress said. She was getting impatient.

"We've lost track over the years. But I know that he would have come here. Recently."

The woman shook her head. "Thousands come here every week, every night, *mein Herr*. One could not be expected to remember all of them."

"My friend would have been up here, in one of these rooms, meeting with Germans."

The woman's eyes narrowed. "Your friend is not a German?"

"No," Mahoney said. "He is an Englishman. Robert Marshall. A tall fellow. Mustache. White hair . . ."

"I am sorry, *mein Herr*, but there are too many people for me to remember one." She turned and scurried down the corridor.

Mahoney watched her go, then he shook his head and glanced at the door. It was half open. One of the men stood there, and the others around the table were looking up. None of them was smiling.

"I am sorry to have caused a disturbance," Mahoney said apologetically.

"May I help you, *mein Herr*?" the man in the doorway asked curtly. He was short, somewhat rotund, and very prosperous-looking in a gray, pinstriped, three-piece suit. Mahoney guessed him to be in his fifties. The others in the room were dressed similarly and were of about the same age. Bankers, perhaps. Lawyers.

"I am looking for a friend," Mahoney said.

"You are not German. American?" the man said with a hint of disdain in his voice. One of the men around the table got up and came to the door. He pulled it the rest of the way open.

"What is it, Otto?" the second man asked. He looked at Mahoney. "Who are you? What are you doing here?"

"He is an American," the first one said. "He is here looking for a friend."

"There are no Americans here," the second man snapped. He was completely bald. A heavy gold chain went from a buttonhole in his vest to his watch pocket. He had cruel eyes.

"My friend is British, actually," Mahoney said. "I don't expect he is here at this moment, but I suspect that he may have been here a week ago. I was hoping to find someone who might have seen him."

"There are no British here, either. This is not a place for foreigners. Do you understand?" the bald man said. He stepped out into the corridor. He was half a head shorter than Mahoney, but he was very powerfully built. He had a dark, drooping mustache, and the cords stood out on his thick neck. His tie was snugged up, but Mahoney could see that he had unbuttoned the collar button.

"Begging your pardon, but I suspect he was here," Mahoney said respectfully. He felt as if he were very near a high-tension wire. These men were hiding something, but Mahoney wanted to find out just how important it was to them.

"He is not here, do you understand that?"

"Marcus," someone from within the room called sharply. The bald man half turned but kept his eyes on Mahoney.

A third man came out into the corridor. He was much smaller than the bald-headed one, and his eyes did not seem so mean. He even managed a slight smile.

"Pardon me, *mein Herr*, but I do not think we can be

of any help to you. We know of no American or of any British person here in these rooms. Not today, at least not this week. Certainly not in my memory.''

''His name is Robert Marshall,'' Mahoney said. ''I'm sure he's been here often. He must have been.''

''I think you are mistaken, *mein Herr*. No one by that name has ever been here . . . to my knowledge. Perhaps you are confused—this is a big city.''

Mahoney started to protest, but the smaller man held him off.

''No. Now I think you must go downstairs, to the garden. I will send a beer down to you.''

Mahoney looked toward the room. ''Perhaps one of your friends inside might remember.''

''We are very busy just now, *mein Herr*. I would like to get back to my meeting,'' the smaller man said. He was losing his patience. He grabbed Mahoney's arm and tried to push him away.

Mahoney pulled out of the man's grasp and started to step around, when the bald man slammed his fist into his stomach. The air was driven out of Mahoney's lungs, the pain excruciating. He staggered backward, his hat falling to the floor.

The smaller man grabbed his arm again, or else he would have fallen. Some of the others came out into the corridor, and as Mahoney doubled over, his stomach heaving, spots before his eyes, he tried to focus on them. They all looked like bankers or chief executives of large companies. And they all looked very worried.

''That was stupid, Marcus,'' someone said.

''He would not go away!''

''He will call the police,'' someone from within the room offered.

''Let him. What does it matter now?'' the one who hit him replied. ''For all we know he is a fugitive himself. He has the look.''

Mahoney began to catch his breath, although there was a deep sickness inside of him. He felt as if he had been run over by a truck. He finally managed to straighten up.

"Are you all right?" the man holding his arm asked solicitously.

Mahoney nodded.

"Can you manage on your own?" the smaller man asked, releasing Mahoney's arm. He retrieved Mahoney's hat and handed it to him.

Mahoney nodded again, but he looked directly at the bald man. He managed to smile. "I will remember you . . . to my friend."

The bald man shook his head in disgust, then turned and pushed his way back into the room. Mahoney looked at the others.

"I will remember you all to Sir Robert," he said. He turned and, hat in hand, shuffled down the corridor to the stairs.

☆ TWENTY-THREE ☆

It was the same evening. Mahoney had retrieved his automobile from the parking garage near the airport, and then had shakily headed north past Regensburg up toward Nuremberg. As darkness fell, and Mahoney the elder tried to hold himself together long enough to find a safe refuge, Mahoney the younger held the telephone to his ear until he heard the tenth ring, and then he hung up.

Renelaux was gone. But it made no sense that even Madame Renelaux was not at home to answer their telephone.

John had checked into an inexpensive hotel the previous night. He had wanted an independence from Renelaux. And he had wanted to make it somewhat more difficult for the man to keep track of him.

Renelaux had not been overly happy by the switch, but he had not objected too loudly. John figured that his wife had begun to get tired of his presence in their apartment.

John had agreed to keep track of his father—who had disappeared again—and to keep in contact. But Renelaux had not checked in with his office at NATO this morning, and there hadn't been any answer at his apart-

ment near the Gare du Midi where John was calling
from a phone booth. He didn't know what he should do
now. Call Conwell? Telephone Langley, try to get word
through to the DCI?

He stepped out of the phone booth and walked out of
the busy railroad station.

The weather continued to hold, although it was very
cold. There was a lot of traffic for a Sunday night, but
then it was still early. Not yet eight o'clock.

John stuffed his hands deeply into his coat pockets
and strolled up toward the Rue de l'Argonne as he tried
to figure this out. Nothing was as it seemed to be. But
his father had intimated that this was normal for the
business.

It wasn't that John was particularly naïve, although
there was a certain charming touch of it in him; it was
simply that he was not used to the baser aspects of human nature. He would not have listened to moraliz-
ing, and neither would his father; no namby-pamby
preachers who said the road to salvation lay in the patient devotion to Sunday mornings—not for him—but
he was beginning to get a glimmer of what the real world
was all about. "Everyone screwing everyone else," one
of his instructors—or had it been one of the students?
—had told them. His father was worried about his own
back door and wanted Renelaux out of the picture.
Malcolm Conwell and even the DCI had gone along
with it. Renelaux, of course, was certain that Sir Robert
had defected. Probably to East Germany. He wanted to
use John's father as bait. As point man.

Meanwhile, everyone had disappeared on him, and
John was getting the feeling that he was being used, and
badly so. He was getting tired of it.

The Renelaux apartment was in a block of pleasant,
four-story stone buildings with iron gates out front.

John passed it once, on the opposite side of the
gloomy, tree-lined street, glancing up at the windows.
They were dark.

Around the corner he stepped into a narrow cul de sac where the Renelauxs kept their automobiles in a garage. He looked inside. Both the blue Opel and Madame's maroon Mercedes were there.

It was odd. He would have thought one of the cars would be gone if the Renelauxs were not at home. Something wasn't right.

He reached inside his coat and withdrew his pistol as he hurried back out of the cul de sac. He stopped in the shadows at the corner and studied the street in front of the Renelauxs' building.

There were several cars parked on both sides of the street. It was impossible to tell from here if there was someone in one of them. Someone watching. Waiting.

It made him very nervous now to think that he had blindly stumbled right past them all without ever once thinking to cover himself. Christ!

He pocketed the gun but kept his fingers curled around the grip. He started down the street, walking casually, glancing inside each car as he passed it. He was very jumpy now. His nerves were strung out. He had a bad feeling about this. Something had happened, and goddammit, he hadn't been ready for it.

Many apartments in the neighboring buildings on both sides of the street were lit up. Watch the roof line for a movement, he had been taught. Look in the back seats of each vehicle as well. Watch the apartment windows. A movement of a curtain. Or a curtain that seems to fall at an unnatural angle. You will develop in time, if you survive, a certain sixth sense. You will be able to smell a post.

At the end of the block he crossed over to the same side as the Renelauxs' building and started back. But there was nothing. Empty parked cars. Nothing else.

He went through the iron gate, mounted the steps, and pushed the button for the Renelauxs' apartment.

A tan Volkswagen van clattered noisily past, then turned at the end of the block.

John rang the buzzer again. In the distance, somewhere across the city, he heard a siren. Whether it was a police car, an ambulance, or a fire truck, he could not tell. But it was a lonely sound. He was a long way from home. He shivered.

He rang the bell for the apartment above the Renelauxs'. It was answered immediately.

"Yes, who is it?"

"Monsieur Renelaux's buzzer is not working. I must get in . . ."

The door lock buzzed, and John pushed through, crossed the vestibule, and took the stairs up two at a time.

The old man from the apartment above hung over the railing on the landing. "Tell them I will not tolerate the noise," he called down. He was angry.

John stopped and looked up. He could hear music playing.

"All day with the radio. It is driving us mad. We will call the manager. They do not answer."

"Oh, Christ," John swore under his breath. He wanted to bolt, but he held himself in check. "*Oui, monsieur.* I will inform them," he said instead.

"See that you do," the old man shouted, and he went back into his own apartment. John heard the door slam.

He pulled out his pistol and raced the rest of the way up to the Renelauxs' apartment, flattening himself against the wall to one side of the door.

He reached out and knocked on the door. The music from within was very loud. There had been no lights showing from any of the windows. Christ.

He knocked again, this time louder. Still there was no answer.

He was too late. He knew damned well he was too late. He pocketed the gun and put his shoulder to the door. The frame gave a little. He backed up and smashed his shoulder into the door with all of his strength. The frame gave way suddenly, spilling him inside the apartment.

The lights were off, but in the light from the corridor he could see that the place had been destroyed. He fumbled with his left hand for the light switch as he closed the door. The music was very loud, and there was an odd, metallic odor hanging in the air.

The lights came on, and his heart leaped into his throat.

Pierre Renelaux lay on his side, his left arm outflung, a trickle of blood down the side of his neck from behind his right ear, most of his forehead on the opposite side gone. He was dressed only in his bathrobe.

Beyond him, just at the narrow corridor that led back to the bedrooms, Madame Renelaux lay on her back, her nightgown hiked up to her thighs. She had been shot three times, once in the chest, once in the neck, and the third time in her right cheek. There was coagulated blood everywhere.

For a long time, his stomach heaving, John remained by the door, staring stupidly at the destruction. He kept seeing the cabin going up in flames; he kept visualizing what it must have been like for his wife and children.

Finally, though, he came out of it. This had happened hours ago. Perhaps this morning. He shut off the stereo, then went to the telephone and picked it up with his handkerchief. He dialed with the end of his pen.

The OD at embassy security answered.

"This is John Mahoney. It is urgent that I speak with Mr. Conwell."

"You're in luck, sir, Mr. Conwell just came in."

Conwell was on a moment later. He sounded breathless. "John? Where are you?"

"Pierre Renelaux and his wife have been murdered."

Mahoney arrived late in Nuremberg, and he spent the

night in a small hotel on the north side of the city, not too far from the airport. As he lay on his back on the bed, conscious of his body, of his heartbeat, of his breathing, and of the aching pain in his chest and stomach, he listened for the occasional truck passing on the highway. For that night at least, he would try to hold himself against jumping to any sort of a conclusion. It would not be so easy. There was such a preponderance of suggestions all pointing toward the same notion that it was difficult not to settle into the comfortable groove of firm belief. For a time, as he tried to sleep, he turned his own attitudes over in his mind. There was no good reason, no real reason, he supposed, for not letting the facts point to their own logical conclusions, except that he wanted the information to first bed itself more firmly at the back of his mind. He wanted to give whatever intuitive powers he had, a chance.

He woke early. His stomach and chest were very sore; a large, ugly-looking bruise had formed just below his solar plexus. He cleaned up in the bathroom at the end of the corridor, then checked out and drove immediately to the airport. He booked a seat on the next flight to Berlin, which was scheduled to leave at nine. It gave him an hour for coffee at the stand-up snack bar. He left his car in the long-term parking area, paying ten days in advance. The car would not be missed until then. It gave him time before any hue and cry arose.

Tegel Airport hit him all at once, like the flash of a jet directly overhead followed almost instantaneously by the tremendous thunderclap of sound. Airplanes, baggage-handling trucks, airport officials, and people seemed to be everywhere at once, each adding their decibels of sound to the general din. Since he had come in on an internal flight, there were no customs checks, so he was able to simply retrieve his bag and cross the madhouse terminal to the banking counter. He changed

the last of his American dollars and Belgian francs into
German marks, then went outside where he got into a
cab.

"*Guten Morgen,*" the cabby said with his very flat
Berliner accent as he pressed the meter button and
smoothly accelerated away from the curb.

It had been a long time since Mahoney had last been
in Berlin. He supposed there would be changes, and yet
the city had always seemed to him to be timeless in the
respect that no matter the age, the city was always in
some sort of political turmoil.

These days, as far as he understood it, one of Berlin's
chief problems was with its guest workers, as they were
called. Turks, Italians, and Yugoslavs were imported to
the city to work in the factories and to do the manual
labor that a lot of Germans were beginning to feel was
beneath them. They caused a lot of trouble.

Also, over the years there had been a steady drain of
young, educated people who felt the confines of Berlin
were too stifling.

The young people who had come into the city in their
stead were the malcontents, the misfits, the punkers
with their orange hair, the space-cadet girls in their aluminum pajamas, the young opportunists in their mini-
skirts and see-through blouses beneath which their sad
little breasts were plainly visible. Ever present, of
course, were the American soldiers, seemingly every second or third one of them wearing a cowboy hat.

"Is the Frühling am Zoo still there?" Mahoney
asked. It was a pleasant hotel he had stayed at some
years ago.

"Oh, yes, of course, *mein Herr*," the driver said,
glancing at Mahoney's image in the rearview mirror. "It
is on the Ku-damm. Very central."

"That will be fine, then," Mahoney said, settling
back.

They passed a highway project. A couple of dozen
dark-skinned men were working. Most of them were

probably Turks. A safety barrier of plywood had been erected, blocking part of the excavation. Someone had written a message on it with paint: *Lebe einzleln und frei, wie ein Baum, aber Brüderlich wie ein Wald.*

Mahoney sat back again. The bit of poetic graffiti at the construction site summed up what he knew of the Berlin spirit these days. It read simply, *Live alone and free, like a tree, but in the brotherhood of the forest.*

There wasn't much else, of course, that the Berliner could think. It was the only attitude possible to him that would make his life tenable.

They came down through a corner of Wedding and into the Tiergarten area. The wind had come up. It whipped tree branches, blew dust in long swirls, and from the looks of the graying sky, it was bringing something in with it from the northwest.

Kurfürstendamm—Berliners called it Ku-damm—was a broad avenue divided by a narrow, tree-lined median strip. It was busy with Monday noon traffic. They passed the zoo, which was on the west side of the Tiergarten itself, and the driver expertly wheeled around the block, coming up to the front entrance of the hotel.

"Hier ist das Frühling am Zoo," the driver said.

Mahoney reached over the seat with a hundred-mark bill. The driver started to make change from his leather purse.

"How long have you lived in Berlin?" Mahoney asked conversationally.

The driver looked up sharply. "Too long," he said. He counted out the change, but Mahoney refused it.

"Danke," the man said.

"You are a native?"

The driver laughed. "No, of course not. I am Austrian. I am going back to my home next week."

"You're leaving Berlin?"

The driver reached back and opened Mahoney's door from the inside. "Yes, naturally."

The remark was startling. "Why is that?"

The driver just looked at him blankly for a moment. "I am Austrian."

"Danke schön," Mahoney said at length, and he got out of the cab and went into the hotel.

He got a pleasant single with bath on the fifth floor overlooking the zoo. After the bellman had left, Mahoney rang for a sandwich and a pot of coffee, and while he waited for it to come up, he took a bath and changed into his last clean clothes.

His meal came, and he handed over his laundry to the room service clerk, who promised to have it back no later than six that evening.

The tray was set by the window, and Mahoney relaxed for a while as he ate, watching the strollers through the park, the animals in their cages, and the traffic on the Ku-damm.

Beyond the zoo was the Tiergarten, a lovely, large, sprawling park. The Reichstag was still there, beyond. It was an old, sad building. A reminder of the past. It was just in this area that the Reich Chancellery was located, beneath which was Hitler's bunker. He had been here, too, after the fighting had stopped. It made him shiver to think about it.

There was the other thing, just visible from his window if he looked closely. It was just beyond the Reichstag. Just across the Potsdamer Strasse. Something from which he averted his eyes. He was not ready for it at this exact moment. And he didn't want to see the thing from here, from this angle, from this distance.

He watched the people in the park bundled up against the wind, but enjoying their fleeting moments nonetheless, as he ate his sandwich and drank the very good coffee.

He figured he probably had a couple of cracked ribs, so he held himself very carefully as he left his hotel room, and out on the Ku-damm he began walking slowly toward the east, up past the zoo and into the Tiergarten. It was getting on to late afternoon, and traffic still had not slowed down on the broad avenue, nor had the flow of pedestrians seemed to have abated much. Berlin was a city very much alive, but already Mahoney was getting the impression that Berliners could be likened to people on a roller-coaster ride. The faster it went, the more they screamed and pleaded for it to stop. But the next time around they were not satisfied with the same ride, and they clamored for more—for bigger and better and faster. When they got it, when they were hurtling down the tracks, around the steep curve, over the precipice, they screamed and pleaded for it to stop.

Of course everything was different from the way it had been in 1945. Then the city was a rubble heap. Hardly an undamaged building stood anywhere within the city. But the Berlin of the 1930s before the war had come, had to have been vastly different from the plastic, mad roller-coaster ride of today's Berlin. For men such as Sir Robert, who had come to this city then, who had apparently loved Germany, this would be a travesty, a mockery, like spitting in church.

Mahoney walked up to the east-west avenue called Strasse Des 17 Juni. Before the end of the war it had been Chaussee Strasse. Then and now it ran through the Tiergarten, choked with traffic but with a hint of forests, and fields, and picnics, and another time on both sides.

Turning the corner onto the street, Mahoney was stopped in his tracks. His heart bumped, and there was suddenly a hollow, sick feeling at the pit of his stomach. For just a moment he knew that he was inside Sir Robert. For just an instant he was certain that he felt exactly what Sir Robert felt each time he came to this point.

Two blocks to the east, rising up out of a very busy traffic circle, was the top of the Brandenburg Gate, the four horsemen galloping away.

Below it was the obscenity that the East Germans
called the antifascist protective barrier. The death strip,
as it was known on the west side. The wall. The single
most important and clearest signal of the differences
between the East and West that had ever been devised
by the twisted mind of man. It divided not only a city,
but it separated an entire country, a people, from each
other. The horror stories of husbands trying to reach
wives, of brother cut off from brother, of mothers who
never again were to see their children were legion. More
than a hundred miles of concrete, barbed wire, electric
fences, floodlights, patrols, and vehicle traps had
transformed West Berlin from the capital city of a nation into an island surrounded by hostile, envious
people. The crime was that Berlin's enemies were Berliners on the other side of the wall.

Mahoney willed himself to move forward, past shops
already starting to put on their lights because of the
deepening overcast, past pedestrian traffic flowing
around him on the broad walk, past traffic on the street
heavier now that it was close to rush hour.

Beyond the wall was Unter den Linden, which had
been one of the prettiest streets in the world. But also
beyond the wall were places with names such as Ho-Chi-
Minh Strasse, Karl-Marx Allee, and Leninplatz. Hitler
had brought this down on his people. Forty years afterward the effects were even more terrible than they had
been at the very end of the war.

As he walked, Mahoney could well understand Sir
Robert's sense of outrage. Of betrayal. Of helplessness.
There was little doubt in Mahoney's mind that Sir
Robert had returned to Germany. Had been returning
to Germany for years now. If not here to West Germany, had he gone over to the East? But what was there
that was closer to his ideal of Germany? How was it
nearer the sense of the 1930s in the East than here?

Stanford Hall had said that Sir Robert hated the Russian presence as much as he hated the American occupation. It still made no sense, although Mahoney was convincing himself that Sir Robert had indeed gone to the East. Not only that, but the man had set up deadly roadblocks behind him against anyone who might try to follow. In Brussels with the Arabs through a friend who went by the name al-'Usta. In England by the assassination of Hall.

But if Marshall had gone to East Germany, what was he doing there? Had he turned the Genesis Plan over to the East German government? If that were the case, why hadn't they responded to the clear threat as Gaddis and Sir Howard Scott and everyone else in NATO expected them to? There were so many questions left unanswered. The really important questions were still to be discovered.

He crossed Potsdamer Strasse, and he was suddenly in the lee of the wall, the Brandenburg Gate rising above him.

There was no entrance here to the eastern sector. Checkpoint Charlie was around the corner to the southeast on Friedrich Strasse. There were others, but not here. Here was only the obscenity itself.

It was getting very cold. Mahoney hunched up his collar and turned finally to walk away, a dozen conflicting emotions rising inside of him from rage to sadness, from helplessness to fear, and from wonder at such an incredible folly to disgust at such Machiavellian madness.

An old man, thin, slightly stooped, stood on the corner, staring at the wall. His overcoat was dirty and threadbare, and his gray trousers were baggy and spattered with mud. He was hatless, his thinning white hair blowing in the breeze.

As Mahoney approached he could see that the man had been crying. Around him traffic flowed, mindless of the wall, mindless of what lay beyond it, mindless of what it represented. This one, however, was the exception.

"It is terrible," Mahoney said, approaching him.

The man looked up. His eyes narrowed. But then he nodded. "Yes, it is. But no less understandable."

"You were here before the wall?"

"Yes, for a very long time before this thing," the man said. "I have been here. I have seen it all." Broken veins crisscrossed his thin, lined face. He had done a lot of drinking for a lot of years. "We built this, you know. We Germans." He stared again at the wall and then up at the horsemen atop the gate. "Brick by brick we put it up. Those of us on the west as well as the others . . ."

"You worked on the wall?" Mahoney asked.

"No, of course not," the man spat. "But I allowed it. We all did." The expression on his face was intense. "It must come down, it must, before it is too late."

"It may already be too late, my friend."

"No, no," the man said, stepping back as if Mahoney were the devil.

☆ TWENTY-FOUR ☆

Le Sex Shoppe was farther out on the Ku-damm, in what was described by the habitués as the racy end of the strip. It was late Tuesday afternoon when Mahoney showed up, nearly twenty-four hours since his disturbing visit to the Brandenburg Gate.

That evening, using several cut outs on foot, by cab, and even by bus, he had made his way over to the Schweitzer Hof Hotel on Budapesterstrasse, where he made two telephone calls to the same number back in the States: the first from the lobby shortly before eight; and the second an hour and a half later from a phone in the hotel's luxurious fitness rooms. He had worked hard all that evening to hold himself in check, to hold his excitement to a manageable level. But each time he thought of it, each time he contemplated the one thing that could not be, the one notion that was nearly outside the realm of reason—and yet the one idea that seemed to fit all of the facts—he felt his blood sing, and he knew that he was close. He had risen early that morning, and after a leisurely breakfast at his hotel, he bundled up and took a tour of the famous zoo. After lunch he walked back up to the wall and followed it as far as Checkpoint Charlie, where he stood for more

than an hour, watching the traffic crawl through the
barriers, the East German soldiers surrounding each
automobile, opening its trunk, checking under, around,
and within every compartment with dogs presumably
trained to sniff out explosives and with electronic devices presumably scanning for weapons or perhaps for
radio transmitting devices. He had had a short, fitful
nap in his room in the afternoon, after which he had an
early and meager supper.

Le Sex Shoppe, judging from its display in the window, dealt in everything from crotchless women's
panties to erotic books, magazines, and devices . . .
guaranteed to increase your pleasure. But there was no
or your money back.

Just inside was a small vestibule furnished with only a
tiny desk behind which sat a tired-looking woman in a
very scanty costume. A door led to the back. The walls
were adorned with a number of enlarged, full-color
photographs of good-looking young men and women
engaged in various sexual activities.

The woman behind the desk looked up and smiled.
"Good evening, *mein Herr*. Have you visited with us
before?"

"No," Mahoney said.

"There will be a twenty-five-mark deposit that will be
applied to anything you should purchase inside. Of
course, should you merely have come to browse this
evening, the deposit is nonrefundable."

"Yes, I understand," Mahoney said. He paid his
deposit and went through the door at the back.

It was dark in the narrow corridor. Black lights il-
luminated garish paintings on the wall and legends at
doorways. Iron circular stairs led up to a balcony as well
as down to the basement.

A good-looking young woman wearing nothing but
the scanty top of a see-through nightie approached.
"Good evening, *mein Herr*. Was there something special you were interested in?"

"Yes, I have come to see a friend."

"Your name, *mein Herr*?"

"Buhle." Mahoney used the cover name Bindrich had given him.

"Of course, *mein Herr*. Just down the stairs and straight back," the woman said, and she turned and disappeared into the shadows.

Mahoney made his way down the stairs, and then along a very dark corridor to a steel fire door. He knocked.

It was opened a moment later by a man Mahoney guessed to be in his late forties, with a red face, thinning fair hair, and round, surprised eyes. He was dressed very well in an expensive-looking Italian silk suit.

"Any trouble getting here?" he asked. His accent was California.

"None," Mahoney said, stepping into a dimly lit corridor, the twin of the outer one. The door closed and locked behind him.

"Felix Salmon," the red-faced man said, sticking out his hand. Mahoney shook it.

"You're chief of base here in Berlin, I presume?"

"You got it. And I don't mind telling you, Mahoney, that you've shook up Bonn. The chief of station threatened to have my ass if this wasn't pulled off without a hitch. And I do mean without a hitch. Pressure from on high. You know how it is."

Salmon led Mahoney along the corridor through another steel door and finally up a flight of stairs. Mahoney figured they were at the rear of the building. The door at the top opened into an alley, confirming his suspicion. A dark gray Mercedes was parked there.

"We've got a place set up for you down near Zehelendorf, on the Grosser Wannsee."

"How about my hotel?" Mahoney asked, climbing into the passenger side. Salmon got in behind the wheel.

"You've already checked out," Salmon said. He

hesitated a moment. "Look, can I call you Walt, or something?"

"Wallace."

"Sure thing," Salmon said. He started the car and they pulled out of the alley and turned right on the Kurfürstendamm, merging smoothly with traffic. "We got your description and sent one of our boys over to get your things and pay your bill. He's damned good. A local thespian at the Schiller. Likes this sort of gig now and then. Of course they're half blind at the Frühling. Piece of cake."

"Have you been told what I need?"

Salmon kept his eyes on the road. Traffic was heavy just here. "Sure," he said. "You want to go over. You need a background. It's simple, but . . ."

"But what?"

Salmon glanced at him. He shook his head. "They tell me things, Wallace, and they don't tell me other things. I just follow orders, for the most part."

"What the hell does that mean?"

"Don't get testy on me. I got the call on you early this morning, and I do mean early. So I set up the meet, got the safe house ready, and arranged your checking out. Beyond that I was told to hold everything."

"Who else will be there?"

Salmon shrugged. "Don't know. I was told to expect some company."

"Right," Mahoney said dryly. This was the twenty-fifth. Sir Robert had been missing for a full eleven days. Each hour that passed made it that much more difficult to unravel this business. Each delay was one more added difficulty. Still, he could not do it alone. Not from this point. Which meant he had to play by their rules. At least for the moment.

They passed Halensee, then through Wilmersdorf into the Grunewald forest, and finally Zehelendorf, which during the final months of the war had housed many of the German High Command's functions. Many of the officers had been moved down here to escape the heavier concentrations of bombing raids in the city proper.

The overcast had deepened since yesterday afternoon, and already it was getting dark. They turned off the Avus, went a quarter of a mile along a residential street, then went along a beach resort area, turning a half mile farther onto a gravel road, the trees close on both sides, the darkness even deeper there.

It was a large house, three stories, dormers and gables, a half-dozen chimneys rising above the roof line. Mahoney spotted it through the trees, and then they came up the long driveway and stopped in front.

"What is this place?" Mahoney asked.

"We call it the Sugar Shack. It's sometimes used for visiting VIPs who want to get away from it all. One of the Nazi High Command generals owned the place. Spoils of war."

Mahoney got out of the car and sniffed the cold air. He could smell the pines and woodsmoke from at least one of the chimneys. Here in this place, in the area surrounding Berlin, the war did not seem forty years ago. For a long, still moment, as the CIA chief of Berlin base got out of the car and came around, Mahoney wondered if Sir Robert had found a place such as this where time seemed to have stopped. Where it was easy to imagine you were back in 1930 or 1940.

"Just inside, Wallace. They're waiting for you, I suspect."

"Right," Mahoney said. He preceded Salmon up the walk, and they entered the house.

They were met in the stairhall by a tall but dumpy-looking man with a thick shock of very black, wavy hair. Mahoney figured him to be in his mid-thirties. He had a feral look about him that was somewhat disquieting.

"They're waiting in the study," he said.

"Everyone's showed up?" Salmon asked.

The younger man's eyebrows rose. "Yes. *Everyone*."

"Like you to meet Fred Trailer, one of the best legmen in Europe. Wallace Mahoney."

Mahoney and Trailer shook hands.

"Bob is on the road," Trailer said to Salmon. He pulled his jacket back to reveal a walkie-talkie on his belt.

"Bob Poole is probably tied for the best field man in Europe," Salmon explained. He motioned Mahoney toward the stairs, and they went up.

At the top they turned to the right, and a familiar figure loomed out of the darkness at the end of the corridor. Mahoney was taken aback for a moment.

"Good evening, sir," Don Page said.

Mahoney's eyes went to the study door and then back. "You've been reassigned?"

"No, sir."

"I see."

Salmon was grinning. "I don't mind telling you, I was damned surprised myself. Isn't often we get a visit from the DCI himself. And especially not under cover."

Mahoney left his hat and coat in the corridor, and he and Salmon went inside.

Sylvan Bindrich, looking definitely worried, sat in an armchair. Malcolm Conwell sat on the couch across from him, the same worried look on his face, and John was at the fireplace, poking the burning logs. He turned.

"Hello, Dad."

"The night is full of surprises," Mahoney said.

Salmon closed and locked the door behind them.

"I hope not too many more," Bindrich said. He rose and Mahoney crossed the room to him. They shook hands. "How are you holding up?"

"Fine for now," Mahoney said. He glanced at Conwell and nodded his greeting.

The study was large. Heavy floor-to-ceiling drapes

along one wall concealed what Mahoney figured were probably French doors leading out to a balcony. There were some books, but not many. A few trophies on the wall. Some photographs of heavyset men in Lederhosen in the mountains. A desk, and the usual grouping of furniture. The fireplace was going well, and the room smelled pleasantly of woodsmoke without a closed-in, stuffy feeling.

They all sat down, and while Salmon poured them coffee and schnapps, Bindrich inquired about Mahoney's health and about his plans for afterward.

Mahoney distinctly remembered his previous impression that Bindrich was in over his head as DCI being strongly reinforced at that moment. No one thing or comment pointed to it. A gesture, a movement of a hand, a raising of an eyebrow, a jutting out of the lower lip. Together, however, they presented a not so subtle picture of a man strung out.

Conwell seemed worried, too. Salmon seemed surprised, and John was definitely eager, though worried, like a young puppy might be with his first scent of a wild pheasant in the field.

Don Page was no field man, but he was a steady hand, and Trailer and Poole were unknowns. Perhaps they were as good as Salmon claimed. But Mahoney doubted if they could match the pair he had once worked with.

When they were all settled, Mahoney in another easy chair, Salmon perched on the opposite end of the couch from Conwell, who had primly crossed his legs, Bindrich nodded. John remained by the fireplace.

"Needless to say, your telephone calls were extraordinary."

"Especially in light of recent happenings," Conwell added.

Mahoney turned in his seat so fast he nearly fell out of the chair. "What happenings?" he snapped.

"Take it easy, Wallace," Bindrich said. "We're all

convinced now that there is something more to this than meets the eye. Your instincts may have been right all along.''

"You had disappeared," Conwell said. "There was no way to contact you."

"Renelaux and his wife are dead," John broke in.

Mahoney turned to his son. "When?" he asked tersely.

"Sometime on Sunday. They were both shot to death.''

"What sort of a weapon was it? Has it been determined?''

"A large caliber. Probably the Russian handgun," Conwell said.

"Was their apartment searched?" Mahoney asked.

"Yes . . . yes, it was, Dad."

"But it wasn't Demin's people," Conwell hastened to add. "We've had a constant watch on them. It was not they who were responsible, otherwise I would already have nailed the bastards.''

"I didn't think it would be," Mahoney said thoughtfully. "I think you'll find it was Thomas Langdon."

"The newspaperman?" Conwell asked.

Mahoney nodded. Another piece of the puzzle had been dropped into place for him. As disturbing as the news was, it had not been out of context.

"Well, now," Bindrich said. "We're all here. You owe us an explanation for the charges you've made."

Knowing a fact, and being able to do something worthwhile about it, were two different things, Mahoney thought. And yet the knowing, in this business, usually precipitated the action. Several days ago he had still contemplated turning his head and walking away from the affair. But not now.

He looked up. "Sir Robert Marshall was not kidnapped. At this moment, however, he is somewhere in East Germany.''

"You said that on the telephone," Bindrich said.

"Has he the NATO Genesis Plan with him? That is what's important here."

"Yes."

"And Langdon is working for him? Covering his trail?" Conwell asked.

"Yes."

"That tears it."

"He's sold out to the East Germans. Goddammit, is that it, then?" Bindrich asked. He ran a hand across his eyes. "What's to be done?"

Mahoney shook his head. He looked up at his son whose eyes had gone wide. John knew. Or at least he was guessing on the right track.

"Sir Robert hasn't defected to the East Germans," he said.

"To the Russians, then. What does it matter?" Bindrich snapped.

"Not to the Russians."

Bindrich looked at him. "What the hell are you trying to tell us now, Wallace? He wasn't kidnapped. Did he defect or didn't he?"

"He wasn't kidnapped, and he did not defect."

Bindrich was clearly exasperated. "I did not come all this way—and you cannot imagine how difficult it was —to be led around in circles. You have something to say to us, and evidently you have something in mind, otherwise you would not have telephoned me with wild stories about the collapse of the EEC—and all of Europe, for that matter. We're here, Wallace. Talk to us."

Mahoney took time to light a cigar, using the delay to order his thoughts, to figure out what exactly he was going to say, and in such a manner that he'd be understood and believed.

"Sir Robert Marshall is and always has been a man of principles," he started weakly. "A seeker after causes. I assume you've all read the file . . ."

Bindrich and the others nodded.

"He is a man of high emotions that seem not to have been tempered either with age or by his experiences."

"It's called the Peter Pan syndrome," John said.

"What?"

"It happens to a lot of men. They never grow up. They're always out there looking for a new adventure."

Was it that simple? Mahoney wondered. Perhaps, but he doubted it. Sir Robert was anything but a simple man.

"It actually began fifty years ago," Mahoney said.

"Spare us a history lesson . . ." Bindrich said, but Mahoney ignored him.

"He came from a privileged family. Money. Tradition. God, king, and country—in that order. And a military background that his father wanted augmented in his son."

The student Robert was sent to Heidelberg to study at the university, to hobnob with Germans. Hopefully some of the Prussian military spirit—the way of thinking, the carriage and bearing, the tradition and discipline—would merge with his own careful, British upbringing.

"Why not the Prussian military academies, then?" Bindrich asked.

"Not for foreigners, and they wanted him to absorb some of the tradition; they did not want him to become a part of the German officer corps."

And it worked, of course. But in a somewhat different fashion than anyone thought it might. Robert very simply fell in love with Germany. He was young, impressionable, and very much in love with the idea of the underdog rising. And Germany is beautiful. Her mountains, her lakes and rivers. And her politics were exciting.

He had to return home eventually to complete his schooling. It was expected of him. But the damage had been done. Beyond everything else, though, Robert was and is an honorable man.

He made a wonderful soldier. He had the correct name, the right connections, he married the perfect woman for his position, and he had the proper schooling. But all the while there was this love for a nation, for a people other than his own. *Gemütlichkeit*, which can't really be translated into another language, was a concept that the young Robert Marshall took completely to his heart.

"There is none of that on his service record," Conwell said. "He was no traitor. He fought the Nazis, and he distinguished himself doing it."

Mahoney held himself from making a snap comment. He felt as if he were a choirmaster leading his group through a particularly difficult passage. In time they'd come to understand the uniqueness of the whole. But first came the individual notes.

"While in Germany, he learned the language from top to bottom. The *Hochdeutsch* of the university as well as the *Plattdeutsch* and *Schwäbisch* and *Bayerisch* of the hinterlands. He was all over the country. He knew the people."

"He was also schooled in England. Even taught at Oxford, from what I understand," Bindrich said.

"Yes, that too, but you have to know his spirit, his will, Germanic if you will, before you can understand what comes next," Mahoney said. He leaned forward slightly. "And it's not too far separated, you know, the British and the German spirits. The Scots don't like to admit it, but the bagpipe, after all, was a German instrument long before the clans took it up."

The student Robert came first. Later the young soldier-cum-statesman Robert was sent back to Germany during the thirties to scout out the mood of the people. To see about this business of National Socialism and the Austrian Adolf Hitler. Whitehall used him as a valuable source. His superiors understood that in Robert Marshall was a man who could perfectly understand what was happening in Germany far beyond a mere proficiency of language. He could feel the people.

"He spoke with Hitler. On many occasions. In Munich in the early days. Then at the Berghof and the Eagle's Nest. He tried to convince the man that Germany had a place in European politics; Germany could be the unifier of all Europe. The great buffer between the West and the Soviet presence to the east."

"Everyone was scared silly of Stalin," Bindrich said. "Though there weren't many who'd admit to it."

"It was then that Sir Robert suffered his greatest defeat, his worst embarrassment, the most difficult time in his life," Mahoney said.

Hitler's troops overran the Polish border. The war had begun, and Sir Robert was devastated. Now he had to fight the very people he loved.

"He was a Nazi after all?" Salmon, who had not seen any of the files and who was playing this simply by ear, asked.

"No, of course not," Mahoney replied. "He always has had a much wider view than that. Germany could have had a place in the leadership of all of Europe. Her place was there at the head of a common European government. National Socialism, killing Jews, and even the war itself were all preventable, in Sir Robert's mind. Hateful travesties born of the Versailles Treaty that had hamstrung Germany."

"So he fought Germans," Conwell said. "Is he still fighting them? Was his thinking altered?"

"On the contrary; his position was solidified. After the war, he taught at All Souls. I spoke with a colleague of his, a man who was a young historian at the time, who advanced the notion that Sir Robert decided the war was his fault. He had not been able to talk Hitler into a course of politics instead."

Conwell started to laugh, but then something else crossed his mind, and a startled look came into his face. "My God. You were there, at Oxford?"

"Friday night."

"What is it?" Bindrich demanded, alarmed.

Conwell turned to the DCI. "An All Souls College professor of history was murdered . . . on Friday. He turned back to Mahoney. "Stanford Hall?"

Mahoney nodded. "I was there when it happened. He went to answer the doorbell and was shot to death. I never saw the man or men, but I heard a car take off."

Conwell started to get up, but Bindrich waved him back. "Sit down, Malcolm. There's more."

"There's more," Mahoney agreed. A lot more.

Conwell sat back. He was clearly unhappy. "Are you saying that Langdon killed Stanford Hall, and then killed Pierre Renelaux and his wife?"

"He may have been responsible," Mahoney said. "He also has a link with the Brussels metro police. You should know that. His contact is a homicide sergeant, Jean Rubaix."

Again a startled look crossed Conwell's features. "Renelaux had contact with Rubaix."

"The common denominator," Mahoney said.

"That means all of NATO was at his feet."

"Certain aspects of the Alliance. Day-to-day security arrangements, for one."

"With Oliver Horne?"

"Rubaix had contact with Horne."

"But why?" Conwell asked. "What was there for him to gain by killing a history professor? And why Renelaux and his wife?"

"Stanford Hall was murdered in an attempt to prevent him from doing what he had already done. Namely tell me about Sir Robert's love for Germany, and his notion that the war had been his fault."

"And Renelaux and his wife?"

"I can answer that," John said. They all turned to him. "Pierre was convinced that Sir Robert had defected to the East. Specifically East Germany. If my father is correct, and if Sir Robert is in East Germany at this moment—for whatever purpose—then Pierre

Renelaux was coming uncomfortably close to the truth.
Madame Renelaux was just there when it happened. She
got in the way.''

"We're trying to run down not only a defector, but
we're also hunting a murderer," Bindrich said heavily.
"The East Germans have to be in on it. They must have
arranged all of this.''

"I think not," Mahoney said.

"No?"

"In fact, I think the East German government either
does not know the full extent of Sir Robert's plan, or
they are at a loss as to what to do about it.''

"But you do know?" Bindrich asked.

Mahoney nodded. "I believe so."

✴ TWENTY-FIVE ✴

To this point Mahoney had not touched his coffee, and he violently disliked schnapps. His cigar had gone out, and just now he felt very stiff and old. He reached for his coffee, but Salmon was up and scooped the cup away from him.

"I'll just warm it up, sir."

"Don't bother," Mahoney said. He really hadn't wanted the coffee in the first place.

"What's your pleasure? German beer? Cognac?"

"Kentucky sour mash whiskey," Bindrich said.

A slow grin spread across Salmon's face. "I think that can be managed. How do you like it? Soda? Water?"

"Straight up, no ice," Mahoney said.

Salmon put the cup on a sideboard and scurried out of the study, leaving Conwell, Bindrich, and John all staring after him. "What's gotten into him?" John asked.

"He smells field work," Conwell said. "I've known him for several years. He likes the outdoors."

They were silent then for a minute or so. Mahoney listened to the sounds of the house. Music was playing from somewhere, perhaps from a television set. As far as he knew, however, the only others in the house were Don Page out in the corridor and Salmon's man, Fred Trailer, downstairs. He could also hear the rising wind outside. It sounded cold. It certainly sounded lonely.

"Where does that leave us, then?" Bindrich asked, bringing them back to what was at hand.

Mahoney had been thinking about another aspect that could be attended to. Conwell would be the one for it. Insurance? he wondered. Or would it merely compound an already incredible risk?

It was, in part, the contacts Sir Robert made while he was at Oxford that led Mahoney to his conclusion. He held a number of seminars on modern history and military interventionism with Rhodes scholars, many of whom were Germans. The cream of the crop, so to speak.

It was there that he developed his idea that the war had been his fault. That had he had more . . . charisma (Mahoney stumbled over the word now, as he had before) he would have been able to do a better job convincing Hitler to take the more moderate course.

"My God, what conceit," Conwell said, naming the one failing that Mahoney had attributed to the Brussels chief of station.

"Not so much a conceit as a genuinely held belief," Mahoney said. "He knew Germany, understand, and he knew Hitler . . . who was, after all, nothing more than a lowborn Austrian."

"But with magnetism," Conwell said.

"Indeed. With a terribleness of purpose. Sir Robert felt that had he been stronger he could have swayed the man. He did not, and the war resulted."

"He taught that pap?" Conwell asked.

Mahoney wanted to slap him down. But again he held himself in check for the more moderate course. It was the night for moderation. Bindrich could read his frustration.

"What about afterward, Wallace? There still is a lot of territory to cover. A lot of years," the DCI asked reasonably.

Afterward came his overseas postings, including the British embassy in Bonn as senior military liaison to the budding German military forces. Then came the business with Edward Juengst's KgU, which led to the Munich lawyer's death.

Until that moment, Sir Robert had been definitely very much involved in the German political scene. He had known and hated Reinhard Gehlen. But he had had a respect for Juengst.

"Both men were trying to pierce the terrible border that had been placed between two halves of a once proud whole. Gehlen was working for a new master, of course, but Juengst was serving the people. Gehlen was self-serving. During the war he wore a Nazi uniform and spied on the Soviet Union. Afterward he worked for the Americans, still spying on the Russians. Gehlen gave a damn for nothing, I suspect, other than his own survival. Juengst, on the other hand, was such an idealist that he couldn't possibly understand the mechanism for his own survival. All he could see was the wall—and the chance to help people over it."

"It's a wonder our boy didn't emigrate and become a German politician," Conwell said.

"He's not a leader himself . . . He's a . . . kingmaker," Mahoney said softly.

Bindrich started to say something, but Salmon came in at that moment, bearing a tray with a bottle of cognac as well as a bottle of Kentucky whiskey, and several glasses.

He stopped, conscious that something significant had just happened.

"Well," he said.

"Just get on with it, Felix," Bindrich said.

Salmon did as he was told. He poured them each a

drink and handed them around. Mahoney sipped his. The whiskey was passable.

After Juengst was found shot to death in his car beside the autobahn on his way to see Sir Robert in Bonn, it began to get complicated. At least it did for Sir Robert, who had been affected by the presence of the wall to such an extent that it became an almost debilitating affliction. He was recalled to London for a time, then was sent to Paris with NATO . . . as a tactical strategist on the staff of the Supreme Allied Commander, Europe. Afterward, when NATO headquarters was moved to Belgium, he followed along and did the same thing. But then he took his retirement and moved to head up the Nuclear Defense Affairs Committee.

"Then one day he walked off with the Genesis Plan," Conwell said. "You tell us he's gone across the border, but *not* to sell his secrets. What, then?"

"The Genesis files may just very well be happenstance," Mahoney said.

"I don't know if I can buy that, Wallace," Bindrich put in. "It has everyone upset, to say the least. It's the only reason the President agreed to wait on . . . the other matter."

Salmon was duly impressed. Conwell and John already knew about the recall.

They had, however, finally come to the point where Mahoney figured he could make his pitch. They would either believe him or they would not. In the old days, he supposed, he wouldn't have given a damn if they believed him. He had had, in many ways, a cavalier attitude about life around him that didn't always entirely square with his actions. His wife used to tell him that he was her mixed-up old man. Gray hair, varicose veins, and no clear idea, sometimes, of who or what he was after. A Don Quixote chasing after windmills. It was the same comparison he had used in trying to classify Sir Robert.

He took another drink of the whiskey and held his glass out for more. Salmon was quick to pour him a second.

Over the past days—hadn't it been months? years?—Mahoney had thought and rethought what he would say if and when he got to this point. *He just said good-bye. It was odd. He might've said, "Have a good weekend, Maggie." Or perhaps, "Don't be an old nag." Something like that. Not "Good-bye." Robert sends his love. He is safe and well. Sir Robert-the-Jerk.*

Sir Robert the revanchist? The re-gatherer of territory lost to an enemy? The unifier?

For a terribly long time Mahoney held his thoughts in stasis. Or rather he held that single concept motionless, while around it he let the facts that had led him to it revolve, just as the liquor in his glass revolved as he swirled it.

They were waiting for him. He looked up.

"Consider eight separate incidents," he began.

"No more history," Conwell groaned.

"This is recent history," Mahoney said. "Beginning with a murdered Arab in Brussels last week."

Conwell sat up.

"I was followed from NATO by four men in a gray Mercedes. Arabs. I managed to cut one of them out and confront him. There was an accident as I was questioning him. But I established two things: one, that he was most likely a Libyan; and two, he was carrying a Graz Buyra, wanting to make us think he was working for the Russians."

"Holy shit," Salmon said.

"Meanwhile, Sir Howard receives a tape telling us that Sir Robert is alive and well. The tape comes from an Arab. A Libyan. And over the past few months Sir Robert supposedly met with an Arab gentleman by the name of al-'Usta."

Bindrich knew the next part.

"I went to Tripoli, of course, where al-'Usta—not the one Sir Robert met with—was killed in an assassination that was also meant for me . . . but me as an American banker, a hated capitalist. Set up by Langdon."

"Langdon?" Conwell asked. "How?"

"I don't know how, but I do know why. The Libyans at the moment are our bogeymen. Tell someone from the CIA that Qaddafi is in on a plot, and you have a believer. Send that American into Libya, and three-fourths of the country wants to take a potshot at you."

John nodded. "That's one."

"Two. Lady Sidney receives a telephone call—that she fails to record for the SIS—from a man claiming that her husband sends his love and that he is all right. He speaks in English but has a German accent. Oxford English, perhaps."

This was obviously news to Conwell. John looked guilty. He or Renelaux had not told the chief of Brussels station about the intercepted telephone call.

"Three. I've already given you what information Hall passed on to me. He was killed in an attempt to prevent him from talking. But it was a German connection again."

"Then you came here to Berlin, on Saturday."

"Heidelberg. I wanted to see Sir Robert's student records. They were gone. In Berchtesgaden I went up to the Berghof as an ordinary tourist—a fishing expedition, actually, because I had no real idea what I might find—but I bumped into the same vague fear in the caretaker there that I had seen in the eyes of the university people in Heidelberg. My guess is that he was there, at both places, and recently."

"That was four and five," John said.

"In Munich I went to one of the major daily newspapers where I asked to see the clippings file, if there was one, on General Sir Robert Marshall. The file had already been checked out."

"Who had it?" John asked.

"The newspaper's chief correspondent for East Germany."

"Christ," Salmon said softly.

"Seven. I went to the Hofbräuhaus next, where I was beat up."

"For what, in God's name?" Conwell asked.

"I poked my nose where it shouldn't have been poked. A group of businessmen were meeting in one of the private rooms. I asked if they knew Sir Robert. If he had been there. They told me no. I insisted. Maybe I just pushed too hard. But one of them punched me, and I was invited to leave."

"Are you all right, Dad?" John asked, his voice soft but with a lot of intensity in it.

Mahoney smiled. "I'll live," he said.

"And eight is the murders of Pierre Renelaux and his wife," Conwell said.

Mahoney nodded.

"And that suggests what to you?"

Mahoney got up and took his drink over to the fireplace. John stepped aside, making room for him. They looked into each other's eyes, and Mahoney, the elder, winked. John grinned uncertainly.

"After Edward Juengst's assassination, Sir Robert was sent back to London. Later he was posted to Paris and finally Brussels."

"We know all of that," Conwell said.

"He did a lot of traveling in those years, I suspect."

"Traveling?"

"To Germany. Munich, Hamburg, Frankfurt, Hannover, the Bonn-Köln-Düsseldorf area. And West Berlin, of course. As well as the smaller towns. It was a big job."

"To do what?" Bindrich asked.

Mahoney turned back to face them. "To do the very same thing he is almost certainly doing now in Leipzig, and Dresden, and Magdeburg, and Rostock."

They all held their silence. It had begun to rain, or sleet. Mahoney could hear it beating against the windows.

"To speak with the bankers and the manufacturers, with the bureaucrats and politicians, and with as many of the high-ranking military officers who were old enough to remember a time of a whole Germany."

"He is preaching."

"Exactly, but not to the public. He'll leave that to others. I think he's preaching revanchism to some of Germany's leaders. To her real leaders. And this time he thinks he has the charisma to succeed that he didn't have in the thirties."

"Impossible without a hue and cry going up," Conwell said.

"You think so?" Mahoney challenged.

"Yes, I do. The newspapers would have gotten on to it. Salmon or his people here in Berlin would have heard something. It would have come out. And that's here in the west. On the other side they'd just kill him."

"Germany went a long way toward rearming after the First World War without anyone on the outside finding out."

"That was different," Conwell argued. "They were a unified people then."

"Do you think the wall has made them any less unified today? They all still speak German," Mahoney said, playing devil's advocate.

"With English on one side and Russian on the other as a mandatory second language. The wall, in its years, has put more than a physical barrier between the people. It's placed a sociological and economic barrier as well. The East Germans are the have-nots, while the West Germans are the wild-eyed capitalists spending themselves into oblivion."

"And the have-nots sooner or later come to resent the foolish haves? Is that what you're saying?" Mahoney asked.

"Something like that."

"They don't begin to resent their masters?"

"The East Germans resenting the Russians?" Conwell asked.

"As well as the West Germans resenting the Americans."

Salmon sucked in his breath.

"What is it?" Conwell snapped.

Salmon shook his head. "Nothing . . . nothing at all," he said. But there was something; they all could see it.

"The East Germans resent their masters because of the wall, because of the relative lack of freedom they are allowed, and because of the hardships they have had to endure. For the most part, East Germany has had the lowest standard of living of any predominantly white industrial nation."

"And they don't resent West Germany as well?"

"They feel that if their country were reunified, they could moderate Western excesses."

Conwell was crossing and uncrossing his legs. "All right," he said at last. "If I went along with that, and I can understand East Germans chafing under the bit, that does not explain West Germany. They have it made here."

"Do they?" Mahoney asked.

"I . . ." Conwell began, but he cut it off.

"They're not a particularly happy lot here in Berlin," Salmon said.

"Besides economic troubles, it takes two powers to produce a separation," Mahoney said. "It takes two for a war. A war, I might remind you, in which NATO's latest scenario says the hell with Germany. She will become a wasteland. The war to end all wars. Tanks and guns and finally nuclear weapons finishing in an undefended West Germany what was left undone by the Second World War."

Conwell said nothing. Mahoney turned to Bindrich.

"There's a ninth point," he said. "It was actually the first I came across but the last to understand."

No one said a word.

"Germany is a member of NATO. Their military and political representatives understood the significance of the Genesis Plan scenario. None of them objected. There was no hue and cry, as Malcolm suggested. No veto. No screaming back to their people with the message that they had been sold down the river. Isn't it obvious to you that something must be happening?"

Conwell got up. He went to the drink tray where he poured himself a stiff shot of cognac. There was a disdainful look on his face. "An entire country cannot possibly hide something like this from the rest of the world, Mahoney." He shook his head. "We have our people operating here. We work hand in hand with the BND. Interpol cooperates across borders on a daily basis. There are newsmen from nearly every station in the world here. Television networks, radio stations, the works." He shook his head again.

"The entire country would have no need to hide anything," Mahoney replied. "The entire country would not have to know until the very end. Only a few key men and women in government, business, and the military need know everything."

"To do what, for God's sake? Mount a coup d'état in East Germany? Don't you think the Soviet tanks would roll?"

"No coup. Those days are past, in Germany. No, there'd be parliamentary pressure to become independent once again. Economic pressure. On both sides of the wall."

"You think the Russians would stand for it?"

"West Germany pulls out of NATO, and East Germany withdraws from the Warsaw Pact. Publicly. Loudly. That might be the first move."

"The Russians are already there in East Germany. They're already in place."

"East Germany asks West Germany for aid. The crack in the wall becomes larger. Who would the Russians on German soil attack? The U.S. would no longer be involved in West Germany to the extent it is today. But think of this: there are more nuclear warheads in Germany than in any other country in the world, except for the United States and the Soviet Union. Missiles. Bombs. Nuclear cannons. All here. Waiting to be used . . . waiting to be . . . seized?"

"Impossible," Conwell sputtered.

Bindrich stared open-mouthed at Mahoney.

"The military leadership in East Germany, although Soviet trained, is still German."

"Sir Robert, an Englishman, is preaching this revanchism in East Germany?"

"After having done it for years here in West Germany."

"Nothing has happened here because of it!"

"Hasn't it, Conwell? I think the German reaction— or *lack* of reaction—to the Genesis Plan scenario is a clear indication."

"I can't believe this," Conwell said, throwing back his drink.

"France is not interested in helping us, which means we'd pull back to Italy, and of course to England. The Soviet Union would withdraw to Poland, which unless I miss my guess, would again become a unified Germany's first objective."

Mahoney turned to Salmon. The man flinched. "You were about to say something earlier, Felix. What was it?"

Salmon felt very uncomfortable, it was clear. Bindrich nodded for him to answer. He looked at Mahoney. "We, that is the chief of bases around Germany, have our quarterly get-togethers in Bonn. Pep talks, you know."

Mahoney did. It was standard procedure everywhere within the CIA. Individual station or base chiefs

gathered on a regular basis with their next higher
echelon for policy discussions. In broad strokes they
would discuss the principal thrust of their activities for
the region, their major targeting, and any major problems. In turn, the heads of broad regions, such as the
chief of Germany, would report back to Langley. He
nodded.

"It came up again at the last meeting that the quality
of intelligence we're receiving from the Germans—from
the BND—has generally been declining in the past year
or so."

Bindrich sat forward. "I saw that report. It was put
down to budgetary problems on their part. We offered
to increase our technical aid, but they declined."

"Which means nothing—" Conwell started to say,
but Bindrich continued right over him.

"What do you want to do, Wallace?"

"Go into East Germany, find Sir Robert, and bring
him back."

"Why?" Conwell snapped. "What can one old man
do?"

"Look what he's already done!"

"It took him years."

"In a democratic country with a free press. It won't
take him very long in East Germany. He'll make contact
with the right people—the decision makers—and the fall
will come very fast."

"I say leave him," Conwell growled. "We're alerted
now to this fantastic scheme of his. We're ready. It
can't possibly happen."

"There's always the Genesis Plan scenario," Mahoney said softly. "Sir Robert took it with him."

"What if he's not there?"

"He is."

Bindrich sighed deeply. It was clear he was very tired.
It was also clear that he wanted to pass the burden of
decision. But that was impossible. His desk was on the
top floor. He was answerable now only to the President

and the Congress, neither one of whom he could bring this problem to.

"How do you want to work this?" he asked finally.

"You cannot be serious, Mr. Director," Conwell sputtered. "This is insane!"

Bindrich looked at him. "I don't agree, Malcolm." He turned back to Mahoney.

"Salmon can provide me with an identity as a businessman, perhaps, and the proper visas to get over. I'll need a car."

"A driver?" Salmon asked.

"No. I'll do this alone."

"That's too dangerous," Bindrich said.

"I'll go," John volunteered.

"Alone," Mahoney said forcefully. He turned to Conwell. "I want you to return to Brussels and approach Konstantin Demin for a meeting."

Conwell's eyes widened. "What?" he asked incredulously.

Insurance, or was it compounding the risk? Mahoney wondered. "I'll need thirty-six hours from the time I cross."

"For what?"

"To make contact with Sir Robert and start out."

"And then?"

"I want you to sit down with Demin and tell him everything we've said in this room."

Salmon whistled. John shook his head in wonder. Bindrich sat stock-still. Conwell turned white.

"Are you crazy?"

"Look, I'm not a policy maker, but I'm sure we don't want a reunited Germany," Mahoney said. "A new Germany with a very effective secret service these days. With a viable air force that includes nuclear weapons. With the will. The Versailles Treaty may have hamstrung Germany in the twenties. But think what we have done to them. We have torn apart their country. Turned German against German. They have forty years of hate to catch up with." Mahoney shook his head. The room was very still. "We would like the wall torn down, of course. And we'd like free trade between the two countries, but we want them as two separate countries. Two separate peoples. For balance. And I'm saying nothing new. It's been our policy all along. It's the *only* policy. A Germany with Messerschmitts, and Panzer divisions, and guns and tanks is one thing. But a Germany with the capability of embroiling the entire world in a nuclear holocaust is another . . . totally unacceptable thing that must be stopped at all costs."

Conwell licked his lips. "He's right."

Mahoney just looked at him.

"Perhaps old Marshall thinks he can save Europe."

"We're still fighting Germans, it seems," Bindrich said.

"No," Mahoney replied tiredly. "Only an old man with delusions of a time past and maybe the . . . charisma, this time, to make believers out of just the right people who can do something about it."

At the rear of the house was a long, broad porch that had been screened in. Mahoney had put on his overcoat and gone out for some fresh air. It was very cold, and the rain was falling in earnest now. By morning, he suspected, it would turn to snow.

Salmon had gone back into town to get everything set up for Mahoney's crossing. He seemed eager to get on with it. He was somewhat disappointed that he could not go along, although he realized that under no circumstances would he, as chief of base, have been allowed to cross.

Malcolm Conwell, still muttering under his breath, had left for Brussels after a long, private talk with Bindrich. He agreed to do as he was told, although coming that close to his Brussels nemesis would be as dangerous, according to him, "as putting matter and antimatter in the same room.'' The signal would be sent from Berlin to Brussels at the exact moment Mahoney crossed over. If all went well, that would happen sometime tomorrow in the late afternoon or early evening. The meeting with Demin then would take place a day and a half later, sometime in the early morning of Friday the twenty-eighth.

John had been the most difficult to deal with in the end, although he had had the least to say of all of them. Mahoney wanted him back in the States. Bindrich wanted him at least back in Brussels, but in the end it was agreed that John would help Salmon and his two field men monitor East German military and police communications, as well as the border crossing point where Mahoney would be coming out.

The plan was for Mahoney to cross quite openly into East Germany in Berlin, at Checkpoint Charlie. Hopefully with Sir Robert in tow no more than thirty-six hours later, he would make egress at Eisenach, far to the southwest. If there was trouble, alternatives would be arranged. South of Eisenach, near the very tiny town of Vacha, someone would be waiting to lead Mahoney and Sir Robert through the woods and across the border.

As much as Bindrich had wanted to remain, he realized that his presence there would jeopardize the entire operation. He had left an hour ago on Mahoney's promise that once the operation was completed, Mahoney would personally make the all's clear call to Langley.

Alone, Mahoney sniffed the air, listened to the falling rain, and thought back to other times and places like this one, on the eve of some action. He was melancholy.

☆ TWENTY-SIX ☆

To every operation comes the moment of truth. Agency wags love to cite one example after another: one depended upon blind luck; another on a steady progression of investigative events; and still another—in Mahoney's case—on intuitive genius in its purest form.

Later, they called Sir Robert "Genesis Man." Almost whimsically, the code name described the purloined NATO war scenario book, as well as the certain understanding that the old man had tried to create light where there had been darkness, order out of chaos, a unified Germany out of a shattered, occupied nation.

If Sir Robert deserved such a title, which was arguable, then Mahoney deserved no less than the approbation he received as the one who had created the heavens and the earth. If it took him slightly longer than six days, no one noted the distinction.

Into the morning hours, Mahoney kept to himself in the Grosser Wannsee safe house as the rain did indeed change to a very wet but wind-blown snow. Later, he went back to the kitchen where with Trailer's help he brewed some coffee to go with his Kentucky whiskey. Finally, up in the room he had been assigned, he ranged through his thoughts much as a forest ranger, worried about lightning-induced fires, might explore his *Wald* in search of the vulnerable spots needing protection. He replayed his conversations over and over again in his mind, listening, as if for the first time, to Lady Sidney's refined agony of her loss, listening to the likes of a jealous, confused Maggie Byrne and a distrustful, frightened Stewart Merrick. He reviewed every nuance of his brief conversation with Langdon, the *London Daily Mail* journalist who almost certainly was Sir Robert's handmaiden. He recalled in nightmarish, larger-than-life detail the death of the young Libyan in the dark doorway at the Gare du Nord, and the subsequent adventure with al-'Usta in Tripoli as well as the dangerous meeting with Detective Inspector Richard Matin. Mostly, though, Mahoney's mind ranged forward and backward over General Sir Robert Isley Marshall's life. Just as a very good actor might wish to steep himself in his character preparatory to his major role so that he might completely understand his charge, Mahoney tried to place himself in Sir Robert's shoes.

Sir Robert was a lover of Germany, Mahoney reasoned, who wanted a peaceful, stable Europe. But it was the Germany of fifty years ago. The Germany of the 1930s. The *Gemütlichkeit* of Sir Robert's youth.

He was gone now. Disappeared into the maw of East Germany. Where to look? Where to seek the man whose image would be on no television screen, whose voice would be on no radio broadcast, whose story would not be repeated in any newspaper?

What trail would such a man, a kingmaker, leave?

Would it be toward Poland, a country he must have instinctively hated? Could it be toward—or rather against—the Communists, whom historically no German liked or trusted?

Sir Robert thought of himself as a righter of wrongs. Fighter for causes. A motivator of leaders. A prime mover. As a sort of supereffective Chamberlain, Sir Robert was on the ultimate shuttle diplomatic mission.

Sir Robert had traveled to Munich, the one city that

seemed to symbolize the Germany of the thirties. He had evidently met with business leaders there. Yet Munich today was nothing more than a tourist city, now symbolizing the present and nothing that was the old Germany.

Berlin was a special case, Mahoney reasoned. It was the spearhead of the warriors. The end result of the terrible war that in Sir Robert's mind should never have been fought. It was a constant reminder of his failure. The true Germany was somewhere else.

For a time, during the very early morning hours, Mahoney allowed himself the luxury of no conscious thought. Of relaxing to a West German FM radio station that played easy listening music.

It came to him, finally, just before the gray dawn, in a complete package as he knew it would, given time. And he rose from where he had been lying on the big, comfortable bed and went down to his son's room. He knocked on the door and went in.

If Munich was the symbol of the Germany of the thirties, and if Berlin was nothing more than the arena where the two superpowers flexed their muscles, there had to be representatives of the two present-day Germanys. They'd have to be subnational examples. They'd have to be Sir Robert's targets. His special cases.

Bonn, in the west, represented West Germany at its worst. The city had been all but created by the Allies. Berlin could not be the capital of a Western Germany, so a new capital had been created. Sir Robert had spent a lot of time there. Were there still ties?

If Bonn was the Western symbol of the new Germany, then what was the East's? Certainly not East Berlin, although it was considered the Paris of the socialist world. No, not East Berlin.

The city would be Karl Marx Stadt. Formerly known as Chemnitz, it was south between Leipzig and Dresden, and coincidentally on the E63 autobahn to Eisenach. Where Bonn was a city of politics, symbolizing the democratic processes of the West, Karl Marx Stadt was and always had been a city of the worker, which is why it had been renamed.

To Sir Robert, Bonn would symbolize all he hated about what the West had done to his Germany in restitution for the war. Karl Marx Stadt would represent all that the Russians had done in the east.

It was where he would go, Mahoney reasoned. To Chemnitz.

John turned from where he had been staring out the window. "Can't sleep?" he asked. He reached over and turned on the table lamp.

Mahoney came in and shut the door.

"You're going to have to go down to Bonn first thing in the morning."

"You're asking for my help?"

Mahoney smiled, a little sadly. He nodded.

At dawn, John Mahoney was driven to Tegel Airport where he took the first flight to Köln-Düsseldorf, the takeoff delayed more than an hour because of the rotten weather. The flight was terribly bumpy, but John kept thinking about what his father wanted him to find out. The logic, as far as he could see, was brilliant. Yet he could understand why his father wanted confirmation before he crossed the border.

He hired a cab to take him down to Bonn, to the ornate town hall and city records building off the Sandkaule. It was raining here, and very dark. John paid the cabby and hurried across the broad marketplace, the sidewalk café tables all deserted, up the stairs, and into the building through the tall, glass-fronted doors. He stopped to ask the way and was directed to the basement where, he was assured by an older man who almost certainly was an attorney, the city's records hall, including property ownership, were located.

The busy counter, staffed by an older man and four

women, was beyond frosted glass doors at the foot of
the stairs.

John had to wait nearly five minutes in line before it
was his turn.

"*Guten Morgen*," one of the young women clerks
said pleasantly.

"Do you speak English?" John asked.

The woman nodded. "Yes, a little," she said.

"I'm trying to locate some information about a
British subject who may own property here in Bonn."

An odd look came into her eyes. "This man's name,
mein Herr?"

Something was wrong. John could feel it. "Robert
Marshall," he said, lowering his voice.

The woman nodded. "*Moment, bitte*," she said, and
she turned and went to the man who had gone back to
his desk.

Several other people had come in, and they stood
behind John. The other clerks at the counter were busy.
The room suddenly seemed stuffy. Closed in. A trap?

The man looked up at John, then came up to the
counter. He was smiling.

"Good morning, *mein Herr*. It is my understanding
you wish to see certain property records?"

"Yes. I am trying to find information about property
held by Robert Marshall. He is a British subject."

"Unfortunately it is not possible to open those
records just now, *mein Herr*."

"I don't understand."

"There has been a hold. A previous request." The
clerk glanced up at the clock. It was a few minutes
before twelve. "If you would care to wait, *mein Herr*. It
will only be a very few minutes. The gentleman who has
made the request will be here. Perhaps he will be able to
answer your questions."

"When was this request made?" John asked.

"I couldn't say for certain. Sometime just this morning, I believe. It came from upstairs. You understand."

"No, I don't understand," John said. The other people in the crowded room were looking at him now. The clerk was trying to be patient.

"I believe it is a police matter, *mein Herr*," the man said, leaning forward confidentially. "If you wish to wait. . . . Perhaps I can call upstairs and you can speak to someone in authority."

John's mind was racing. Sir Robert almost certainly had sent someone here for his records. By why at just this moment? It could not be a coincidence. It probably meant that the Berlin operation had been spotted and had been figured for what it was—the work-up to a crossing.

"That won't be necessary," John said nonchalantly. "In fact, I doubt if I will wait."

"I understand, *mein Herr*."

"But could you tell me the name of the man who is coming for the records?"

"That I would not know, *mein Herr*. As I said, the request came from upstairs. It may be best if I do call up . . ."

"No, it's not necessary," John said, backing away from the counter. "I have another appointment. I will come back later."

"Maybe that would be best . . ."

John sidestepped toward the door, and as he stepped out into the corridor he looked back as the clerk picked up the telephone on his desk.

Sir Robert had been years here in West Germany, making his contacts. With military men, with politicians, with businessmen . . . and with the police?

John hurried up the stairs and out the front doors. It would not do for him to get caught here in Bonn by men on Sir Robert's side. There was no doubt in his mind he would end up with a bullet in his brain. Just like Pierre Renelaux.

He started down the stairs to the sidewalk, when a metallic blue Mercedes 500SEL slid up to the curb and a vaguely familiar man jumped out.

John stopped. He knew the man. He had seen him speaking with Renelaux. It had been John's first night in Brussels. He had been at the Renelaux apartment when this man had shown up.

He suddenly knew who it was!

"Langdon," John called out, hurrying the rest of the way down the stairs.

Langdon had just come around from the driver's side, the car parked in a no-parking zone. He looked up as John rushed across to him. For a moment there was a totally blank look on his face, but then he realized who it was.

He had killed the Renelauxs. He had murdered Stanford Hall. He had helped obscure Sir Robert's trail. And he was here now to pick up Sir Robert's property records.

"You," Langdon hissed. He reached inside his coat and pulled out a gun. But John was on him, grabbing his wrist.

"Don't!" John shouted wildly.

Langdon jerked back, and the pistol went off, the shot going over John's head. A woman screamed. John shoved Langdon back against the side of the Mercedes, bending his gun arm down.

"*Achtung! Polizei!*" someone shouted from above and behind.

John had his hand around the pistol when it went off again, and Langdon suddenly went limp in his arms, blood coming from his lips, his body sagging to the street.

Another woman screamed as John stepped back away from Langdon's body and turned around. He had the gun.

There were a lot of people on the stairs and at the door. A uniformed police officer was at the top. He started to raise his pistol.

Instinctively John raised his gun and snapped off a

shot, well above the policeman's head. The crowd was scattering, getting in each other's way. The cop dropped down flat.

John spun around, yanked open the Mercedes's door, and slid in behind the wheel. The keys were in the ignition; Langdon had not planned on being there long. The car started instantly. John slammed it in gear and jammed the accelerator pedal to the floor as the window in the back door, just inches from his head, shattered.

The car shot away, and John just had time enough to glance in the rearview mirror at the confusion behind him as he maneuvered the heavy luxury car through traffic and around the corner onto Dorotheenstrasse, which led to the southwest.

The urge was to keep the car moving forward, to race away from the square as fast as he could. But he slowed down immediately, by the training manual, and turned the corner again in two blocks. Do not make yourself conspicuous. Easy. Easy. He found the controls for the electric windows and powered down the shattered rear window. He would call less attention to himself.

Cold air and rain instantly filled the car. In the distance behind him he could hear the sounds of many sirens. The search would rapidly expand outward.

He turned the corner again, and a half block later turned down a narrow side street where he pulled over to the curb and shut off the engine.

Pocketing Langdon's gun, he leaped out of the car and hurried in the opposite direction, hailing a passing cab one block later on Kölnstrasse.

"The airport in Düsseldorf," John said, sitting back and low so that he would be less noticeable from outside.

"*Jawohl, mein Herr,*" the driver said, and they headed out of the city, the gathering excitement of the sirens falling behind them.

John looked at his hands. They were rock steady. It had been Langdon all the time. Once they got clear of the city, he would have to call Berlin. He would have to get word to his father not to cross. Langdon, on Sir Robert's orders, had killed Stanford Hall, had killed Pierre and Madame Renelaux, and had arranged for the deaths of the American banker and al-'Usta in Tripoli. John knew that he should be feeling something now. He had just killed a man.

He looked up as they passed a big sports stadium on the right. God help him, he felt nothing.

Mahoney sat in Salmon's dark gray Mercedes, the Berlin chief of base behind the wheel. It was a little past three in the afternoon. They were parked around the corner from the Berlin Museum, in clear view of Checkpoint Charlie a block and a half to the north. Bob Poole had left around noon to pick up the van in Frankfurt and get it ready for their operation outside Eisenach. Fred Trailer had gone ahead into East Berlin to make Mahoney's arrangements. They had not heard from John yet, and Mahoney was starting to get worried. He kept it to himself, however.

"You'll take the bus across," Salmon said, never taking his eyes from the checkpoint. "Less conspicuous that way. You'll be required to change at least twenty-five marks into East German currency, *Mark der Deutschen Notenbank*. But I wouldn't change more than fifty MDN at the border. You'll need more, of course, but you can do it at the hotel."

"Isn't Western currency more acceptable?" Mahoney asked.

"You betcha, and you'd stick out like a neon sign in a dark closet," Salmon said. "Low-key. If your boy expects someone to be coming over, it's just the sort of thing he'll be watching for. It'd mark you for certain, sir."

"Right," Mahoney said. But what about John? He was afraid something had happened.

"The drill is easy. Security has been loosened up over there, so things are much simpler. You'll check into the new Swedish Palasthotel where you will have dinner and a few drinks at the bar. You will retire early to your room, where you will muss up the bed, dirty up the bathroom, and then get the hell out of there. Fred will have the car waiting for you. White Mercedes. Dent in the right front fender. It'll be in the hotel parking garage. Slot four-five-four, same as your room. You have the chit with your papers. There'll be luggage, plenty of gas and coupons, and even some camping gear, just in case."

Mahoney looked at the man. He was leaving something out.

"Oh, yes," Salmon added. "There'll be a gun. In the front seat springs on the driver's side. Russian. Bit of poetic justice."

If he were picked up in East Germany, chances are he could talk or buy his way back out. If he were caught with a weapon, he'd never get out. There was no question of it.

Yet Mahoney was not so naïve as to believe that he could count on simply walking up to Sir Robert, chatting, and then, arm in arm, leading him back out. It was the one factor he had not discussed with Bindrich. In fact everyone had stayed away from the subject until the mention of the gun now.

"The Palasthotel business will give you an eighteen-hour head start. Your bill is paid in advance. But leave at least twenty-five marks for the maid. It'll probably be late afternoon before she says anything. By that time you'll be long gone. If they decide to start looking for you, nothing will begin to happen until tomorrow night, or possibly the next morning. By then, with luck, you and Sir Robert will be across."

Mahoney couldn't find fault with it.

"As soon as you're in, Trailer will be coming out. We'll meet Poole at Frankfurt. We'll be monitoring

GDR communications from the van outside Eisenach."

"And if there's trouble?" Mahoney asked.

Salmon looked at him. "Let's hope there isn't any. But if there is, we'll play it by ear. We've got quite a bit of satellite time on the comms, so we should be able to sort it out. We won't leave you in the lurch . . . I promise you that."

The telephone buzzed. Salmon picked it up. "Yes?" he said. He listened for a couple of minutes, glancing at Mahoney from time to time. "He's planning to come to Frankfurt or go directly to Eisenach?" he asked sharply. "All right, see what you can do to calm things down. I'll call Bonn."

Salmon hung up and shook his head. "It was your son. He just called my people from Düsseldorf."

"What is it?"

"Sir Robert evidently has property in Bonn after all, although John never saw the records."

Mahoney held his silence.

"Thomas Langdon showed up. There was a struggle. He was killed."

"Christ."

"Your son is wanted by the federal police on a charge of murder. He's on his way to Eisenach now. If he's picked up, it'll blow everything."

"Is there anything you can do about it?"

"We're trying. But my suggestion to you is, scrub the crossing until we can straighten things out."

"No," Mahoney said. "Sir Robert will know that Langdon was killed. He'll know someone is coming after him. The longer we wait, the deeper he'll go. If we wait too long, we'll never reach him."

"But you can't go over now, for Christ's sake!"

"Get Trailer out. I'll take the car and leave immediately."

"They'll be waiting for you!"

"It's the chance I'm going to have to take," Mahoney snapped. He should have known better. And yet send-

ing John down to Bonn had accomplished what he
wanted it to. It had proved beyond the last shadow of a
doubt in Mahoney's mind the Bonn-Karl Marx Stadt
connection.

Salmon glanced at his watch. He seemed like a man
backed against the wall. He had wanted action. He was
getting it now, but it didn't seem to suit him.

"Trailer will be at the hotel by four. I've no way of
getting a message to him. You'll have to meet him."

Mahoney nodded.

"Tell him the story, and tell him to get his ass out
now! I'll be waiting here for him," Salmon said. He
shook his head. "Goddammit," he swore. He stuck out
his hand. Mahoney shook it. "Good luck, sir. And I
sincerely mean that."

"Right," Mahoney said. "We'll see you in Eisenach
tomorrow evening at the very latest."

Mahoney got out of the car and started toward the
bus stop.

Salmon powered down his window. "If there's any
trouble, get the hell out. It's not that important," he
called.

Mahoney did not turn back. He could not get his
mind off his son. He only hoped that John could stay at
large until Salmon got to him.

The crossing at Checkpoint Charlie was an anticli-
max. There were a lot of West Berliners on the bus
heading across to the State Opera House, and the
Grenztruppen who boarded the bus to check papers and
make the twenty-five-mark-per-person exchange seemed
bored and indifferent.

Mahoney paid only the twenty-five marks and
showed his well-used passport in the name of Conrad
Buhle, an American from Milwaukee, with the proper
GDR visa.

If he were to be stopped driving across the country,

his papers would show that he had crossed at Eisenach, and had made stops in Dresden and Berlin besides Karl Marx Stadt as a representative for Associated Technologies, an American firm specializing in control devices for manufacturing equipment.

He got off the bus at the edge of Alexanderplatz, a vast shopping center, and then with his coat collar up, his hands deep in his pockets, he made his way across to the Palasthotel, getting thoroughly wet and chilled to the bone in the process.

East Berlin was quite different than he thought it would be. Gone was much of the evidence of poverty and oppression. Gone was the heavy, dark feeling that had pervaded the city as recently as ten years ago. Although East Berlin didn't have the glamour of many Western capitals, the people seemed prosperous. They seemed happy. Busy. Almost carefree. There was even a lot of automobile traffic, though most of the cars were very small, cheap-looking Soviet or East German models. The shop windows were filled with consumer goods.

It was just a few minutes before four when Mahoney entered the busy lobby of the hotel. It was a gleaming showplace. Well-dressed men and women seemed to be everywhere, mingling with men in uniforms. It could have been the lobby of a good hotel in any Western city . . . but one at war. Here there was a definite air of militarism.

He took the elevator down to the parking level, and when he stepped off he glanced at his parking chit. It was marked 454.

He started down the first row of cars when an older model white Mercedes 280SE, a dent in its front right fender came around the corner. Fred Trailer was behind the wheel.

He pulled up and started to roll down his window, but Mahoney hurried around to the passenger side and jumped in.

"What's wrong?" Trailer asked, alarmed. He wore khaki slacks and a dark brown leather jacket.

"Let's get out of here—now!" Mahoney snapped. "You must get back across the border. Salmon's waiting for you."

"What about your reservations . . .?"

"I'm leaving immediately."

"You're not coming out?" Trailer asked, backing up, turning around, and heading back up the ramp to the exit.

"No. Salmon will explain it to you."

Trailer glanced at him. "Do you want me to stay with you, sir?"

"No," Mahoney said. His mind was racing ahead.

The attendant paid little or no attention to them as they drove out, then turned the corner. A block from the hotel, Trailer pulled over.

"I'll make it on foot from here," he said. "Are you sure about this?"

"Absolutely," Mahoney said.

"The gun is under the seat."

"Right."

"Good luck, then. We'll see you in Eisenach," Trailer said, getting out of the car. Mahoney slid over behind the wheel.

"Right," Mahoney said again, but his mind raced forward to Karl Marx Stadt and what he thought he would find there, and he drove off even before Trailer had rounded the corner toward Checkpoint Charlie.

✮ TWENTY-SEVEN ✮

Malcolm Conwell was one of what former Vice-President Spiro Agnew once called the effete, East Coast intellectuals. He was a Harvard graduate, had served on Henry Kissinger's staff for a time, and had come to the Central Intelligence Agency on a recommendation from his father, a former Senator from Connecticut.

Opinion was divided on him; there were those who felt he brought a certain class to the corridors at Langley and who felt that if he never became DCI, he'd at least rise to assistant director. It was expected of him. There were those, however, who felt Conwell was so impressed with his own credentials that he had never once stopped to examine the subtleties of any task at hand.

He was aware of both opinions, of course, and on this late Wednesday afternoon in Brussels he was glad that he was of the former group. He *was* an East Coast intellectual, with breeding, upbringing, education, and most importantly, background.

He sat in an easy chair sipping a very good white wine in a suite at the Europa, one of the finer luxury hotels on the Rue de la Loi. It was very near the headquarters of the European Economic Council.

The trip to Berlin had been upsetting, no less so for

him for the brash actions that Wallace Mahoney contemplated. Robert Marshall came from an old, established family, but he was from the wrong side of the Atlantic, after all. There was no reason to expend any more American money, effort . . . or possibly blood on the project. It could be stopped now.

The bell rang. Conwell nodded to his field men who flanked the door. One of them opened it, and Konstantin Demin, the KGB *resident* for Brussels walked into the room like a Sherman tank moving through a poplar woods.

Conwell rose, putting down his wineglass. "Good evening," he said.

Demin stopped, realizing all at once that he had probably walked into a trap. When he had agreed to speak with Conwell, it was to have been alone, no field men. He backed up a step, his right hand reaching for his jacket.

"Wait," Conwell said, holding out a hand. "I've called you here merely to talk. We have a mutual problem."

Demin stayed his hand. He looked like a cornered animal. He was very dangerous at this moment. "I don't know what you are talking about," he growled.

"Sir Robert Marshall. He is, at this moment, in East Germany. Karl Marx Stadt. And he is going to have to be . . . dealt with."

Felix Salmon stood in the rain beside his Mercedes in the lee of the Berlin Museum, a pair of powerful night binoculars to his eyes, trained on Checkpoint Charlie. Three buses had already come across. Salmon had watched them coming through, and watched as they stopped on this side to disgorge some of their passengers. But not Trailer.

"Come on," he said to himself.

There was a military jet transport waiting at Tegel with supposed hydraulic problems. As soon as he and Trailer were safely aboard, the problems would disappear and they would be given clearance to take off for Frankfurt where Bob Poole was waiting with the communications van.

From time to time Salmon had to lower the glasses and wipe the lenses with his handkerchief because of the rain that was beginning to turn to sleet.

It was dark now. The brilliant lights around Checkpoint Charlie were very harsh.

Another bus was coming. He could see it through the barriers, moving very slowly, making each turn very carefully, just yards now from the western zone.

Salmon stiffened. There was some activity on the other side. Powerful spotlights on the towers suddenly swiveled around to the bus as a dozen East German border guards came running.

The bus stopped and the door opened.

Salmon stepped forward. His rage impotent. Something had gone wrong. Something had happened over there. He knew damned well it would be Trailer. The man had gone through once too often. Someone had recognized him.

Several of the *Grenztruppen,* their weapons at the ready, climbed aboard the bus. Others stood around, waiting, looking expectantly up toward the windows.

The sharp reports of gunfire came to Salmon over the wind, and he flinched.

A half-dozen shots, no more. So sharp. So goddamned final. And then nothing. Salmon almost willed himself through the lenses and across the intervening distance to the bus.

Four soldiers clambered off the bus, followed moments later by two more, dragging a body . . . a man wearing a dark brown leather jacket. It was Trailer.

Salmon lowered the glasses. If they knew about

Trailer, then it was possible they had found out about Mahoney. But there was no way of warning him. No way now of pulling him out.

Salmon looked once again through the glasses. An ambulance was coming, but Trailer was almost certainly dead. And there wasn't a damned thing he could do about it. Officially Trailer did not exist. Officially he had not been in the Eastern zone. Officially he was a nonperson.

Salmon turned, got into his car, and hurried out to Tegel Airport. They'd have to salvage something out of this operation.

Mahoney drove fast despite the sleet and dropping temperatures that iced up the bridges along the auto-bahn route from Berlin to the outskirts of Dresden and then west toward Karl Marx Stadt. The heavy Mercedes was very good on the highway and not once did he con-sider slowing down because of the conditions.

He kept turning over in his mind the one item in this business that did not seem to fit anywhere. On the tape Sir Howard Scott had received, the speaker mentioned a fortnight. Fourteen days, which was only a few more days from now, for the general to be heard from. At first he thought the business of time was a ruse. Something to put them all off. To lull them into a sense of believing that if they were making little progress, it would not matter because the business would be over in a couple of weeks. But now Mahoney was worried about that final bit that did not seem to fit. Sir Robert had spent years developing his notions about Germany and from the fifties on, even more years speaking with Germans about unification. Apparently he had built up a circle of believers. But something had precipitated Sir Robert's sudden drastic move. He knew, of course, that his disappearance with sensitive NATO documents would produce an immediate, widespread search. He

must have understood that sooner or later they'd catch
up with him. In East Germany. Fourteen days? Was
that how long he suspected he could remain at large?
But there was more. Mahoney could feel it around the
edges. There was the one thing that they were all missing. The one bit that would drop the fortnight business
into its proper slot. But for the life of him he could not
figure it out.

It was shortly before eight o'clock when Mahoney finally came into the center of the manufacturing city. It
seemed like a ghost town, the sleet making the distances
soft and putting halos around the streetlights along the
deserted streets. Traffic was almost nonexistent, and he
did not see a single person on foot for three blocks.

Just off the downtown area, Mahoney pulled up in
the driveway of the Kongress Hotel in a block of drab,
nearly featureless office buildings.

He was disappointed, in a way. If this was Sir
Robert's eastern stronghold, if his thinking had been
correct, then he had expected something more than this.
But what? Crowds at a Nuremberg-style rally? Banners
proclaiming German independence? Sir Robert's men
posted on street corners?

There was no doorman. Mahoney got out and entered
the hotel. A couple of military officers stood talking
with a civilian in the otherwise deserted lobby. They
glanced over at him but then went back to their conversation.

Mahoney approached the desk. An obsequious little
man in morning clothes came from a back room.

"*Guten Abend, mein Herr.* You have reservations?"

"No, I do not," Mahoney said tiredly.

"Ah, Englander," the clerk beamed. He brought out
a registration card.

"American," Mahoney said. He laid his passport on
the counter.

The clerk opened it and glanced at the photo and at
the visa in the back as Mahoney filled out the card in the

name of Conrad Buhle. When he was finished the clerk
pinned the card to the passport, which would be picked
up by the police in the morning, and then selected a key
from the slots behind him.

"You have a car, *mein Herr*, that you wish to have
parked?"

Mahoney took the key. "Yes, but I can get it myself,
if you will direct me."

"Of course," the clerk said. "At the east side of the
building is a parking lot. There is no need to lock your
automobile here, of course."

"Of course," Mahoney said. He turned away from
the counter, but then as if he had just remembered
something, he turned back.

"Mein Herr?" the clerk asked.

"I will wish to place a local telephone call from my
room this evening."

"Of course."

"And later I will wish the use of a conference room.
There will be a meeting."

"Of what nature, your meeting, *mein Herr*?"

"It is a business meeting of a confidential nature,
perhaps only two or three people. I would like privacy
and security."

"I understand, *mein Herr*." The clerk brought out a
key on a yellow tag. "Your room is on the fourth floor.
The conference room you wish to use is on the second
floor. Twenty-one." He handed Mahoney the key.
"Would you wish for service? Perhaps coffee, perhaps
something stronger?"

"It is not necessary," Mahoney said.

"I wish for you a successful meeting," the clerk said.

Mahoney went back across the lobby and out to his
car. He drove it around to the side parking area. Then,
sure that no had followed him from inside, he reached
under the front seat and found the gun. It was taped in
place. Carefully he peeled the tape loose from the
springs and pulled the gun down and out.

For a minute or two he stared at the big gun. It was a Graz Buyra. It looked very deadly. He left the tape loosely on the gun, then stuffed it into his suitcase from the trunk, went back into the hotel, and entered the elevator. As the doors closed the military officers and the civilian turned to look at him.

His room was small and shabbily furnished, but very clean. It had a small bathroom with a shower stall but no tub.

After Mahoney splashed some water on his face, he picked up the telephone. Seconds later the clerk was on the line.

"Yes, Herr Buhle, your telephone call?"

"I do not know the number."

"It is all right, sir. Whom do you wish to call?"

"Robert Marshall," Mahoney said with no inflection whatsoever in his voice.

There was a very long silence on the line. Mahoney could hear some sort of a noise in the background that sounded like a motor.

"I will have to look up that number, *mein Herr*, and call you back if I find it."

"It is not necesary," Mahoney said.

"No?"

"No. I wish merely to pass along a message to Herr Marshall for him to meet with me here, in the conference room, at ten."

"This evening?"

"Yes, this evening."

"I will look for the number, *mein Herr*."

"Do that," Mahoney said. He hung up, then took the big handgun and tape out of his suitcase and stuffed it into his coat pocket.

There was no one in the corridor when he left his room, nor did he meet anyone on the stairs or in the second-floor corridor as he went down to the conference room he had been assigned.

He opened the door with his key and flipped on the

lights. It was a small room with a medium-size conference table in the center. Several poorly done paintings of workers in factories adorned the walls. Coffee
cups and serving pots were stacked on a side table. The
room smelled of cigars.

Mahoney made sure the door was locked, then he
went to the head of the table and sat down. He pulled
out the gun, made sure it was loaded and there was a
shell in the chamber, and then taped the weapon to the
underside of the table just above his knees.

Insurance, he told himself when he was finished.
Perhaps he'd not have to use it.

There were a lot of lights at the border crossing, made
blurry by the heavy rain that was falling. John Mahoney
was parked in a rest stop above the autobahn. There
were a lot of trucks parked there already despite the
early hour. It was because of the weather, he supposed.
The Cortina's windshield wipers flapped back and forth
as he watched traffic below on the autobahn. The crossing reminded him of the toll roads in Illinois where you
had to stop and pay a toll before entering. Only here the
border police were searching every fourth or fifth car,
and nearly every truck.

He had rented the car in Düsseldorf and had driven
immediately to the Eisenach crossing. So far he had had
no trouble since Bonn, although he was still shook up
about it.

He glanced in the rearview mirror as a Ford Econo-
line van came up from the autobahn and drove to the
far side of the rest stop, beyond the Esso station and
restaurant, then parked.

John turned around and stared at it. The van's plates
were German. They began with the letters DK. It was
the communications van.

He shut off the engine, got out of the car, and crossed

the parking area on foot, hunching up his coat collar as he leaned into the wind.

The windowless van was dark when he reached it. He started around to the driver's side, when someone stepped out from behind, and he felt the muzzle of a pistol against his cheek.

"*Was wollen Sie hier?*" a familiar voice asked.

John half turned, his hands raised.

"Oh, shit," Salmon said, lowering the gun. "I didn't know who the hell you were."

"I'm parked across the way. I saw you come in . . ." John started, but he bit it off. Something was wrong. Drastically wrong. He could see it in Salmon's eyes. "What is it?"

"He went over anyway. Fred Trailer was killed coming back across."

It took a moment for the significance of that to sink in. Along with Langdon's presence in Bonn it could only mean one thing. "They know he's coming in?"

"It looks that way."

John looked toward the border crossing, then back at Salmon. "We have to help him! Get him out of there!"

"Just hold on, John," Salmon said. "Bob is linking up with the satellite. We'll see if anything is going on. Besides, you have enough troubles here as it is."

"You know goddamned well they're waiting for him!" John shouted. He stepped back, looking again toward the brightly lit border crossing. "I'm going over. You have to get me over."

"One of our people has been killed already. I'm not throwing you away—"

"I'll cross on my own, then, and take my chances," John said.

"You're going to do as you're told, goddammit! You'll not be helping him by charging across the border. You have no idea what he's running over there."

"I know that if Sir Robert is anywhere near Karl

Marx Stadt, he'll have my father killed! I know that much!"

The rear door of the van opened, and Poole stuck his head out. The smell of warm electronics wafted out.

"What'd you get?" Salmon asked.

Poole was staring at John. "Nothing," he said softly. "Not a damned thing. Radio silence, I suspect."

"Christ," Salmon said.

"Trailer wasn't an accident," John said.

"Neither was Langdon," Salmon snapped. His mind was working furiously. "Your father's plan was to stay at the Kongress Hotel. He was going to try to contact Sir Robert. Set up a meeting."

"Can you get me across the border?"

"Yes. But if there's any trouble inside, you'll have to use the Vacha route. Do you understand?"

"Yes," John said. His heart was pounding. His father was alone in there. And probably walking into a trap.

☆ TWENTY-EIGHT ☆

Alone again in the field as he had been for most of his career, Mahoney waited in the hotel conference room on the second floor, listening to his own internal clock ticking off the seconds. It was just a few minutes before ten. He had managed to get some rest, although he was still tired, and he was hungry now. Sir Robert had not returned his call, of course, but neither had the clerk called to deny or confirm receipt of the summons. Sir Robert was here in Karl Marx Stadt. Mahoney could almost feel his presence, just as he had felt that he was close in Heidelberg, the Berghof, and finally Munich. The man had property in Bonn, and somewhere very near here, he had a house, perhaps looking down upon the twin of two cities he despised most in the world.

"Bring my husband back to me, Mr. Mahoney," Lady Sidney had pleaded.

But he no longer knew if it were possible. Power corrupts, absolute power corrupts absolutely. Lord Acton. Sir Robert Isely Marshall?

In the old days Marge might have said that he worried too much. Not worry as in the traditional sense of concern. But worry as in the sense that a dog will worry a bone, gnawing on it, turning it end over end, playing with it, until at last it becomes nearly unrecognizable.

Had he done the same with the business of Sir Robert? Had he assigned more reality to the man than was ever there? Was Sir Robert nothing more than a very old man at the end of his career, so fearful of his pending retirement, of being sent off to the dustheap, that he had regressed, as so many old men do, to a time when as a small boy he had to do something startling to guarantee attention? Was he, in the end, nothing more than a senile old fool who had done a terrible, terrible thing and now knew of no way out?

He was a seeker after causes, after all. A believer in men such as Edward Juengst. Fearful of the power of Hitler and yet ashamed of his own lack of talent to sway him.

Mahoney had told himself all those things over and over again. Nothing, however, altered the fact that Stanford Hall had been brutally murdered. Pierre Renelaux and his wife had been shot down. Al-'Usta was dead, as was a young Arab in a dark doorway in Brussels. All of it turned Mahoney's stomach. This was not war. There was nothing justifiable here.

But Mahoney had come to the battleground, after all. It was the most amazing thing of all. He had been led here, as if by the nose, with a lot of noise but with little or no resistance.

He reached up under the table and felt for the big handgun. It was there. Even the feel of it was deadly.

The door swung open at precisely ten, and a tall, intense-looking man came in.

"Mr. Mahoney?" he said pleasantly.

Mahoney had signed in as Buhle. This man was from the general. "I was expecting Sir Robert."

"Yes. I have been sent to fetch you. Sir Robert is at his home . . . along with a few other gentlemen who would like to meet with you." His excellent English had a definite Oxford accent.

Mahoney remained seated within easy reach of the big gun. "I wish to meet with Sir Robert here."

"I'm afraid that will not be possible, *mein Herr*," the man said. He half turned as if he were going out, reached into his coat pocket, and when he turned back he had a pistol in his hand.

"Will you shoot me down here?" Mahoney asked, his voice very calm. Inside he was seething. Sir Robert had been ahead of him nearly all the way. Stanford Hall had been his only serious mistake.

"It is not my order to harm you, Mr. Mahoney, only to bring you to a meeting with the general."

Mahoney leaned forward, his hands out of sight beneath the table. He groped for and found the automatic. "If I do not wish to leave?" he said. He pulled the tape loose.

"Please, *mein Herr*."

The automatic came loose. "I have my coat upstairs," Mahoney said.

"You won't be needing it. We have a pleasantly warm automobile just outside the front door."

"Someone will see us leaving the hotel," Mahoney said. It was maddening. He had the gun, but he couldn't do a damned thing with it. Not with Sir Robert's goon standing right there.

"There is no one here this evening," the man said. He turned and glanced out into the corridor.

At that very moment, Mahoney quickly slipped the automatic into his jacket pocket and stood up. He kept his hand on the grip, his fingers curled around the handle.

The dark man motioned with the pistol, then stepped aside to allow Mahoney to pass.

There would be others at the meeting. They would probably search him before they allowed him near Sir

Robert. So what was the use of all this dangerous drama?

"It's getting late, Mr. Mahoney. They are waiting."

There simply was too much at stake. Too much had already transpired for him to leave it alone. Bindrich understood. Salmon, he suspected, did, although Conwell did not.

Mahoney moved around the table, stepped out into the deserted corridor, and started immediately toward the stairwell without bothering to look back. Downstairs, he crossed the empty lobby and stepped outside. A black Mercedes, its engine running, was waiting. The driver, a tall, fat man, jumped out, hurried around and opened the rear door. He looked Arab. Mahoney stared at him, stepped across the walk, got in, and the door was closed. There were no handles on the inside. No way of opening the door.

The driver, who almost certainly was the man Lady Sidney thought was al-'Usta, and the man with the gun got in the front, and they pulled away from the hotel and headed out of the city.

There had been no trouble crossing the border at Eisenach, and John Mahoney made it the 110 miles to Karl Marx Stadt on the E63 autobahn in less than an hour and a half, pushing the Cortina to its absolute limits through the terrible night.

He entered the city from the northwest, the lights on the tall stanchions along the gentle curve of the exit ramp nearly as bright as those at the border. There had been very little traffic on the superhighway until he came within ten miles of the city. Then he began to see a lot of military vehicles. All of them converging here.

There was trouble. He knew goddamned well there was trouble. The markings on the sides of the military truck were Soviet . . . not East German.

He took Langdon's pistol out of his pocket and laid it

beside him on the seat. Salmon had not asked if he was armed, nor had he offered a weapon.

His last-minute instructions had been simple: "Pick him up at the hotel and then get the hell out of there."

John had not said a thing. He had climbed into his car, started the engine, and left.

He passed through the downtown section, then turned off the square and drove the final few blocks toward the hotel.

The city was quiet, suddenly, and John began to feel that he was too late, that there would be nothing for him to do.

He came around the corner before the hotel and pulled up short. His father had just stepped out of the main door, hesitated a moment, then crossed the walk and got into a car. The driver slammed the door, and a second man, who had also come out of the hotel, got in the front. A moment later the car pulled away from the curb.

The night was very dark, what few city lights they passed, dull, indistinct balls because of the rain and the mist. Then they were in the country, driving very fast along a winding road. Mahoney got the impression that the driver and the other man were frightened, or at the very least in an almost reckless rush to carry out their orders.

They crossed a bridge, and then the road began to climb as it wound back and forth through what probably were the hills that led up into the Erz Mountains, the driver obviously very intent now on what he was doing.

Finally they slowed way down, turning down a very narrow lane that led through the trees.

The house was very large and brightly lit. They saw the lights through the trees before they actually saw the house itself, but then, suddenly, dramatically, they seemed to burst out of the dark woods and into a broad clearing around which a vast, sweeping drive led up to the mansion.

The place was right out of some Germanic tale of barons and princes and the Prussian aristocracy. Fitting, Mahoney decided, for Sir Robert's purposes, and all the more ostentatious for its location here in East Germany. Sir Robert—or the people on this side who he knew were powerful—owned this place.

A dark thought crossed Mahoney's mind as they came around the driveway and stopped at broad marble stairs that led up to the grand entrance. Perhaps Conwell had been correct with his speculation back in Berlin. Perhaps it was already too late.

The rear door opened, and Mahoney got out of the car. He was very tense. If they were going to search him, it would happen now. He did not know how they would react when they found the gun. He put his hand in his pocket, his fingers curling around the trigger. The wind just here was very strong and cold.

"Up the stairs, Mr. Mahoney," the man who had come for him said.

Mahoney looked at him for a long moment. This was all wrong. Surely Sir Robert understood basic security measures. Or was he simply too arrogant, too overconfident, to think he could be threatened here?

Mahoney preceded him up the stairs, across the broad veranda, to the massive, carved wooden doors that swung open as if they were automatic.

They went inside to a vast stairhall, stag and boar heads on the walls, stained-glass windows, highly polished marble floors, dark wooden beams and paneling. The total effect was nearly overwhelming. German wealth in its rawest display.

A door opened to the left of the broad staircase, and General Sir Robert Isley Marshall came out and strode across the hall. The general was a lot taller than Mahoney had imagined he would be, well over six feet.

But he was certainly much thinner than Mahoney thought he would be. He wore some sort of light gray suit that looked like a military uniform but without any brass buttons, medals, or insignia of any sort. His face was thin and angular, dominated by a beak of a nose and topped with thick white eyebrows and longish white hair.

His presence was nothing less than commanding. Charismatic, the word came to Mahoney. He completely filled the vast hall with his presence. He seemed to be everywhere at once, even though he came straight across. There was a slightly sardonic grin on his paper-thin lips.

Here was another Douglas MacArthur, Mahoney thought. He had met the famous general in New York in the late forties. Both men had the same aura of command, of terrible responsibilities behind those eyes that were far beyond the ken of ordinary mortal men.

Here was another FDR, another Kennedy promising a Camelot.

But above and beyond all of that, the man looked positively radiant. He was alive!

"Good evening, General," Mahoney said.

"Wallace Mahoney? Central Intelligence Agency?"

Mahoney inclined his head.

"You, sir, have caused me some consternation. And I believe, at least as an indirect result of your interference, I have temporarily lost contact with one of my ablest lieutenants."

"If you are referring to Thomas Langdon, General, he is dead. It was an . . . unfortunate accident in Bonn. At the city hall."

"I see," he said. "And now . . . the moment of truth? Now you will tug at my heartstrings by mentioning my wife's tears, by recounting the devotion of my friends, by parading here duty, honor, and country?" Sir Robert shook his head with his own private amusement. He turned to the man who had brought Mahoney from the hotel. "Leave us now, Dietmann. I will call for you later."

"Yes, sir," the man said. He turned on his heel and left.

Mahoney never took his eyes off the general's. There was anger there. Irritation. And a trace of . . . fear?

"Chemnitz, I'm told, was once a beautiful city," Mahoney said.

"And Bonn is a Paris," Sir Robert snapped. "Why have you come after me?"

"To fetch you home, actually," Mahoney said. "And to bring back a certain . . . NATO document you took."

"The Genesis Plan," Sir Robert said. He chuckled. "No one on God's earth would believe such an amazing farce. I destroyed it."

Mahoney blinked. "You destroyed it?"

"Yes. I burned the bloody thing at a campground outside of Heidelberg ten days ago. No one saw it but me." He shook his head. "No one should ever see it," he added.

Sir Robert's voice was suddenly strained, as if he had been doing a lot of talking just recently and it was catching up with him. But the tone of his voice was becoming almost petulant. Mahoney decided he was disappointed.

"Then what are you doing here, General? Why did you leave?"

"You can ask me that? Here?"

Mahoney looked beyond the general toward the door across the hall. Someone stood there, in the shadows.

"Stanford Hall took it as a joke, you know," Mahoney said.

"Unkind cut," Sir Robert snapped. "The foppish bastard wouldn't raise a little finger to defend his own. He was not fit to be an historian."

"Or you an Englishman?"

"I'm here to save Europe, you cretin."

The man was buried deep within a shell. Ordinary

means would not get to him. Perhaps nothing would.

"Sir Howard Scott?"

"Will you actually parade names past me like this?"

"Maggie Byrne?"

Sir Robert smiled. "Ah, Maggie Byrne. A sweet if incompetent woman. Her brother is a heroin addict, you know. I've supplied the lad with the stuff for years. Maggie is devoted."

"And your wife, General? Why did you bother getting a message to her that you were safe?"

Sir Robert stared at Mahoney as if he weren't seeing him but was looking at some inner image. It seemed as if he were trying to catch his breath.

"Have you ever been in battle?" he asked.

"My own personal wars, but no major battles," Mahoney admitted.

"Your own personal wars," Sir Robert repeated. "You understand, then, the meaning of commitment?"

"Yes, I do," Mahoney said. "But my understanding does not include the ends justifying the means."

Sir Robert laughed again. "No?" he said. "I won't argue that point with you. Suffice it to say that I feel a sense of commitment to my wife. She has nurtured me all of these years. She deserves some little comfort."

"You're not that cold, you bastard," Mahoney said, suddenly angry. He had a vision of a lovely woman coming down the stairs, her hand trailing on the banister.

"Dedicated."

"To what? To a reunified Germany? Don't be a fool, General."

Sir Robert straightened up. "You think the DDR is in love with the Russians? What have they brought here other than fear? And how has the Federal Republic gained from the American presence? The war will be fought on German soil. You read the plan, didn't you? This time the destruction would be complete, German against German. And let me tell you, there would finally be nothing left of Europe. Or of Britain, for that matter."

"They are two separate countries. Two separate peoples now," Mahoney said. The figure was still at the doorway.

"I did not expect you to see, of course."

"The Germans you have spoken with understand you?"

"Naturally."

"The businessmen in Munich? The ones at the Hofbräuhaus?" Mahoney said, his words like hammer blows. "The ones with fear in their eyes?"

"They fear only men such as yourself."

"You have your followers?"

"Yes."

"And you will lead them to a confrontation . . . to a glorious new Germany?"

Sir Robert looked at Mahoney for a long time, the oddest of expressions on his face. He shook his head. "You still don't understand, do you?"

"You're an old man. You've had a long, distinguished career. You've had your disappointments, but then you've had your triumphs. Let it go. Return home. Your wife needs you."

"Howard can have her."

"You son of a bitch," Mahoney said. There was no spark of human warmth in the man's eyes. He was a different creature than the one Sir Howard had described. Completely different from the man his wife loved.

"They've been in love for years. Don't you think I know that?"

"Your friend has been in love with your wife since you were teaching at Oxford. Since before that, even. Yet all your wife can speak of is you. She wants you back."

"She won't have me, not until I have finished here," Sir Robert snarled.

"No," Mahoney said. "I don't suspect she will. But you are coming back with me."

"Not yet," Sir Robert said.

"General," the man from the doorway called.

Sir Robert glanced over his shoulder. "*Moment, bitte,*" he said. He looked back. "It will be very soon, now. Three or four days. The first of November."

"For what?"

"You don't understand," Sir Robert said. "Why do you suppose I left Brussels when I did . . . with what I did?"

"You can explain that later," Mahoney said. He pulled out the gun and pointed it at Sir Robert.

"I left with the war scenario because I wanted to make bloody well sure that someone would come after me—and keep coming after me."

"What?"

"I may have been lying . . . about burning the Genesis files. Someone else will have to come after me if I fail. In a few more days."

"And then what? Are you telling me you plan to return then?"

"No, of course not! Within three days the selection of the next chancellor of Germany—of a unified Germany —will have been completed."

"You?"

Sir Robert laughed. "I'm a Brit, not a German leader."

"General," the man by the doorway called again.

His voice! Suddenly Mahoney recognized it, or thought he did. But it was a voice . . . from the West. From Bonn.

Sir Robert read Mahoney's recognition from his face, and he smiled. "Yes. He is the man for Germany now. Not a Nazi during the war, but not a traitor either. He remained to help rebuild a West Germany. And now he will build a unified Germany."

"You recruited him."

"It wasn't hard."

It was finally clear to Mahoney. His insides were churning. His hand shook. There would be terrible upheavals across all of Germany. On both sides of the border. Economic chaos would reign. Order would break down. Out of the ashes would rise a new order. Sir Robert could very well be right. Mahoney had a sudden vision of a unified Germany . . . complete with nuclear weapons.

"Come meet the others," Sir Robert said. Ignoring the gun in Mahoney's hand he turned and started back across the hall.

They would have to be stopped! With Sir Robert dead . . . with the other one dead, and with the American and Soviet governments understanding what had nearly happened, it would end.

Mahoney raised the automatic, cocked it, and pulled the trigger.

The hammer fell with a sharp snap on an empty chamber.

Sir Robert stopped at the door and looked back. He beckoned.

Mahoney desperately yanked the automatic's slide back. The gun had been unloaded. There were no shells in the clip. One of Sir Robert's people had searched the hotel conference room, had found the gun, and had unloaded it.

✵ TWENTY-NINE ✵

John had stopped well down from the house, within the darkness on the narrow road that led up from the highway. Careful not to drive off the side of the road, he managed to get the car turned around. It was very cold. The rain was beginning to turn to spits of snow, and the wind whistled in the trees. It was cold in another way, too—lonely, depressing, without any human warmth, he felt, all the way back to the border. The war was being fought here and now.

When his eyes had finally become accustomed to the darkness, he started up the driveway toward the house, his shoes making very soft crunching noises on the gravel. Twice he stopped and looked back over his shoulder. The first time he could see the soft gleam of the chrome bumper, but the second time he could see nothing other than the dark woods, and he continued.

A hundred yards later the driveway opened suddenly onto a clearing, across which was the large, Teutonic house, lights at several of the windows. John pulled up short. The Mercedes he had followed from the hotel was parked in the front. From where he stood he could not tell if anyone was behind the wheel. Nor could he tell if anyone stood in the shadows around the house.

There would have to be guards, John thought. They could not be so arrogant as to not post sentries. Or could they?

He waited a full five minutes in the darkness, watching the house, the car, and the grounds, watching for a chance movement, a stray bit of light from a cigarette, perhaps, a dark shadow moving past one of the lighted windows. The cold was penetrating. He hunched up his collar, but it wasn't enough. The rain seemed to soak into the very marrow of his bones, causing him to shiver.

Twice he reached into his pocket and withdrew the pistol he had taken from Langdon, but then put it right back. He took the gun out a third time and finally moved away from the protection of the woods. Pistol in hand, keeping low, he raced across the clearing, directly to the Mercedes.

He expected at any moment to hear an alarm, hear the baying of dogs, the sound of men shouting, of gunfire directed at him. But there was nothing other than the wind and his own labored breathing as he raced the hundred yards or so.

He pulled up behind the big automobile. There was no one in or around it. They were all inside. With his father.

The keys were in the Mercedes's ignition. He opened the door on the driver's side, took them out and pocketed them, then he hurried around the front of the car, up the main stairs, and then angled left across the broad veranda, away from the front door.

Light came from a large window at waist level. John flattened himself against the rough stone of the building and just eased around the edge so that he could see inside. His grip tightened on the pistol.

It was a large room. A fireplace directly across, a grand piano to the right, couches and wing chairs on either side, paintings on the walls, a large arch to the right leading out into the stairhall. Two men stood just within the room. They were talking.

John ducked below the level of the window, scrambled past it, then straightened up and hurried to the end of the veranda, which continued around the side of the house.

Halfway back were French doors. Light spilled out onto the veranda from inside. Shadows moved back and forth.

John's heart was pounding as he carefully approached. His father would be there. He knew it! But who else?

Sir Robert laughed, his voice echoing through the stairhall.

"Don't be tedious, Mr. Mahoney," he said. "You came all this way to unravel your little mystery. Take the last few steps."

Mahoney pocketed the useless gun. He glanced toward the living room. The chauffeur and the man who had brought him from the hotel stood just within the arch. They were looking at him.

He slowly crossed the stairhall where Sir Robert and the other man stood waiting for him.

He had recognized the voice, but the shock of recognition when he finally saw the man's face was no less for it.

"I believe you must know Peter Sturm, former ambassador to the United States from West Germany," Sir Robert said.

Sturm's was the one face and voice from Germany today most recognizable by anyone in the world. His dramatic mane of thick dark hair, graying at the sides, his heavy eyebrows, his dark penetrating eyes, his firm mouth and solid build, were *Germany*. Nothing less.

He looked a little sad, even somewhat frightened, Mahoney suspected.

"I am sorry you had to come here like this, Mr. Mahoney," he said.

"Do you understand what has happened . . . the people murdered . . . over the past two weeks, and the significance of those acts?" Mahoney asked.

Sturm nodded. "Yes, I do. But I believe you do not . . . you *cannot* understand, Mr. Mahoney." He looked at Sir Robert, then went into the room.

Sir Robert motioned Mahoney inside, then followed him in, closing the heavy door behind them.

It was a study. Smoke-filled. Close. A fire burned in the fireplace. A big leather-topped desk dominated one side of the book-lined room. A concealed wet bar was open to the left. Straight across were French doors, the curtains open.

A dozen men stood or were seated around the richly appointed room. Their presence like this was something of a shock to Mahoney. He recognized many of them. The director of the BND—West Germany's secret service. Two others from the Bonn government. The leaders of West Germany's top four industries. The others were East German.

They all had the same look as the businessmen at the Hofbräuhaus in Munich. A certain disdain, but beyond that a slight fear, as if despite what they had done to date, they understood the implausibility of what they were trying to accomplish. As if they understood the dangers. Maybe even the futility.

"Gentlemen, Wallace Mahoney, the Central Intelligence Agency, the first to break through," Sir Robert said.

A tall man in an East German army uniform, general's pips on his collar, stood by the fireplace. He shook his head. "Hopefully the last," he said.

"Thank God, at least, he's not KGB," one of the West German industrialists said.

"Would it have made any difference?" the East German general snapped.

"Gentlemen, please," Sir Robert said.

"We still must decide what to do with him," Peter Sturm said. he stood beside a wing chair, his left hand resting on one of the wings.

"He will have to be eliminated, of course," the East German general said.

Sturm shrugged. He turned to Sir Robert. "Robert?" he said.

Mahoney had the absurd notion that he wasn't present in this room, that in fact he was watching a movie of the happening. It was old footage of the Beer Hall Putsch. He felt as if he could move around or speak to himself, and the actors on screen would take no notice of him.

He thought too about Lady Sidney, and he wondered how many other wives, how many other families or lives were being left behind so that these men could pursue their goal of a reunified Germany.

"It simply will not matter in a very few days," Sir Robert said.

"But they know he is here. His people must be waiting for word."

"It doesn't matter. They will never ask the KGB for assistance. It would be unthinkable. Yet that is the only course at this moment that could possibly affect us," Sir Robert said. He turned to Mahoney and smiled.

"There are enough people who know what is happening to stop you," Mahoney said.

"No," Sir Robert replied flatly. "You may have suspected about me. But you cannot have known about Peter. Or the others."

Bindrich knew at least the basics. NATO was on alert. Nothing would come of this. It could not.

Mahoney started to raise his hand to beckon, when the French doors crashed open and someone barged in, the cold wind whipping through the study.

Someone shouted. Someone else leaped up, knocking over a chair. Sir Robert leaped toward the door, but Mahoney instinctively shoved him back.

"General!" John Mahoney shouted, raising his pistol.

Everyone scrambled to get out of the way. Sir Robert

pulled a gun from his coat pocket and started to turn back.

"No!" John shouted, dropping into a crouch, both hands on the pistol, his arms outstretched in the classic shooter's stance.

Sir Robert stopped not quite around, and held very still.

"I don't want to hurt anyone," John said breathlessly. He was obviously very nervous. His hands shook.

"Easy, John . . ." Mahoney began, when someone knocked urgently at the study door. Sir Robert flinched.

"General!" the chauffeur shouted.

Mahoney nodded toward the door. Sir Robert was looking at him, his eyes wide and bright, his lips pursed, the automatic steady in his hand.

"General!" the chauffeur called again.

"*Alles ist in ordnung*," Sir Robert called out.

For a beat everyone stood like that. The only sounds were those of the crackling logs in the fireplace and the wind through the open French doors.

"Sir?" the chauffeur called uncertainly.

Sir Robert was looking at Mahoney. "It is all right. Leave us."

"Yes, sir," the chauffeur said.

Mahoney held his breath, listening. There was nothing. Carefully he moved away from Sir Robert to the door, and he turned the latch.

"You will not get out of here alive," Sir Robert said. "Certainly you will not get to the West."

"You are coming back with us," Mahoney said. This was an exceedingly dangerous situation. Sir Robert was probably correct. But they had come this far. And now, somehow, John was here.

"You don't understand . . ." Peter Sturm said. He was distraught.

"Let them go," the East German general snapped. "They won't get across the border."

For a moment it seemed to Mahoney that Sir Robert would acquiesce. His gun hand wavered, and the harsh expression in his eyes began to soften. But then the man's resolve seemed to return.

"There's a car out front . . ." John started, when Sir Robert, his eyes wide, spun around and brought up the automatic.

"No!" John shouted and fired three times, the first catching Sir Robert in the chest with a tremendous smack, shoving the man backward, his own gun going off reflexively, the shot hitting the desk. John's second shot, seemingly in slow motion, caught Sir Robert in the side of his head, blood, bits of bone and white matter splattering against the bookcase, driving the man against the wall. John's third shot went wild.

Peter Sturm shoved Mahoney aside bodily and tore at the door.

John fired, catching the would-be chancellor of a unified Germany in the spine.

The East German general had leaped to the desk and was fumbling in a drawer.

John spun around and pulled the trigger, but the hammer fell on an empty chamber.

Mahoney scooped up Sir Robert's automatic, and from a kneeling position fired, catching the general in the throat, sending him backward, the pistol he had come up with falling to the floor.

There was a commotion out in the stairhall. The chauffeur was shouting something. Mahoney jumped up, shoved one of the West German industrialists aside, and started across the room, when one of Sir Robert's guards appeared at the open French doors on the veranda.

John stepped aside at the same moment the guard fired, the shot catching John in the shoulder. Mahoney fired twice, hitting the guard in the chest, driving him back out of the study.

The others in the study had hit the floor. Mahoney grabbed the back of John's sodden coat and propelled him out onto the veranda, over the fallen guard. They raced around to the front, turning the corner as two

shots were fired at them from the French doors, and
then they were stumbling down the stairs, across the
walk to the Mercedes.

"I have the keys!" John shouted.

They ran around to the driver's side, where Mahoney
tore open the door and shoved John inside and across
the seat.

He turned and snapped off another shot toward two
figures running across the veranda, then he got behind
the wheel, took the keys from John, and fumbled them
into the ignition.

The rear window erupted in a spray of glass as he got
the car started, slammed it into gear, and then they were
accelerating wildly down the long circular driveway.

They plunged into the darkness of the woods, and
suddenly John's car was blocking the road. Mahoney
yanked the wheel sharply left, and the big car slewed
half off the road, sideswiping the other car with a
tremendous crash, but then they were past, and seconds
later on the highway back toward the autobahn.

The final hours of that night would forever remain a
blur in Mahoney's mind, although his son, despite his
wound, claimed to recall every single detail, including
his father's explanation for Sir Robert's final, grand
delusions, and the fact that in the end he had been
cheated out of his dream.

John's wound was deep, but the bleeding had all but
stopped. They were not followed, at least for the moment, and just past Eisenach they turned off the autobahn and followed the country lane ten miles farther to
the village of Vacha. Here the border was less than a
hundred yards away. It was nothing more than a pair of
tall wire fences topped with barbed wire and patrolled
by foot soldiers.

Vacha was their alternate route out, in case there was
trouble. Salmon had given them directions to a man
who would guide them across.

Beyond the village, Mahoney turned out the headlights as they turned down a narrow path back to a
house at the edge of the woods.

"This is it," John said weakly.

Mahoney stopped the car and turned to his son. "Are
you all right? Will you be able to make it on foot?"

John managed a smile. He nodded.

A certain pride welled up in Mahoney's heart for
what his son had become, and yet there was still that
same nagging fear that this business would burn John
out, would irrevocably change him into a hateful shell
of a human being, an automaton controlled by men who
cared more for their political aims than the lives of the
people who did the dirty work.

Let go, old man. Mahoney could hear Marge's words
as if she were right there beside him.

"I don't think you're an incompetent old fool," John
said softly. "I was just angry. You were taking over."

Mahoney smiled wistfully.

"I'm . . . I'm sorry, Father . . ."

"Does that mean you'll come see me for advice from
time to time?"

John grinned. "Only if you'll promise not to take
every one of my assignments."

Mahoney nodded wryly, then looked toward the
house. It was dark. No lights shone from the windows.
If their contact was waiting, as Salmon said he would
be, he would have heard the car.

Something was wrong now.

"What is it?" John asked.

"I don't know," Mahoney said. "Stay here." He got
out of the car, pulled Sir Robert's automatic from his
pocket, and went up to the house.

It was still raining, and the wind rustled the trees. The
border was very close, yet without help, without a
guide, they'd never make it through.

Mahoney tried the door. It was unlocked. He slowly
pushed it open.

Just inside an old man lay on his back, his head in

a puddle of blood. Mahoney's stomach flopped. This was Sir Robert's country. This and West Germany. He had known someone was coming across. Evidently his people knew about this contact, and they had murdered him.

Mahoney pocketed the gun and hurried back to the car.

"Is he gone?" John asked.

Mahoney slammed the big Mercedes in gear, turned it around, and headed back toward the road that led back to the autobahn.

"He's been shot to death."

"Christ!" John said. "Do you think it was Sir Robert's people?"

"Probably."

"What are we going to do?"

Mahoney took a deep breath and let it out slowly to clear his chest. He looked at his son. "We're going to cross at Eisenach, the same way you came in."

"They won't let us out!"

"I have a passport. You'll go in the trunk. They probably won't check," Mahoney said. It was a desperate hope, actually; he knew that. But at this moment it was their only one. Already the alarm had been sent out from the house outside Karl Marx Stadt. Already whatever was left of Sir Robert's organization would be fanning out, hunting down the two Americans—father and son—who had shattered the dreams for a new Germany.

They passed through the dark village of Vacha, and then minutes later they were back to the entrance to the autobahn, which swept in a wide circle down hill.

To the west they could see the lights of the border post, although they could not see the buildings or the actual checkpoint because of the falling snow. It was coming down very hard.

Mahoney pulled up short of the entry ramp and set the parking brake. He shut off the headlights and turned to his son.

"It'll only be for a few minutes, John," he said.

John said nothing, but he nodded. His complexion was very pale. He seemed uncertain.

"Right," Mahoney said. He shut off the motor, took the keys out of the ignition, and then went around to the trunk.

John got out of the car and came back as the trunk lid came open. He and his father looked into each other's eyes. Then without a further word, Mahoney helped his son into the trunk and closed the lid.

Before he got back behind the wheel, Mahoney again looked toward the lights shining through the snow-storm. Their freedom was so close.

The entrance ramp was very slippery, so Mahoney drove slowly down onto the autobahn itself, then carefully accelerated toward the west.

Two Soviet Army troop transports rumbled past him toward the border crossing, and he slowed way down.

Soviet Army trucks. Here. So close to the border on this night. Why?

He glanced in the rearview mirror as a pair of head-lights came up behind him. He slowed down more, but the lights held back. Whoever was there did not want to pass him.

The border crossing was suddenly just there ahead. They were boxed in now. And Mahoney had a very bad feeling about this.

A dozen Soviet Army troops had leaped out of the trucks, and three Soviet officers were talking with the East German border guards, when the checkpoint came into view. A fourth Soviet officer stepped out into the brightly lit holding area and held up his hand for Mahoney to come to a halt. Two of the armed troops broke away from the others and came over.

Mahoney brought the big Mercedes to a complete halt and powered down the window. The Soviet officer came around, his two troops directly behind him.

Mahoney held out his passport with his left hand,

while with his right he reached for the automatic on the seat beside him.

"If you will just get out of the car, sir," the Russian officer said in English.

For a very long second or two the significance of the officer's use of English did not strike Mahoney. But when it did, it was like a lightning flash. He thought immediately of Conwell, already back in Brussels. Had the man spoken with the Russian, Konstantin Demin? Was it possible?

Mahoney shoved the automatic aside and carefully got out of the Mercedes. The guards stepped back a pace, and the officer glanced inside the car.

The other officers and troops were busy with the East German border guards. There seemed to be some kind of an argument. Straight down the highway, through the barrier to the west, Mahoney could see a half-dozen automobiles parked just beyond the border post. He could vaguely make out a number of people standing there. Watching. So close. So damned close!

"Please to open the trunk, sir," the Soviet officer asked.

Mahoney's breath caught in his throat. "There is nothing there . . ." Mahoney started.

"Please . . . the trunk, sir," the officer insisted.

The troops behind him did not seem hostile, but they were obviously alert.

Mahoney nodded, then turned and reached inside the car for the keys. His eyes fell on the automatic in the seat. But then he backed out with the keys and went to the trunk, the officer and troops with him.

"There is nothing here," Mahoney said.

The officer said nothing.

Mahoney slowly opened the trunk lid. His eyes met John's. The Soviet officer motioned for his two troops to help John out of the trunk, and Mahoney had to step aside as they pulled his son out.

John swayed on his feet, and Mahoney had to take his

arm. He could not read anything in the Soviet officer's eyes. Nothing at all. No emotion whatsoever. This could easily be a setup.

"There are people waiting for you, I believe, sir," the officer said. He stepped back and motioned toward the border. "You will have to go on foot," he said. "We may not help you."

Mahoney looked from the officer to his troops, and then toward the other officers and Soviet troops still engaged with the East German guards.

"Say nothing," the Soviet officer cautioned. He motioned toward the border crossing again.

Mahoney nodded, and he and John started through the snow toward the frontier crossing less than fifty yards away. As they walked past the East Germans and the other Soviet troops, no one looked up at them.

They passed under the striped barrier on the eastern side and slowly crossed the twenty yards or so of no-man's-land between the two zones.

Ten yards away from the West, a man stepped forward and raised the barrier. It was Salmon; Mahoney could recognize him now.

And then they were across, the West German barrier lowering.

Mahoney turned back and looked toward the east in time to see the Soviet troops and officers climbing back into their trucks. Already the East German border guards had gone back into their frontier post building.

✭ THIRTY ✭

As the Lufthansa jet from Frankfurt touched down for a landing at Brussels's Zaventem Airport, Mahoney had the strangest feeling that this was two weeks ago, and he was starting the entire business all over again. For three days he had refused to budge from his rooms at the luxurious Frankfurt Sheraton by the airport. Bindrich had telephoned his cautious congratulations after Salmon had done the debriefing, and asked when he'd be returning. There was still the matter the President wanted to discuss, though not as urgently now that the election was so very close. John had, in the end, agreed to return to Washington, but only after his father had given his ironclads that he would limit his stay in Brussels to a few hours and then take the very next flight back to the States. John had his debriefing and new schooling to go through, but afterward they planned on taking a very long vacation together. The mystery of the appearance of Soviet troops was explained when Conwell admitted he had jumped the gun in telling the Brussels KGB *rezident* about Mahoney's plans. The Russians had no desire to release their hold on the Germanys . . . no more than the Americans had. Conwell, of course, was recalled.

The airliner taxied to the terminal, but Mahoney held back, preferring to be the last off rather than fight the crowd. Sir Robert, he was thinking, had simply been a man whose time had run out . . . or had very nearly run out, and it had probably frightened him that he could not look back and total his life in the positive column.

Mahoney got off the plane, smiled at the pretty stewardesses, then was passed through customs with no trouble on the strength of his diplomatic passport.

He headed across the terminal toward the cab ranks, sad in a way for the irony of his thoughts. Sir Robert could have had, in his retirement, all that Mahoney had ever wanted.

"Monsieur Mahoney," someone called from behind.

Mahoney stopped and turned as Detective Inspector Richard Matin materialized out of the crowd.

"You have time for coffee with me before your Washington flight leaves," Matin said, taking Mahoney's arm.

"I was on my way out to Anderlecht . . . to see Lady Sidney," Mahoney said. There had been nothing in the newspapers, of course, about what really happened. Just that Sir Robert had been found dead outside of Frankfurt. An apparent suicide. The East Germans promised to return his body in a few days, after an autopsy. Lady Sidney had been informed, and so, Mahoney assumed, had Matin.

"I am sorry, *monsieur,* but that will not be possible. Lady Sidney has returned to England with her daughter, and with Sir Howard Scott, of course."

"I see," Mahoney said.

"In any event, you would not be allowed from the airport. We think it would be best that you return home now. This business is finished. Thank God."

Mahoney looked into the inspector's eyes. There was a great sadness there. A sorrow. And a little bewilderment. But then Matin had mentioned he was close to retirement.

"Jean Rubaix was found dead last night," Matin said.

"He wasn't murdered . . . ?" Mahoney asked, alarmed.

"*Non,*" the Belgian policeman replied. "No. I found him. It was definitely suicide."

"I see," Mahoney said.

"I wish only to know about the young Arab."

"At the Gare du Nord?"

Matin nodded.

"Thomas Langdon killed him."

"And Langdon was shot to death by an unidentified man in Bonn."

Mahoney nodded. Perhaps it was best he went home now. He was really getting to hate the lies. "Did you see Lady Sidney before she left?"

"Yes, right here at the airport, in fact. We talked. She will do well. She is a lovely lady."

"Yes, a lovely lady indeed," Mahoney agreed, but then he was thinking about another lovely lady in another time and in another place. . . .